KU-441-011

The Body in the Mist

NICK LOUTH

THE BODY IN THE MIST

CANELO

First published in the United Kingdom in 2019 by Canelo

This edition published in the United Kingdom in 2019 by

Canelo Digital Publishing Limited
57 Shepherds Lane
Beaconsfield, Bucks HP9 2DU
United Kingdom

Copyright © Nick Louth, 2019

The moral right of Nick Louth to be identified as the author of this work
has been asserted in accordance with the Copyright, Designs and Patents
Act, 1988.

All rights reserved. No part of this publication may be reproduced or
transmitted in any form or by any means, electronic or mechanical,
including photocopy, recording, or any information storage and retrieval
system, without permission in writing from the publisher.

A CIP catalogue record for this book is available from the British Library.

Print ISBN 978 1 78863 550 9
Ebook ISBN 978 1 78863 223 2

This book is a work of fiction. Names, characters, businesses, organizations,
places and events are either the product of the author's imagination or are
used fictitiously. Any resemblance to actual persons, living or dead, events
or locales is entirely coincidental.

Look for more great books at www.canelo.co

Printed and bound in Great Britain by Clays Ltd, Elcograf S.p.A.

For Louise, as always

Chapter 1

A few miles south of Exmoor National Park in Devon, dusk had reclaimed a damp and misty November Wednesday. Detective Inspector Jan Talantire drove up Winsford Hill on the A39, then passed the sign for Furzy Hill, the hamlet's bright red phone box caught in the beams of her headlamps. The ping of fresh gravel hailed the underside of her car as she found the narrow turning, heading north past the kiosk towards the moors. A body had been reported lying in a ditch on this quiet, unlit country lane. On her ten-minute drive north from Barnstaple, she had guessed the likeliest story. A walker or cyclist, hit by a speeding car, whose driver panicked and then drove away. The classic hit-and-run.

A patrol car was parked 20 yards beyond and downhill, its sweeping blue lights cutting the mist like a lighthouse warning shipping away from deadly rocks. Constable Clifford Willow had already taped off a three-yard section of hedgerow, in the shadow of a five-foot high drystone wall. Sitting in the rear passenger seat of his patrol car was an elderly woman in rainproofs and a woolly hat, with a small dog on her lap. Willow's radioed report had referred to Mrs Muriel Hinkley, a dog walker, finding the body. This must be her.

Talantire parked her unmarked Toyota on the other side of the road from the crime tape, and 50 yards beyond it. She peered into the gathering gloom, and then in the interior light of the car checked her Ordnance Survey map. This was a half-mile long side road to nowhere with a gate to a derelict farm at the end, and an overgrown public bridleway across moorland beyond. From the boot she donned plastic overshoes and gloves, and lifted a small rucksack containing a packet of evidence bags, a digital camera and a can of blue spray paint. She turned on a powerful inspection lamp and made her way back towards the patrol car, which was parked half on the verge right next to the crime scene tape. A beginner's mistake.

'Willow,' she called. The young uniformed policeman stood up from where he had been peering into the ditch. She could just make out the outline of the body, face down in the blue strobe.

'Yes, ma'am?'

'Definitely dead?'

'Yes, ma'am. Head's all crushed. No pulse. So told the ambulance not to hurry.'

'Okay. But you parked in the crime scene.'

'Sorry, ma'am,' he stepped towards the car and opened the driver's door.

'Don't move it now, you'll only compound the problem. Did you check for tyre marks first?'

'No, ma'am. Sorry, ma'am.'

'Did you find a bicycle?'

'No, ma'am. It's pretty foggy. Is there a bicycle?' In the light of her torch, he squinted uncomfortably, youthful brows knitted. Only a year out of training, and already seemingly forgetting everything he had been taught about crime scenes. Still, at least he knew there was still lots to learn. PC Nick Kite, smartarse of 15 years standing, well, you couldn't tell him anything. Thought he knew it all. He'd make the same mistakes every time, and when you pointed them out, just look back with surly resentment.

Talantire knelt down and shone the torch around the front and rear of the patrol car.

'There is often a bicycle in a hit-and-run, Willow, but our hitter-and-runner will often throw it over the hedge or wall. To try to disguise what has happened. Which makes him a tosser as well.'

Willow's eyebrows were now so knitted that his eyeballs almost overlapped.

'But our hitters-and-runners-and-tossers are usually too scared to touch a body.' She stood up. 'No tyre tracks here except yours, lucky for you. And no recent bike tracks that I can see.'

She shone the torch back up the road towards the phone box. There were a pair of magpies waddling in the road, one of them pecking at something. Half a dozen crows softly silhouetted on the telegraph wires were cawing in anticipation. More were gathering. Must be something to eat.

'Did you check by the phone box?' she asked.

Willow shook his head. Talantire moved up the lane towards the telephone kiosk. She wanted to see exactly what kind of roadkill had drawn the magpies. The inspection lamp illuminated a long, dark, sinuous trail a few inches wide. She followed it, taking photographs every few feet. The road was rough and gravelly, the fresh surface only a week or two old. It was damp too, but should not be as wet as this. Not enough to make this

3

reflection, redolent of spilled gloss paint. Not mud. She knelt and looked more closely. Definitely blood. Lots of blood, with traces of hair and flesh.

She stood and gazed upwards, trying to see beyond the mist. Rain was forecast, likely as not within the next half-hour. It could destroy the evidence. She sprayed a small arrow on the road, level with the deposit, and marked the letter A. With a latex fingertip, she wiped a lump of human flesh and smeared it into an evidence bag. 'Willow,' she yelled. 'Call CSI at Exeter. Get the small evidence tent out of the boot of my car and set it up over the body. And put some booties over your shoes. And give me some more crime scene tape, we're closing off the whole road back up to the phone booth. Move quickly, now. We're expecting more rain.'

Willow responded immediately.

She advanced right up to the phone box. The magpies, now scattered, had indeed found some human remains. More blood, more hair. A piece of dental bridgework, two bloodied molars connected by wire, now bent. She marked the position with the paint spray, photographed the teeth, then dropped them into another evidence bag, which she tagged with the road position. Gradually she worked her way up the bloody smear, calibrating each scouring of human skin with a unique marker corresponding to its position.

It must have been an awful way to die. Hit here, by the phone box, and cheese-gratered beneath the vehicle, face in contact with the gravelly road for many yards at considerable speed, before rolling away, and dying in a ditch. This back lane near Furzy Hill, connecting three farms and a back way into the hamlet, probably had one vehicle movement per hour, if that. That movement would be a tractor, probably, during daylight hours. Once it was dark, next to nothing. That was good luck and bad. Good, because few vehicles if any would have disturbed the evidence. Bad, because the chance of securing a witness was poor.

Talantire carefully checked all along the verge from the phone box down to where the body still lay in the ditch. A vehicle had mounted the grass, briefly, leaving a deep impression of a thick, chunky tyre of a width common on a 4 × 4. That sideways steering twitch matched a deflection in the stripe of blood on the carriageway. She took more photographs, then shone light into the ditch. A damaged black shoe, its sole torn off but uppers still laced, lying upside down. She photographed it, then picked it up. Dry inside. Not here for long, then. She slid it into an evidence bag and added it to the rucksack. Finally she made her way back to the body. It was face down, but the misshapen and fractured skull, matted with blood and hair, was obvious even from the back. The body was clearly male, dressed in an anorak and corduroys, the clothing partly shredded and bloody around the upper body.

'Okay, so not a cyclist, then,' she said, to no one in particular. Willow had given the victim the once-over for ID, but she needed to be a bit more thorough. She delved into pockets, slid up the cuffs of shirt and trousers looking for tattoos, finding only a wristwatch, which she removed. Once finished, she bagged up her evidence gloves, then made her way over to the patrol car and opened the rear door. The elderly lady and her dog looked up, alarmed. She was white-haired but robust-looking, with glasses and a weather-beaten face.

'I'll need to go home soon, because my husband expects his dinner sharp at six,' she said.

'Buy him a tin opener for his birthday,' Talantire responded. 'It's a small price to pay for a bit of freedom. So about this body. What time was it you found it?'

'Ten to four,' she said. 'Billy boy found him, didn't you?' She scratched the mongrel's ears. 'It didn't half make me jump. Poor man.'

The DI asked what route the woman took on her walk, and she described a two-mile loop that she undertook every day. 'I like it because we're only on the road for a short while, and I can let him off the lead.'

'Did any vehicles pass you on your walk?'

'No. Not one today.'

The detective looked up as two more police vehicles arrived. Willow hadn't yet enlarged the taped-off area, so she ran towards them to try to stop them before they passed the phone box. Having failed, she then yelled to stop them parking on the verge. The passenger-side window on the first vehicle rolled down, revealing the grizzled face of Detective Chief Superintendent Bob Parker, and beyond him the grinning countenance of PC Nick Kite.

'Detective Inspector, did you just call us moronic fuck-wits?' Parker said, the slightest of smiles playing on his lips.

'No, sir,' she replied quickly. 'I think you must have misheard. Would you be kind enough to reverse back well beyond the phone box? You've driven over part of the victim's head, which seems to be spread over a large area. We don't want to suffer a loss of face.'

Once Kite had reversed the vehicle, the DCS emerged to listen to Talantire's theory. 'Sir, the evidence points to the pedestrian being hit at speed, just by the phone box, by a big enough vehicle for him to be caught underneath for several seconds, which explains the injuries and the gory deposits on the road. The driver swerved briefly once, mounting the verge, perhaps trying to free the obstruction, but may have driven over the skull. The impact dragged off a single shoe, which I found there,' she indicated with the torch. 'At some point in the next ten yards, the driver swung back to the right, and the body rolled a few feet into the ditch where this lady found him.' She indicated the witness.

'Do we know who the victim was?' Parker asked.

'Nope. No obvious ID.'

'No wallet or phone?'

'No, sir. No receipts, envelopes—'

'Jewellery or tattoos, rings?'

'No. A wristwatch, just an ordinary Seiko, damaged in the accident, time stopped at 3.41 p.m. No tattoos visible. I don't want to move the body until CSI has been.'

Parker gave her a scowl as if it was her fault. He wandered down to talk to Willow, leaving the overweight figure of PC Kite apparently checking emails in the car.

Talantire made her way back to the phone box. It was in better condition than most, recently repainted, with clean unscratched glass panels. Obviously no longer owned by BT. There was a reason for that – it had no telephone inside. According to a notice on a panel, the kiosk had been adopted by Furzy Hill Community Group as a free library, and to prove it there were three shelves of paperbacks and some kiddies' crayoning books. With a slight smile, Talantire closed off the entire road beyond it with tape, and wrapped the box up too, finishing with a bow as if it was an overlarge Christmas gift. Like a well-behaved child, she would wait until the morning before unwrapping it to find what evidence the better light of a new dawn revealed.

–

Talantire rarely minded working through the night when there was a case that demanded it. Her partner, Jonathan, a freelance graphics whizz seven years her junior, was often to be found in his home office in the small hours, and they would work side by side in silent harmony. But unlike her, he was always back in bed asleep from 5 a.m. until 10 or 11. Many of Jan's colleagues were of a jobsworth mindset, who grumbled about working through a tea break, yet alone the night.

By midnight she had spoken either face-to-face or by telephone to the three farmers whose land bordered the lane. No one had seen or heard anything. By 3 a.m. CSI had been and gone, and the body was in a mortuary at the Royal Devon and Exeter Hospital. By four, forensics services at Bristol had identified the tyre type that had run over the verge, and by five she had arranged with the Devon and Cornwall Constabulary media office for coverage on the morning radio news, with an urgent appeal for witnesses. The only trouble was there were no names. Not only did they not know the vehicle or who was driving it, they had no idea who the victim was either. Not only was he without wallet, phone, receipts or papers, he also had no recognizable face.

Most of it had been left on the road. What was left looked like a grisly parody of a Halloween zombie. Unless they got a good break with the DNA, this was going to seriously impede getting a quick ID. The detective, half dead with tiredness herself, had stayed with the body as paramedics wheeled him into the hospital mortuary, then stepped outside into the corridor, finding a seat for a quick doze. She awoke as the duty medic, a chubby middle-aged man whose name badge said L.F. Chaudhry, came out.

'Anything you can tell me?' Talantire asked, checking the wall clock. She'd slept for half an hour.

'Cause of death is likely to be head injuries. You don't need to be a doctor to see there are compound skull fractures.'

'Any idea of the time of death?'

'About 13 hours ago, counting back on the body temperature.'

'So maybe 3.30 to 4 p.m.' That matched exactly with the damaged wristwatch.

The doctor nodded. 'Roughly. We can corroborate with rigor mortis if you need a more precise timing, but the rectal thermometer reading is generally pretty accurate. Hit-and-run, I understand?'

'Yep. Found face down in a ditch,' Talantire said. She explained about the lack of ID.

The doctor shook his head, appalled. 'Some drunk, running someone down, not even stopping to see whether they are alive.'

'I hope it was a quick death.'

'I would think so,' Chaudhry replied. 'No one survives those head injuries.'

–

It was gone six but still dark when Talantire drove out of the car park at Barnstaple police station intending to go home. Short of detective backup, she had left PC Willow with enough homework to keep him busy for hours. A list of the five vehicles that had been reported stolen in the county in the last 24 hours, registration details to be distributed throughout the region, and a list of all the garages in the area that might undertake emergency vehicle repairs. Mechanics at these facilities were advised to keep an eye open for bloodstains on the underside of any vehicle. Though she had found no indicator or headlamp glass at the scene of the accident, there was still a good chance that bulldozing a human body for 30 yards up a rough country road would cause some damage to wheels or suspension. Two of the stolen vehicles would have been perfect candidates for what she had seen. A 2012 Ford Ranger pickup, stolen in Barnstaple itself on the afternoon of the crime, and a Cherokee Jeep pinched in Exeter town centre two days earlier. She was just turning into her own street, stifling a yawn, when the call came through from the incident room. The woman who owned the Ford Ranger had just stumbled across it when her sister was driving her home. It had been abandoned by the allotments in Bear Street, just round the corner from where it had been stolen. The delighted owner had, unfortunately for forensics, driven it home.

'Did she just find it?' Talantire asked, looking at her watch. It was 6.37 a.m.

'No, at 4.15 p.m. yesterday. But she only just told us. She says whoever took it seemed to have run over a badger,' the operator said. 'You're the nearest officer, are you able to take a look?'

Talantire yawned extravagantly and said, 'Okay, I'll be there in half an hour.'

She was already certain. That was no badger; it was human remains. She'd call the recovery people and get the vehicle brought in.

Sleep would have to wait.

–

Three hours' sleep had given Talantire that kind of buzzy, spaced-out look often seen in the eyes of drug users. Back at Barnstaple police station by ten, she lurched into the evidence room, gripping a large coffee in one hand and the door frame in the other. PC Willow was already there, wandering the small warehouse with a stack of brown paper evidence bags, trying to find the correct shelf on which to file them.

'What have you got there, Clifford?'

'The clothing that the hospital doctor cut off the hit-and-run victim.'

'Has it all been signed off by CSI?'

He squinted at the large paper labels, his pale brows furrowed. 'Yes, they're done with it.'

'Right, then, I want to take a look. Let's see what we can find,' she said, taking the stack of envelopes like so much dry-cleaning, and signing them out. Willow followed as she headed for the storeroom set aside for evidence examination. This was supposed to be of laboratory-standard cleanliness, but there were rumours PC Nick Kite ate takeaways there during the night shift while watching football on a portable TV. She unlocked the door, sniffed for the tell-tale aroma of fish and batter and, detecting none, unrolled a fresh sheet of plastic from a wall-mounted dispenser to cover the table. Once suited up in Tyvek suit, booties and gloves, she unsealed the largest of the packets and slid out the victim's heavily damaged and bloodstained zip-up fleece. It was torn at both elbows and at the collar where most blood was dried on, and impregnated with lumps of gravel sticky with tar. Using a magnifying glass, she looked around the seams and turned the waist pockets inside out for lint. She did the same for shirt, trousers and underwear.

'So what do you think, Clifford?' Talantire asked. 'You want to be a detective, so tell me something.'

'It's a mess, ma'am.'

'There's no denying that. Was he an M&S shopper, do you reckon?'

Willow looked at each of the items in turn.

'Dunno.' He looked up, puzzled as to why the detective in charge would care.

'Precisely. There are no labels, Clifford. No brands, no washing instructions, nothing. They've been unstitched or cut out. Don't you think that's a bit odd?'

'Maybe.'

'I haven't got CSI's report in yet, but we'll see what they think.'

The final three packages were different – smaller but heavier. Talantire picked one that was labelled 'sole of right shoe, fragment'. She recalled that the victim had been found with only the uppers of one black shoe on his foot. The sole must have been found by CSI somewhere in the ditch. She opened the envelope and slid out the leather sole, torn stitches attached. It was almost unworn, with a couple of tarry gravel fragments lodged in heel treads.

'New shoes. And he clearly walked at least a few steps on the road, right Clifford?'

He looked back at her, mystified.

'It's not the only way to arrive is it? For example, if he was chucked out of a car boot already unconscious, and then run over, he wouldn't be so likely to have this gravel stuck in his heel, would he?'

Talantire watched the light of understanding spread like a slow and rather dim dawn down Willow's features. 'I'm with you now, ma'am.'

She looked again at the sole. There was a brand name, partially obscured on the sole by something the victim had trodden in.

Talantire leaned in with the magnifying glass, feeling woozy. 'What do you reckon he trod on, Clifford?' She passed the lens across.

'Chuddy, ma'am.'

'Chewing gum, right. That's a very useful find. Recently discarded, because it's still light grey rather than black, and still looks pliable.'

Willow grimaced. 'But no flavour left, is there?'

Talantire just stared at him. 'I wasn't proposing to eat it. Do you know, Clifford, that in 2017 a 1981 cold murder case was solved by DNA in saliva found within an old piece of chewing gum?'

He shook his head.

'What I'm saying is that this piece of discarded gum could be a useful repository of evidence, should we need to know where our victim had been spending time in his new shoes.'

Chapter 2

Next day

Smeared jewels of red tail lights snaked ahead into the darkness and the rhythmic lament of the wipers made only the briefest impression on the rain. A Friday evening, heading out of London to the south-west. Like everybody else on the planet, or so it seemed. They had the radio on because they were not speaking. Craig Gillard's hands gripped the wheel, arms straight, as if he were racing, but they had only moved a few yards in half an hour. Sam eyed her husband of two years. They had argued, uncharacteristically, for three junctions round the M25. Now 12 miles along the M3, a heavy silence lay between them.

It had begun with a phone call to their home on Wednesday evening. Gillard had just got back from a particularly rough day. A man's suicide on the railway track at Worplesdon, just outside Guildford. Initial reports were that he may have been pushed. Gillard had taken statements from a number of upset witnesses, and had been there when the news was broken to the man's wife. His final commute, as it turned out. He had lost his job months ago and had never told her, just continued to make the journey until the day his season ticket ran out. It seemed an appropriate day to throw himself under a train.

Sam had assumed that that was why Gillard had been irritable that Wednesday evening. He had not thanked her for the special meal she had cooked. Gazpacho followed by seafood paella and zabaglione, which was quite a tricky dessert. He hadn't noticed the new blouse she was wearing, nor remarked upon the fact that she had lit candles at the dinner table. She always made allowances for the stress of his work, the things he had to see, the people he had to deal with. Criminals, obviously. She coaxed him to talk. That usually helped. But the long phone call he received just before dinner, which he had taken out of hearing up in their bedroom, seemed to have made things worse.

'Who was that, Craig?' she had asked.

'Tricia. Auntie Trish,' he said with a roll of his eyes.

Sam remembered her from their wedding. She was a tiny little fluttering bird of a woman, about 70, with quick bright eyes and an enquiring mind. But she could certainly talk for England. They had a standing invitation to visit her in Barnstaple in Devon, one that Gillard had always seemed determined not to accept. 'What did she want? Is she all right? You were on there a long time.'

'Timing my calls now?' he had snapped. Seeing the look of shock on her face, he immediately apologized, blaming the stress of the day. She had put her arms out to him, but felt that his embrace was perfunctory, the kiss on her ear absent-minded, the pat on her back merely a genuflection. His mind was elsewhere.

'So what did she want?'

He looked away. 'Usual family stuff.' His expression telegraphed it was anything but usual, but she had let it lie.

Next day, from work, he had texted her the idea of a long weekend away in Devon. Friday evening to Monday afternoon. Brilliant. That had been her response. She was on a flexi day on the Monday. It would work well. Sam was surprised, because she was normally the one dragging him away from work, making all the arrangements for time away. This time Craig said he would sort everything out. 'There's no need to book anywhere,' he had said. She wondered if he was making amends for his coldness the day before.

Sam had been on an overnight shift at the police incident room on Thursday, so it was only when he got home from work on Friday afternoon that she was able to ask him exactly what they would be doing.

'Don't get too excited,' he had said with a grimace. 'We're spending the first night with Trish, and then we're staying with dreaded Barbara on a farm by the North Devon coast. Near Exmoor.'

'Exmoor! That's fantastic,' Sam said, imagining a wild, rocky coast with coves and headlands to explore.

Gillard looked at her and raised his eyebrows with unreleased knowledge. 'We've also got to visit my uncle Philip, in a care home. A bit tedious, I'm afraid.'

'I don't mind at all,' she had said, and meant it.

The good mood endured while they packed. The forecast was vile, a named storm due in on the Saturday, with gusts of a hundred miles an hour on exposed coasts. And Sam soon discovered they were going to be staying on a very exposed coast. There was no point in taking any rock-climbing gear; instead they would settle for some good blustery, coastal walking. Fabulous.

It was only when they had started the journey, and when Sam brought up the subject of Auntie Trish again, that the atmosphere soured once more. Had Craig and Trish been cooking up this long weekend on the phone call together, she wondered. She asked him.

'No, Sam. Nothing like that. Barbara, Trish's sister, had her car stolen on Wednesday afternoon, and someone used it in a fatal hit-and-run.'

'Oh God,' Sam said. She had heard of mad Auntie Barbara before. 'How tragic.'

'She's very upset, of course.'

'Have they found who did it?'

'Not yet. That's where the story gets a little muddy,' Gillard said, turning to her. 'When they interviewed her, they asked if she had been driving it. She's denied it, of course – no surprises there. But she drinks like a fish, and from memory drives like a loon, so who knows?'

'What are they expecting *you* to do?'

'Yes, exactly,' Gillard said, tapping his fingers on the wheel. 'It's almost like they want me as some kind of referee, just because I'm police. If she's worried, she needs a lawyer. I told her. I can't really help her. I'd rather not be involved.'

'Oh, Craig. She's your aunt, she probably just needs a bit of reassurance.'

'Barbara? You've got to be joking.' Gillard barked a sceptical laugh and shook his head. Nothing was said for a while. 'Trish told me that Barbara had a drink-driving conviction a few years ago, and only escaped a ban because she runs the farm pretty much single-handedly. So it's not surprising that the local fuzz might think she made up the story of the car being stolen.'

'Who was the victim?'

'That's the thing. They don't know. I don't have any contacts in Devon Police, but the news stories I googled were pretty lurid. Reading between the lines it seems the bloke was dragged along the road for a long way underneath the car.'

'How horrible. Well it can't be her, surely?'

Gillard's eyebrows arched. 'That only shows that you've never met her. All I know is that this is going to be a complete pain in the arse. Trish has high expectations of what I can do, and I'm sure I'm going to disappoint her. Sam, be warned, this weekend may not be all that much fun.'

'That's all right,' Sam said, squeezing his leg. 'I'm here to support you. Through thick and thin. Did you get any flowers? Or a present for Trish?'

Gillard looked at his wife with an air of bafflement.

'We're going to stay with your relatives, Craig, to be fed and watered and you're arriving empty-handed!'

Gillard turned away and mouthed an expletive, but the shape of his mouth was a giveaway: *For f—— sake.*

'I'll buy some flowers when we stop.'

'Don't waste your money.'

'Why are you being so horrible?' she said. 'They're your flesh and blood.'

At that point they were tailgated on the fast lane by some big 4 × 4, and although Gillard pretty quickly moved the car over into a gap in the middle lane, when the big vehicle swept past, he swore at it. That was most unlike him. He never took bad driving personally. Something had definitely got under his skin. It was when Sam persisted and asked if something was the matter that he retorted: 'Leave it alone, Sam, please, would you?'

For the next half-hour they said nothing, just letting the inanity of the teatime radio shows wash over them. Gillard tuned to BBC Radio 4 for the news. The full impact of Wednesday's surprise mini budget was being detailed. A return to austerity, big cuts that might well affect policing. Only two days ago they had heard that an agreed pay rise to boost recruitment had been scrapped because of pressure from the Treasury and the new chancellor of the exchequer. That was another depressing conversation if they wanted it.

At the Camberley turn Sam risked a conversational gambit, reminding Gillard of a pub in the town where they had spent their third date, a wonderful evening. 'What was that place called?' she asked.

'Lamb and Flag,' he said, tersely.

'I remember when we were there, you told me about spending summer holidays in Devon when you were young.' She smiled, trying desperately to raise the mood, to get him out of his fug.

'Yes. Two summers at Hollow Coombe farm. Must be some of the steepest farmland outside Wales,' he said. 'Only really suitable for sheep. A hardscrabble living and no mistake.'

'What were the names of the dogs that you liked?'

'Ah yes. Bosun and Bedgelert. Lovely animals. I used to race them up to the sheep paddocks, but they always won. I was only seven.' He smiled, and his eyes lit up. 'It was my first recollection of countryside.'

'Happy memories?' she asked, trying to elicit some more.

'Poor bloody dogs. Long dead,' he said.

'Mr Gloomy today, aren't we?'

He didn't reply and his gaze returned to the road. Sam recalled why it was that Craig would have been there. His parents had temporarily separated, one of several such interruptions in a difficult marriage. His late mother Margaret would typically go off to friends in Essex during one of these intervals, and Craig and his older sister Viv would be parked with relatives for a week or two at a time. It must have made for a difficult childhood. Craig's father worked long hours and couldn't even boil an egg, yet alone look after the children in his wife's absence.

'Did Viv come with you to the farm?'

'No. Viv didn't like Barbara. Not after the first time. She wouldn't go. She ran away from home to avoid it. I'm not surprised. My mum wouldn't go back either. Bad memories, that's all she would tell me. Mum ran away from home as a teenager, went off to London. Barbara ended up running the farm on her own, and resented Mum having a freedom she never did.'

Sam watched her husband, hoping for some more details. None were forthcoming. She recalled the stories of Craig's mother having a wild time in Soho in the Swinging Sixties. She had been a waitress at Ronnie Scott's, briefly been a backing singer, had an affair with an ageing actor, and then finally ran into Craig's father at a bus stop on the Holloway Road. Her death from breast cancer in 1988, at the age of 40 and when Craig was still only 21, hit the family like a thunderbolt. Craig had said it was probably the main reason he never went to university. The photographs Sam had seen of Maggie, as she liked to be known in her younger days, showed a vivacious, fashionable young woman with a winning smile who had modelled herself on Jean Shrimpton.

The contrast with photographs Craig had shown her of Barbara could not have been starker. An imposing, matronly woman, the second of the four, who in almost every picture wore a stained leather apron and wellies, as if she had just returned from an abattoir. It was hard to believe the pictures were from the 1980s. She looked more like a Victorian throwback, with her pinched, careworn face, stern slanted mouth and unruly bun of dark hair. She seemed to gaze past the camera, drawn by one wayward eye that had a strange milky mark the size of a thumbnail.

'Is she blind in one eye?'

'Yes and no.'

'Well she either can see out of it or not,' Sam laughed.

'She was dragged under a harrow when she was four. She has scars, but the eye is still there. She always said that she never completely lost her vision, though it was impaired. She always said she was just able to see different things from before.'

'Different things?'

Gillard looked at her and then turned away, his face tightening. 'She said she knew what you were thinking. Don't laugh, I've seen evidence of it.'

Sam watched as her husband overtook a lorry and then pulled back neatly into the inner lane, sending a great wave of spray into the verge.

'She must have been pretty scary.'

'If you were seven, she certainly was. But she had a tough life. She ran that farm for decades on her own. Even with one eye not working properly. There's not much she couldn't do.' Gillard licked his lips, swallowing the lower one. 'A tough woman. Had to be, for that place. Her father, my grandfather, was a complete bastard. Died before I was born. Threw himself off a cliff while drunk in 1964, on his wedding anniversary, leaving the family with unmanageable debts.'

Gillard's eyes remained on the road but as she watched they softened, some memory coming to them momentarily. Sam didn't say anything, just soaking up new knowledge about the man she loved. They were quiet again as they drove through Wiltshire, until they passed Amesbury. Here the A303 was narrowed by roadworks, and then finally reverted to single carriageway in each direction. Ahead of them was a dawdling van with only one rear light working. Sam wouldn't have overtaken. It didn't seem safe to get past, but Craig was such a confident driver, a brilliant judge of distance. He accelerated, foot suddenly heavy on the gas, gear changes unusually firm and rapid.

'My mother had a name for her,' he said suddenly, glancing across at Sam as they whizzed past the van. 'Barbaric Babs. There was always something...' He searched for the right word. 'Something wild, almost primitive, about her.'

'She never came to our wedding.'

He let out a slight laugh. 'It was either her or Trish. There were years when they wouldn't be in the same room together.'

'When was the last time you saw her?'

'The very last time, about 30 years ago at Mum's funeral.'

'Did she never marry?'

'No.' Gillard laughed. 'She would have been a bit of a handful. Now Trish, she did marry. Howie, she called him. Howard Gibson. I only met him twice. He was an oil worker, worked away on the rigs for most of their marriage. A big friendly Scottish guy. They divorced, well, about ten years ago. But they're still on friendly terms, and she has retained his surname. He lives in Thailand now, has a big family over there apparently.'

The talked about other things for half an hour, watching the rain running across the windows, the branches of roadside trees bent by the wind, the confetti of leaves cartwheeling across the road.

'Barbara got into trouble with the law several times. Not just the drink-driving. She broke the jaw of a neighbouring farmer in a pub fight about fence lines. I suppose she would have been in her 30s at the time.'

'I always guessed that criminality ran in your family,' Sam chuckled.

'You don't know the half of it,' Gillard said softly, almost to himself.

'You can always tell me.'

He turned to her and grinned. 'I might just do that.' He took the next left turning, a farm track, whose stark leafless hedges rattled in the wind.

'Why are we here?'

'For a view.' They braved the rain and the wind and skirted puddles to reach a metal gate, and he offered her a pair of binoculars. 'We're half a mile away, and its back on the other side of the A303, but if you climb a couple of rungs you can see over the hedge.'

Sam peered through the lenses and was amazed to see huge silhouetted stones. 'Stonehenge! I've never been here.' The sky was the colour of pewter, and the ancient monument imposed itself across the soft greys of the landscape, as if stamped out of ink.

Gillard put his arm around Sam and apologized for being in a bad mood. He brushed tendrils of wavy damp hair from her face and kissed her hard, his warm hands on her cool cheeks. 'You're everything to me – you do know that, don't you?'

She nodded. 'So you say.'

'It's just my family…' He shook his head. 'They've been at war for decades, with one thing and another. It just never seems to get resolved.' After a few minutes looking at the stones, they returned to the warmth of the Vauxhall.

'Oh. And this family business?' Sam reminded him, as she was clipping herself into the seatbelt. 'Do you want—?'

'To tell you what it is?' He snorted, started the car and drove off. He chewed his lips for a long time before responding. 'If I start, I shan't stop.'

'I don't mind.'

'You know what I told you about my mum?'

'She was the youngest, wasn't she?'

'Yes. She hated her father for his violent drunken outbursts, his black depressions, and the way he treated her mother. Like I say, she ran away as a 16-year-old and never went home. It was the early 1960s, and she had a great time in London. But family has a way of reaching back to you even when you think you can escape it. The way she met my dad for example. She should probably have never married him, because in some ways my father resembled her own. Hence the bad marriage.'

'At least ours is better.'

Gillard smiled. 'Remember me talking about my uncle Philip, Trish and Barbara's older brother?'

'Yes.'

'He was a vicar in a tough parish in Liverpool as a young man, then became linked to some radical causes during the Thatcher years. He presented a very successful TV series in the 1980s too, about homelessness.'

'You mentioned that.'

'When he retired, he bought a big old place at the seaside in Lynton. But the stairs got too much for him after he had a stroke and struggled to walk. Ten years ago, he moved into a caravan at Barbara's farm, just a few miles away, but his mobility worsened and two years ago he was moved into a care home. He's now confined to a wheelchair and losing his marbles a bit. Alzheimer's, I suppose. We'll be seeing him, I expect, though my aunts are in dispute with the care home, so I'm not sure what will be happening. I'm not sure if it's an official complaint about the way he's been looked after. They would probably have pulled him out but neither of them can cope with him any more.' He smacked his palm on the steering wheel. 'I think Trish and Barb are at loggerheads about it, just as they are about almost everything. There's been decades of backbiting and sniping.'

'They'll have to agree eventually,' Sam said.

'Well they have agreed on one thing as regards Philip. Can you believe Trish asked if we had room to look after him?'

Sam stared open-mouthed at him. 'Look after your uncle? Was she serious?'

'To be honest, Sam, if I gave her half an inch of opportunity, Philip would be shoved straight through our front door in his wheelchair and tipped onto the mat.'

'Oh God. I don't think I'd like that. Still, poor bloke.'

'Feeling guilty yet?'

'A bit, I suppose.'

'Welcome to the family,' Gillard said. 'That's why I warned you not to expect too much fun from this weekend. By the end of it, if I can get the rest of my family to stand in the road, I'll probably be tempted to do a hit-and-run myself.'

Chapter 3

It was eight o'clock on a Friday evening and, apart from a couple of uniformed officers joking around the main desk, Barnstaple police station was quiet. The minor collisions of the evening rush hour had been dealt with, while the first town-centre drunks typically wouldn't be echoing around the corridors until close to midnight. DI Jan Talantire leaned back in her creaky office chair, sucking a pencil and enjoying that blessed calm while reading the CSI notes on the hit-and-run.

The paperwork was proficient but terse, factual but utterly lacking in conjecture when tying in the injuries documented at the hospital with the evidence recovered on site. CSI had also noticed the labels removed from the clothing, but had not noted the chewing gum. On the other hand, there were extensive notes on the wristwatch and the fact that the smashed timepiece had frozen the recorded time at 3.41 p.m. They had also looked up the shoes: Cottrell Edge, made by Clarks, smooth black leather, size nine, 60 quid or thereabouts, available all over the country. Their fingertip search of the ditch and surrounding grass verge had brought forth nothing new. No wallet, no phone, not even a receipt.

'You don't want to be identified, do you?' Talantire muttered to herself. 'You just want a bit of privacy.' She logged off, yawned, and looked at her watch. Time to head home for a long-overdue early night.

Ah, she forgot. Just one last thing to take a closer look at.

The vehicle.

Talantire signed out the keys to the secure warehouse unit next to Barnstaple police station's car pound, and suited up in Tyvek and booties. With a printout of the CSI report in hand, she walked out into the chill night and slid open the warehouse's creaking metal door, flicked on the light and made her way inside. A 2012 Ford Ranger pickup is a hefty vehicle, and under the flicker of strip lighting the midnight-blue double cab pickup dominated the space. Weighing nearly two tons, 15 feet long and over 6 feet high: get hit by it and you'd know all about it. She fired up the big inspection lamp and knelt before the blood-smeared radiator as if inspecting holy stigmata. Smears of gore and hair still marked the front edge of the chassis, especially on the blade-like lower edge of the number plate.

CSI had noted extensive traces of skin, hair and blood in numerous places, and the 15 numbered yellow tags marking those places were still in situ. She grabbed a mechanic's wheeled creeper trolley and lay on it, scooting herself carefully under the front of the vehicle. She played the light above her, into the intricacies of the vehicle's chassis and engine compartment. Talantire was no mechanic, and didn't know the names of most of the parts she could see, but she could recognize blood in most circumstances.

There was plenty of it here, tagged and noted.

Playing the light into these complex cavities she spotted a flexible hose, with something else dangling in the shadow above it. It was a gobbet of dried gore, the size of a thumbnail, suspended by a hair. And it looked like there was a tiny screw protruding from it.

CSI had missed it.

She pulled out a pair of tweezers from the breast pocket on her Tyvek and tried to reach it. It was awkward, and however she angled her wrist and elbows, she found she couldn't do it without touching surrounding areas and disturbing CSI's precious tags. Perspiring in the crackling plastic suit, she slid out and rifled the police toolbox. She found nothing narrow enough to do the job. Next she opened the driver door, released the bonnet catch and, leaning over the engine, tried to get it from above. No dice.

Eventually she had an idea.

She walked back into the rear door of the police station and the evidence exam room. This time she was going to rely on Kite's slovenly habits. She opened the flip-top bin and, sure enough, found the detritus of a McDonald's meal. With it was a milkshake carton and a couple of fat and thankfully uncreased straws. She extricated them, washed them in the kitchen and taped them carefully together. She then blew through them to dry them out. Returning to her previous position, she lay on her back on the trolley underneath the engine. Fitting the extended straw to her mouth, she then threaded it up so it could reach above the hose. When the tip touched the lump, she sucked in sharply, and felt the air cut off. She prayed that this piece of the hit-and-run victim was sufficiently cohesive to not find its way in pieces down to her mouth.

She gradually tried to extricate the straw and, on the eighth or ninth attempt, whatever it was suspended from gave way, and a piece of a dead man fell with a plop onto her cheek.

She popped it in a clear evidence bag and then slid out to take a look at it.

Underneath the dried flesh was a tooth, a lower incisor, with a neat screw protruding from the bottom. A dental implant.

She marked it up, stowed it in the evidence refrigerator, and then, after washing her cheek, succumbed to a brief fit of the shudders.

Definitely time to go home.

Chapter 4

Once you leave the M5 just before Tiverton, the rolling wooded countryside of Devon begins to emerge. Sam looked out to the right as Gillard drove into the blustery darkness, the dual carriageway of the A361 taking them close to the southern edge of Exmoor. Unseen, ten miles north beyond the moor and ancient woodland, was the Bristol Channel, wind-whipped and choppy on a night like tonight.

It was just before 10 p.m. when they got into Barnstaple. Trish lived in a rambling white-painted detached house on the edge of town, sandwiched between a disused petrol station and a garden centre. When the house had been built, in the 1850s, there were only open fields around it, but now it had been caught up in the town's inexorable expansion. Gillard explained that Trish had never got over Howie leaving her. 'He still sends her postcards, and they talk on the phone. But there's a kind of wistfulness when she talks about him, and having kids that Trish always wanted for herself. She's bound to mention it herself, but don't be surprised if she gets upset.'

Trish welcomed them both at the door. She was only five feet tall, dressed in sequinned woollens, wearing lots of silver jewellery and tottering on tiny glittery shoes of the type that might be found in a fairy story. Losing herself momentarily in Gillard's embrace, she then hugged Sam, scanning her face with bright enquiring eyes.

'Oh, you are *such* a pretty thing,' she said, holding her by both wrists. 'I was so sad not to be able to stay for long at your wedding.' She leaned into Sam's ear and breathed: 'They thought the cancer had returned. But I beat it, with a bit more surgery.' She then continued with a volley of questions about the weather, the traffic and their health, as she led them into an overheated lounge.

Gillard passed across a bunch of flowers they had found at a service station in Wincanton. Sam had bought wrapping paper to spruce them up a bit, but to her eye they still looked a bit second-rate. Nonetheless, Trish seemed delighted to get them, and said how kind they both were. Sam counted four cats: a large ginger and white, plus three tortoiseshells. Trish introduced them in order: 'That is our marmalade, Napoleon – he's in charge. There is Lucretia, Billericay and Griselda. They've all had their bits taken away too,' she hissed conspiratorially in Sam's ear. 'Watch out for the litter tray, it tends to move about a bit. Mottram likes to tug it around with his teeth. It could end up anywhere, couldn't it, Mottram? Best not put your foot in it.'

Sam hadn't noticed the Jack Russell terrier Trish was addressing until he barked. He was sitting on the sofa, and then ran away out of the room. There were family photographs propped up on every surface, and a pinboard full of postcards. On a sideboard she recognized a younger Trish, Barbara looking formidable even as a 40-year-old, and a school photograph of a young Craig, his hair carefully brushed across his forehead.

'This was Philip at 31,' Trish said, handing her a studio portrait in black and white. Her brother had wavy fair hair, a firm jaw and a ready smile. He was standing with one foot on a chair, his hand gripping a pipe in his mouth, looking as incongruous to modern eyes as the jacket and tie he wore with his pale cable-knit sweater. 'He was quite a handsome fellow, wasn't he?'

'He looks like a naval commander in civvies,' Sam said. To her the staged pose reminded her of the knitting patterns from the 1970s which were now turning up on retro greetings cards. 'Do you remember him, Craig?' she said, offering him the picture.

'Not really. Of course I knew about him. That famous TV programme.'

'Oh yes,' said Trish. 'People still remember that. He still gets letters to the farm. He was also in demonstrations in the 1990s. Trying to stop shopping centres being built. He was quite a radical. Got a photograph of him somewhere chained to a bulldozer.'

'What was the show called?' Sam asked.

'It was called *Poverty*, dear. It was on Thames TV at half past eight on a Tuesday. Always started the same way, with a camera coming up to someone on a park bench at night, sleeping in cardboard boxes or under newspaper. Then Podge would pop up from under the newspapers and ask: "Do you know what it's like to lose your home?" He would interview rough sleepers, very gently, and tease out these amazing stories. There were lots of former soldiers, even someone who had once been really high up in the civil service. It was very interesting.' She looked across. 'Did you ever see it, Craig?'

'I did, a long time ago. It was ground-breaking stuff. That kind of social commentary was well ahead of its time.'

Trish interrupted. 'He met Michael Heseltine, John Major, lots of VIPs. The archbishop of Canterbury, though I can't remember which one. Of course, he never met *her*. He never liked her.'

'Mrs Thatcher,' Gillard explained.

'Bit before my time,' said Sam with a smile.

'Well, the homeless are still with us, dear. Podge did some good things, despite everything. But most people have forgotten about him now.'

Despite everything? It seemed a curious allusion. Sam caught Gillard's eye, and a raised eyebrow which showed he too had picked up on it. Trish put the photograph back, and then wiped her fingers on her skirt as if they were soiled. 'Well, we're going to see him tomorrow.'

'Trish, this dispute with the care home,' Gillard said. 'You thought someone had assaulted him. You did say you had pictures.'

'Oh, I completely forgot.' She put a hand over her mouth, then trotted off into the kitchen. She returned with her mobile phone.

Sam glimpsed between the two of them the images Trish had caught with her phone. There were mottled discolorations – mauve, yellow and green – visible on the old man's neck, plus a really nasty vertical cut behind one ear that had scabbed over. But what struck her wasn't his injuries, but his expression. He was looking at the camera, his soft brown eyes wide, like a frightened rabbit. He looked absolutely terrified.

'When were these taken?' Gillard asked.

'The morning after. I went straight round.'

'But when was that?'

'More than a month ago now. It's all healed up.'

'Was it another resident at the home? I mean, these look to me like a strangulation attempt. Much more serious injuries than I expected.'

'I don't know. The staff say it wasn't them. The manager, Mrs Dickinson, had them all in for interviews, and they all denied having anything to do with it.'

'So who first reported the injuries?'

'It was at breakfast. This lovely chap called Fitz, well, he is actually a West Indian. But he is very nice. Anyway, he reported it.'

Sam permitted herself a small smile at Trish's attempt to redress a perceived prejudice, one that she assumed they shared.

'What did Philip say?' Gillard asked

'Well, he was still in his pyjamas when I arrived. Fortunately he can still dress himself, though it takes a while. And I noticed these marks. "What have you done to yourself?" I asked him. And he said. "I'm sorry, I'm so, so sorry." Then he started to cry. Oh, I did check after you asked, Craig, and there isn't any CCTV. But they are planning to install it eventually.' She smiled, and led them through to the dining room where a huge spread had been laid out on the table: quiche, ham sandwiches and raspberry cheesecake.

'Trish, I'm still really surprised you didn't report the home to social services. Or even the police.'

'Well, I threatened to, of course. But then Mrs Dickinson and I, we had a discussion.' She smiled as she bit into a slice of raspberry cheesecake.

'She offered you a discount on his fees, didn't she?' Gillard asked.

Trish didn't reply and continued to chew. But her sparkling eyes radiated a kind of satisfaction.

–

After the meal and the washing-up Trish led them up narrow, creaking stairs lined with family photographs and showed them into their room. It was small and fussily furnished, reeking of potpourri. The high, rather small double bed was heaped with sequinned cushions, and hosted the recumbent form of Napoleon, the marmalade cat, whose arch expression indicated displeasure at being disturbed. Sam went to shoo the animal off the bed, and earned herself a hiss. With a long languorous stretch and a dismissive glance at each of them, Napoleon strode slowly to the edge of the bed, jumped lithely to the floor and marched out, swinging his long ginger tail slowly from side to side. No sooner had he exited then the door opened further and a plastic cat litter tray entered followed by the Jack Russell terrier who was proudly holding it in his jaws.

'Mottram, *they* don't need it, you silly thing,' Trish called from the landing. 'They are people, not cats.' The dog, one ear cocked for his mistress's advice, offered the tray to Gillard and Sam in turn with a wag of his tail. Finding no takers, he trotted out, still carrying the well-used cat facility.

Gillard closed the door and exchanged another meaningful glance with Sam.

'She seems nice,' Sam said, the bottom half of her face a contradictory grimace of horror. 'Did you see there is a

36

knitted cosy for the spare toilet roll? And one for the air freshener?'

'Trish means well,' Gillard said, looking round the room at the knitted bedspread, the weighted doily dust covers for the jug of milk and sugar bowl on the tea tray, and the little corn dollies which hung from the mirror. 'But it is a bit Hans Christian Andersen.'

After Gillard had struggled to turn the radiator down, they undressed, turned off the light and squeezed together into the squeaky bed.

'Are you going to tell me a bedtime story?' Sam whispered.

'I certainly could,' he said enfolding her in his arms. 'But if I told you the story Auntie Barbara told me when I was seven, you wouldn't get a wink of sleep.'

'What story?'

'About the time she was cornered by the wolf of Exmoor.'

'Sounds scary.' She slid her hand under his pyjamas. 'I think I prefer Jack and the Beanstalk.' She gave him a gentle, intimate caress. 'There, I found it.' They dissolved in a fit of suppressed giggles as he gently slid on top of her.

–

After being woken at seven by Napoleon scratching at the door, Gillard and Sam were lured downstairs by the smell of bacon. Trish watched them each consume a full cooked breakfast, but ate nothing herself.

'I've got a small errand to run, then I'll go and make friends with the local constabulary to find out what they know about the hit-and-run,' Gillard said. 'I'm sure I'll be about as welcome as an outbreak of the plague, so don't expect too much.'

'I'm sure you'll be able to straighten it out, dear.'

Gillard had to wait 45 minutes at reception at Barnstaple police station for Detective Inspector Jan Talantire. He had already looked her up on the Devon and Cornwall Constabulary website, so recognized her immediately as she walked in. If he had not done so, he would have pigeonholed her as a mid-ranking business executive in her late thirties: expensively coiffed, in a smartly cut white blouse, black trouser suit and houndstooth jacket. He knew from what Sam had told him how much those highlight hairdos cost. Talantire was on the phone, but had instantly eyed Gillard and turned her back to shield her confidentiality. After keeping Gillard waiting another five frustrating minutes, she hung up, turned and offered a brief but firm handshake. 'Thanks for the email, Craig, if I may call you that. There were some good questions. But come on, you're experienced, you know the score. Given your links to the Antrobus family, I can't share any of our thinking about this case so long as there is the slightest uncertainty about who drove that vehicle.'

'I understand perfectly,' Gillard said. 'I'm not here to make life difficult, but if I can help in any way, I'm available. You've got my contact details.'

She smiled. A keen intelligence shone in her brown eyes 'We could always do with more hands on deck, just not from you, or on this particular case.' She paused, and he felt her scrutinizing him. 'I looked you up. Quite an impressive track record. Solved the Martin Knight murder case. Must have been tricky, given your connection to Mrs Knight.'

'It was.' Gillard immediately realized what a sharp brain this woman had. Picking the only other case in which he had a conflict of interest, asking around enough to discover something not mentioned in any of the official reports.

At that moment a young uniformed constable emerged from the door and called out to her. 'Forensics called, ma'am.' He waved a piece of paper. 'We've got a match for the fingerprints on the can. Bit of a likely boy—'

'Willow, zip it,' Talantire said, flicking her fingers away from her to indicate the young constable should return through the door he'd so foolishly entered by. She excused herself to Gillard, then followed the PC, closing the door behind them.

-

Talantire was furious. She snatched the piece of paper from Willow's hand and quickly scanned it. These were the results she'd been awaiting. Half a dozen different sets of prints from inside the vehicle, one matching the owner, one matching a known local bad boy. She looked up at the PC, then pointed a thumb over her shoulder, through the now closed door. 'Do you know who that is?'

'Yes, he introduced himself earlier, a Detective Chief Inspector...' The constable screwed his face up trying to remember the name.

Talantire helped him out. 'Craig Gillard, from Surrey.'

'That's the one. I saw him up at the crime scene this morning. He was quite helpful.'

'The crime scene! Clifford,' she said, gripping the constable by the shoulders, 'that detective is the nephew of Barbara Antrobus.'

'Is he? Is that why he's come all the way down here?'

Talantire nodded, waiting while the cogs in Willow's brain slowly turned. She found herself fervently wishing that Avon Police up in Bristol would hurry up and allocate the promised two detective constables to help her while DS Charmaine Stafford was on maternity leave. 'Did he cross the crime tape? If he did, I'll bloody nail him.'

'No, we chatted outside the cordon.'

'You chatted, did you? So what did he want to know?'

'Just about where the body was, what condition he was in. He asked whether we had done fingerprints on the car, tyre analysis, and established whether the locks had been forced.'

'I hope you didn't answer any of those questions.'

The constable looked sheepish. 'I didn't see any reason not to. He showed me his card, mentioned your name, so I thought he was part of the investigation.'

Stupid boy. 'Willow, from now on, do not tell him anything. On principle, okay? If it turns out that Barbara Antrobus was the hit-and-run driver, you might well have compromised any chance we have of getting a clean case to the Crown Prosecution Service.'

'But we got all the fingerprint results through. And the fingerprints from the can in the car, they match Micky Tuffin. That's what I was telling you—'

'And broadcasting to everyone sitting in reception,' she said.

'He's a bad 'un, Micky Tuffin,' Willow said. 'Regular car thief. Right from school.'

'Your school?'

'My year, my class. I know all about him. I had the desk in front.'

She rolled her eyes. 'For God's sake.' She leaned back against the door, momentarily closing her eyes. 'Okay, thanks for letting me know. Was he a friend?'

'You're kidding,' Willow said, grinning. 'I hated him. We had a punch-up during year nine.'

'All right, to be squeaky clean, I'm still going to have to keep you away from that side of the investigation. Christ, another conflict of interest. Confine yourself to dealing with the leads that come in on the victim. Keep off the driver side of the investigation.'

Angry now, Talantire dismissed the young constable, turned on her heel and went out to confront Gillard.

He was nowhere to be seen.

Chapter 5

Gillard drove out of the police station car park just after ten feeling quite pleased with himself. In two hours he had probably found out as much as he was going to about the investigation, and with his cover now completely blown he was going to have to be more careful. He didn't blame the young PC for blurting out all the details. Gillard had pretty much gathered what had happened from a comprehensive reading of the local press, and the lad had just filled in a few extra details. The most significant of these was that they seemed to have an idea of who it was that stole the car. A drink can found in the footwell with an excellent set of fingerprints made up for what were apparently partial prints found in the rest of the vehicle. He had already heard from Trish that Barbara was outraged to have been fingerprinted during her initial interview. From what he remembered, he would not have wanted to be on the receiving end of Barbara's outrage. She had always been a woman and a half.

When he got back to Trish's house, Sam's expression telegraphed that she had endured about as much small talk as she could bear. While Trish bustled in the kitchen, talking to the cats, Sam took him to one side. 'So glad to see you back,' she breathed. 'My ears are worn out. I've had chapter and verse on Napoleon's trips to the vet's, and she's shown me every single postcard from her ex in Bangkok.'

'Howie married a local woman,' Gillard said. 'Tangmo is half his age.'

'Well, if so, Trish seems to be a woman remarkably devoid of jealousy,' Sam said.

'Really? It was she who told me, years ago. She was spitting feathers at the time. None of Howie's family would speak to him either, apparently. He just buggered off to Thailand after a huge row with Trish and spent the next year and a half in the fleshpots of Pattaya until the divorce came through.'

'What a nice guy,' Sam muttered. 'Well Trish at least has obviously got over her anger. She still misses him, and looks forward to their calls. Howie's brother-in-law Sarawut came over to see her last year, and the whole family is coming over at Christmas. Eight of them, apparently, including his wife's parents. She's already in a flap about where she'll put them all up.'

At that moment Trish came in wearing a coat and reminded them they were already due at The Beeches a few minutes ago.

'Philip gets anxious if I'm late – he thinks he's been abandoned.'

Gillard's offer to drive was declined. 'My car's got the wheelchair lift, and as we're taking him out to lunch it will be easier.'

The Beeches was a sizeable 1930s building not far from the centre of town. 'It used to be a pub,' Trish said as she eased her Nissan into one of the disabled parking slots. 'But it's still run by the same people, which is nice.'

It began to spot with rain as they walked in. They passed an elderly lady with a walking frame standing outside sucking hard on a cigarette. She greeted Trish by name, and coughed out an enormous cloud of smoke.

They found Philip in a crowded lounge sitting on a sofa watching children's TV. 'Hello, Podge,' Trish said. He looked at her quizzically for the first couple of seconds, before recognition swam into his soft, searching brown eyes behind the gold-framed spectacles. He had soft downy hair, a delicate liver-spotted forehead and a charmingly cheeky grin.

'Trish, so lovely to see you, finally.' He turned to the florid overweight woman sitting at the other end of the sofa. 'This is my little sister, Trish.'

'I know, pet, you introduce me to her every week,' the woman said with a Scottish burr.

'But you've never met her,' Philip said indignantly. 'This is her first visit.'

'Podge, I come every week to see you,' Trish said without a hint of irritation. 'And this is your nephew Craig and his wife Sam.' She turned to point them out.

Philip ignored Gillard, but with open mouth appraised Sam from head to foot. It was a nakedly lascivious look, enough to make her blush, and she moved behind her husband to escape it.

'Podge, behave,' Trish said.

A tall dreadlocked care assistant came into the room, offering a cheery hello. All the ladies answered 'Hello, Fitz' in unison. Fitz organized some coffee and biscuits in the quiet of the dining room, and went to fetch a wheelchair.

Fitz helped Philip into the chair and then trundled him into the dining room. After pouring coffee he left and closed the door. The old man's eyes again hunted for Sam, and she retreated from his gaze to stand behind him.

'I'm sorry, dear,' Trish said. 'He's become quite uninhibited. Don't take it personally.'

Sam nodded. Gillard sat himself down opposite Philip and asked: 'Do you remember me? Your nephew.'

'I don't know you,' he said. 'But I'm delighted to meet you.' He held out his hand, which was slender, the skin like parchment. Gillard shook it. His uncle had a surprisingly firm grip.

Trish reached across and pulled down the collar of Philip's shirt. He flinched, and leaned away from her.

'You can't see it too well any more. But there were bruises. Like fingermarks. And there are still scabs, and those deep cuts behind his ear.' She moved the ear forward for Gillard to see.

'Philip,' Gillard said, trying to catch the old man's gaze. 'Who did this to you?'

He shook his head. 'No. No. I'm so sorry.'

'Was it a stranger? Or was it somebody you know?'

'I didn't mean to do it, you know. It wasn't meant to happen.'

'What wasn't?' Gillard asked kindly. 'You can tell me.'

'You can trust him, Podge, he's a policeman,' Trish said.

The old man recoiled as if struck. 'Policeman? No.' He shook his head repeatedly. 'Not the police. No. They won't let me out, you know. Not after this.'

Gillard looked up at Trish, and she nodded as if he should carry on.

'You've done nothing wrong, Uncle Philip. We're here to help you. We just want to find out who hurt you.'

'Did someone hurt me?' he asked, amazed.

Trish gave Gillard an exaggerated shrug. 'He's forgotten.'

'Are you here about Emily?' Philip asked.

'Who is Emily?' Gillard asked his aunt.

She shrugged her shoulders. 'I have no idea. He's been talking about her on and off for several weeks now. Someone he used to know, I suppose. But I'd never heard of her.'

'Who is Emily, Podge?' Trish asked, crouching down to his height. 'Tell me who she is. I'll give you a chocolate biscuit.'

'I don't want a bloody chocolate biscuit,' he roared, and swept the plate off the table, sending his coffee cup flying and spattering Sam's blouse and trousers. 'Not the police, no!' After the momentary shock had subsided, Trish fussed over Sam while Gillard went to fetch a cloth from Fitz.

'He's never been like this before,' Trish said as she dabbed at Sam's blouse with a paper handkerchief. 'I'm so sorry, so very sorry.'

'It's fine,' Sam said. 'Don't worry about it.'

'It's awful that you should come down here for a nice weekend away and be treated like this. It's the first time, you know. Honestly.'

Philip was facing away from them, his wheelchair partially jammed under the edge of the table, but he had turned his head and eyed Sam furtively.

'He's staring at me again,' Sam whispered to Trish.

'Don't worry about it, dear. His mind is going.'

But I expect his body still works, Sam thought. Or at least part of it. As if on cue, Philip started to hum, an ancient pop song that Sam found familiar, but couldn't name.

'He's started doing that as well,' Trish said. 'He's not bad, is he? When he sings, he can hold a note. You should hear him in the bathroom. "Merry Xmas Everybody" by Slade, at any time of year.' She chuckled. 'It's harmless, isn't it, Podge?'

'She's dead,' Philip declared.

'Who's dead, Podge?'

'Emily. Dead and gone.' Then he began to cry, an unrestrained childish wailing which intensified and carried through to the rest of the home. Trish could do nothing to make him stop.

'I'd love to know who this Emily is,' Trish said.

Gillard looked distinctly unenthusiastic. 'We don't even know that she exists. She could be somebody off the telly.' He turned to Sam and said: 'I warned you that this might be an odd weekend.'

—

Fitz came back into the room and suggested they take Philip back to his room. 'What's happened? Some of the other residents are a bit upset by his crying.'

'We weren't trying to upset him,' Trish explained. 'Just wanted to know how he got hurt.'

'I'd like to see the accident book for the home,' Gillard said. 'I assume it has all been logged.'

'I wasn't on duty until later that morning,' Fitz said hurriedly. 'But I reported it and I understand it was logged. Mrs Dickinson, she's the manager, made sure of that.' They all followed Fitz, who pushed Philip in his chair down a carpeted corridor through a newly painted extension and out into a large walled garden. The grounds contained half a dozen wooden chalets, each accessible by a concrete ramp, and dozens of saplings planted within protective mesh.

'This is his room,' Trish said, pointing to chalet number six. 'It's very nice.'

Fitz wheeled the chair along a meandering tarmac path, past flowerbeds and bushes, and up the slope onto a wooden veranda where, through a large glass window, they could see a double bedroom.

'So the old timers basically all live in sheds,' Gillard said as Fitz produced a key to unlock the room.

'They're a bit better than sheds,' Trish said. 'Just as well considering how much they charge for them.'

Fitz grinned. 'Super-luxury sheds, maybe.' Once inside, he showed them the wet room, large-screen TV and the panic alarm. 'There's a care assistant on call 24 hours a day,' Fitz said.

'I understand there is no CCTV?' Gillard asked.

'No, it's not compulsory for care homes. We like to feel we are well enough staffed to look after our guests without the intrusiveness of cameras everywhere.'

'Is the manager around today?' Gillard asked. 'And I'd still like to see that logbook.'

'Craig, don't make a fuss, dear,' Trish whispered, gripping his arm. 'Just calm down.'

Sam smiled to hear her husband addressed like a little boy until she caught the expression on his face. He was livid.

After making Philip comfortable in his room, Fitz led Gillard back to the main office in search of the incident log. Almost as soon as he'd gone, Philip said one word, carefully pronouncing each syllable: 'lavatory'.

'Do you need a hand,' Sam asked Trish, fervently hoping that she didn't. Once again, tentacles of guilt emerged within her, even though she knew that this strange and troubled man was not part of her family, nor her responsibility.

'It's all right, dear, I'm well practised at this, unfortunately.'

While Trish moved Philip into the wet room, Sam looked around the chalet. The photographs she had seen showed vertical cuts behind his left ear, and she wondered how they could have been made. If he had fallen against a door frame, that could explain it. But as she walked around the room, she didn't see any sharp edges. The recognizable tune of another old pop song echoed from the wet room. This was one she knew. 'See My Baby Jive', by Wizzard. She hadn't even been born when it came out, and couldn't recall where she had first heard it.

She went to his bedside table and slid the drawers open as quietly as she could. There was neatly laundered underwear, incontinence aids of various kinds and, at the bottom, a rather well-thumbed men's pornographic magazine. With an involuntary grimace, she closed the drawer. I was right, she thought. God's practical joke: the most practical functions of the body seem to break down first, but what at his age should be useless desires, like sex, seem to march on for ever.

'Been having a nose around, dear?' Trish was standing on the threshold of the wet room. Sam flushed.

'Sorry, I was just wondering if he could have banged his head on one of the drawers,' she lied.

Trish gave a rather supercilious smile. 'Of course, a bit of detective work on the sly. You were sort of in the police yourself, weren't you? One of those hobby bobbies, I gather.'

Sam bristled. 'I was a PCSO, a community support officer. It's harder work than you might imagine. Now I'm a civilian officer taking calls in the incident room.'

Trish peered out at the weather. 'I'm sure it's all very useful, dear, helping out our hard-pressed bobbies,' she said dismissively, before going back into the wet room and skilfully reversing out the wheelchair and its occupant. 'If you're wondering who hurt him, I think I can let you in on the secret.'

'You know?'

'Yes, I told Craig on the phone when I rang him. Barbara. It's bound to have been her. Such a temper. Every family has one mad sibling, and she's my cross to bear.'

'What makes you think it was her?'

'Ah well, dear. I've lived my whole life in this family; you don't know anything about us. I bet your husband hasn't talked much about us, has he?'

It was true. Sam didn't know what to say.

'I thought so,' Trish said. 'Well you're going to meet her for lunch in a few minutes so you can judge for yourself.'

Chapter 6

All Britain's unidentified bodies are listed on the police Missing Persons Unit. It is a public resource run from a website where anyone can type in an age, description, ethnicity and various other details and see elements of the case files. DI Talantire slouched in her chair at Barnstaple police station and eyed the details that PC Willow had entered for their nameless corpse: a rough age, 60–65, white European ethnicity, height five foot eleven, grey hair, shoe size nine and some generic clothing description, as well as details of the location where he was found.

The site usually carries images of the dead, but in this case injuries to the face were so severe, and so unhelpful to identification, that her superiors had decided not to include them, not even on the sensitive images files which the public could opt to look at. No tattoos, no piercings; a few moles but nothing outrageously memorable. The nearest to anything distinctive was that he was uncircumcised and had mild haemorrhoids. If those two details jolted somebody's memory she would be surprised. Even the eye colour was not obvious given the damage he had suffered. Further details would have to await a full autopsy. Three days after his death, the victim of the hit-and-run incident was clinging grimly to anonymity.

Talantire worked her stub of pencil over and over around the top of her knuckles and back again, before jamming it back in her mouth for a ruminative chew. She switched the screen to the charitable website Missing People. Altogether she had amassed the details of 629 British people who were missing and approximately matched the description she had. When she had narrowed it down to those missing for less than a month and in the south-west, she was down to 19. The answer would probably lie amongst those.

The regional radio alert had triggered hundreds of calls and emails, mostly of people missing in the last few days. But as so often with appeals to the public, the vast majority of responses were for those of the wrong age, and in some cases the wrong sex. Willow had struggled manfully to whittle down the list of possibles to 25. She looked down the list. Two men, roughly the right age and height, both reported missing on the day the body was found, one from Falmouth, the other from Bristol. There was also a wild card: a keen walker from Potters Bar in Hertfordshire who had been missing three days and was a regular visitor to Devon. She had requested DNA samples from the local police force in each case.

The victim's DNA tests, including mitochondrial to give a precise ethnicity, would be back on Tuesday. She would be very surprised if the body retained its secrets for long after that.

The bang of the door behind her and a shout of greeting prompted her to whirl the chair around. 'Oh Charmaine, how are you?'

'Bloated, blotchy and knackered,' said DS Stafford as she waddled into her boss's office and sat down heavily.

'Boy, are you pregnant,' Talantire exclaimed. The baby bump was like a basketball on the woman's previously lissom frame.

'Just a month to go,' she said. 'I'm bored out of my mind reading magazines about romper suits and breathing exercises, so I thought I'd come and give you a hand.'

'Fantastic,' Talantire said. 'Are you past the stage of feeling pukey?'

'Well past, fortunately.'

'Good. I need you to cross-check details of the missing against our dead body.'

At that moment PC Willow knocked on the half-open door.

'Ma'am, there's something else I forgot to tell you. When I was talking with that Gillard fellow this morning, he pointed out that someone had left a bunch of flowers tied to the fence behind the phone box. I'd not noticed it, had you?'

'It wasn't there on the day of the accident.'

'He was quite proper and said he didn't want to trespass on the crime scene or anything, but asked if I knew who'd left the flowers. So I said I didn't know because I'd not noticed them. So then he says I should check for a label because this could easily be the hit-and-run driver feeling a bit guilty or possibly a friend or relative of the victim, and suggested I take some pictures and pass them around the florists in the area, and see if we can get some dabs of the cellophane they are wrapped in.'

'And did you?' Talantire asked sharply. She had to admit that Gillard's suggestions were spot on, but she was simultaneously annoyed to be wrong-footed.

'I took a couple of pictures, but I got a call from the super soon after, and I drove off forgetting to pick up the flowers.'

Talantire stared at Willow. 'Did you ever see that programme *Dad's Army* on the BBC? Bit before your time, but it ran for years.' Her eyes slid sideways to Stafford, who was sniggering quietly.

'Yeah. Are you going to say that I look like Private Pike? Everybody says that.' He looked almost proud at the comparison.

'Okay, show me the pictures,' she sighed.

He got out his phone and swiped until he found the images he wanted. 'They seem a bit fuzzy for some reason.' He showed her.

'You took them into the sun. They're almost useless. You can't even tell what the flowers are.'

'Well, there are yellow and white ones.'

'Why didn't you use flash to fill in the foreground?'

'I thought it would be automatic,' he said.

Talantire closed her eyes. *Stupid boy.*

–

Early that afternoon Talantire drove back up to the lane where the body had been found. It was a beautiful spot, with breaks in the hedgerow giving views across fields and the rising moorland beyond. The crime scene tape was intact, and the phone box still done up with its festive blue-and-white bow. She knelt down and shone her torch inside the booth. It was a well-stocked little library, with a few dozen romance, historical fiction and crime thrillers, many of their pages curling from the damp. Nothing inside seemed out of place. She had asked CSI to dust the kiosk door for fingerprints, but had been told there were none. She untied the tape, heaved the door open, and stepped inside. She carefully inspected the inside for bloodstains, or even a dropped phone or wallet. Nothing.

The lack of ID on a hit-and-run victim seemed so strange. Looking through previous cases of unidentified bodies, Talantire had seen that they basically fell into two categories. One was the suicides, where precious personal items had been left behind at home, often with a note. The second quite distinct category was murders where the perpetrator had removed the victim's ID, either before the crime or after.

It was hard to see how this could be a suicide, unless there was a co-conspirator who had agreed to run him down. That would be just plain weird, and overly complex, when less than half an hour's drive away to the north there were cliffs easily high enough to do the job.

The idea of murder was more intriguing. If this was an inner city, or even a busy thoroughfare, it might be a tenable theory. Wait for someone who regularly walks a particular route and run them down, then take their ID to gain a bit of breathing space.

But the holes in the murder theory for a place like this were enormous.

Firstly, though there might be a scattering of walkers, either locals or tourists at this time of year, no killer could rely on them being here. The only regular users of this lonely road at this time of year would be dog walkers like Muriel Hinkley and a couple of farmers. If it had been summer rather than a rainy afternoon in late autumn, that list could have included the owners of the two holiday cottages in Furzy Hill less than half a mile away. But

Willow had established they were both unoccupied at the moment, and the doors and windows seemed secure.

Secondly, all bar dog walkers would probably be within a vehicle, not on foot.

Thirdly, if the victim was a dog walker, where was the dog? He had been carrying no poo bags, lead, treats or any of the other accoutrements. Moreover, the faithful pooch would presumably not have gone far. Any local dog walkers would soon be missed. In fact, she would have expected this to be solved already if that was the case.

Fourthly, the body hadn't looked disturbed. None of the pockets were inside out when she had got there. It didn't seem that the lack of ID was anything but random.

Talantire shrugged and got back in her car. She had already started the motor when, to her horror, she saw the remains of the floral tribute still tied to the fence by the phone box. She killed the engine and made her way across. Calling up on her mobile phone the fuzzy images recorded by PC Willow, she compared it to the wilted rotting mass before her. Yes, there were some yellow and white petals. There was no card, but as the rather astute DCI Gillard had pointed out, the cellophane wrapping might well still harbour fingerprints, if the repeated downpours had not eradicated them. She got a paper evidence bag from the boot, donned latex gloves and carefully cut the raffia that had been used to tie the bouquet to the wooden upright. She then separated the damp, rainspotted wrap, and slid it into the envelope. It was a long shot and no mistake.

The Stag Inn was a big chain eatery, a sprawling and characterless modern pub by a roundabout, perfectly set up for disabled access. After previous embarrassments with Philip, Trish explained she had booked a table in the family section where unexpected racket was part and parcel of the experience. They were allocated a large table, with a thick sheaf of plastic menus offering a bewildering variety of meal deals. They had a great view of the very large car park, and each time a vehicle came in they all looked up to see if it was Barbara. They were just about to order when a battered Mitsubishi Shogun roared into the car park in a cloud of diesel fumes and pulled up just a foot from the window, blocking out half the light to their table.

'That's her,' Gillard breathed. They watched the formidable-looking woman, wearing an eyepatch under her spectacles, clamber out, slam the door and march in.

'Craig,' she bellowed. 'Come here and kiss your auntie.'

Sam watched as her husband dutifully rose to his feet and was engulfed in her matronly bosom as she planted kisses on both his cheeks. 'And you must be the lovely Samantha?' she said, pulling her into a rough embrace and laughing uproariously. 'My, she is nubile,' she boomed, winking at Gillard.

Sam's gaze was drawn past Barbara, where Philip was cringing in horror, sinking down in his chair. His hands were shaking. She looked up to try and catch her husband's eye, and saw that his face showed a paler shadow of that same expression. A wariness, if not something more.

'Now, we're moving tables,' Barbara announced, seizing the handles of Philip's wheelchair and moving further into the restaurant. 'Don't want to be in the family section.'

'But Barbara, I booked this,' Trish said, trailing behind. Sam and Craig exchanged bewildered shrugs. Barbara loomed over a young waitress and firmly pointed out the table that she wanted. Her argument, that it was still quite early and there was plenty of room, brooked no opposition, and she soon had three members of staff scurrying around rearranging chairs to make room for Philip. 'And I'd like a pint of cider please, straight away.'

For the next half an hour, Barbara totally dominated the conversation, broadcasting about the problems with her sheep flock, the new ram that she had bought and wasn't up to the job – typical male – and how behind she had been in getting organized for the tupping. There was a great deal of detail about expenditure, the poor market price for lamb and particularly for wool, which was hardly worth shearing, and the uselessness of the police – here she rested a beady eye directly upon Gillard – for failing to catch the thieves who had stolen not only her quad bike, but had siphoned off half of her diesel from the storage tank.

'If I got hold of them, I'd thrash every one of them myself, then toss every last one of them off a high cliff,' she announced. 'None of this police caution nonsense. Physical punishment.' She looked at each of them in turn, daring them to disagree. None did.

Sam was amazed that the subject of the fatal hit-and-run had not arisen. 'Craig? Aren't you going to mention…'

He shook his head slightly, as if a fly had landed on his nose. 'Not now.' Sam took the cue and shut up.

The food arrived, and Barbara organized its distribution. 'Philip will have the soup and some apple pie. He doesn't need a main course.' She had brought with her a large towelling bib, one with a plasticized gutter at the bottom. As she reached across to tie it around his neck, Philip started whimpering. 'Oh do stop making a fuss, you silly sausage.'

Sam looked at her husband and could see that Craig was working up to saying something. It was obvious he was having to overcome some anxiety. She could understand why Craig was annoyed, irritated and even disliked this woman, but she had definitely seen fear too. If her husband could face down the head of the Albanian mafia, what possible hold could this batty old lady have over him?

Barbara turned to Sam, as if she had just spoken her thoughts out loud. 'You might be wondering how Philip got those cuts and bruises,' she said, turning to face each of them in turn. 'I know you, Trish, will have had no doubt about them.' She laughed. 'And I suppose that, not the theft of my car, is the real reason, Craig, that you're finally down here to see us two mad old bats.'

'Well, Barbara, it's been absolutely years—' Gillard began.

'Oh do shut up, I'm not stupid. You don't want to be here, do you? No, of course you don't. Look. I've discovered something rather incriminating about our wonderful innocent brother. I'm going to show you. Don't ask me to tell you what it is in advance because I can't bring myself to. But what I had to do was to rub his nose in it. And I'm afraid I might have been a little too vigorous.'

'He had severe bruising around his neck, and a nasty cut behind his ear,' Gillard said. 'Did you do that?'

'Oh, for goodness' sake, I get bruises like that every day on the farm. Don't be so bloody dramatic.'

'Barbara, it actually looks like you tried to kill him,' Trish said, her eyes like daggers.

'Nonsense. I looked after him for ten years, Trish. Every meal, every day. And when he could no longer look after himself in that last year, I carried him in a wheelbarrow down from his caravan to the farmhouse and wiped his bottom as required, and I lugged him back again, come rain or storm. While you, madam, were coveting his property. So if anybody wanted him dead, I'd wager it would be you.' She pointed a ringed finger at her sister.

'Please don't argue,' Gillard said. He knew there had long been contention about what would happen to Philip's old home in the Devon seaside town of Lynton.

'You could go to jail – for grievous bodily harm, on top of everything else,' Trish retorted. 'Bloody lunatic.'

'Trish, please,' Gillard said, gripping his aunt's arm. 'This isn't helping.'

Barbara flipped up the eyepatch and gave Sam the full benefit of the milky pale-grey orb. 'So, young lady, what you think of us obscure Devon rellies? Did he tell you we were inbred? Did he tell you we were rural simpletons, to be visited like reptiles in a zoo? Careful, they bite!'

'No, nothing like that. He didn't tell me much at all.'

'Hah! Not surprised about that,' she said, and reached forward and pinched Gillard's cheek quite roughly. 'There's more of us in you than you will ever admit, isn't there, Mr Detective?'

Gillard stared down at the remains of his meal and his eyes flashed anger. 'You're right, Barbara,' he said, his voice dripping with sarcasm. 'We should never have come. I should have just called the local police, got them to come up to the farm to sort you out. And your drunken driving.'

Barbara roared with laughter. 'Oh the police have been up all right. Rode a couple of them in my time, though don't know why I bothered. They still like to sniff around, if they think a bit of surplus shoulder of lamb is going after Easter. But solve a crime? Hah! Forget it. They're not going to pin that accident on me. It's ridiculous.'

Trish was crying quietly, dabbing her eyes with a tissue. A waitress, a tiny little slip of a thing, wandered up to the table and asked if they had enjoyed their meal.

'Well, his soup was out of a tin, wasn't it?' Barbara barked. 'And that chop was never local pork. The texture was too coarse. It had been fattened too fast, you understand? And there wasn't enough fat on it. Proper pork has a good layer of fat which transmits the flavour.' She waited in vain for a response, and then folded her arms impatiently. 'You do eat food, don't you? Not a vegan, I hope.'

The waitress shrank under each assault. 'I'll tell chef.'

She was about to go when Barbara took a firm grip on her arm. 'And is that chef Ian Foster today?'

'Yes, actually.'

'No point telling him, then, my lovely. I've known him since school. He shouldn't be left in charge of a toaster. Now fetch us the bill, and give it to this nice gentleman down from Surrey.' She pointed at Gillard.

After the waitress had gone, Barbara said: 'I knew it was Ian when I saw his Land Rover. He bought it off me 12 years ago.' She wiped Philip's mouth roughly with a cloth she had brought for the purpose, untied his bib, rolled it up and stuffed it in a plastic bag.

'You two can come with me now,' Barbara said, indicating Gillard and Sam, 'and I'll drop you back to pick up your car later this afternoon. 'Trish, you follow on behind.'

Barbara marched out to the Shogun, which was caked in mud almost up to the door handles. 'Sorry about the mess,' Barbara said. 'Back to the old car, I'm afraid, now the police have grabbed my new one.'

'I'll sit in the back, Craig,' Sam said. 'You talk to her up front.'

'Thanks,' Gillard mouthed, sarcastically.

Sam had been in some dirty vehicles in her life, but nothing prepared her for this. There was mud, paint, tar, dog hairs and what looked like smears of dried blood on the seats. 'There's an old fertilizer bag to sit on,' Barbara said 'It's in the back. Watch out for Henrietta.'

As Sam turned to reach into the rear space, a large horned creature with slotted eyes and rancid breath stood up and pushed its snout towards her. Sam's cry of alarm brought forth remonstrance from Barbara.

'It's only a nanny goat, my lovely. She won't bite. Well, she might nibble your clothes.' Barbara fired up the engine, revved hard and then turned to Gillard. 'I took her to the vet this morning. She's got mastitis again.' The vehicle thundered out onto the road, under a sky that was darker than the bruises on Philip's neck. 'It's going to be bad tonight,' Barbara said, then laughed.

Sam leaned as far to the left as she could in the seatbelt, but she was still caught in the miasma of the goat's putrid breath, and its filthy beard still hung over her shoulder as Henrietta strained forward to see where they were going.

At every turn they clashed heads, so that Sam was forced to keep her hand between her head and the animal's jaw. Barbara, who had downed a pint and a half of strong cider over lunch, drove at breakneck speed, barely stopping at junctions, while commenting on the shortcomings of other road users, most of whom she seemed to know. After half an hour, with the rain now lashing down again, the Mitsubishi turned into a narrow sunken lane between drystone walls and high thorny hedgerows. The undulating, rutted lane took them up a steep wooded hill, the treetops thrashed by a gathering wind. Flocks of crows wheeled and dived around the highest points.

'That's Martinhoe Head,' Barbara shouted. 'Hollow Coombe farm is just down to the north-west. This here's Donnie Westbrook's land.'

'I think I met old man Westbrook when I was a child,' Gillard said.

'You may well have done. I also hear you like rock climbing, Craig. There's Trentishoe Slab just here on the seaward side. Three deaths and fourteen serious injuries in thirty years.' She laughed. 'It's very crumbly, apparently. The bolts just slide out of the rock.'

'I think I read about it,' Gillard said. 'It's closed now, isn't it?'

'Certainly is,' Barbara said. 'Fool of a hobby if you ask me. Enough danger in life without asking for more.' After three or four spine-juddering bounces, the Shogun crested a ridge, and suddenly the North Devon coast was there for them to see, with a watery light sparkling off the Bristol Channel.

'It's beautiful,' Sam said.

'On a good day you can the South Wales coast. On an overcast night, you can see the red glow of Port Talbot steelworks on the underside of the clouds. Like the devil's furnace. Probably the only unionized one old Satan has.' She laughed.

'How wonderful to live here!'

'You may say that,' Barbara said. 'But you can't eat beauty, and a fine view won't pay the bills.'

Sam soaked up the scenery. Rugged headlands, rough rock-strewn pastures, stony coves and wind-bent trees were stripped of their foliage by the buffeting wind. In the distance, sharply downhill, she could make out a low white farmhouse with numerous outbuildings.

'There we are,' Barbara said, bringing the vehicle to a halt in a farmyard. The moment she opened the door, the thunderous roar of the distant surf swept in. Before Sam could move, the goat jumped into the seat next to her and was butting on the window to be let out. Barbara complied, and the animal jumped down and sped away. 'Won't catch her for a couple of days,' she said, as she watched the animal tear away up the hill.

Once Trish arrived in her Nissan, they picked their way through the waterlogged yard into the farmhouse, leaving Philip behind in the vehicle. Everyone was told to leave their mud-caked outdoor shoes in a big, dank entrance hall. There were a dozen mouldering coats and two dozen pairs of wellingtons. Barbara gave them all thick woolly socks from a bucket so they didn't get chilled feet on the stone flags. After a steaming cup of tea, sipped in front of a roaring coal fire, Barbara announced that she would show them what they had come to see.

'I hope you've got a strong stomach,' she said to Sam.

They all donned borrowed wellingtons and trudged out into the farmyard, where heavy rain was now beginning to fall. They climbed up a steep, well-used path beside a drystone wall, and after crossing several planks laid across muddy patches, entered a different field via a rusted metal gate. The slope got steeper, and near the top of it was a mildewed caravan in a clump of nettles behind a rusting wheel-less saloon car that looked as if it had just died while towing it.

'Uncle Philip's caravan,' Gillard said.

'It's been there many, many years,' Barbara said. 'He lived in it for most of the last ten years. That's his old Jaguar, believe it or not.'

The caravan had been jacked up on one side with breeze blocks to make it level, and more of the blocks were used as steps. Dozens of bin bags of animal fodder and blue plastic sacks of fertilizer had been crammed underneath the caravan, which looked as if it was resting on a series of pillows. Barbara led Gillard up and fumbled for keys to open the lock. Once inside, she flicked on a light switch and beckoned for Gillard, Sam and Trish to follow.

'I can't believe he lived here for so long,' Trish said. The caravan's floor was lined with muddy newspapers, and the beds were stacked with grubby blankets and bags of old clothes. The caravan reeked of damp, and there was black mould on the ceiling. A fold-down table with a laptop on it stood beyond the bed, and it was to this that Barbara led them.

'All this stuff has been here basically untouched since he moved into the home,' Barbara said. 'But when I decided to take an Open University course, I thought I'd use Podge's laptop. I've no real skills with computers,

65

but the accountants in Ilfracombe have been on to me for years to put my farm accounts onto them. I'd already run some electric up here for him, so I thought it would work.'

She sat down on a stool at the laptop, an ancient Dell that was at least two inches thick. 'So I logged on, like the woman at the library showed me, and after a bit of ferreting about came across this little lot. Craig, take a look.'

Sam watched as her husband peered over Barbara's shoulder at the screen. His eyes widened. 'These are bad, Barbara. Some of the worst categories.'

'Then there's this,' she said, clicking on a different folder.

'Good God. You didn't warn me.'

'There's more,' Barbara said, clicking on a fresh tab.

Sam peered over his shoulder and immediately shied away. 'Oh my God.' The images were grainy, and no faces were shown, but it was clear enough that the girls in the pictures looked to be around mid-teens, involved in adult sexual acts with the same largely unseen, but clearly adult male.

'I don't think I'll look, actually,' Trish said.

'Is that man your uncle Philip?' Sam asked Craig.

'No,' the two aunts said in unison.

Sam eyed Barbara and Trish, who were looking at each other, and at Gillard. She felt some kind of complicity, some knowledge they shared that was being withheld from her.

'You know who this is, don't you?' Sam said.

No one replied. 'I can see why you thumped him,' Gillard said to Barbara. 'Considering everything.'

'How did he get hold of it?' Trish asked Barbara.

'I have my suspicions,' she replied.

'Would the police prosecute him, even though he's got Alzheimer's?' Sam asked.

'Well, it would be down to the forensic medical examiner,' Gillard replied. 'But no, he's clearly not fit to stand trial. However, the existence of images of child abuse always indicate crimes committed by those who took the photographs.' He eyed Barbara and Trish. 'I have to report it,' he added, almost apologetically. 'Despite the family embarrassment.'

Barbara folded her arms. 'To think that I brought him his dinner every day, cleaned up for him, looked after him. And he got hold of this… filth.'

Gillard looked around the caravan and saw a plastic bag. He reached for it, tipped out the clothing within, then carefully used it as a glove to unplug the laptop, finally easing the computer into it without leaving his finger-prints. Gillard then turned to Barbara. 'When I report this, you have to be prepared to admit to the assault on Philip.'

'My little nephew would turn me in?' she asked. 'My little bedtime soldier.'

Gillard bristled, and a vein on his forehead throbbed. 'I will do what I have to do. So perhaps you could tell me precisely what you did do to him.'

Barbara stared at him, her jaw set. 'It was eight o'clock on a Tuesday evening. I had just discovered this and I was furious. I drove down to the nursing home and let myself in through the back gate into the gardens. I never saw anybody. I went to the chalet, put him in his chair, wheeled him to the car and brought him here.' She stopped and, removing her spectacles, wiped her good eye with her forearm. 'You know why I did this. You know why this matters to me.'

Gillard said nothing, but he couldn't hold her gaze.

Barbara continued. 'I was already furious by the time I got him here. I parked at the bottom of the steps and carried him up in the wheelbarrow. He was bleating like a lamb. I think he knew. His memory may be gone, but his sense of guilt was sizzling like bacon. All this saying sorry that he does.'

'So you showed him the pictures?'

'Yes. I wrapped my hand in his hair and forced him. He didn't want to look, not with me, though no doubt he spent hour upon hour looking at them when he was on his own. The filthy beast.'

'And you hit him?'

'I picked him up by his throat and smashed his head into the metal door frame of the caravan a couple of times. I think I wanted to kill him at the time. But obviously I didn't.'

Gillard opened his mouth to say something.

'Young man, don't you dare. Don't you even dare say that to me. After what I've been through. After all I've done for him.' She exploded into action, smashing her fist into the side of the caravan so hard the entire vehicle rocked. It left a dent in the panelling.

Chapter 7

By early evening, Gillard and Sam were back at Trish's house, while Trish went off to deposit Philip at the care home at the other end of town. As soon as they were alone in the bedroom, Sam tentatively asked Gillard what that last exchange with Barbara was about. Gillard didn't reply but the muscles in his jaw flexed and a vein stood out on his temple. 'Family secrets, Sam. Christ, I should never have come back here.' He braced his hands on the dressing table and glowered into the mirror. To Sam he looked older, troubled and careworn.

'Craig, your aunts recognized the abuser, didn't they?'

He sighed. 'I think they have their suspicions. It explains a lot of things.'

'What things?'

He didn't reply.

'Well, we've both got to stay with the old bat for the next two nights,' Sam said, angrily stuffing the clothes back into her rucksack. 'It would be nice for me if I knew what was going on.'

'I'd tell you if I could, really I would.' He turned to her and apologized, scooping her up into his arms. 'Look, there is a fantastic coastal path that runs through the farm, and you can get down onto the beach. It makes for a great run. I'll take you there.' He kissed her on the nose.

'Don't try to get round me like that,' Sam said, avoiding the perfunctory kiss. 'You can't just change the subject.'

Gillard sighed. 'I will tell you, but it's painful stuff. I need to get my own head round it first. Some things aren't easy to face.'

'Well, I've always got a listening ear for you. You just need to use it sometimes.' In the extended silence that followed, she decided it was probably best to change the subject. 'What about the laptop?'

'I'm going to have to take it in at some point. This is turning into a bloody busman's holiday,' he said with a shake of his head.

'Little bedtime soldier, eh?' Sam chuckled, and dug him in the ribs.

He whirled on her. 'Don't.' He gathered up the rucksack and spare clothing, and marched past her down the stairs, cursing under his breath.

'Aren't we having a lovely holiday?' Sam whispered to herself.

As they loaded the car, they saw Auntie Trish's grey Nissan pull up outside. She was as white as a sheet, and grasped Gillard's arm as soon as she emerged from the car.

'Are you all right?' he asked.

'Bit of a near miss on Alexandra Road,' she said. 'A van pulled out without looking.' Then she added: 'Do you think this Emily that Podge keeps mentioning is a real person?'

'I don't know, it's almost impossible to tell. It's probably somebody he knew years ago,' Gillard replied.

Trish said nothing for a moment and then said: 'I was just driving him back to the home, and when we drove through the gates he stopped singing, and started whimpering like a child. Crying, really pathetic. He's been doing this a lot recently, which made me think that someone in the home was being horrible to him. But this time he seemed really upset. He hates the place, and feels it is a prison. "They won't let me out, ever, after what I've done." So I asked him what he had done. "Emily," he said. So I asked him who she was. And he replied… He replied…'

Trish was suddenly overcome with emotion, and shook her head while fumbling for a handkerchief.

'What did he say, Trish?' Gillard asked, his arm around his aunt's trembling shoulders.

Her voice was thick, and she had to blow her nose twice before she was able to say what she wanted to say. 'He said: "She was my little girlfriend. And I murdered her."'

Nothing was said for half a minute. Sam said. 'All those photographs, do you think Emily was…?'

'That's my fear,' Trish said. 'Some poor teenager.'

Gillard nodded. 'Well, I think we have to make that detour to the police station tonight.' He stepped outside into the garden to get a phone signal, and Sam watched him walking about in the gathering darkness, his hair being blown by the wind, overhearing him talking to the incident room at Barnstaple. When he came in, he said:

'Let's go in now, get it over and done with. We'll need Trish to come with us.'

-

For all that Barnstaple is an attractive tourist town, the police station on North Walk is as ugly a concrete monstrosity as anything to be found in Britain's crime-ridden inner cities. The duty sergeant, a bespectacled and grizzled officer, showed Gillard and his aunt into an interview room. Sam was left nursing what had to be the worst cup of machine coffee she had ever tasted, sitting on a hard plastic seat opposite a tipsy young woman with glitter on her face and an obscenely short silver skirt, who was regaling someone on her phone with a blow-by-blow account of tonight's disastrous hen party.

After almost two hours, Sam had heard more than she could ever want to about the sexual conquests of this mythical Tiffany, whose party it was, and how towards the end things had got out of hand with someone called Scrumpy Jez. Sam was more than relieved to see her husband emerge, minus the laptop, but steadying a rather wobbly and tearful Auntie Trish.

'I think this woman needs a stiff whisky,' Gillard said.

Once they were settled in a quiet recess of a local pub, he recounted the police interview to Sam. 'They're taking it very seriously. As I said, there's no immediate action likely to be taken against Philip. A duty doctor, the forensic medical examiner will have to assess whether he is fit to be interviewed. However, if it turns out that there is someone missing called Emily, they will probably have to attempt to interview him at some stage.'

'What about Barbara's assault on your uncle?'

'It never came up,' Gillard said, glancing at his aunt. 'Did it?'

Trish shook her head and blew her nose. 'The policewoman was ever so pregnant,' she said. 'She should have been at home.'

'She's a nice woman, DS Stafford,' he said. 'She did a quick check on local cold cases. There are no children called Emily missing in the county. So that's good news, I suppose. Though I'd like to do a more detailed nationwide check myself when I get back to the office.'

'So it's over to Barbara's now?' Sam asked.

'After we've dropped Trish back, yes.'

'You know something,' Trish said tearfully. 'I spent months with Philip, trying to get him to engage his mind, to connect with reality and retrieve the memories of his life. But after what he said tonight, that confession, I find myself hoping that I've been unsuccessful. Hoping that what he said was just a fantasy. Because the alternative explanation is unbearable.'

Chapter 8

A storm was gathering as Gillard drove Sam down the sunken lane to Hollow Coombe farm. Large raindrops splattered across the windscreen, and twigs blew across in the glow of the headlamps. The car's digital clock showed 9.17 p.m.

Sam stared out at the spooky shapes of the trees, whose branches waved above them. Gillard wrestled with the steering wheel as the car lost its grip on one muddy incline, but then finally they were over the ridge, and heading down to the westward path. The headlamps picked out sheep huddled together by a tumbledown stone wall. One ewe, the wrong side of the wall, ran ahead of the car, leading them at a panicky trot towards the farm. Gillard had again been largely silent on the journey, responding to Sam's questions with what seemed like a feigned enthusiasm for an early-morning run. Finally, in the shelter of the farmyard, they extricated their belongings and hurried towards the warmth of the house. They were met at the door by Barbara, who bade them warm up quickly in front of the fire.

The farmhouse was little changed since it was first built in the 1680s. The black and white diamond-pattern kitchen tiles and the thick stone flags of the dining room were original, as was the great low oak beam which shouldered the weight of the stone-tiled roof, and had to be ducked by both Gillard and Barbara. Two boisterous collie dogs, Captain and Sergeant, shared a large basket by the huge open fire.

'I'd normally put you in one of the caravans,' Barbara said, 'but we've got a couple of young German tourists in the best one, and it's a bit too wild of a night for most of the other wagons. So you can have the spare room here, but you'll have to watch your heads. It's quite a low ceiling.'

She wasn't exaggerating. The door to the room was barely four feet high. 'Built for the seven dwarfs,' Gillard grinned as he ducked under the lintel. The ancient bed was a cast-iron monster that surely must have been built inside the room, because there was no way it would have gone through the door. The windows were tiny, and didn't close properly, and the lumpy whitewashed plaster was crumbly. There was an active community of woodlice underneath the bed. But the room, being next to the main chimney, was toasty warm. When Sam sat on the bed, she disturbed a brass warming pan under the blankets which contained two hot fire bricks.

'Wow, never come across anything like this,' she said.

Barbara bellowed up the stairs to say dinner was ready, and they both descended with their thick borrowed socks on to sit at the battered oak table. Barbara served huge ladles full of venison casserole in cider, with butternut squash, parsnips and baked potatoes so crisp the darkened skins shattered to the touch.

'What's this?' Sam asked, as Barbara poured pinkish fluid from a flagon into her wine glass. 'It's my own hedgerow wine. Sloes and rosehip, nettle and comfrey. Best not overdo it,' she said with a cackle. 'It's quite strong.'

She herself already had an earthenware mug full of a brown cloudy liquid. 'Rough cider – a bit too rough for you two, I expect.'

Over dinner Gillard explained what had happened at the police station and what the next step was likely to be. It was nearly eleven by the time they finished. While Gillard stepped away to take a call on his mobile, Sam offered to help with the clearing up and ended up with a tea towel in her hand.

'So, ready for babies?' Barbara said without preamble. She made it sound like she was offering dessert.

'Pardon?'

'You don't want to wait too long.'

'I'm only 34,' Sam retorted. 'There's plenty of time.'

'Best pop 'em out when you're young. It's like with sheep. It's always the older ewes that have trouble in lambing, that produce the malformed young. We had one last season with two heads. Didn't live 15 minutes,' she said.

'I'm not a sheep,' Sam said emphatically. 'And I assure you I'm not going to be producing two-headed babies.'

'No, 'course not, my lovely.' She paused. 'Still, our family hasn't a great record. There's no grandchildren on our side. Craig's sister Viv produced a daughter. Met her once. She didn't look right to me.'

'Charlotte? She's lovely. She's studying fashion.'

'Too skinny. Like an emaciated gazelle. It's all this vegan eating, I suppose. Trying to put the likes of me out of business.'

'I don't think she is a vegan. She was eating a doner kebab when I last met her.'

Barbara looked out of the window and said, 'It's going to be a belter tonight. Listen to that wind. And it's the new moon tomorrow.'

'Why does the new moon matter?'

'Chances are we'll get a visit from the beast. If he comes, it's often during the new moon, when it's darker.'

'Is this the story that you used to scare Craig with when he was little? About the wolf?'

Barbara turned to Sam and gripped her by both shoulders, her fingers like iron. 'It's not a story! The Exmoor wolf exists, believe you me. It takes nigh-on a dozen of my ewes every year, tears them open. Guts everywhere. I can show you the photographs.'

Sam gulped. 'Well, it could be dogs. They attack sheep.'

'I know what I know. And I've seen him. I cornered him in the derelict barn. He had a newborn Devon closewool, and there were tufts of wool everywhere. I could hear the mewling, but underneath it there was a low growl. Boy, he was big. I saw them yellow eyes, narrowed. He went for me and I whacked him with a shovel, but it hardly slowed him down.' She paused and the good eye bored into Sam's head. 'I can see you don't believe me. Listen to me, girl. You're young and you don't know everything.' Barbara didn't have her patch on and the milky eye was weeping. 'Right. Come on, get a coat and some wellies. We're going out.'

Barbara shouted out to Gillard, who was still on the phone, and said they would be back in a minute. She bustled out to the cloakroom with Sam following, waterproof in hand. They booted up and Barbara donned a huge green coat, stained with sheep droppings. The sound of the coat flapping immediately brought the two collies panting into the hallway. 'Yes, boys, you can come too,' Barbara said.

Sam slipped into her anorak and pulled on a woolly hat. They went out through a door on the cliff-facing side that Barbara had to push hard against the buffeting wind. In the darkness she shepherded Sam and the dogs out, then let it slam. They were within 50 yards of the cliff edge, and the explosive roar of the surf detonated in Sam's ears. Barbara, stout stick in hand, led the way down through the long, soaking grass, pointing out the wire fence which marked the cliff edge.

'Hundred feet down here,' Barbara bellowed. Sam looked out at the roiling sea and beyond the quick-silver lacework of incoming surf that ran from horizon to horizon. The power of the wind was incredible, and she had to brace herself against every body-checking gust. Barbara marched left, westwards along the top, crossing a rickety wooden stile and then following a path which turned inland and climbed sharply. Gillard's aunt may have been over 70, but she was still fit. Sam, pretty athletic herself, struggled to keep up.

'All this,' Barbara yelled, indicating land back to the farm and beyond, 'is Hollow Coombe land. Been in the family more than 200 years. We've fought to hold on to it, against the landlords, against the bailiffs, against the taxman, and against all sorts of ruffians. It's in our blood.' Once Sam had caught up, Barbara turned and marched on, reaching a rocky promontory, where the wind was more powerful still. The wire fence here was more substantial and marked with danger signs. Tied to the wire were the emaciated bodies of a dozen crows, rotted and desiccated. Many of the feathers were gone, revealing just bone, tendon, claws and beaks.

'Ugh, what are these?'

'I put them there as a warning,' Barbara said. 'Crows are the devil's bird, not above pecking the eyes from a newborn lamb. They herald trouble.'

She looked out to sea, as if she somehow expected to see the arrival of whatever it was she feared. 'There's been a lot of jackdaws recently. Big buggers, with black caps and grey ruffs. I got more shotgun cartridges last week,' she said conspiratorially. 'I'm ready.'

'Who will take the farm on when you retire?' Sam asked.

Barbara dug her hands deep into the pockets of her coat. 'No idea. Find me a kid today who likes to get up at four in the morning seven days a week. It's hard graft, and not enough pence in your pocket to make a jingle. Who'd want it?' She strode on, taking a narrow, shadowed path down between gorse bushes.

'Barbara, it's really dark. I can't see where I'm going,' Sam said.

'Townie eyes,' she retorted. 'Don't know how to look, except where someone else shines a light. No wonder most city people don't notice anything around 'em, except what's on their phones. I tell you what's wrong with this world, girl: the Internet. Everyone peering deeper and deeper into a narrower and narrower foreign place, drawn down into hell like my brother.'

'Shouldn't we be going back? Craig will be wondering where we've got to.'

'I just want to show you this one place,' Barbara said, guiding Sam along the path and over a series of protruding tree roots. They reached the cliff edge where the fence had fallen away. It looked down a hundred feet into a rocky cove.

'My old dad, Jacob Antrobus, threw himself off here onto the rocks in 1964.' She looked over the edge, as if she still expected to see him there. 'He was smashed to pieces.'

'Oh my God,' Sam said. 'That's awful.'

'It was. But good riddance too. He was a bad 'un.' She then led Sam inland on a winding stony path that reached a huge basin of a rock between a pair of wind-bent holly bushes. She pulled out a lightweight torch and illuminated a cairn in the centre of the rock.

'My baby is under the left-hand holly. I come to talk to him every day. Well more than half a century dead now,' she said, kneeling at the stone, caressing its surface as if it was a polished headstone. 'Lived less than two hours.' Barbara knelt and tenderly kissed the ground. 'There now, you rest easy. Don't let the storm fret you. Your old mum is not far away.'

Sam felt tears prickle her eyes, and put a hand over her mouth.

–

The rain was lashing down by the time they got back to the farmhouse. Gillard was standing at the doorway, petting the dogs which had run on ahead. 'I was wondering where you had both got to.'

'I've been shown a bit of family history,' Sam said, sweeping a rain-drenched hunk of hair from her face.

After they had warmed up in front of the fire, they went to bed. Sam and Craig snuggled up together in the huge bed, sparring for control of the hot patch where the bed warmer had been. Gillard gallantly surrendered control, settling for holding his wife close and nuzzling her neck. The wind was really howling now, and there was a fierce cold draft from the ill-fitting windows. The draw and crash of the surf carried in, as if they were sharing a room with a particularly heavy breather. As they were dropping off to sleep, a door banged in the distance, stopped, then banged twice again. Sam incorporated the sound as best she could into her dreams, which were an unsettling mixture of dead babies and drunken farmers. It was a movement by Gillard in the small hours that awoke her.

'Did you hear that?' he whispered. She raised her head.

'What?'

'A door.'

'I heard one banging in the distance, hours ago.'

'No, there's someone moving about. Up here.' He slid out of bed, slipped on a pair of tracksuit trousers and grabbed his LED inspection lamp which he had put by the bed in case of power cuts. He opened the bedroom door and peered into the corridor. Under the door Sam could see the brilliant bluish light of Gillard's lamp. He was gone for only a minute before sliding back into bed.

'What was it?'

'Very strange. There's no one there, but there were wet footprints – or should I say sock prints – coming up the stairs, leading into Barbara's room.'

'Maybe she'd gone outside.'

'These socks were huge, way bigger than mine.'

'So some bloke is in there with her?' An involuntary groan of distaste crawled out of Sam's throat.

'Don't jump to conclusions,' Gillard said. 'Especially not those ones.'

–

The morning dawned with the sound of movement. Sam lifted a bleary eye and saw a shaft of watery sunlight piercing the room. Gillard wasn't there, but there was definitely some kind of conversation going on out in the corridor, the click of latches and the thud of stockinged feet on stairs. A couple of minutes later he reappeared, fully dressed. 'Ready for a run?'

Sam groaned, but it was only five minutes later when they were both warming up in their running gear on the steps that led to the cliff edge path. The wind was still blustery, and there were dove-grey clouds overhead, but out at sea the sky was a pale scrubbed blue.

Gillard led the way, and was soon joined by the dogs, Captain and Sergeant, who bounded along at their sides. They passed the headland where old man Antrobus had died, and found a rough path which descended to the cove. There was a narrow shelving beach, with sand at the water's edge leading to crescent-shaped fans of small pebbles higher up. 'It's low tide for the next hour,' Gillard said. 'It wouldn't be safe to do this at high tide.'

They ran for an hour, sucking in the fresh tangy air, weaving round headlands, splashing through the shallows and exploring some of the narrower inlets. Finally, they raced up a series of steep wooden steps which led gradually up to the clifftop. The view from there was magnificent.

After each wave crashed on the shore, the suck of the undertow was like rhythmic inhalation.

'God, I feel so much better for that,' Gillard said as he caught his breath.

'Me too,' said Sam. They embraced, and found a bench to sit on while they recovered. 'Craig, I want to talk. I've felt shut out almost since we arrived. In fact, even before we arrived. I know there are lots of secrets in the family. I don't want to pry, but I just feel that you're bottling something up, something important. Would it help to talk about it?'

'Would it?' He rested his elbows on his knees, cradling his head while he squinted out to sea. It was a few minutes later when he spoke. 'I came out here with Viv the first summer, when I was seven. We had a great time, running wild. But even then Barbara was very tough – she was probably not yet 30. She probably had to be; she was doing everything herself, since her father killed himself. Her mother was disabled with multiple sclerosis, and getting worse. Trish had moved away to Barnstaple. The farm was in debt, I mean mortgaged to the hilt, and there were these two kids, me and Viv, who'd been foisted on her. So she worked us, pretty hard.'

'What kind of work?'

'Carrying fence posts from the yard, right up to the high edge of the farm at Dulverton Wood. I used to run them up in a wheelbarrow. Viv learned how to milk a cow. There was one afternoon, I think, when Barbara was run ragged and Viv made a mistake, and then cheeked her aunt. Barbara dragged her to the barn and gave her the strap. She had a Scottish tawse that her own father had used on her, and it cut Viv, and scarred her. She was ten years old, but she said she would never come back here and she never did.'

'Did she ever use the strap on you?'

'No, not the strap. She was harder on Viv than on me. Something Viv hated. She was envious of how she treated me, but she shouldn't have been.'

'Why?'

'Because the following year, when I was there without Viv, Barbara abused me.'

'Oh God, Craig.' Sam embraced him. 'I thought it was something like that. There was no other reason for you to be scared of her.'

'Sam, you know me too well.' He kissed her neck and stroked her hair.

'So what exactly did—'

'Don't ask, Sam, please don't ask me that.'

–

Craig and Sam arrived back at the farmhouse to find a classic English breakfast underway, with three strangers sitting at a table groaning with food. One was a very tall, dark-haired and hollow-cheeked youth wearing white earbuds. He was introduced as Peter. Next to him were the German tourist couple Axel and Irena. They were fair-haired, almost identically dressed in square framed spectacles, fleeces and trainers, and spoke excellent English. Barbara bustled in, carrying a hot plate of black pudding, bacon and caramelized mushrooms, and hurried out again to bring in scrambled eggs and grilled tomatoes.

Axel described how the caravan they were in lurched backwards and forwards in the storm. 'We thought it would turn over. We have never felt a storm like it.'

'It was very frightening,' Irena said. After a sociable half an hour, they cleared up together, crowding into the kitchen to share the washing-up, except Peter. Sam watched as the dark-haired youth slipped away, plugged into music. She followed him, and saw that he ascended the stairs and slipped into the bathroom next to Barbara's room.

Returning to the washing-up, she kept an eye out for him, but was interrupted when Gillard reminded her that they were due at the care home in a half-hour. The previous day Trish had asked if they would play Monopoly with Philip. It was one of the few things that he enjoyed, and according to Trish, would often help his mind to focus.

'Do we have to go?' Sam asked. 'He makes me so uncomfortable. And those disgusting photographs...'

Craig sighed. 'I'd rather not, but Trish hopes that she can find something out about this Emily. If she even exists. I did promise we would go.'

As they drove the 40 minutes back to Barnstaple, Sam asked: 'So who was it with the big socked feet last night? The quiet lad, or the randy German?'

Gillard smiled. 'I honestly don't want to think about it. If Barbara has found someone to make her happy at her age, then good luck to her, whoever it is.'

'Sometimes, Craig, for a detective you have no sense of curiosity. I think there is something strange about Peter. The way he looks at your aunt.'

'A detective's hunch?' he asked with a smile.

'Feminine intuition,' she replied, tapping her nose.

Chapter 9

At ten o'clock on a Sunday morning, DI Jan Talantire would have preferred to be almost anywhere else than in the basement interview room with Micky Tuffin. She was just glad that she had DS Charmaine Stafford and experienced duty solicitor Patrick James with her when faced with this six-foot oaf who reeked of BO. Tuffin had been plucked from his mother's sofa yesterday evening in a raid led by PC Nick Kite. Tuffin had been drunk. After putting up a bit of a fight, he had been held in the cells overnight. He was dressed in a faded grey T-shirt and trackie bottoms, and a pair of stained Crocs, but no socks. Two huge dark patches of sweat garlanded his armpits as he leaned back in the chair and stared at Charmaine Stafford's bump.

'Who's the daddy, then?' he asked.

Stafford scowled at him, but didn't answer. Talantire did: 'Don't be disrespectful, Micky. We've got some serious questions to put to you.'

'Like where were you at 3.40 p.m. last Wednesday?' Stafford asked.

'On a bench outside the NatWest with me mates, probably.'

'Planning a bank robbery, were you?' Talantire asked.

'Ha ha, very funny. Don't give up the day job,' Tuffin scowled at the detective.

'Have you got anyone who will vouch for you?' Talantire asked.

He pursed his lips. 'Davy maybe, big Jim probably.'

Talantire stared at him. 'Did you hear about the hit-and-run outside Furzy Hill? Some poor pedestrian was dragged up the road 30 yards on his face and left for dead in a ditch. A powerful car that was, a big Ford.' She tapped the photograph in front of her. 'Just the kind of thing a petrolhead like you would like. Stolen from the car park of an old people's home.'

'You can't think I had anything to do with that,' he said, a frown of incredulity looped over his heavy brows.

'Come on, Mickey, you have a long history as a joyrider,' Talantire said.

'When I was young. But not now.'

Talantire nodded. 'Yes, you've matured and moved up in the world. Some class B dealing, cheque-book theft, shoplifting. Seriously, Micky, it's time they threw the book at you,' she said. 'No more suspended sentences. Put you away for a while.'

'I didn't do it,' he said.

'If you didn't do it, how come your fingerprints are all over a used cider can found in the rear footwell of the car?' Talantire gave him a little smile.

'You don't have to answer that question, Mr Tuffin,' Patrick James said.

'Well I can, if it's that car, the big Ford. Show me the picture again.' Stafford passed across the photograph of the Ford Ranger. 'Pete Yates gave me a lift in it last Saturday.'

'Who is Pete Yates?'

'Oh dear, oh dear, our detective hasn't been doing her homework, has she?' Tuffin leaned back again, chuckling to himself. 'You just can't get the staff, can you?' he said to Stafford.

'Answer the question, Tuffin,' Talantire growled.

'Pete Yates is a mate of mine. He works at that rundown old farm with the madwoman.'

'Hollow Coombe farm?' Talantire asked.

'That's the one. He is well in with the owner. She lets him use the car.'

'That's not what she said. She told us that she is the only one insured to drive the vehicle, and that nobody else uses it.'

Tuffin shrugged and leaned back, casually sniffing at his own armpit then recoiling a little.

'Going back to last Saturday,' Talantire said. 'You claim that the reason we have your dabs on a can in the back is because you got a lift from Yates?'

'Yeah.'

'And you were having a drink and then you tossed the can in the car?'

'Yeah.'

'Are you sure it was a Saturday?' Stafford asked.

''Course I am. He said he got it for the evening, and come to my house then we drove down into town to see some mates and maybe pick up some girls.'

'What time?' Talantire asked.

Tuffin shrugged. 'Eight, maybe.'

'So the only time you were in this vehicle, ever, was the Saturday before the hit-and-run? And you were not in it at any time on the Wednesday?'

'That's dead right.'

'We can check all this out, you know, Micky,' Talantire said. 'If you're lying, we will get you.'

'It wasn't me, simple as.' An idea could be seen forming on his face. 'There's a camera outside the bank. Look at the CCTV.'

'Oh we will, don't worry,' Talantire said. 'And right now, we're checking all through that car for any of your DNA.'

After they let him go, and the solicitor had departed, Stafford turned to Talantire. 'It's not often they suggest CCTV, is it?'

Talantire nodded. 'Mickey Tuffin is a habitual liar, but on this occasion, I might believe him. We got a lot of unidentified prints in that vehicle, as well as those of Barbara Antrobus.'

'I'll get on to the NatWest,' Stafford said. 'That'll settle it one way or another.'

'And get Peter Yates in for a statement. Kite can take it,' Talantire said.

–

The Monopoly game was all set up when Craig and Sam arrived at The Beeches. Trish, who claimed she detested board games, was sitting there with the Scottish woman, Moira, who once again had to suffer Philip's introduction of Trish as 'my sister, who never comes to visit me'. Philip had forgotten who Craig was, and ignored Trish's introduction of him to instead ogle Sam. 'Will you play with us, young lady?' he asked.

Sam reluctantly agreed. She knew why they were doing this but wanted to stay as far away from this repulsive man as possible.

It soon became clear that games made Philip Antrobus unusually sharp. He volunteered as the banker, counting out the money without difficulty, keeping track of who was owed rent, and on his own account playing a fiendishly acquisitive game, eventually mortgaging Mayfair in order to afford Vine Street, which gave him control of everything from the jail to free parking, including the Electric Company. Sam, with few properties, was happily languishing in jail, but had to leave on this, her third, turn. She would have to roll at least ten in order to avoid all his properties, unless she was lucky enough to get a seven for community chest.

'Ha ha, I've got you now, Emily,' Philip cackled, rubbing his hands together with unrestrained glee. 'I hope you've got plenty of money.'

'I'm Sam, not Emily,' she corrected him.

Philip looked up at her and realized he had said something wrong. 'Sorry, slip of the tongue. Is Sam short for Samantha?'

'Yes.'

Craig and Trish shared a glance. 'Who is Emily?' Trish asked, as Philip watched Sam jiggling the dice in her hand. He ignored them.

'Well, Samantha,' Philip said. 'You can't stay inside for ever, but leaving is pretty perilous. I've even got the station, Marylebone.' He pointed excitedly to the middle of his row of properties. 'That is always Margaret's favourite, as I recall.' He looked to Trish for confirmation. 'She always goes for the stations, doesn't she? King's Cross,

Fenchurch Street, Liverpool Street.' Suddenly he looked up. 'How is she? I've not seen her for years.'

'Podge, she died 30 years ago. In 1988. Don't you remember?' Trish said.

For a moment he looked panicked, then a memory clearly returned. 'Right,' he said absentmindedly. 'I remember now. Was I at the funeral?'

'You read the eulogy, dear,' Trish said gently. 'It was very good.'

'Oh God.' He seemed momentarily lost in sadness.

Sam rolled the dice, an eight. She counted out the squares.

'Aha! Marlborough Street, one house.' Philip squinted through his glasses at the title deed in front of him. 'That's, um, £70. Come on, cough up, young lady.' He snapped his fingers.

'Podge, who was this Emily that you've been mentioning?' Trish asked. 'Your little girlfriend.'

His face tightened and his eyes narrowed. 'I don't know who you mean,' he said, primly.

Sam collected up the money and passed it over. Philip counted the notes she had given him out loud, stacking each on the correct colour pile in front of him.

Carefully and slowly, Trish took hold of her brother's wrist. 'Podge, please tell me about Emily.'

His eyes flashed up, sharp and shrewd. For a second, they all saw within them that he had the intelligence and the recollection of who Emily was and knew exactly what had happened to her. 'No, no, no, no.' He swallowed his lips as if they might speak of their own volition. Then he began shaking his head in denial.

Chapter 10

Back at Trish's house in the late afternoon the three of them had a council of war over coffee and biscuits. 'He has good days and bad days,' Trish said. 'This was a good day, a very good day. And when I saw his face, I think he knew exactly what we were asking, and why he shouldn't tell us anything.'

Gillard said: 'Last night as I mentioned, Trish, I rang some of my colleagues at Surrey Police headquarters. I gave them the name Emily, and asked them to look through cold cases on the Police National Computer. It might also be worth looking through the missing persons database for clues.'

'Well we should be able to find out pretty quickly, then,' Sam said.

'Not without a surname,' Gillard said. 'We don't have any kind of timeframe for this either. The older it is, the more problematic it may be, because of poor record-keeping. I mean he could have killed someone even back in the 1960s.'

'So what do we do next?' Trish asked.

'I think we keep at him,' Gillard said. 'We've got most of Monday. Sam and I have to be back by late evening. Every shred of information we can get from Philip will diminish an awful lot of haystacks that we would otherwise have to look through in search of needles.'

'How can I help?' Trish asked.

'I need a list of all the addresses that he has lived at since he left home. All the employers he worked for, which churches he was based at, that kind of thing.'

'I don't know if I or Babs could tell you much about the early years. Once he left to go to university, which I suppose was 1958, the next thing we really knew was that he had jobs in industry, then went to India for a couple of years in the late 1970s. I know that because I still have the postcards. I know he lived in Kidderminster for a while, but not exactly when or where. He didn't join the Church until the early 1980s to my knowledge.'

'Did he ever marry?'

'No. He had a few girlfriends, I think. Couldn't tell you any of their names.'

'Not an Emily amongst them?'

'No. I'd definitely not heard that name from him before. He's got heaps of old stuff in the loft of his house in Lynton, but there are tenants in there. That would be a major expedition.'

'I'm after quicker answers at this stage,' Gillard said.

'The great thing, which I've just realized,' Sam said, 'is that because he forgets who we are, he won't become any more guarded about what he knows. He's only started to mention Emily in recent weeks and months, right?'

'Yes, that's right,' Trish said.

'Well, we could expect that as he gradually loses his inhibitions, and forgets why he shouldn't tell us, we'll learn more about what he recollects.'

'Until he finally forgets everything,' Gillard added.

'It doesn't seem to be working that way, does it?' Sam said. 'The older memories seem to be strong, but it's the newer experiences and his sense of judgement that are being eroded.'

'That's certainly true about his judgement,' Trish said. 'Years ago, of course, when he was in the Church, his behaviour was absolutely proper. None of these ogling shenanigans. But in the last few years, well, I can hardly begin to tell you.' She stared around the room. 'I used to take him for pub lunches regularly, but he started to gawp at barmaids and make inappropriate comments, once or twice really lewd. It was embarrassing all round. That's why I wanted us in an obscure corner of the family room yesterday.'

'It's interesting,' Gillard said, 'that he's not obviously looking at teenagers, but at young women. Yet the images we found on the laptop were all of kids around 13 or 14.'

'I can't explain that,' Trish said.

'Let's try him on another game of Monopoly tomorrow. See what we can learn,' Gillard said. They all agreed.

–

The wind was intensifying and the rain coming in squally gusts as Craig and Sam drove back to Barbara's farm. They stopped on the brow of the hill and watched the last watery rays of the sunset being extinguished by roiling clouds. The farm downhill and to their left had been well-sited to avoid the worst of the weather. It nestled in a slight hollow, as if it had its back to the north-westerly gales, the two arms of outbuildings enclosing the yard. As they approached, Peter, the tall, dark-haired lad they had seen at breakfast, emerged from an old stable, chewing gum and still plugged into his music. He mounted a quad bike, which he started and then roared off up the hill.

Gillard pulled up next to Barbara's old Shogun, and he and Sam made their way carefully through the muddy yard into the house, expecting to be greeted by the dogs. The house was quiet and there was no sign of Barbara, but there was a delicious aroma of cooking coming from the range. Sam soon discovered a giant casserole, on low, in one of its four ovens. She filled up the ancient metal kettle and fired up the hob to bring it to the boil.

After tea, Gillard said: 'Fancy a walk? Barbara must be out there somewhere.'

Sam peered out at the rain which was now thrashing against the windows. 'We'll have to wrap up or we'll get drenched.'

Five minutes later, in heavy rainproofs and big boots, they started on the path up past Philip's caravan, which took them to the main track running parallel to the cliff from one end of the farm to the other. It was pitch black now, and Gillard's torch illuminated the horizontal specks of rain. They saw lights ahead, and the silhouette of a quad bike. When they got there, they found Peter and Barbara kneeling, looking at something.

'Oh my God, there's something dead,' Sam said. In the light of the torch they could see glistening entrails and flecks of wool, leading to the carcass which was in a bank of nettles. Barbara stood and greeted them grimly.

'That's the second ewe today,' she said, pointing into the nettles. 'Guts torn out. This one was probably pregnant.'

'How do you know?' asked Sam.

'Tupped last week.' She picked up the carcass, a strong hand in each gory flank and showed the rear end to them. 'See the wax trace still? Stripe of orange? That means she was done the week before last. The ram wears a little chest harness with a wax crayon sticking out, different colour every week. If he mounts, he leaves a mark, so we get to know which sheep are carrying, and when they'll be due.'

'Was it dogs?' Gillard asked.

'We didn't hear nothing,' Peter said, the first words they had heard from him. 'And you usually do.'

Barbara looked up, balefully. 'Dogs don't do this. They chase, and snap and exhaust the animal, but they don't pull it to pieces. Not these days, at least. They're too well fed.'

'It's the beast again,' Peter said, looking up to the sky. 'It's time.'

Gillard stared at the youth. 'What do you mean, it's time?'

'New moon tonight.' He nodded, as if it was an obvious connection.

'You don't still think—?'

'Craig, we've had decades of this. Look over here.' She pointed her torch at a section of muddy ground. There was a huge paw print, almost the span of a man's hand. 'That's no dog.'

'It could be a very big dog.'

'That's what the police have always said, but no. I found its scat on several occasions. You could just see from it that it has been living wild. Berries, coneys, weeds for digestion. More like badger poo in composition, but I know where all the badger latrines are on my land.'

'So this is the wolf?' Sam asked.

'Of course. He'll be lying low somewhere, probably looking at us now, certainly scenting us.'

'Still here?' Sam asked in alarm.

'He's as cunning as the devil himself,' Barbara said. 'But I'm laying a trap for him. I've had enough, really I have.' She pulled a plastic bag out of her pocket, and with her ungloved hand scooped up the bloody, glistening viscera. 'And this is the bait.'

–

Over dinner, Barbara regaled them with stories of the moors and the history of the beast of Exmoor, which many other farmers believed to be a puma. 'There have been an awful lot of sheep killed over the years. That's a fact. And here's another fact which is a lot less elusive. None of the farmers round here can get insurance cover any more because of our history of claims.'

Sam and Craig shared a bottle of wine, while Barbara glugged down at least two pints of strong cider. 'I'll go a bit easy, because I may be going out later. If the wolf comes.'

'I'll come with you,' Gillard said.

'And me,' Sam added.

Barbara banked up the fire until it was roaring, and they all sat around until it had burned down to glowing embers. Gone midnight, and the wind outside was really howling; doors somewhere were banging. Every so often the noise rose to a keening.

'Hundred miles an hour, that'll be.' Barbara nodded, as if satisfying a prediction.

Sam yawned and said good night. Gillard followed her up a few minutes later. The bed warmer was welcome, and

Sam soon snuggled up to the warmth of her husband's body. She dreamed of the cold and the wet and a pair of amber almond eyes. She awoke with a start, bathed in sweat. Gillard wasn't next to her. She put the light on, and then heard his voice in quiet conversation on the stairs.

She slipped on a thick pullover and her running trousers, and emerged onto the stairs. Gillard was at the bottom of the staircase, dressed to go out, and Barbara was next to him. He looked up at her and his face was pinched, worried, somehow different.

'It's foul out there, Sam. No need for you to get soaked as well.'

Before she could reply, she heard the dogs whining. Captain and Sergeant were keening – long, high plaintive cries. They were pacing about, clearly disturbed.

'He's calling them, just like I said,' Barbara said to Gillard.

'I can't hear anything,' Sam said.

'But they can,' Barbara said. 'If I was to let them out, they would fall under his spell. I learned that lesson years ago. He's the alpha male, organizing the pack.'

Gillard said goodbye and blew her a kiss as they clattered out into the storm. Sam had to admit to being a little scared – of wolves, and the dark. The comfort of being warm and dry held her too. However, she was too wired to return to bed. She went down and curled up on the sofa in front of the glowing embers of the fire. She pulled the dog basket to her, but the animals would not settle. Captain, the larger of the two border collies, kept whimpering and looking around anxiously, his ears swivelling like radar. Sergeant watched his older brother and whined continuously.

'You can certainly hear something, boys, can't you?'

A huge gust hit the house like a thunderclap, and somewhere glass fell, broken. Doors banged and windows rattled. The rain pounded on the roof and poured in twisted silvery ropes from the overflowing gutters. A growing knot of anxiety built in Sam's chest, and she began to feel stupid for not joining Gillard. This was the twenty-first century, and she could look after herself and probably look after him too, especially as this strangely powerful family seemed to disarm him. Finally decided, Sam grabbed the biggest torch she could find, went to the coat room, and donned all her wet-weather gear and boots. Then she stepped out into the storm.

–

The moment she opened the farmhouse door, Sam felt it almost torn out of her grasp. The power of the wind seemed to suck her out into the yard, now a lake of mud. She splashed through, relieved that it was only a couple of inches deep, and squelched up the very slippery path towards Philip's caravan. In the broad beam of the torch she could see the pale sidings of the caravan, shivering and rocking in the wind. Many of the fertilizer bags that had been underneath it were blowing up the meadows towards the trees. Turning to her right on the main track, she looked to the western edge of the farm. A faint flash of light came to her from a barn a few hundred yards up near a section of woodland. She made for this, the rain now lashing directly into her face, running down her neck and underneath her jersey.

'Craig!' she yelled 'Are you up there?' She could hear no reply. As she got closer to the barn, she could see that it was a vast, partially derelict building, with huge vertical panels of corrugated metal, some dangling by just a couple of rivets, clashing and banging in the storm. In the light of her torch she could the reflections of hundreds of eyes: Barbara's flock was corralled inside, behind a barricade of straw bales. They were running backwards and forwards in panic. The flashes of torchlight within became a little clearer, and suddenly caught momentarily in a lateral arc was a creature: black, powerful, crouched, wreathed in its own breath. And then it was gone.

The wolf. It exists.

'Craig. Craig!' Her voice sounded thin and pathetic against the fury of the storm, and she turned around, expecting at any moment the leap of the creature, the tearing of its teeth into her flesh. Now she really didn't know what to do. Part of her was frightened and wanted to rush back to the farmhouse, but another part of her wanted to press on and find her husband, to be with him. In this storm, in the screeching wind, the thunderous surf, every childhood fear seemed justified. Wolves, monsters, bogeymen. This was their territory, their time of day. She cast about her, looking for the wolf in the beam of her torch. Finally, she moved onwards to the barn.

At the far end of this creaking, screaming structure, beyond a stack of bales, she caught sight of a tall hooded figure in the light of her torch. 'Craig!' She yelled again, and summoned the courage to vault over the bales and into the building. The noise was immense, rock-concert loud, metal screeching as the wind plucked and bent each sheet. She sprinted towards him, scattering sheep as she did so.

As she mounted a bale to get a better view, the figure re-emerged from a stack ten yards ahead, holding a spade above his head like an axe.

It wasn't Gillard.

The stranger brought the weapon down hard on whatever was at his feet. A deafening, high-pitched shriek came from somewhere nearby. Suddenly this all felt terribly wrong. Sam swung her torch to the right, and in its beam just caught a figure leaping at her. Then: impact. She was knocked from her feet by strong arms and crushed to the floor. An immense shuddering crash hit nearby, and her screams were stifled by a filthy, bloody hand clamped across her face.

Chapter 11

The weight above her shifted, giving her space, and her reflex defence was to swing the torch still in her hand at the dark head above. Her wrist was caught by superior strength and bent back. 'Don't panic, my lovely. You're like a startled lamb.'

Sam blinked at Barbara, who had been sitting astride her, and was now standing aside to let her get up. 'Who was that man?' Sam croaked, wiping muck from her face. 'And where's Craig?'

Barbara ignored the question. 'Didn't you hear me yelling for you to stay back? I could see the roof was going. Look.' She pointed to the door-sized sheet of quivering corrugated iron, impaled in the very straw bale that Sam had been standing on. 'That would have been you, sliced in half. We can't stay this end. Other panels may go soon enough.' Barbara pulled Sam to her feet and led her by torchlight to the far end of the barn. There she finally recognized Peter, the farmhand. At his feet was a scene of carnage. Three or four dead sheep, some of them ripped to pieces.

'I had to put two out of their misery,' Peter said to Barbara, waving the spade.

'It's the devil's work.' She eyed the carnage. 'Two good breeders, the other was one of last year's lambs. Am I never going to be rid of it?'

'Was that really a wolf? I saw something,' Sam said.

Peter shrugged and turned to his employer.

'I told you,' Barbara said. 'But you wouldn't believe me.'

'Why don't you shoot it?'

'I've tried, believe you me, but it's hard to get close enough,' Barbara said, turning towards a cone of light moving down the hillside towards the barn. 'Craig, did you see where it went?' she bellowed at the hooded figure striding towards them behind the light.

'I ran after it to the western edge of the farm, but it escaped under a fence and through the woods. It's too fast for me.'

Sam, overjoyed to hear the reassuring voice of her husband, had one overriding question 'Is it a wolf?'

Gillard shook his head. 'No, of course it's a dog. An Alsatian cross, big and lean and mean, bigger than a wolf, if that's any comfort. It could well have been living rough on the hills for a while.'

They all looked at Barbara, whose set jaw indicated she did not agree. 'I've lived on this farm all my life, and I know.'

'Whatever you say, Barbara,' Gillard said.

'She saved my life,' Sam said. 'Pushed me out of the way when the roof down there was collapsing. A huge sheet of metal fell down, right where I'd been standing.' Only then did she notice the bloody gash in the shoulder of Barbara's coat. 'Oh, you're hurt.'

'I'm all right. It just caught me on the way down.'

'We should get you a tetanus shot,' Gillard said.

'I don't have time for any of that malarkey. I got the farm to run. I want photographs of all those dead sheep. Did you get one of the beast, Craig?'

'Only of its rear end, disappearing into the woods. But there's plenty of evidence. I'll come with you tomorrow to make the report.'

'To the police? Waste of time. They'll send up some whelp of a hobby bobby with a keep-dogs-on-leads sign. And that will be that.'

Sam, insulted, glared at her. She could quite see why this family had torn itself to pieces.

–

In a lane beyond the copse at the far western edge of the farm, a Land Rover was parked in darkness just below the crest of the hill. A sinewy, dark creature was crashing through the dense woodland 200 yards away, racing towards the vehicle. A man, cloaked in raingear, emerged from the vehicle and gave a long low whistle which spurred the animal to even greater speed. The brindled beast, with yellow eyes and bloodied jaws, leaped the high fence at the edge of the wood and jumped into the open rear compartment of the vehicle. The man closed the door behind it, returned to the driver's seat and released the handbrake to allow the vehicle, using only sidelights, to coast down the hill unseen and unheard.

–

Monday morning. Detective Inspector Jan Talantire arrived at Barnstaple police station in a foul mood. It was gone eight, there were five people waiting outside and the door was still locked. PC Nick Kite should have been there an hour ago to open up, she thought. She herself had spent half an hour clearing her own drive of fallen branches and the unpleasant contents of next door's over-turned wheelie bin before she could even get her Renault off the drive and to work, but knowing there had been a storm, she got up earlier to do it. It was no good trying to rouse Jon at this time. He was affably useless until midday, though she loved him no less for that.

Until the cuts a few months before, Barnstaple police station was a 24-hour operation, with an overnight custody sergeant for the dozen refurbished cells, a resource which now largely went to waste. The drunkards and wife beaters who would otherwise have been held there were now driven to Exeter, soaking up staff time which should have been used on front-line policing.

So where was Kite? She wouldn't normally welcome looking at his pasty fish-wrapper face, but any help would have been welcome. She had been promised the NatWest bank CCTV images would be couriered to her first thing, but now she would have to deal with all this first.

She had barely left her own car before some angry middle-aged woman strode up to her and reported a burglary at her house. 'I couldn't get through on the non-emergency line,' she complained. Talan-tire fended her off while she unlocked the door and showed those waiting onto the seats by the main desk. Among them waiting were Barbara Antrobus and DCI Craig Gillard. Over the next half-hour she manned the place single-handedly. Kite called in, saying a falling tree had crushed his brother's conservatory during the night, so he would be late. The uniform superintendent was stuck on a train in Dawlish, where a landslip had blocked the line, and a high-sided vehicle had overturned and blocked the main road off the motorway, which was occupying the time of four officers and two patrol cars. But probably the biggest difficulty was that two mobile phone masts had come down on Exmoor, including the relay used by the emergency services. As far as she could tell, the entire Devon and Cornwall Constabulary were running around like headless chickens.

Craig Gillard walked up to the desk, where she was surrounded by a gaggle of people attempting to simultaneously report incidents. 'I can help you with some of the basic paperwork if you like,' he offered.

And so he did. Twenty minutes later, PC Clifford Willow sauntered in, his face wide with surprise, bringing in a couple of civilian members of staff.

It was almost eleven before Gillard and his by-now incandescent aunt were able to give details of the dog attack on the farm. Talantire looked at the incident report that Gillard had filled out at the desk. It was a model statement. 'Thank you for your help, Craig. As you are probably aware, we won't get round to this for a day or two, given the storm.'

'Then you need to get more bloody staff,' Barbara growled.

'Tell me about it. In fact, as you're here, I'd like to ask you a couple more questions about the hit-and-run.'

'Oh for God's sake,' Barbara said, banging down her fist on the counter. They were ushered into an interview room, while Talantire briefed Willow on what had so far been reported.

'Right,' Talantire said, pulling up a chair at the interview room table. 'I just want to clarify a few things.'

'Is it all right if I stay?' Gillard asked.

Talantire shrugged, then nodded. 'It's just for the witness statement. Right. So, Miss Antrobus, you said that you were at The Beeches care home visiting your brother last Wednesday when you noticed your vehicle had been stolen. What time did you arrive?'

'Half past one. And I noticed it was gone at a little before four. That's when I phoned in to report.' She tapped the statement in front of the detective. 'Like it says.'

'And you really left your new Ford unlocked, with the keys in the ignition?'

'Yes. It's a habit, see. My old pickup won't lock, and I often used to leave the keys in. It's not worth stealing.'

'Obviously not a good idea with your new vehicle.'

'No, but I had my hands full. I was intending to go back and lock it.'

Talantire nodded. 'There have been thefts from vehicles in that car park before.'

'I know. Mrs Dickinson told me. There's no camera, but it's not exactly inner city, is it?'

'So you didn't see or hear the vehicle being driven away?'

'No. The car park is round the corner from the main lounge.'

The detective looked down at her statement again. 'And later on, you found the vehicle yourself, on Bear Lane.'

'Yes, by the allotments. It was when my sister was driving me home. Seeing as I couldn't drive myself home, because my car had been stolen.'

'Were the keys still in it when you found it?'

'No. But I always keep a spare in a magnetic box on the underside of the pickup.'

'And your sister will confirm all these details, I trust?'

'I hope so. She was there. She was there at the home with me and Podge.'

'Podge?'

'My brother Philip, it's him who's in the home. We were playing Monopoly with him. There were other members of staff who saw us.' Barbara was leaning across the desk in an attempt to intimidate. Talantire was not impressed. Despite that bizarre scarred eye, it wasn't going to work. Perhaps time to show her.

'It's still pretty convenient, isn't it?' Talantire held Barbara's disconcerting gaze. 'Your car is stolen, used for a short time by somebody else in a hit-and-run, and returned to a place less than two minutes' drive away where you could pick it up on the way home—'

'What do you mean "convenient"?'

'What I mean, Miss Antrobus, is that it appears a very considerate thief took your car. Joyriders normally attract attention, cause considerable damage and quite often abandon the vehicle in some lonely spot, and frequently set it ablaze.'

'He's not that considerate. He mowed down a pedestrian.'

'Are you sure it wasn't you that mowed down—'

The heavily ringed fist that shot out and struck Talantire on the nose was so quick that the first she knew about it was when she was lying on the floor, still in the chair, the metallic taste of blood in her mouth. Above her, Gillard was struggling to subdue his aunt. He had her face down on the table, his knee in her back, her arm twisted up behind her.

'Get your hands off me, you bloody idiot,' Barbara bellowed.

'You always have to bring the house crashing down, don't you?' he yelled. 'You've really gone too far this time.'

'Let me go, young man, or I'll tell you something you'll regret knowing. Something you should have known long ago.'

'You slippery bitch,' Gillard replied, his face twisted in anger. He leaned harder with his knee and twisted her arm even further up her back, forcing an animal growl from the woman, who was wriggling like an enraged eel.

'Okay, go easy on her. I don't need you to snap her arm off.' Woozily, Talantire climbed to her feet. Gillard's face was dripping blood where three parallel scratches had raked from ear to mouth.

The door burst open and PCs Kite and Willow stood there, amazement draped on their faces.

'Lock her up,' Talantire croaked. 'Lock her up and throw away the key.'

As Kite and Willow got a grip on Barbara, Gillard stepped back to leave them to it. His aunt's hair had come undone, a great dyed black waist-length mass. It cascaded down her back and arms, giving her a bestial appearance. She managed a solid blow into the younger constable's face, which almost took him down, while even the bulkier figure of Kite struggled to keep her still.

'Let me go! I've got ewes to look after, and a farm to run.' She bit Kite on the cheek, prompting Gillard to step in again, an arm around his aunt's neck to close her jaw. Somehow, even though she was being held on her back on the table, she managed to get an arm around his neck too, trying to bite him.

Talantire, amazed at the woman's strength, managed to grab hold of a flailing leg which had already kicked Willow in the side of the head. The woman, locked in a vicious embrace with Gillard, whispered something to him and then laughed. He hesitated and allowed her to escape the neck hold.

Eventually the two local policemen managed to manhandle the struggling, spitting woman off to the cells, from where her shouting and screaming and hammering on the door filled the entire police station.

'Christ Almighty,' Kite said as he and Willow returned from the cells. 'If she's like that sober, what would she be like fuelled up?'

Talantire held a handkerchief to her nose, which she feared was broken, and looked around the room. Kite's cheek was swollen and bleeding, as was Willow's temple. Gillard's cheek was torn and covered in spittle, but to Talantire it was clear that wasn't the worst damage he had suffered. His face was pale, his eyes wide.

'Thank you for your help with that,' she said. 'What did she say to you?'

'Just an insult,' Gillard answered with a brittle smile. 'I thought I was used to it. Obviously not.' The Surrey detective seemed to pull himself together. 'I've got to go now. I've got an urgent appointment to play Monopoly with an old man.' With that he hurried out of the door before they could ask him any more questions.

Chapter 12

Sam looked up when Gillard walked into the games lounge at The Beeches. He looked gaunt and angry. She, Philip and Trish were already sitting around a large coffee table playing Monopoly with another resident, George, who had a portable oxygen machine to help him breathe.

'We decided to start without you,' she said. 'God, what happened to your cheek?'

'Barbara threw a complete wobbler during interview, punched Talantire, and has been arrested,' Gillard said.

'Oh for crying out loud, no,' said Trish. 'She's got such a temper.'

Philip interrupted. 'Would you like to join us?' he asked Gillard. 'Let me introduce my sister Trish, and her delightful friend...' He looked at Sam. 'What was your name again?'

'Her name is Sam. You've already introduced them,' rasped George, rolling his eyes. George had a viral heart condition and according to Trish was not expected to live long. He had ulcerous swollen legs, which his oversized sandals and loose socks failed to fully disguise. To Sam he smelled as if he had already died, yet his strong voice and robust irascibility told otherwise.

Trish pointed out to Gillard his counter, the iron, still on 'Go', and passed across the wodge of cash they had dealt out for him at the start. 'Your go.'

Gillard rolled the dice and got a four.

'Hah, income tax,' chuckled Philip. 'Two hundred pounds before you even get going.'

'Barbara didn't go down without a fight. She didn't like the accusation that she might have been driving the hit-and-run car.'

'Of course she wouldn't. She was here, with us,' Trish said. 'Wasn't she, George?'

'Yes, that's right,' he rasped. 'The whole afternoon.'

'If you're going to play, young man, you have to concentrate,' Philip said to Gillard. 'If you don't pay your taxes, you'll be in trouble.'

Once they settled back into the game, Trish started to ask some of the questions that Gillard had helped her prepare the evening before. 'Podge, when did you learn to drive?'

He looked up. 'Don't remember exactly, early 1960s,' he said as he rolled the dice.

'I remember that you had some job as a salesman.'

He looked up at her suspiciously. 'Why you want to know that?'

'I'd forgotten. I was just telling Craig here about what you used to do before you joined the Church.'

'It's all ancient history,' Philip said, then reached across the Monopoly board. 'I'll buy the waterworks, as no one else has got it. They might work better than mine.' He grinned.

Trish shared a glance with Gillard. He's way too sharp today, his aunt seemed to be saying. Sam's eyes followed as the two of them left the table for a moment, leaving just George and Philip.

'Stop looking up her skirt, you old pervert,' George whispered.

'I wasn't,' Philip responded. 'And how much do you want for Park Lane?'

Sam stepped away while the two old men bickered over the price, but she could still feel Philip's eyes on her. That man gave her the creeps, with an intelligent malevolence hidden behind those bright little eyes.

'Excuse me,' she heard Philip's voice say softly behind her. 'Lavatory.' The word was even more attenuated this time.

Sam turned and saw his eyes on her. 'I'll fetch Trish.'

'It's all right, I can manage as long as you manoeuvre me round the tight corner at the end and hold the door open.'

Lost for ready excuses, and unable to see where Trish had gone, Sam took the wheelchair, pressed off the brake with her foot and trundled the old man down towards the toilets along a stiflingly hot corridor which smelled of burnt dust. As he'd said, the corner at the end was tricky, and the fire door beyond it had a strong spring. Once she got him through into the disabled toilet, he pushed the door closed behind them. 'Samantha, would you be kind enough to undo my trousers?' he whispered. His expression suggested he'd said something seductive.

A shiver went through her. 'I thought you could manage,' she said.

'I can wipe my own arse, is what I meant. Obviously I'm not a circus acrobat.'

'I'll fetch Trish,' she said huskily.

He jerked the wheelchair backwards to block the door. 'No, don't fetch bloody Trish. Come on, one day you'll be like this and someone will have to help you. It's hard enough feeling your body falling to bits day by day without having to beg.' His eyes crawled down her body, lingering on her breasts.

Sam folded her arms instinctively. 'You're a manipulative old man, and I don't like you.'

'You wouldn't have said that when I was 30,' he replied. 'You would have begged for what I've got.' Suddenly, with both arms braced on the wheelchair handles he began to rise to a standing position. He was six feet tall, and somehow broader than she had appreciated.

'Philip, please. Let me out, please.'

'You see, young lady, I told you that you would beg.' He let go of the wheelchair and began to unbuckle his belt.

Chapter 13

Gillard was in conversation with Trish, Fitz and Mrs Dickinson, the manager, when they heard alarmed voices. He ran back to the lounge, where he found Sam in a state of some distress.

'Philip's had a fall and banged his head. I think he might be unconscious.'

'Where?' Fitz said, looking around the room.

'In the toilet. He asked me to take him to the toilet.'

Fitz ran on ahead as Sam hurried back along the corridor with Craig and Trish. 'I do hope he is all right.'

'So do I,' said Trish. 'You should have come to fetch me.'

Behind her back, Sam looked up at her husband, and gave him a shrug of bewildered horror, as if to say: how on earth did this happen?

The door to the disabled toilet was wedged almost closed. With a hefty shove, Fitz was able to get a partial glimpse inside. 'The wheelchair is on its side, and stuck between Philip and the door,' he said. He grunted as he reached in with one arm. 'Ah, that's it.' Finally, he was able to jiggle the chair and insert his slender frame through the gap.

'Sam, how did you get out?' Gillard asked.

'It wasn't stuck like that when I left,' she said. 'The chair wasn't on its side—'

'Call an ambulance,' Fitz shouted from inside. 'He's banged his head on the washbasin and is bleeding.'

Gillard ran to get some bandages from the office while Trish dialled 999. As the call rang out, they could hear Fitz asking the old man what had happened. 'It was her,' came a croaky voice. 'She pushed me over.'

'I did no such thing!' Sam retorted.

Trish's face tightened as her call was answered. 'Ambulance, please, and police. Someone has just attacked my elderly brother in his nursing home.' She looked up at Sam with a glare of pure hatred. 'Yes, we know who it is. We have the suspect here.'

–

While Fitz worked on Philip, Gillard eased himself into the bathroom, then folded and extracted the wheelchair, so that the door could be properly opened. The moment he emerged, Sam, horrified at the accusatory looks she was getting both from Trish and Mrs Dickinson, took him to one side. To Gillard, Sam's fury was utterly convincing. 'That crafty old pervert has been eyeing me up ever since I got here,' she said. 'He chose his moment, took advantage of my pity, and then tried it on.'

'So you didn't push him over?'

'Of course I didn't – he was standing, just about to expose himself to me, and I tried to push past his chair so I could get out.'

'So he fell?'

'No, he was holding onto the wheelchair—'

'What do you mean he was standing?' Trish yelled. 'He can't stand – he's a paraplegic. What nonsense you're talking, girl. You just took it out on an old man.'

'He was standing when I left,' Sam retorted. 'It was only as I got out of the door that I heard the crack of his head, and then I couldn't get back in.'

At that moment the paramedics arrived and Fitz showed them into the disabled toilet. A minute later the police arrived too. 'This is the one you want,' Trish said, pointing to Sam. 'She did it.'

Chapter 14

Monday

It was early evening when Sam's interview with DI Talantire at Barnstaple police station finally ended. As she left the interview room, she saw Craig had been patiently waiting for her by the desk, and she flung herself into his arms.

'How was it?' he asked her as he stroked her hair.

'Horrible, just horrible. They clearly don't believe a word I said.'

'It's their job to be sceptical,' Gillard said as he led her out into the car park. The wind was up again under a slate-grey sky. The remnants of sleet lay like pellets of polystyrene across dozens of windscreens.

'Talantire and her pregnant sidekick DS Stafford went at me time and again. "Come on, we understand how tempting it must be when some filthy old pervert leers at you. Come on, admit it, you gave him a shove, didn't you?" It was all that kind of stuff.'

'Standard practice, I'm afraid. How was the duty solicitor?'

'He didn't say a word. I think he was looking at his phone most of the time.'

Gillard harrumphed his disapproval. 'But anyway, they haven't charged you?'

'No. They want to interview Philip first.'

'Then you're probably off the hook,' he said. 'Philip is in no state to be interviewed, particularly now, and they know it. He's got a concussion and plenty more bruises to add to his collection. By the time he's ready, he may well have forgotten about the whole thing.'

'He's a nasty old bastard, Craig.'

'Yes, that's been quite a revelation to me. I knew what Barbara was like, but him…'

'I don't think Trish will ever speak to me again,' Sam said.

'Be grateful for small mercies,' he laughed. 'It'll save you wearing earplugs.'

'So what's happening with Barbara?'

'She's been charged with aggravated assault and will spend tonight in the cells. They'll probably give her police bail tomorrow, on condition she stays at the farm. Philip is spending the night in hospital, and Trish will fetch him in the morning.'

'Well that's something.'

Gillard eased the Vauxhall out of the car park and onto the main road out of town. 'I'm going to get you home, and we can try and forget about some of this.'

'Nothing would make me happier. I never want to go back there again.'

'Neither do I,' Gillard muttered. 'Not after what Barbara said to me.'

'What did she you say to you?'

He sighed. 'I don't know, it's probably nothing. But unfortunately, I can't check now because I handed in the laptop.'

'Is it about the photographs?'

'Yes. They weren't recent, you know. And they tell a story. But there are so many pieces still missing.'

'So what did Barbara say?'

'Like I say, it was probably nothing.'

'Was it—?'

'Not now, Sam. I'm not ready to talk about it.'

It was a while before Sam felt the confidence to ask the question that was more important to her than anything else. They were just on the brow of a hill, the lights of Barnstaple sparkling behind them. 'Craig? You do believe me about the Philip thing, don't you?'

He turned to her and smiled. 'Completely, Sam. I trust you utterly. It's because I know who you are. You wouldn't lie to me.'

She looked back at him, and realized that after this weekend, she couldn't say the same about him.

–

Midnight on Monday at Barnstaple police station, and one light in one office still burned. It had been one of the busiest days that Detective Inspector Jan Talantire had ever endured: a huge disruption from the storm, a backlog of incident reports, a flaky performance by colleagues who seemed to use any excuse not to turn up, a bloody nose from Barbara Antrobus and finally this allegation of assault against Samantha Gillard. At least the old boy didn't seem to be too badly hurt. Just confused and bruised, but it could have been a lot worse. The chances were that the CPS would not be interested in prosecuting her without some independent corroboration. Especially given that she had been a serving officer with an exemplary record. The documents emailed over from Surrey Police confirmed that.

Talantire sighed and logged into the Police National Computer, and looked up Barbara Antrobus's file. PC Nick Kite, who had spent all his years of service here and knew the family, had told her that there had been plenty of previous arrests. The records confirmed it, from 1960 onwards: shoplifting, assault, assault occasioning actual bodily harm, drink-driving, driving without due care and attention. The rest of her family, bar her late father, were clean. Philip had some motoring offences, Margaret had a drunk and disorderly in London. All of it was decades ago.

She logged off and picked up the Jiffy bag that had lain there untouched since the morning. She held it up in the light. Yes, it looked like the CCTV disc from NatWest bank. She was dog tired, desperate for sleep, but this was important. Micky Tuffin's supposed alibi for Wednesday last week. It would make life so much simpler if it didn't stand up.

She slid the disc into the PC. The picture was quite clear, showing a pedestrianized shopping area with several benches. She slid the arrow to 3 p.m. Sprawled on one bench, in the far-right corner of the fisheye-lens picture, was an obese man wearing a filthy anorak, tracksuit bottoms and flip-flops. Big Jim, Tuffin's mate. As she watched the footage unspool, he bent to retrieve some cans from one of several plastic carrier bags grouped around the bench, revealing a wedge of hairy bottom.

'Jesus Christ, that's enough,' she said, and hit fast forward. At 3.16 p.m., amid the frenetic movements of shoppers scurrying back and forth, another large figure sprinted into the shot, heading for the bench. Talantire slowed the video to normal, but she already knew. Micky Tuffin. She cursed under her breath. She fast-forwarded through the rest of the footage until both Mickey and Big Jim left at 4.18 p.m. Muriel Hinkley had found the body at 3.50 p.m. Temperature and rigor mortis measurements, plus the watch, showed the victim had been dead less than half an hour at that point. That put it beyond doubt. You cannot be in two places at once.

Mickey's alibi held water better than the Thames Barrier.

With a heavy sigh she flicked through the witness statements from The Beeches. Two members of staff had seen Barbara Antrobus arrive at about 1.30 p.m. She was joined a few minutes later by her sister Trish according to three witnesses, including another resident, George Butler. Miss Antrobus's call reporting her vehicle missing was logged at 3.57 p.m. from the care home landline, and was separately witnessed by at least two other people.

She had to admit that was a pretty watertight alibi too.

She wrote down the name of every suspect whose fingerprints had been found in the car. Micky Tuffin: alibi. Barbara Antrobus: alibi. Trish Gibson: alibi.

Peter Yates.

No alibi. And he had failed to turn up for a requested witness interview with PC Kite at the station on Sunday afternoon. Time to haul him in. Tomorrow.

—

Despite the blue skies and sunshine, Talantire was not in the best of moods on Tuesday morning, having to drive up to the farm to fetch Peter Yates. If he was being evasive, it could take quite a while to find him up here on the edges of the national park.

But she was in luck. She came face-to-face with him on the track leading to the farm. She was in her unmarked car and he was riding a quad bike with a bale of straw strapped to the back. Yates showed no awareness that this visitor to the farm wanted to speak to him. She had to open her car door to stop him manoeuvring around her. He stared at her, revving the vehicle, seemingly waiting for her to get out the way. Talantire stepped up to the quad bike, reached over the handlebars and killed the engine. She then removed the key and showed him her warrant card. She mimed the action of wanting to speak to him. He finally got the message and removed his earbuds.

'Are you Peter Yates?'

He nodded.

She introduced herself, then said: 'Park that here, you're coming with me to the station. Something you should have done two days ago at 4 p.m.'

'But someone's got to look after the beasts,' he said.

'I've caged one beast for 24 hours: your very own employer. I can easily cage you too.'

Half an hour later, Peter Yates was sitting in the same smelly interview room at Barnstaple police station that Micky Tuffin had occupied, with the same duty solicitor. But Peter looked far more nervous than Mickey had.

'Right,' Talantire said, 'Let's get the formalities underway.' She began by reminding Peter of the crime she was investigating and confirming his home address, which turned out to be with his parents in a suburb of the town. She then asked him to produce his driving documents. He showed her a provisional licence.

'So you've not passed your test?'

'Failed couple of times,' he said morosely.

'Do you drive any of your employer's vehicles?'

'Only the quad bike and the Massey Ferguson – on the farm, like.'

'What about her cars?'

'I've driven the Shogun when Miss Antrobus has been in it, teaching me.'

'Not alone?'

'Well, maybe on the farm a few times, just rearranging bits and bobs. But not the Ford. I'm not allowed.'

'Where were you last Saturday night, between 8 and 11 p.m.?'

'Why are you asking about Saturday? I thought you were here about something that happened on Wednesday.'

'Please just answer the question,' she said.

Peter thought for a long time, his dark, impenetrable eyes unfocused. 'Mickey's told you, hasn't he?' he replied.

'Told me what?' she smiled.

'That I let him drive Miss Antrobus's new Ford when she was out.'

'And did you?'

Peter hung his head, his cheeks becoming almost cadaverously hollow.

'Did you drive it yourself at all?'

'No, I'm not covered.'

'Is Mickey covered?'

'Yes, he can drive anything.'

'What would you say if I told you that Micky Tuffin is banned from driving, and currently has no insurance valid for any vehicle, even that little moped he uses.'

Peter looked shocked. 'He told me—'

'—a pack of lies, I'm afraid.' Leaving this to sink in for a moment, she added: 'So what was the motivation for this joyride on Saturday night?'

Peter was biting his nails. 'Miss Antrobus don't often leave the farm, but her sister invited her out to Exeter to see a film. I mentioned it to Mickey, who said he could come up on his moped, then we could use the car and meet some girls he knew in Barnstaple, have a few drinks. You know.'

'And did you?'

'We had some drinks, yeah. No girls to speak of.'

'Did you at any time drive the car?'

'No. Mickey did.'

'And he returned the car to the farm?'

'Yeah, I knew we had to be back by eleven. The film finished at ten so they could have been back in an hour.'

Once she finished noting it down, Talantire looked up at him. 'So, on to the main point, where were you on Wednesday afternoon?'

'I was here at the farm, from about midday.'

'Was anybody with you?'

'Not until Miss Antrobus came back, at half six.'

'This is a very important question, Peter: did you drive the Ford Ranger on Wednesday afternoon? And did you hit-and-run down a man by the phone box at Furzy Hill?'

Peter shook his head emphatically. 'No, I did not.'

'Peter, we've got a thumbprint on the steering wheel looks very like the one we just took from you not half an hour ago. What have you got to say that?'

'It wasn't me.'

–

Talantire wasn't satisfied with this explanation and wanted to see more about the way this gangly youth lived. She led him to a patrol car and had PC Kite drive them to Yates's parents' home. Mr Yates was at work, but Peter's mother, a small and rather mousy woman in her 50s, was horrified that her son would have got into any trouble.

'We're just checking things,' Talantire said to her. 'It's nothing to concern yourself with too much at this stage.' Peter's room was as untidy as any adolescent's, with posters of heavy metal bands, a couple of electric guitars and some fairly serious-looking home recording gear. Talantire directed Kite to take his laptop and any other portable electronic gear. After questioning his mother, Talantire established Peter stayed overnight half the week at Hollow Coombe farm. 'It's because of the early mornings he has to do,' Mrs Yates explained.

'Right, we can go back up to the farm now to check your accommodation there,' Talantire said. It was the first moment when the youth had looked truly frightened. She already guessed why that was.

They arrived at the farm only half an hour after Barbara. 'What do you want *now*?' she yelled as she opened the door. 'They've only just let me out.'

'Don't get into a lather,' Talantire said. 'We've come to search his room, in case it was him who was driving your car.'

'He doesn't drive my pickup,' Barbara said. 'Not the Ford.'

Talantire smiled. 'Well, we'll see where the evidence leads us. Now, if you would show us the way.'

Peter and Barbara exchanged nervous looks before she said: 'I'll get you the key to the caravan.' She led the two police officers and Peter up a steep muddy pasture, past the caravan that had belonged to Philip Antrobus, to one that was larger and in better condition.

'This is where he sleeps, on those days when I need him in early,' Barbara said, unlocking the door and flipping on the light switch. The interior was neat and tidy, with folded unmade bedding, clean curtains and an array of recently washed dishes in the kitchenette.

Talantire stepped inside, wiped her feet on the mat, and looked around. 'Do you really sleep here, Peter?' she asked. 'It's a bit tidier than your place at home. In fact, it doesn't look like anyone has slept here recently.'

'I got an Airbnb rental coming in tomorrow, that's why it's been tidied up,' Barbara said. 'The farm needs every bit of income it can get, since we're losing so many sheep to wolves,' she added, emphatically.

Nick Kite let out a wolf-type howl, and then grinned at Barbara.

'That's enough of your nonsense,' Barbara replied, pointing a finger right in his face. Her knuckles were still grazed and scabby.

'So where is his stuff?' Kite added menacingly.

'He's got a sleeping bag in the farmhouse, and some toiletries in the bathroom,' she said.

Fifteen minutes later, when Talantire and Kite were on their way back to the police station, Kite said: 'There's something funny going on there, if you ask me.'

'Takes all sorts,' said Talantire.

'But what a family, eh? First, Barbara Antrobus wallops you over this nonsense about the sheep, then her aged wheelchair-bound brother is beaten up in his old folks' home by his nephew's wife, a former PCSO at that.

And neither sister reckons they have anything to do with knocking down this poor bloke in their car.'

'There's a pretty good alibi.'

'Nah.' The PC waved his arm dismissively. 'Listen, Jan. I know this Antrobus tribe of old. I wouldn't trust any of them as far as I could throw them.'

Chapter 15

When Talantire arrived back at Barnstaple police station on Tuesday afternoon, DS Charmaine Stafford welcomed her with news of the DNA tests. The full range of mito-chondrial analysis on the hit-and-run victim showed a man of predominantly European origins, with Nordic and Irish connections. The standard DNA test showed no matches to anyone on the UK DNA crime database.

'That doesn't get us very far,' Talantire said.

'I was wondering if we could do a familial DNA test to see if he's related to anyone on the database?' Stafford said.

'No, I've some experience of trying to do this when I was based in Bristol. You can only do specific match-ups, you can't trawl the database hoping to catch a connection. There's not enough information retained on the records.'

'I traced the Clarks shoes,' she said. 'They were part of a batch shipped to Dubai duty free in March. So this bloke clearly is an international traveller.'

'If he's foreign, that would explain why nobody here has missed him.'

'This just came too. I haven't had time to look at it,' she said, passing across an A3 sealed envelope addressed to Talantire. 'Full works from the autopsy.'

The DI opened it and read the summary. It gave the man's blood type and a full health rundown. 'He had mild cirrhosis of the liver, and as we've already been told, haemorrhoids.'

Stafford chuckled, and held her stomach.

'This is interesting. The lungs indicate he had smoked years ago but given up, which contradicted the fact there were traces of nicotine in his blood.'

'Maybe he was on e-cigs, or patches,' Stafford said.

'Good point. Or maybe just needed a fag.'

Talantire returned to the toxicology document. 'His blood showed traces of zolpidem, "which showed recent use of this imidazopyridine" whatever that is. "Examination of his fingernails and bones showed cadmium, zinc and lead, in unusual concentrations, though not at dangerous levels. These may indicate some kind of environmental or work-related exposure and we recommend specialist analysis for more detailed results".'

Stafford googled zolpidem. 'It's a sleeping pill, basically.'

'It is probably not significant, but I'm going to ask the pathologist. I think the work-related contaminant angle could be very useful too.'

-

Talantire was once again in the warehouse unit, kneeling before the Ford Ranger. Next to her squatted Mike Robinson of the CSI unit, a powerful inspection light trained on the smears of gore and hair which still marked the front edge of the chassis.

'From what we know,' Robinson said, 'the victim was hit sideways on and tried to somehow cling on to the radiator, which is how the sole of his left shoe got trapped here. He fell backwards, the front left wheel ran over his right forearm, then his skull, and he got pulled underneath, except his shoe held him in place until his leg fractured.'

'So that's how his left leg got so badly twisted?' she asked.

'That's what we think, yes, and it matches what Dr Chaudhry told us about the injuries. The vehicle must have been doing nearly 30, and there is no evidence of braking or evasive manoeuvres during the collision, bar that one twitch up onto the verge. If the brakes had been applied at that point, we would have expected to see smudging of the tyre imprint on the verge, but they are clean and crisp.'

'So you think this could have been deliberate?' Talantire asked.

'Well,' he blew a sigh, 'it's a big leap to impugn motive based on incompetent driving. I used to spend most of my time looking at RTAs, and it's amazing how oblivious drivers can be. I had one case where an elderly male driver towing a caravan knocked over a cyclist and was completely unaware. He did another 4 miles with bits of the bike scraping beneath the caravan before stopping.'

'It doesn't surprise me.'

They moved around the vehicle together on hands and knees, and then inside, with Robinson pointing out all the fingerprint locations, which Talantire cross-checked on the CSI report on her clipboard. Those on the steering wheel were of Barbara Antrobus who had found her abandoned vehicle and had presumably obliterated the dabs of the thief when she drove it home. The fingerprints of her sister Tricia were found, along with Barbara's, on some door handles inside and out, the rear door and glove compartment.

'What about Peter Yates?' she asked.

'Partial prints inside and out, particularly on the tailgate, as I mentioned. No surprises there, given his work on the farm. But there is, significantly, this partial print on the steering wheel.'

'We can't put him behind the wheel on that alone, can we?'

Robinson shook his head. 'We need more.'

Talantire suddenly remembered. 'Ah, Mike. Did you get any prints from the flower cellophane pinned to the fence at Furzy Hill?'

'Nope. Nothing at all.' He turned his attention back to the car. 'There are still a few unidentified partial prints, including one on the glove compartment. I'd really be happy if we could get that identified. Dust and mud samples from the mats inside matched those from Ms Antrobus's farm. There were various animal hairs, which have been identified as cat, dog, sheep and goat.' He smiled.

'Bit of a Noah's Ark,' Talantire responded.

'The clothing worn by the victim had also been contaminated with animal hairs, though this time just feline.'

'Can you do anything with that?' Talantire asked.

Robinson laughed. 'There are eight million cats in the UK, so it's unlikely to be a breakthrough clue. It's definitely got to be easier to ID the victim. So how is that going?'

Talantire sighed. 'Not good. He's Mr Nobody. Nobody knows him, nobody saw him, nobody's missed him. We've got the Centre for Anatomy and Human Identification at the University of Dundee doing a facial reconstruction, but they warned us that because of the damage it will inevitably be fairly approximate. We know he was about 60 to 65 and in decent health, apart from the haemorrhoids and the mild cirrhosis.'

Robinson chuckled. 'So he might not have been able to sit down comfortably but otherwise would have lived quite a long time had he not been dragged up the road on his face underneath a massive 4 × 4.'

'That's right. We're pretty sure now that it's nobody local. We've got CCTV from the railway and bus station, and of course we've no idea what type of face we're looking for. There are no obvious matches with the clothing he was found wearing, except the shoes as I mentioned.' She turned to him. 'Here's something weird, Mike. All the washing and manufacturer's labels on the clothes had been cut off.'

'Maybe an allergy?'

She shrugged. 'We've asked car park owners in the area to notify us of any vehicles parked on that Wednesday and since unattended, but there are no leads there either.'

'What about DNA?'

'Ah yes. More disappointments. We had two men, roughly the right age and height, both reported missing on the day the body was found, one from Falmouth, the other from Bristol. There was also a keen walker from Potters Bar, three days gone, not quite tall enough, but who knows how this body has been stretched. Sadly, the DNA says no. It's not any of them.'

Robinson eyed her cautiously as he heaped further ignominy on the enquiry. 'I hear you haven't charged the driver of this beastie either?'

'Nope. The alibis all stack up, for the Ford's owner as well as our favourite joyrider. There is a possibility that an employee of the owner was driving it, but I don't think we can prove it. We're going to do a reconstruction and drive an identical vehicle around next Wednesday at the same time the Ford was stolen. See if it jogs any memories.'

'Are you getting heat from Exeter?' Robinson said.

'Absolutely.' She smiled. 'But I can handle it, for now at least.' She turned away as Robinson stopped to check his phone.

'Hold your horses,' Robinson said as he read an email. 'This will interest you. You know that piece of chewing gum you found on the sole of the victim's shoe? The lab has managed to extract some DNA. It belongs to Peter Yates.'

'Wow,' Talantire said. She thought for a moment. 'That means our hit-and-run victim has at least crossed paths with Barbara's employee.'

Robinson screwed his face up sceptically. 'Or he might just have walked in the same pubs that Yates and Tuffin visited the previous Saturday and trod in it then. Doesn't prove anything.'

Peter Yates. To Talantire, he exuded innocence, but she could be wrong. On this occasion, given that everybody else had an alibi, it would be helpful if she were.

Chapter 16

Friday

The first few days he was back in Surrey, DCI Gillard was swamped with work: a major fraud at an engineering company in Woking and a stabbing at a bus stop in Carshalton. In some ways he was quite happy to shunt aside the unpleasant weekend that he and Sam had experienced in Devon, to throw himself into the drudgery of a normal workload. It wasn't until the last afternoon of the working week that he could summon the energy to think about Philip Antrobus. He clicked on the folder on his PC desktop that had been left for him by DC Colin Hodges. This was all the cold-case information he'd asked for. Perhaps it would give some clue as to whether Emily was a real person or a figment of his uncle's imagination. He scrutinized it, and realized how much more work there was still to do.

At home in the evening, he rang Trish. He'd been meaning to mend fences with his aunt about Philip's accident and Sam's involvement. Trish said that her brother was now back in the care home but seemed a little more confused than usual. 'I'm used to him forgetting when I last came to see him, but at first he didn't even seem to recognize where he was.'

'Hopefully he'll recover quickly,' Gillard said. 'Sam is ever so sorry about what happened, as you know.'

His aunt was uncharacteristically silent as Gillard retold Sam's version of events. 'She would never manhandle, shove or hit a vulnerable person, I can assure you of that,' Gillard said.

'Why did she lie?'

'She didn't.'

'She most certainly did. She said Philip had stood up. Craig, believe me, he can't stand, ever since he had a stroke ten years ago. The bit of his brain that controls his lower back and beyond doesn't work. Physio helped his comfort and muscle tone, but that's all.'

'Well I can't explain that. But I do assure you of Sam's good intentions.'

At this Trish softened. 'Well, she does seem very nice, overall. And Philip can be an awkward tyke, as we all know. A doctor came to The Beeches on Tuesday and assessed Philip as being "unfit to be detained".'

'That's three days ago. Why didn't you tell me this before?'

'Well, I thought you would know. Aren't you friends with that woman detective? Barbara said you two were very pally.'

Gillard closed his eyes and silently counted to ten. 'Do you have the precise wording?'

'Let me open the letter, dear. Yes, unfit to be detained on both physical and mental grounds. He was also judged unfit to give evidence on mental criteria.'

'That's pretty much what I expected.'

'Poor Podge didn't react at all well to being shunted into the office and asked a load of official-sounding questions, especially when he was told that the doctor was working on behalf of the police. He seemed to think he was already in prison, and kept asking me to take him home. He said sorry a few times and asked the chap if he'd come about Emily. The doctor picked up on it, and asked him who she was, but Podge didn't say any more. I told him we didn't know either. So he made some notes and that was that.'

Gillard sighed. 'I've been giving this Emily story a lot of thought. He doesn't remember the surname, does he? It would really help.'

'No. I've asked him several times.'

'Searching just on a Christian name isn't easy. My colleague has had a quick look at the cold-case murder list going back to 1960. Now, excluding those relating to the Troubles in Northern Ireland…'

'Why exclude them? This Emily could have been from Northern Ireland.'

'Well yes, she might have been. But I excluded them quite simply because they are 90 per cent of the country's unsolved homicides. That's 3,000 people whose lives were ended, in many cases by known perpetrators. In all probability, because of the Good Friday Agreement, no one will ever be charged. That's quite a price to pay for peace. Still, there are specific characteristics relating to most of those killings which allow us to classify them as "Troubles-related". Ignoring them, we have fewer than 50 women and girls from the British mainland believed to have been murdered since 1960, and where we have no conviction. Not one of them was called Emily.'

'So it isn't true. That's such a relief, Craig.'

'It's unlikely to be true, certainly. But that's not the end of the matter. I also looked at the missing persons database. I searched for the name Emily and found thousands of references over the years.'

'My goodness, I had no idea.'

'Yes, an awful lot of people – 250,000 – go missing each year in the UK. It's a staggering number, isn't it? Most of them will eventually turn up unharmed; some never do, but are assumed to be alive. And in the middle are a significant number who are dead, either from natural causes or suicide. Very few, proportionately, turn out to have been murdered. But every life is important, which is why we are prepared to take the time to make sure. However, with children we are on firmer ground. Disappearances of children are reported quickly, are taken seriously and are almost always resolved. That's true now, and it was generally true in the past. I went back to 1970 and couldn't find records of any youngster called Emily who was under 16 when she disappeared and is still unaccounted for. That's not a cast-iron guarantee, but it does seem unlikely that he murdered a child.'

'Thank goodness. I couldn't bear it if he had.'

'What he actually did do is less certain. But we're not going to start at that speculative end of the enquiry, because we could spend a heck of a lot of time getting nowhere. I'm going to ask you to spend some time finding out everything you can about your brother. That will eliminate most possibilities. Do you have a tape recorder?'

'I do somewhere, yes.'

'Good. I'm going to email you a list of questions. Now I understand he has got a lot of stuff still stored at his old house in Lynton, is that right?'

'Yes, but it's in the loft, and I can't get up there.'

'Is there anyone you could ask to help clear his stuff out?'

'Not really.'

'What about Peter, Barbara's farmhand? He's young and agile.'

'I wouldn't trust him, Craig. Besides, it's family stuff. I don't want any Tom, Dick or Harry poking about up there.' The silence lay like a corpse between them for several seconds. 'Would you—?'

'I'm extremely busy, Trish.'

'Have you spoken to Viv?'

'Yes. But I think you can guess her response.' Gillard's older sister had been scathing when he suggested that she visit her aunts. He had a feeling he knew where this conversation might end up; he just wanted to explore every other possibility first.

'Oh, I see.'

'I'll ring Talantire and let her know that I'm looking into the Emily angle.'

'The doctor is coming back again on Monday to see if, after a couple more days' rest, Philip would be fit to give evidence. I don't think they'll give up, and then they'll look into all these terrible photos. I don't know, Craig. I'm finding all this very stressful. If you could just—'

'Okay, I'll come down and have a look myself at some stage.'

'That's very kind of you, dear. What time tomorrow should I expect you?'

Gillard gritted his teeth. 'Trish, I'm not coming tomorrow.'

Trish's voice had started to waver, the precursor to tears. 'I don't know, dear, my brother and my sister in trouble with the law, and no one here to help me. I've had to see the doctor to get extra tablets—'

'Okay, Trish, okay.' He sighed.

'So I'll expect you both by teatime tomorrow, then? I've got a nice bit of pork loin to roast, that'll do perfectly.' She said goodbye and hung up.

Sam had been watching television but the explosion of swearing and the slamming down of the phone interrupted her concentration. 'Craig, what's the matter?'

He thundered downstairs and relayed the message.

'I suppose I have to go. I'll have to take Monday off. It's the last thing I want to do, but I suppose I can't let the mad old bat suffer alone. Fortunately, I've still got 17 days leave which human resources has been on at me to take before the end of the year.'

Sam blew a sigh. 'I'm coming too. I've got another day owing.'

'You said you never wanted to go there again.'

'I don't, obviously. I'd rather bang my head against a brick wall for a fortnight than spend five minutes listening to Trish wittering on. But let's face it, Craig, you are utterly defenceless against both those cardiganed wolverines. Particularly the emotional blackmail. I want to be there to look after your interests. You need protecting.'

Saturday

'Now this is Howie's brother-in-law, Sarawut. I met him in Exeter when he came over from Thailand,' Trish said, showing Craig and Sam a picture on her phone. 'I spoke to him yesterday, and he's hoping to come and join us for Christmas. His son Buma is a junior trader at a bank in London, doing derivatives. He is ever so clever.' This was about the fiftieth photo of Howie's extended family they'd had to endure since arriving half an hour ago.

'I think we should get on and go to tackle this loft,' Gillard said, looking at his watch. It was nearly six. 'We've only got limited time.'

'Of course, but we'll have to have the roast pork first. It's nearly done. There's a lovely bit of crackling on it.' She bustled back into the kitchen, followed by two of the cats.

Gillard put out his arms to Sam and pulled her into an embrace. 'I promise you a proper weekend, somewhere relaxing, to thank you for your stalwart temperament in coming here to back me up,' he whispered. Napoleon, the dominant ginger cat, stared up at them from the sofa with narrowed green eyes, as if he was taking it all in, ready to report overheard details to his mistress.

The meal was delicious, conversation muted by the firecracker crunching of pork rind. 'Very fluffy roast potatoes, Trish,' Sam said between mouthfuls.

By the time they had finished it was gone eight, and Trish said: 'I suppose it's too late to disturb the tenant now. We'll go tomorrow before we go to see Podge in the afternoon. We might find some possessions that jog his memory.'

Sunday

For most of his ecclesiastical life, Reverend Philip Antrobus had lived in church properties attached to the various dioceses where he was based. But when he retired from an active role in the Church of England, he returned to North Devon to buy and renovate a rundown eighteenth-century townhouse in Lynton.

Trish, Craig and Sam were standing outside the imposing three-storey whitewashed building, overlooking the small picturesque harbour with its bobbing yachts and gently tapping lanyards. Trish rapped sharply on the brass knocker and, after a minute, the door opened. An unsmiling middle-aged woman with mousy hair and glasses showed them in and pointed out the loft hatch at the top of the rickety, twisty staircase.

'Use the slide-down ladder if you're going up,' she said to Gillard. 'Come out of there the wrong way and you'll be straight over the banister onto your head. I don't want to have to clean up the mess.' She stalked out into her kitchen.

'She's an awful woman,' Trish muttered as she followed Craig and Sam up the stairs. 'Don't much like her husband either. Should never have rented the place to them.' Gillard stood on a chair to release the loft hatch, and was immediately deluged in dust and soot.

'You should have put some overalls on,' Trish said, unhelpfully.

'I've got a Tyvek suit in the car. But once you put that on, you start a panic. Everyone expects you're going to find a dead body.' He reached up and slid out the aluminium ladder stored within, extending each section carefully and fixing the clips. Sam passed him the inspection lamp and he climbed up. The roof space was low, filthy and stained by soot. Chimneys at either side had clearly leaked smoke over many decades, and the ancient timbers looked brittle, too fragile to hold up the sagging roof. Only a small part of the attic was boarded, almost all of which was taken up by half a dozen grimy packing cases and two old suitcases. Sam climbed up to join him, and together they spent the next hour going through Philip's belongings.

They found paperwork, a leather-bound photo album, a folder of newspaper cuttings, a vintage typewriter, a broken slide projector, a box with an ancient Polaroid camera, old clothes, bundles of letters received while he was in India, and a mounted scorpion in a glass case.

Gillard examined the camera carefully. 'I wonder if the child abuse pictures were taken on this. It looked to me like some of them were very old Polaroids which had been re-photographed in order to get them onto the computer.'

Sam turned her attention to a smaller red leatherette case, definitely feminine in design. It was covered in aged stickers, one with a Rolling Stones-style open mouth, and had two rusted metal clasps. 'Perhaps we should bring this down for Trish. It could belong to her,' Sam said.

They gathered together the papers, Polaroid camera and photo album, and resealed the packing cases, and with Gillard halfway down the ladder, passed them down to Trish.

'Does this vanity case belong to you or Barbara?' Gillard said.

Trish stared at it. 'It's not mine, and I don't think it's Barbara's. She wasn't the type for a vanity case, even as a teenager. It's pretty old though.'

She stood back and watched as Gillard, kneeling on the landing, attempted to jemmy open the locks with a screwdriver. The metal clasps were stronger than they looked, and it took a couple of minutes to force them.

Finally, he was able to lift the lid. The first thing they saw was a pair of shiny pink PVC high-heeled knee boots.

'Wow,' Sam said. 'Outrageously retro.'

'Definitely not mine,' Trish said, removing the boots and delving into the case. 'Do you remember these?' she asked, holding up a floaty dress with colourful zigzags across it. 'Mother had one in some dreadful nylon material that used to give you electric shocks. A single flaming match and it would probably have gone up like a Roman candle.'

They also discovered a pair of bell-bottom jeans in size eight with an embroidered dart at the ankle, a cheesecloth blouse or two, and some neatly packed underwear.

'This stuff is ancient,' Sam said. 'Like some 1970s time capsule.'

'The question is, why has Podge got it?' Trish asked. 'And why has he kept it all these years?'

'There could be an innocent explanation, I suppose,' Sam said. 'It's not evidence of murder, is it?' They continued to unpack the case and found half a dozen vinyl 45s in their original sleeves, carefully wrapped in a skinny-rib pullover. They included Wizzard, Gilbert O'Sullivan, the Strawbs, and Alvin Stardust, as well as some better-known David Bowie and Slade numbers.

'We already know a lot, don't we?' Gillard said, nodding at the suitcase.

'Do we?' Trish asked.

'A young, fashionable girl, in the 1970s, leaving home, taking her most precious records. And somehow she got separated from all this. From everything that mattered to her from her previous life. This must all belong to Emily. Whoever she is.'

Chapter 17

Back at Trish's house they were joined by Barbara, and they looked together through the paperwork and pictures. Gillard had hoped for a detailed employment history, but apart from some tax forms, which mentioned one employer's name, there were only some household bills for an address that he had clearly lived in during the 1980s in Liverpool.

'That was when he got back from India,' Barbara said. 'He joined the Church, and they sent him off to Toxteth. He was there at the time of the riots.'

Sam picked up the cuttings folder, simply labelled 'Protests 1992–2004'. It was a collection of newspaper articles clipped from various sources detailing Philip's involvement in homelessness protests.

'All right, let's take a look at the photographs,' Trish said. She flicked through the pages of the album, which alternated with bound sheets of tissue paper, giving little oohs and aahs over the earliest scallop-edged black and white prints. There were pictures of her late mother with a newborn baby who could have been either one of the sisters, and next to it a studio portrait of them all, Philip a smartly dressed nine-year-old, Barbara perhaps five, Trish aged two or three and Margaret just a babe in arms, cradled on the knees of her father. Then there was a studio portrait of Philip in his mid-20s. Later on, there were small white-edged colour pictures of three children squinting into the camera on the farm.

Craig and Sam exchanged glances as the two sisters reminisced over the various pictures, bickering over exactly when and where each of them may have been taken. Sam began to feel that she was once again being dragged into a gothic family feud. However, it was a portrait of their father, with his glowering dark features, hooded eyes and knowing stare at the camera which silenced both sisters. A cold hatred seemed to overpower the heat of the room. Barbara reached forward, moved Trish's hand from the page and firmly flipped it over.

'That's enough of him,' he said.

'He seemed a very forbidding—' Sam began.

Barbara silenced her with a glare, and Gillard's gentle hand on Sam's wrist telegraphed that this was not a subject for now, or perhaps any time.

'What's this?' Trish was working away at a picture which seemed to be stuck under the endpaper of the leather-bound album. She pulled out a small colour photo of a girl with long dark hair wearing bell-bottom jeans and a cheesecloth shirt.

'Looks like Sam as a teenager,' Gillard said.

'Those are the same jeans as in the suitcase,' Sam said. 'The embroidered dart is identical.'

'Do you know who she is?' Gillard asked his aunts.

'I have no idea,' Barbara said. 'Someone from the 1970s, I imagine. He had a few girlfriends. But I haven't seen this one before.'

'I don't recognize her,' Trish added. 'But I suppose this might be Emily.'

Gillard nodded. 'We're going to have to play this very carefully. This is what we're going to do.'

Sunday afternoon

Trish and Barbara were sitting with Philip in the garden room of The Beeches, looking out through the bay window onto the lawns and trees that separated the residential chalets. It was the coldest room in the home, and they were confident of not being disturbed by others who generally preferred the warmth of the two south-facing lounges. After they had seated Philip opposite the window, Gillard quietly slipped into a large wing chair within earshot, placed a digital recorder on the arm of the chair, and switched it on.

Philip had already refused the offer of a game of Monopoly, which usually meant that he wasn't feeling at his sharpest. He was still bruised from where he had cracked his head on the washbasin, and had complained of headaches. He clearly recognized both sisters, but at first struggled to remember Barbara's name. The two women started by going through the photo album, pretending they didn't know many of the people in the pictures, and asked Philip to identify them. He was hopeless at the baby pictures, but quite good at identifying members of the family from their teens onwards.

'Now, do you know who this is?' Trish asked. Gillard could tell from her tone that she was showing him the mystery picture.

There was a long pause. 'Emily,' he said softly.

'How old was she in this picture?' Trish asked. 'She looks about 19 or 20.'

147

'No. It's her nineteenth birthday next month. So she's 18.'

'Next month?'

'Yes, on the fourth. August fourth. She's having a party. I'm invited.'

Ask her where, Gillard thought, trying to telegraph the thought into his aunt's mind. *We need to know where*.

'Podge,' said Barbara. 'We're in November.'

There was a confused sound in his throat. 'Are we?' he asked huskily.

'Yes, Podge,' Trish said. 'Look outside. There are no leaves on the trees. Can you tell me when this photograph was taken?'

'It was July,' Philip said. 'At the picnic.'

'What year?' Barbara asked.

'This year I think, or was it last?' Philip asked.

'No, Podge. It wasn't this year. It was a long time ago.'

Gillard had risked turning around to look over the arm of the chair towards the table where Philip sat with his sisters. He was staring at the photograph, held in both his hands. They were trembling.

'I don't know,' he said, in a rising tremolo of uncertainty. 'I don't know what year. She could tell you.'

'Emily?'

'Yes.'

'But you said Emily had died. Didn't you?'

'Emily is dead?' He seemed quite distressed by this revelation. 'I don't think so. I saw her just last week.'

Gillard was willing either Trish or Barbara to ask the question he had prepared for them for this moment: how old are you, Podge? If he was reliving the time when he was with Emily, remembering his own age would help to date the incident precisely. But neither of them asked the question. Instead, they moved on to another.

'Where did you have the picnic with her?' Trish asked.

His reply was enthusiastic. 'In the meadow. There were buttercups, glorious buttercups, daisies and... snake's head fritillaries.' He looked proud of himself for remembering the name.

'Where was it near? What town?'

'Oh. It was off the motorway. I don't remember. It doesn't matter.'

Yes it does! Ask him again. Gillard was giving himself a headache in his attempted telepathy.

Barbara leaned forward across the table. 'Did you kill her, Podge? Did you kill Emily?'

'Shhh. For God's sake.' Philip looked around. 'They might hear.'

'Who?'

'The police. Look, I said I was sorry. I never meant to—'

'Podge,' Trish whispered. 'Tell me. Just whisper it in my ear.'

Philip shook his head emphatically and began to swallow his lips, his hands working nervously on the arms of the chair. 'No, no. I can't. They'll never let me out.' He looked around him and caught a glimpse of Gillard peering around the back of the chair, which seemed to give him a shock. 'Lavatory. Trish, I need the lavatory.'

While Trish wheeled him off, Barbara came to sit with Gillard. 'How did we do?' she asked.

'Not bad. The recorder may have missed some of the quieter exchanges, but at least I've got something concrete to show DI Talantire.'

'Podge will have his regular early afternoon sleep now. We normally wake him up at around 4.30 p.m. He will probably have forgotten everything that happened. That's what normally happens.'

'Okay, so that's when the second part of our plan kicks in. I just hope his short-term memory is as bad as usual.'

—

Sam had taken a while to prepare herself for this role. She had studied the face in the photograph and used her mascara brush and eyeliner to match as much as possible the 1970s make-up style that Emily had worn. Metallic-green eyeshadow had required a trip to the shops, but now, in the visitors' bathroom at The Beeches, she slid out of her own clothes, put on the cheesecloth shirt and hauled on the bell-bottom jeans. They were tight. Very tight. Emily had looked to be only in her late teens, after all, half Sam's age. The biggest worry was that she wouldn't be able to do up the zip, but after lying on the floor inhaling to the fullest extent, she was able to do the trousers up completely. She used her own belt just in case the brass button gave way. Rising to her feet again, she checked herself in the mirror against the picture. Not too bad. As long as she didn't try anything clever. Like breathing.

Walking was the next difficulty. She hadn't attempted to wear the pink PVC boots, which were too small, but had found a pair of platform shoes in her size in the charity shop yesterday afternoon. She tottered around in them to practise, and realized she could only take small steps in any case because of the tightness of the jeans. Finally entering the lounge, she got a little round of applause not

150

only from the two sisters, but from Gillard and a gaggle of elderly residents who had picked up that something was going on. Craig, Sam and the aunts made their way out of the main building and across the garden towards Philip's chalet. The curtains were closed. After a quick rehearsal, Sam flapped her hand to her chest to allay her nerves. Gillard had promised he would be right outside – she only had to scream.

She walked up the steps and tapped on the door. There was no reply. She turned the handle and stepped inside.

Chapter 18

The room smelled stale, and she could hear the rasping rhythm of breathing. She pulled the curtain just a little to let the thin afternoon light penetrate the room and placed the digital recorder, already running, on the bedside table. She switched on the bedside lamp.

The man awaking in the bed, without spectacles or dentures, looked older and more cadaverous than the Philip she had seen before. A plume of bad breath hung over him.

'How are you?' she asked, handing the old man his gold-framed glasses.

Philip tried to sit up in bed. 'Give me a hand, then,' he croaked impatiently as he hooked the arms of his glasses over his ears. 'Are you new?'

'No, Philip, I'm not new. I think you know me.' She reached across and switched the main overhead light on, flooding the room with brightness.

A sobbing, wordless exclamation poured from him. 'Emily!' he rasped. 'Oh my God, Emily.' Tears began slipping down his face. 'I am so, so sorry,' he said. For a full minute he just stared at her, shuddering with emotion.

'It's all right, Philip. I wanted to come to see you.'

'Emily, I am so sorry.'

'Are you?' Sam asked.

'Not a day has gone by when I haven't wished that I could go back and let you walk away...'

Sam's gasp of horror died in her throat.

'They'll never let me out now,' he said, his eyes turning left and right. 'I'll die in here.' He looked up. 'Please sit down, let me hold your hand. Oh, in all my dreams I never guessed you would come back.'

Sam sat primly, halfway down the bed, and mustered a smile.

'Emily, I thought, I really thought you were...'

'Thought I was what, Philip?'

'Gone. After... after...' He shook his head. 'Have you come to accept my atonement?' Tears were dripping off his nose.

'I have. I can forgive you.' The words almost choked her. Sam knew this was not a dispensation that a counterfeit Emily was entitled to offer.

'Emily, you are so beautiful.' He wiped his eyes with his pyjama sleeves. 'There was that song, our song. Do you remember it? It was on the radio. You sang it for me, when we were in the car.'

'Did I?'

Philip closed his eyes and crooned: 'The first time, ever I saw your face...'

'That's a very old song,' she said. 'Roberta Flack, wasn't it?'

'Emily...' He nodded and beckoned her closer, patting the covers. 'This is very, very important. Don't tell my family that you've been to see me. They wouldn't approve.'

She was very conscious of being out of breath. The jeans were unbearably tight. 'It's our secret, Philip. But some of it I've forgotten. Will you remind me exactly what happened?'

'At the picnic, Emily? Don't you remember? That wonderful summer weekend, after I stopped to give you a lift. "He maketh me lie down in green pastures".' He gave her a knowing smile. 'Psalm 23.'

'In all these years I have forgotten what happened.'

'Kiss me, Emily, tell me you forgive me.'

'Forgive you for what?' Sam leaned in close, offering her cheek, but the old man tried to move his head, his foetid breath and dark crusted lips puckering for her own. As she turned her head, the repulsive slick impact landed near her mouth, and then he softly whispered: 'I was so aroused. I couldn't help myself. I forced myself onto you, Emily, inside you. And then when you screamed out, I tried to strangle you.' His fingers were like a bird's claws around her neck, gripping tighter.

A sob escaped Sam, and she had to resist the urge to punch this repellent creature. She held his shoulders away, stopping his open mouth again trying to make contact with hers.

'I remember now,' he whispered, his eyes wide in shock as he told her. 'But I must have been wrong.'

Sam couldn't help it – she wrenched herself from the old man's grasp and fled sobbing from the chalet, his last words ringing in her ears.

'I buried you, Emily. I dug your grave.'

–

When Gillard heard the scream, he tore up the ramp to the chalet, just in time for Sam to fling open the door and throw herself into his arms, sobbing 'It's true, it's true.'

'Where's the recorder?'

'Shit, I left it inside.' While Barbara and Trish went inside to see their brother and try to convince him that he had experienced nothing more than a dream, Gillard led his wife back into the main building. They passed Fitz, the care assistant, coming in the other direction. He glanced at Sam's clothing, and then saw she was upset.

'Are you all right?'

'Just another inappropriate remark from Mr Antrobus,' Gillard said. 'He's getting worse.'

Fitz gave a helpless shrug and said, 'Time for another meeting with Mrs Dickinson, I suppose.'

–

The call from Craig Gillard broke Talantire's reverie. She had been highly sceptical when the Surrey police officer had first mentioned the muddled confession of his uncle to killing a young woman by the name of Emily. If dementia meant Philip Antrobus wasn't fit to give evidence over the possession of child pornography, then she was hardly going to drop everything to pursue his vague recollections of historic wrongdoing. Especially when there was no clear indication of who the victim was. 'Give me a surname and I'll look into it,' she had told him at the time.

However, Gillard's use of his wife in a reconstruction to elicit further memories from the man had been ingenious. The recording Gillard had played over the phone certainly made it sound like Philip Antrobus at least was convinced of his own guilt. Then he asked her a rather surprising question: 'Would it be possible to have a quick glimpse at those child abuse images that I passed across to you on the laptop?'

'I thought you'd already seen them.'

'I have. But there may be somebody on them that I can now identify.'

Talantire sighed. 'Craig, it's not even a live case for us. I'd need a good reason to unseal evidence before then.'

His exasperated sigh showed how disappointed he was.

'Look,' she said. 'I can't promise anything, but I will ask, okay?'

He thanked her and hung up.

Later in the day she mentioned the case to her superior, DCS Bob Parker, who had hit the roof. 'Oh come on, Jan. Keep focused. Until you get me a result on the hit-and-run neither you or your team are to get involved in anything else. And certainly not airy-fairy historic cases. Understood?'

–

Jeanette Dickinson had been the manager of The Beeches care home almost since it opened a decade earlier. As DI Talantire sat in Mrs Dickinson's office she took in the controlled hairstyle, the full make-up and the neat but conservative black trouser suit. The office was a model of organization, and Mrs Dickinson certainly looked fully in charge.

'I had rather more to do with Mrs Gibson than her sister,' she said. 'It was Trish who made the approach about getting Mr Antrobus into our facility. Barbara is a frequent visitor, but not every day, I would say. She's quite loud, as I'm sure you know, so we always know when she's about.'

Talantire scanned the initial statements that Willow had taken the day after the hit-and-run. 'So you say that she was here from 1.30 p.m. until the moment she reported the missing vehicle, just before 4 p.m. from your phone. Are you quite sure?'

'Well, let's say I saw her several times over that period. I can't attest that she was here every minute, though I believe one of the residents, George Butler, saw her during that time. She was playing Monopoly with her brother and sister.'

The next witness that Talantire checked with was Fitz, Marcus Fitzgerald. The dreadlocked care assistant seemed quite nervous about being interviewed again. He confirmed that he had seen both Trish and Barbara playing Monopoly with Philip, and it was he who had manoeuvred Philip's wheelchair to take him to bed in his room at around 3.40 p.m. 'I saw both sisters, but I wasn't there the whole time, so I can't swear to anyone's continuous presence,' he said.

On the whole, Talantire believed him. But it still meant that a continuous alibi hinged on the testimony of four people, three of them from the Antrobus family and therefore not impartial, including one who was unfit to give evidence. That left George Butler, the fourth man around the Monopoly table. The detective stepped outside the office and found Mrs Dickinson again. 'I'd like to speak to Mr Butler now, if that's possible.'

'Oh. Weren't you told? Mr Butler passed away last Thursday. It wasn't a total surprise. He had a very serious heart condition.'

'God, that's awful news,' Talantire said.

She must have looked shocked, because the care home manager gave her the kind of comforting smile that bereaved relatives could expect. She even stroked her arm. 'He's in a better place.'

'Not better for the purposes of reviewing a witness statement,' she replied. Talantire said her goodbyes and went down the steps into the car park, leaving a rather stunned-looking Mrs Dickinson staring after her. She made her way round the red-brick building to the parking spot where Barbara Antrobus claimed she had left her Ford Ranger on the day of the hit-and-run. It was in the shade of a large rhododendron hedge, overshadowed by a holly tree and out of sight not only of the office, but of every other window in the care home. Mrs Dickinson had corroborated the arrival time of the Ford, which coincided with her return from lunch. But there was no other evidence of when it had disappeared from the parking spot.

She cursed softly. The Antrobus alibi looked decidedly more fragile now, but death had robbed Talantire of the opportunity to punch a hole right through it. And Butler's original brief witness statement would presumably be regarded by a court as sufficient to buttress the Antrobus version of events.

Chapter 19

Gillard drove Sam and Trish over to Barbara's farm for the Sunday evening. They took with them the suitcase of women's clothing, the photo album and Philip's personal correspondence, which largely consisted of letters sent to him while he was in India in the 1970s. 'Let me have a look at this little lot,' Barbara said once they were sitting round her large kitchen table.

Trish, sitting on the sofa, continued to go through the clothing in the suitcase. She pulled out a plastic Etam bag packed with underwear, and a pair of fringed leather hot pants. 'Look what I found,' she said. Digging through the pockets she found a lipstick and a small textile purse. Opening it, she let out a gasp, stared at something then let it drop to the floor. 'Oh my God.'

Gillard went over to her and retrieved the purse. Inside it was a dark-green plastic bank card with a large stylized red letter 'A' on the front and a long credit card number below it. The name underneath was Miss E. Speakman, and the expiry date October 1974. There was no issue date. The back was signed with a looping signature.

'It's signed Emily,' Sam said.

'Emily Speakman, and a date. Now we're really getting somewhere,' he said. 'My father used to have an Access card like this. They were the first credit cards in the country, along with Barclaycard.'

Trish had her hands over her mouth in horror. 'All this time, Craig, I thought that Podge must be making it up, that there must be some other explanation. A fantasy, or something he'd seen on a film. But now this. It's proof, isn't it?'

'Well, it's evidence the woman existed at least,' Gillard said.

'Why did he hang on to it for all these years?' Sam asked. 'If he killed her, why not destroy all the evidence?'

'I think he felt guilty,' Barbara said. 'To throw away her possessions, all that was left of her, was to dishonour her memory. I could certainly see why he kept the clothing and the photograph.'

'But he had buried her in his mind,' Trish said. 'I never heard him mention her name until the last few months. He must've been so determined to block her out that it took the Alzheimer's to make him forget why he was doing it. From what he has said, he clearly adored her.'

'Or was simply mortified by guilt,' Barbara added. 'Who knows, it might explain why he went off to India, and on his return joined the Church. He never showed any religious leanings when he was young.'

'That's fascinating,' Sam said.

'I'll ring Talantire tomorrow morning,' Gillard said. 'She said she would take it seriously once we found a surname for Emily. But maybe I can save her some trouble by googling the name.' Gillard whipped out his iPhone.

Chapter 20

PC Nick Kite had parked the patrol car around the back of the old market while he grabbed forty winks. He hated being on nights. The eight-till-eighter was a killer, a mixture of extreme boredom and a smattering of the very worst town-centre policing. Barnstaple was no different from many other British seaside towns in the off season. An all-you-can-drink vomitorium. You could spot the participants a mile off. Even though it was a Sunday, there were always a few. He'd driven past them two hours ago, just before midnight. One crouching girl by the kerb, one standing behind holding her ponytail back with one hand, the rest of her mates standing around, eating from a Domino's box, smoking and laughing as she barked out liquefied pizza into the gutter.

Quieter now. He was supposed to be on duty with Willow, but they had a deal on Sundays and Mondays, the quieter nights. They split the shift. One would do the first half, one the second. He checked his watch. Almost time to drive over to Melrose Avenue, pick up the young PC, then Willow would drive him home so he could go to bed. He reset the seat-back to vertical, checked for the latest reports from the control room, then fired up the Vauxhall Astra and eased the estate car out, ready to turn right onto Alexandra Road.

A car on the major road shot by without any lights on, doing at least 40.

Some things you can't ignore. Kite called it in to control, then flicked on the blue lights and turned left to follow. It was a small blue or black Toyota Yaris, driven by someone wearing a woolly hat but no seatbelt. Kite's flashed headlights had no effect; neither did the siren. Luckily, there was little other traffic, because this driver was a maniac, weaving wildly within the carriageway, and crossing straight over two mini roundabouts. The control room called him back to say that the nearest patrol vehicle was an hour away in Exeter, and the chopper was unavailable because of maintenance problems. So it was down to him. Kite knew the safest thing was to stick close behind and provide all the light and sound possible to warn other traffic of the unlit vehicle's approach until he could find a way of safely overtaking and pulling it over.

Kite was relieved to see the vehicle take the Braunton road, which ran alongside the River Taw. The Toyota sped up to 70 as they ran along the edge of an industrial estate. The road was wide and straight, with few parked vehicles and little night-time traffic, offering opportunities for safe overtaking. Kite knew they were now in the last mile of street lamps. Once they hit the town boundary things could get very dangerous, so it was a last chance to pull him over. Kite put his foot down, pulling level with the Toyota for a sideways glance at the silhouetted driver. Not the boy racer he had expected, but an elderly man in gold-framed glasses, his mouth open, his face frozen in some kind of horror, looking neither left nor right.

The Astra easily out-accelerated the Toyota, got well in front, then slowed gradually, crimping the road space.

Kite's greatest fear was that this crazed old fossil might simply plough into the back of him, which is why he made his manoeuvre as gentle as possible. He glanced again into the mirror.

The Toyota was gone. Vanished.

A second later there was an explosive impact somewhere to his left. 'Jesus, no,' Kite groaned as he slowed to a halt and whipped the car round. The Toyota had buried itself right up to the windscreen in the reception area of Barnstaple Industrial Paints. Kite raced his car onto the forecourt, leaped out and sprinted towards the Toyota. The driver-side door was bent almost in half and there was no chance of opening it, but the glass had frosted and mostly fallen out. The inflated airbag obscured a view of the driver, who, without the benefit of the seatbelt, had been catapulted onto the dashboard. When Kite leaned in and edged the airbag aside, all urgency suddenly ended. From the twisted angle of the neck and spine, it was clear the man was dead.

Kite shone his torch at the man's face. He knew who it was.

—

The phone call to Barbara's landline came just before 5 a.m. on Monday, and awoke Gillard before anyone else. He slipped on his dressing gown and descended the stairs just as Barbara herself emerged from her room, her waist-length hair cascading over her nightshirt. Behind her Gillard could see young Peter the farmhand, his head propped up on one shoulder in her bed. He looked like a cat who'd got the cream.

Barbara took the call with a grim face. Gillard knew it was something very serious.

'That's not possible,' Gillard heard her say to the caller. 'You've got this wrong, surely.' She then listened, her frown deepening.

'That was the police,' she said after hanging up. 'They've just found Philip in a crashed car up the Braunton road. He's dead.'

'Not another hit-and-run?' Gillard asked.

'Not exactly. He was driving, supposedly.'

'What?'

'That's what the police say. But it must be wrong. An officer witnessed the accident.' She invited Gillard and Sam downstairs for a brandy. 'I'll ring Trish.'

An hour later they were all sitting around Barbara's kitchen table in a state of shock. 'How did he even get into the car?' Trish asked. 'How did a paraplegic drive it?'

I told you he could stand up, but you didn't believe me,' said Sam.

'If he could walk,' Barbara said, 'why did I nearly give myself a hernia taking him to and from the caravan to the inside toilet in the wheelbarrow, day and night for years. He's been having a laugh at my expense.'

'Well, the joke's on him now, isn't it?' Gillard said, arms folded.

'Poor man,' Sam said. 'I never liked him. But he was obviously very confused.'

'Him and me both,' said Barbara. 'What I want to know is, was it he who stole my car and knocked that bloke down?'

Gillard shook his head. 'Weren't you here with him at the time?'

'Yes and no,' Trish said, topping up her brandy. 'We had tucked him up in his room for his nap.'

'So he could have slipped out while you were in the lounge,' Sam said.

'You make him sound like a cat burglar,' Trish said. 'He was a confused, elderly paraplegic.'

'Well he did steal a car last night,' Sam said. 'He must have had the gumption to swipe the keys. He wasn't all that confused, was he?'

'This doesn't make sense,' Gillard said. 'I wonder whose car it was?'

'Here's to Philip,' Barbara said, raising her glass. 'He had a good innings, didn't he?'

'Barbara, he may be your brother, but he almost certainly murdered somebody,' Gillard reminded them. He shared a look of exasperation with Sam. 'And we are not going to get any more information from him about it now, are we?'

'That's true. Perhaps his crimes will die with him,' said Barbara. 'That's usually the way in our family.'

–

They were still there at mid-morning when Trish was called on her mobile by Mrs Dickinson. After expressing her condolences, the care home manager quickly moved the conversation on to the process of moving Philip's effects out of the home to make way for someone on the waiting list.

'For crying out loud, we've only known about his death for a few hours,' Trish responded. 'Give us a moment to grieve, please.' After a nudge from Gillard,

Trish asked her: 'The police said that Philip was driving. Did he steal a car from one of your staff?'

'It appears so. It belonged to Jessica, one of the overnight care staff. Fortunately, she is insured against theft. Philip must have stolen keys from her handbag, which would be in the staff room. He had been seen moving about that evening. I have to say I'm impressed that he managed to get himself out of his wheelchair and into the car. We could have saved a lot of staff back pain lifting him on and off the toilet.'

After having got all the limited information that Mrs Dickinson had about the incident, Trish hung up. 'I wonder where Philip thought he was going?'

'To visit Emily, presumably,' Barbara replied.

Gillard sighed. 'If the Barnstaple police had just followed him instead of trying to pull him over, he might have led them to where Emily's body is buried. Or maybe he would have just got lost.'

We'll never know, will we?' Sam said.

Chapter 21

News of the death of the Reverend Philip Antrobus made the local headlines on Monday morning, and was soon on national radio. For DI Jan Talantire, the news simplified her workload. There would be no question now of putting aside the investigation of the hit-and-run to look at either Antrobus's predilection for teenage girls nor the historic murder that he was said to have admitted to. It could all go on the back burner.

She wasn't surprised Craig Gillard rang her that day, but was impressed by how much progress he had made digging into the identity of the woman the retired priest had confessed to killing. 'For all that, Craig, I don't think anyone here is going to be looking at that case for a long time. Feel free to pursue it yourself. Of course, if you really do crack it, someone else will have to go over all your work again to check it before it can be officially put to bed.'

'I'm aware of that, Jan.'

'Me, I get to be tied-up all day with the reconstruction of the theft of Mrs Antrobus's Ford Ranger.'

'Well, you now have a new candidate for the culprit, seeing as he was able to drive.'

The reconstruction certainly generated plenty of interest. The *North Devon Gazette* played a helpful role, tweeting the position of the vehicle every few minutes as PC Clifford Willow replicated its journey of that fateful Wednesday afternoon. Several witnesses rang in to say that on the Saturday before the incident they had seen a black Ford Ranger spinning doughnuts and pulling handbrake turns in the car park of the Coach and Horses in the centre of Barnstaple. But none of them had seen it on the Wednesday.

In the end there was just one relevant witness. A lady phoned the helpline saying she had seen the Ford parked that afternoon in Bear Street, one street up the hill from the care home. When asked about the time, she said she wasn't sure, but it was already quite dark. However, her recollection of the colour of the vehicle seemed imprecise, except to say it was not a light colour, and she had no idea of its registration number.

–

Sam was fidgety during the long drive home from Devon. Craig was being silent and brooding again. The death of his uncle Philip had seemed to stir things up within him. Sam felt bad enough herself, having terrified the old man with an apparition of a young woman he once adored. Whether that played any part in his decision to steal a car in the middle of the night would never be known for sure. However horrible a man Philip had been, they had all played a part in misleading and scaring him in an effort to get to the truth. Whatever he had known but not revealed would now probably never see the light of day unless they could discover another way to find out.

'So what do you reckon the chances are of quickly tracing this Emily Speakman?' she asked as they were heading along the M5.

'Well, I've already done a quick Google search, and there are quite a few of them around these days. There are no murders associated with that name, at least none notorious enough to show up on the Internet, but I'll have to check the cold-case files when I can get on the Police National Computer tomorrow. I've got a bag of the underwear from the suitcase we found, and will get a DNA check done. That probably won't help much if this girl disappeared in the 1970s, but should eliminate some possibilities.'

Chapter 22

Back at work on the Tuesday, Gillard spent a slow day taking statements from half a dozen people at a Woking engineering company where the finance director's PA had been helping herself to the company's money. Or at least that was the allegation. There were at least two other people it could have been.

Although he was the senior investigating officer, most of the work so far had been done by DS Shireen Corey-Williams, a 45-year-old qualified accountant and financial specialist. It was her diligent work that had unravelled the incredibly complex property fraud in the Knight murder case back in 2016. She didn't miss much.

'So here's a conundrum for you,' Gillard said. He outlined the confession of his late uncle, and the discovery of the credit card.

'May I have a look at it?' she asked.

Gillard nodded, unlocked a drawer in his desk and pulled out a paper evidence bag. He showed her the Access card. 'Don't worry about touching it. I've already had it checked for dabs and there aren't any, apart from my aunt's when she found it.'

'It's before my time of course,' Shireen said with a smile. 'So you're assuming that this card belonged to the victim, and presumably wasn't used after her death?'

'Unless it was a robbery, in which case it might have been flagged up at the time. With an expiry date in 1974, it is extremely useful in narrowing down the timeframe we're talking about. But the trouble is that the Access credit card company no longer exists. I checked, and though it was jointly owned by several of the UK clearing banks, it seems to have been closed, although the brand name was bought by MasterCard.'

'You're going to have a problem with this, I suspect,' Shireen said. 'I did some work on a historic fraud case last year. As you know, there are thousands of dormant bank accounts in the country. You can trace accounts which are still open back through the various live transactional and bookkeeping computer systems which kept data on the money going in and out of them, and where, in theory at least, data is never lost. But this is quite different.' She turned the card over in her hand. 'Credit card issuers will eventually close accounts that are inactive or where the debit charge has not been repaid. They would write to the cardholder, of course, but eventually once the account has been closed all the paperwork would go into historic files. Then you are dealing with back-office systems which in the 1970s were kept on paper.'

'I found out where the old head office was, in Southend-on-Sea,' Gillard said. 'There were about half a dozen different offices there for the paperwork, but they've all gone now.'

She nodded. 'There was no particular requirement for banks to keep information about these. When money-laundering regulations came in back in 2007, banks were required to keep certain details on closed accounts for more than the usual six years, but much data had already been discarded. In fact, since the Data Protection Act of 1998, the regulatory pressure has been to shred rather than retain confidential customer data. So the short answer is, you're going to struggle to find anything.'

Gillard shrugged, and gave her a tight-lipped smile.

'Sorry,' she said. 'I wish I had better news. Still, as long as you have the name, there are always other avenues.'

'Yes, when I get a bit more time I shall pursue them.'

Gillard had an email from Trish to say there was an obituary of Philip in *The Times*. When he got hold of a copy, he saw it was a sizeable piece.

> The Reverend Philip Antrobus, who died this week, was a seeker after truth and social justice who reached an audience of millions with his 1980s documentary series Poverty. He was born in 1940 to a struggling Devon farming family. Philip Antrobus, by his own account, was a slow and recalcitrant child, unhappy at school and much preferring the company of comic books to the more educational variety. The oldest of four children, he was expected by his father to take over the farm, but it was a desire to escape from the grinding toil of rural life that fuelled him.
>
> He aspired to Oxford, but ended up reading business studies at York University in 1958. 'I was a great disappointment to my father, but then he was a great disappointment to me.' Antrobus, who in his own words 'qualified as always with E's', pursued a variety of jobs in his twenties, never sticking at one for long and exuding a kind of restless energy. He was briefly engaged in the late 1970s, but he described himself as 'always unlucky in love'. In the spirit of the times he went to India in search of spiritual enlightenment, and

ended up at the same ashram as George Harrison. As he admitted in an interview in 1987, neither transcendental meditation nor musical inspiration rubbed off on him, and he returned to Britain a year later.

He initially became a deacon, then later a full-time clergyman for the Church of England in an unforgivingly tough parish in Liverpool. It was while working there that he became a political campaigner, both against government policies which, as he saw it, 'fostered a hidden poverty and inequality' and against nuclear weapons. He was arrested numerous times on various marches. It was in 1982, during the Thatcher years, that he became a fixture for his 'camp-outs' on public benches near the House of Commons, from which he would be interviewed by student journalists, and later by broadsheet reporters, on the evils of homelessness in a divided nation. It was due to his beguiling demeanour and twinkling eyes, as he saw it, that Thames TV commissioned from him a 13-part series on homelessness.

In later years he became known for activism against what he called 'soulless box' housing developments, and pressing for the preservation of woodlands and meadows for children to play in. In 1989, he and a group of demonstrators chained themselves to earth movers in an ultimately unsuccessful attempt to prevent the building of the Broxbourne Park shopping centre in Gloucestershire. He built a national network of 'peace plazas' in various new housing and shopping developments. He is survived by his sisters Barbara and Patricia. A younger sister, Margaret, died in 1988.

He put down the paper and stroked his chin. So Philip had been engaged. His sisters had mentioned nothing about that, but whoever the woman was should be able to provide useful details of his life then. Assuming she wasn't actually the Emily in question. Nonetheless, it was a new lead worth following up; perhaps someone who came to the funeral would be able to shine some light on it. In the meantime, there was a haystack to search through for Emily Speakman.

–

Gillard began with a family tree website, discovering that between 1950 and 1965 there were 138 births of an Emily Speakman in the UK, including those with alternate spellings of either name. He decided for now to ignore an additional 78 cases where Emily was a middle name. Of the remainder, in 85 cases a marriage was also registered, while just 19 in total had a recorded death certificate. On the assumption that Philip Antrobus had murdered and secretly buried his 18-year-old Emily Speakman, she would therefore not have lived long enough to marry. If she was already married, the name on the Access Card would probably be different, certainly in the 1970s, when it was rare for women to retain a maiden name after marriage. There were 12 cases of Emilys acquiring the name Speakman in marriage between 1970 and 1973, but the youngest was 27 when she became a Speakman, not young enough to be the girl in the picture.

The detective began making notes based on the searches, building up Venn diagrams to underpin his logic. The largest circle he labelled births, and part in, part out, another large circle he labelled marriages; intersecting the two within the largest circle was a smaller circle labelled deaths. Five of the 19 dead Emilys departed this earth in childhood, or at least before 1970, which meant they could be discarded. But what of the rest? He knew there were no cold murder cases concerning an Emily Speakman, and thus the probability was that any murder victim he was looking for was unlikely to be registered as dead. He shaded out the dead circle, and the marriage circle which left 44 unmarried Emilys, once the nine unmarried known dead were removed.

Forty-four names. That was quite a lot to cross-check. He switched across to his saved search on the missing persons database. A couple dozen Emilys, but no Emily Speakman.

Gillard then rechecked his own assumptions: one, that the credit card belonged to the woman Antrobus murdered; two, that the date of her death was no more than three years before the expiry of her card, otherwise why would she be carrying it? Three, that her death has not in any way been recorded or attributed to another cause or person. Four, that the victim had been unmarried at the time of her death. Five, that Philip's recollection of Emily's age, and the photograph he had of her, were accurate.

These were not heroic assumptions, they were entirely reasonable and logical, but it only needed one of them to be wrong and his pool of birth certificates to check would be too narrow.

–

Gillard turned to the paperwork they had recovered from Philip Antrobus's house in Lynton. If he could narrow down where Philip was living and working at the time, it would narrow down where and when he had opportunities to kill. After two or three evenings, and a few phone calls slipped into quiet times during the working day, he was in a position to ring Trish with his findings.

'I've made huge progress on his addresses. Using his driving licence, I've unearthed his DVLA records which record several addresses in Coventry, Northampton and Kidderminster, though it may not be all of them. Your brother passed his driving test at 19, and soon after worked for RCP Engineering, based at their Birmingham office, from 1962 to September 1973. His National Insurance records are being sent to me, which should further home in on where he lived. My guess is that he was living in digs or renting for most of the 1970s, because if he'd owned a home there would have been some mortgage records, and I can't find any. I'd really hoped he wasn't sharing a home.'

'Why is that?'

'Trish, the most likely place to dispose of a body is in a garden, and ideally under a newly built garage, patio or shed. I mean he did say he'd buried her, didn't he? But if you're the lodger or in a shared house, that kind of thing is much harder to get away with.'

'I see what you mean. So what about the employer?'

'RCP has been taken over numerous times, and is now part of a multinational company called AXK Electrical Systems. You will not be surprised to know that they do not retain any records about the kind of work he did, or whether he had a company car. However, when I showed them his P60s that we found in the loft, and some linked expenses claims for fuel and accommodation on his employee number, they were able to suggest that it was very likely he would have been a salesman with a car. They're now looking to see if they have on their pension scheme any employees who might have worked with him.'

'I already thought about that,' Trish said. 'I asked several of his old colleagues to come to the funeral. A very nice man from Thames TV is coming, and some people from his days in the Church. I couldn't track down anyone who knew him before he went to India.'

Gillard continued. 'There was another firm, Johnson Hoists Ltd, that your brother worked at from September 1973 to the middle of 1976. Unfortunately, the P60s and other documentation that you provided haven't got us anywhere. The company went into liquidation in the recession of 1981.'

'Oh, that's a shame,' Trish said.

'However, by looking up the list of trade creditors and their addresses, we have some inkling of the firms that used to do business with Johnson Hoists. If Philip was a sales rep for them, then there's a good chance he visited many of the places I have here on a list. There are more than a dozen locations all across the country, from Leith in Scotland down to Torquay. We're trying to do the same with RCP's list of customers from that time.'

'I can see you really have been thinking about this,' said Trish.

'I have, but it still hasn't really got us very far. Trying to recreate the typical travel patterns of a 1970s salesman is not easy. You won't be surprised to hear that this case is not resourced to the level where we could explore most of these avenues.'

'It's just you, is it?'

'Yes.'

Chapter 23

DI Talantire had not met Dr M.R.V. Wellesley before. The Home Office forensic pathologist was travelling down from Bristol to look at Mr Nobody, whose faceless cadaver was currently in the mortuary at North Devon District Hospital, Barnstaple, and she was waiting in pathology reception to meet him. She idled away the time by attempting to do a Google image search of her visitor, but though she could find plenty of academic references and texts, she couldn't find a single picture. Dr Nobody meets Mr Nobody.

The door of the reception room burst open and a short, corpulent fellow with a blond ponytail, a Megadeth T-shirt and heavily tattooed arms strode in. He had a small rucksack on his back and a briefcase in hand. The DI noticed a lanyard dangling from his neck, but the receptionist apparently did not, and barked a strident: 'Excuse me, can I help you? This is not a public—'

'I'm Wellesley, forensic pathologist. Sorry I'm late.'

The receptionist, unconvinced, examined the proffered lanyard while Talantire introduced herself. They were then both ushered into the mortuary office, where Wellesley set up his ultra-thin Mac laptop next to Talantire's ancient and scratched police-issue Hewlett-Packard.

'Right,' Wellesley said, scanning at high speed the documents listed on his laptop. 'Our Mr Nobody. Age 60 to 65, identity unknown, found dead in a ditch a few miles south of Exmoor National Park.' He then listed the various known facts and dates of the case. 'Toxicology, blood analysis, DNA both standard and mitochondrial, facial reconstruction imaging. I've read all these reports – is there anything else we have not covered that you would like me to know?' He turned an intense gaze on the detective.

'Did you commission a report on the dental implant? I was quite excited by that.'

Wellesley shook his head. 'Don't be. I've got the report, and it's pretty technical, and in the end not very helpful. The type of screw was easy to identify. It's an endosteal, of a design used most commonly in Eastern Europe up until 2012, when it was superseded by a new design. The calcification of the thread indicates the prosthesis has been in place for a number of years.'

'So could our hit-and-run victim be Eastern European?' Talantire asked.

Wellesley smiled indulgently. 'Well, he could be, but this is the point I was coming to. The trouble with implant surgery is that it's a health tourism issue. Lots of Western Europeans visit Hungary or Romania, for example, to get cheaper implants than those available locally. We'd actually be on firmer ground if we were looking at a filling, because patients are much less likely to travel for them. So all in all it's not much help, I'm afraid.'

He pursed his lips, before returning to his laptop. 'I'm not particularly impressed by Dundee's facial reconstruction either,' he said, calling up the three-dimensional image created by the university. 'I suppose it's a human face, but it could be anybody.'

He scratched his head and then moved on to the next document. 'However, I'm quite intrigued by the chemical analysis. Cadmium, zinc and particularly lead may indicate he had worked for an extended period in close contact with petroleum-based products. This could in theory be anything from being a garage mechanics right through to working in an oil refinery, though given the preponderance of lead, I would lean towards the cruder end of the petrochemical production spectrum.'

'Why is that?'

'Refining is intended to remove the more persistent and dangerous of the heavy metals. I would imagine that we can get a precise signature for that environmental exposure. We will need specialist help and I will look into it.'

'We also found cat hairs on his clothing. I don't know if that will be of any help,' Talantire said.

'It is possible to identify types of cat hair. I recall that Leicester University has a mitochondrial DNA database, which can isolate feline lineage with a good percentage chance of success. However, it won't get us anywhere until we are in a position to seek corroboration. For example, if we suspect he came from a particular address, matching animal hairs might underpin that evidence.' Wellesley undid his rucksack and pulled out a white coat. 'I see an initial post-mortem has already taken place at the hospital. But I'd still like to have a little look myself.' As he was doing up the buttons, he stopped. 'I forgot to mention… One more promising avenue, if we still haven't made any progress, is stable isotope analysis.'

'What's that?'

'It's a very fundamental analysis of the chemistry of the body, pioneered at Robert Gordon University in Scotland. Characteristics of the water that we drink and the food we consume reflects the geology they are from, and gets lodged in our tissues and bones. By analysing them at an atomic level, it's possible to say where someone lived. Minerals found in the hair may tell you where they lived recently, while those of the nails, and especially the bones, give a more long-term view.'

'That sounds great.'

Wellesley smiled. 'It's not quick and it's not cheap. How is your budget?'

'Under pressure, as always, but I will ask my boss.'

—

An hour later Talantire and Wellesley were sitting in a cafe overlooking the River Taw. Wellesley was tucking into a thick sausage sandwich smothered with mustard, while the detective settled for a strong coffee. The sight of Mr Nobody's heavily damaged body had spoiled her appetite, but obviously not that of the forensic pathologist.

'Most of my work is of course spent determining the circumstances of a suspicious death,' Wellesley said while chewing. 'This death of course was not initially suspicious in its cause, so the coroner was correct in allowing a local post-mortem. But the investigation into exactly who the victim might be is absolutely fascinating. So do keep me copied in on every detail.'

'I will,' Talantire replied. 'I'm looking at international missing persons, just in case there's an oil worker due back on a rig who hasn't turned up. Something like that.'

Wellesley chewed ruminatively, his eyes resting on the ceiling. 'Here's something else. We've got residues of sleeping medication in his bloodstream, right?'

Talantire nodded. 'Zolpidem, I think it was called.'

'Yes, now this particular imidazopyridine compound is quickly metabolized. So the fact that we were able to detect it means he either took a smallish dose quite soon before his untimely death, or a larger dose some hours before. One of the drugs in this class, Ambien, is entirely eliminated from the body within three hours.'

'So you mean he could have been asleep just a few hours before he was knocked down?'

'Yes. Now, given that he was killed at around about 3.40 p.m., that would mean he was taking the medication, let's say, in the middle of the morning. I think you'll agree that's an odd time to take a sleeping tablet.' The pathologist wiped his mouth with a napkin.

'Maybe somebody slipped him a Mickey Finn,' Talantire said.

Wellesley chuckled. 'Trust a detective to create a crime. No, I was thinking more along the lines of someone who is normally asleep during the day. A night worker, for example.'

'What about someone with jet lag?'

Wellesley pursed his lips. 'Possibly. Though normally a traveller would try to fit in with the time zone they are arriving in. Which would indicate taking your sleep medication at night, when you would otherwise find it difficult to sleep.'

The pathologist soon bade his goodbye, saying he had to be back in Bristol by mid-afternoon.

Chapter 24

It was almost three weeks after their first visit when Craig and Sam returned to Devon for Philip's funeral. Encouraged by Gillard, Trish had done a herculean job of trying to track down Philip's friends and acquaintances from his early years. She had made contact with his former producer at Thames TV, and had been contacted separately by someone who had been homeless whom Philip had been able to help. Both of them had agreed to make the long trip down to Devon, and Gillard was looking forward to talking to them.

They stayed at Trish's house on the Friday night, helping her lay on an enormous spread for afterwards. They all went together to the funeral at St James's Church. Gillard had somehow expected there to be hundreds of people present because of Philip's fame from the TV series. But there were only a dozen attendees, scattered over the first three rows of pews. The vicar who conducted the service also gave the eulogy. 'Philip was one who quietly gave himself to God, to helping the poor and the homeless. For him the ministry was a calling. The TV programme for which he was best known he used not to build fame or status, but to spread the word. Faith, hope and charity. And the greatest of these is charity.'

Trish also said a few words, in which she talked of her brother's effect on people. 'He was not motivated by greed, but by kindness.'

Gillard stopped listening to this litany of untruth, but instead observed the stiffening shoulders of Barbara Antrobus who had to listen to her own sister describe Philip as being untouched by human vice. Yet, for all of his many failings, the lust and the lies, his guilt had clearly forged within him a desire to make amends, something that drove his charitable energy for decades. Despite his polarising experience as a police officer, Gillard knew that very few people are all good or all bad. That combination is what makes us human.

After the service, Gillard sought out his uncle's old colleagues. The first he talked to was a garrulous priest called the Reverend James Hart, who met Philip when they both worked in Toxteth in Liverpool in the early 1980s. 'He was a truly energetic man, very understanding and caring, and took me completely under his wing.' When Gillard asked about girlfriends, and specifically Emily Speakman, he was perplexed. 'I don't recall meeting anyone he was romantically involved with,' Hart said. 'He seemed to me so full of the spirit of the Lord that I couldn't imagine there was room for anything else.' Gillard showed him the picture of Emily Speakman, but he didn't know her.

Gillard also talked with an archdeacon from London, a slightly built man in his late 70s with a soft and faltering voice. He couldn't shed any light on Philip's friendship or acquaintances, except in one very significant way. 'I do remember this. I was quite attracted to him in those days, and had asked him if he wanted to stay at my place overnight. He replied that he was happy to do so. "But you should be aware that, even though my admiration is generally expressed from afar, I like girls, not boys." That was all that was said on the subject. I was disappointed, of course, but it did save a potential embarrassment.'

'But he never mentioned an Emily Speakman?' He produced the photograph. 'We think this is her.'

The archdeacon shook his head. 'I don't recall the name or the face.'

The next old friend that Gillard talked to was Graham Walsh, a former cameraman for Thames TV who had worked with Philip for three years on *Poverty*. 'He was wonderful to work with,' Walsh told Gillard. 'We were filming at night, in parks, open spaces and in the cardboard city around Waterloo Station, and we had to do take after take. Often it was because of noise, or the unwanted attention of some of the other homeless people. And quite often it was very cold. Philip wore these trademark fingerless gloves, so he really did look the part.'

'Were there any girlfriends, or women around him during that time?'

'Not during filming, no. I never really knew anything about his private life after his divorce.'

'His divorce? I didn't think he was ever married.'

'Well, I know that he introduced this delightful Anglo-Indian woman to me as his wife. I met her a couple of times, and then later when I asked about her, he said they were divorced.'

'Do you remember her name?'

'Gosh. Was it Lakshmi? I got the impression that he met her when he was in India. She spoke in this wonderful received-English voice that made her sound like an aristocrat. To be honest, she was gorgeous.'

'Could this be her?' Gillard showed him the photograph.

'Well, she is a super-looking girl too, but no, that's not Lakshmi. I mean Lakshmi did look Indian, even though she didn't sound it.'

'We don't have all his correspondence, but there is nothing mentioning her in his paperwork.'

'Well I really can't help you. He was a very private individual. But I tell you what, I'll ask around among his old colleagues. There's quite a few of us who remember him, mostly retired now, and we meet up for a drink from time to time. You'll have to come and join us.'

It was almost seven and the reception was down to its last few lingering individuals when there came a knock at the door. Gillard answered it and a tall, bedraggled individual with cropped dark hair and a lived-in face stood there. 'This is the right address for the Antrobus funeral?'

Gillard told him that it was, and the man nodded. 'I wasn't invited but I heard about it,' he said, peering over his shoulder into the room.

'What's your name?' Gillard asked.

The man paused for a moment, as if he had not been asked that question for a long time. 'I'm Charlie Wykefield. Philip saved my life.'

Gillard suspended his disbelief for a moment. 'I think you'd better come in.' He took the man's raincoat which had been soaked by an unforecast shower. Wykefield said that he had come down from Preston by coach, then walked from Barnstaple bus station.

Wykefield didn't seem to know any of the others, and Trish had no idea who he was. The man said that he had lived for two years in the cardboard city by Waterloo Station, and had been interviewed on one of the episodes of *Poverty*. 'I was at a low ebb,' he said. 'Philip didn't come across like your usual pious churchman, full of clever words meaning nothing. He let me stay at his digs for a couple of weeks until I sorted myself out. He helped me deal with my debts and introduced me to someone who could help with this.' He tapped the side of his head. 'I was crazy for a long time.'

'That's lovely to hear,' said Trish. 'There's still plenty of food if you're hungry. We had a man here earlier who was a cameraman on the TV series, but he went an hour ago.'

'What year was it you went to stay with Philip?' Gillard asked.

'Well, it would have been the late 1980s,' Wykefield said. 'Couldn't tell you exactly.'

Chapter 25

On his return to Surrey, Gillard wasted no time in registering Emily Speakman on the police Missing Persons Unit website. Beyond the photograph, he had little information to offer. Hair colour: dark; eye colour: unknown; ethnicity: white British. The year of her disappearance he bracketed as 1972–74, with a date of birth guesstimate of 1950–58. Sam, having tried on the clothes, was able to estimate the woman's height as five foot five, and her weight around eight stone. Pretty much every part of the description was drawn from the photograph, so if nobody recognized it, that was the beginning and end of it. Gillard had also sent the picture and description to every constabulary in the country, but doubted that anyone in Britain's busiest and most populous police areas would even look at it, and with good reason. This wasn't a high-priority case, it didn't have the backing of police officialdom, and the person in question probably died in the mid-1970s. If the police couldn't raise the manpower to investigate a burglary that happened yesterday, and often they couldn't, they certainly wouldn't have the time to look into a non-case from almost 50 years ago.

Gillard had known right from the start that it would be down to him. Still, he had been in that position before, and it wouldn't put him off. Once again he googled Emily

Speakman, and got 300,000 results. He cut this to just over 10,000 results when he restricted the search to show only those pages registering both words together. Many of them were for just a few prominent people including a talented Welsh teenage artist and an American business-woman. He switched to the image search, which stretched to a dozen pages and showed no one with any resemblance to the photograph he had.

There were other ways to seek information. Gillard used a Russian email service to set up an account for Emily Speakman, as it asked no ID or verification questions. With the email he then created a Facebook profile for her, fixing her picture at the top and including a request for information. He then shared the post worldwide. There was really no more he could do until someone, some-where, searched for her name or recognized the picture.

It was only half an hour before he got the first of several dozen friend requests, mostly coming from dubious-sounding individuals who had few online friends of their own. A couple of them showed pictures of attractive, and in some cases, partially clad women. Gillard recognized the hallmarks of fraudsters, phishing for confidential infor-mation like date of birth, address and mother's maiden name.

Having heard that Philip Antrobus had been married, Gillard searched the General Register Office for a marriage certificate in his name, but came up short. He was no more successful in researching the Central Family Court for evidence of a decree absolute to nail down the date of a divorce. Graham Walsh, the Thames TV cameraman he had met at the funeral, must have been mistaken. Gillard emailed him, and in response the man said he had contacted other colleagues who remembered Philip, but apart from the name Lakshmi, and recollections of her considerable attractiveness, they had no clue about his wife, who only seemed to be on the scene for a year or two. 'One of my colleagues thinks that they met when they were both in India.'

Suddenly that made sense. Gillard guessed that Antrobus may have gotten married in India. He looked online, and soon realized that there wasn't a unified online source of marriage information for that country. This particular line of enquiry seemed to be rapidly running into a dead end. Instead, at the suggestion of an Indian colleague, he placed an advertisement seeking information about the Rev Philip Antrobus in the classified section of the *Times of India*.

For a week there was no progress whatsoever in enlarging his knowledge of the life of his uncle. Then he got an email from a Superintendent Donald Hunter in Special Branch, subject line Emily Speakman, which tersely asked him to ring his office as soon as possible.

Intrigued, Gillard rang the number and was put straight through to Hunter. 'DCI Gillard, can I ask why you registered a missing person in this name?'

Gillard outlined his late uncle's confession.

'Local police not interested?'

'They seem to have their hands full,' Gillard replied.

Hunter laughed. 'And how are you getting on pursuing this on a freelance basis?'

'Not very well, if the truth be told. I've got an old credit card in the woman's name, but it hasn't got me very far.' In the slight pause that followed, Gillard decided to take the offensive. 'Perhaps I can ask how this came to your attention?'

'I don't think you need to know that. Good luck with your enquiries.' He hung up.

Gillard stared at the receiver.

–

The mysterious phone conversation had piqued Gillard's interest. Why on earth was the name Emily Speakman of interest to Special Branch? That is the arm of the police which works most closely with the security services like MI5 and is involved in protecting VIPs. Gillard had a contact who was a constable in Special Branch in London, doing diplomatic protection work. He messaged him and asked for a discreet check into why enquiries about Emily Speakman might be ringing alarm bells. They exchanged two or three phone calls over the next couple of days, and then suddenly his contact ceased to return his calls.

That evening Gillard confided in Sam that he seemed to have run into some kind of official obstruction. 'I'm not getting anywhere with this,' he said. 'I really don't know what to try next.'

'Maybe there's a spy called Emily Speakman,' she said.

The truth, which took another two days to emerge, was every bit as astounding.

–

The call came to Gillard's personal mobile at just before 10 on a Sunday evening. 'Hunter speaking. We have some news for you. I just need to confirm some security details.' Gillard was then required to confirm his police tag number and his date of induction into the service. Having done so, Gillard was put through to another man who had a silky-smooth upper-crust accent. 'I work in the office of the chancellor of the exchequer, and your Speakman enquiry has come to her attention.'

'Does Emily Speakman owe *that* much tax?' Gillard asked.

'Ah yes. Very good, very good indeed,' he said. 'I understand that you found a credit card in the name of Emily Speakman, is that correct?'

'Yes.' Suddenly the penny dropped. 'It's her, isn't it?'

'Yes, it's me, Detective Chief Inspector, and I believe the card may be mine.' The new, female voice on the line was the same one he had heard delivering the budget speech just a few weeks earlier. The Right Honourable Emily Cavendish MP, Chancellor of the Exchequer. 'Speakman was my maiden name.'

'That makes sense, ma'am,' Gillard said. 'I think I saw your profile in a newspaper article when I was researching the name. The piece must have mentioned your maiden name, but I discarded it for obvious reasons.'

'Obvious?'

'Well, you're still alive for one thing.'

'Of course,' she chuckled. 'Your energetic and persistent enquiries and the picture were brought to my attention by one of my security people. Let me get this straight: do I understand correctly that someone has claimed to have murdered me?'

'Well, not necessarily you, ma'am. My uncle, Philip Antrobus, confessed to having killed someone called Emily, and just before he died identified her in the photograph. Of course, he had dementia and we can't rely on his judgement. If I may be so bold, I don't see much of a resemblance.'

'No. I'm afraid I didn't look quite that good even in those days.'

'Have you ever seen this person?'

'I don't think so, but I do recall losing an Access credit card when I was a student back in the '70s. Someone stole my handbag in a pub. Was your uncle a thief?'

'Not that I'm aware of, ma'am. He was quite a prominent churchman.'

There was a pause. 'Good God, not *the* Reverend Philip Antrobus? Who died just recently? I saw his TV programme. It was quite influential on housing policy in the 1990s. I think I may even have met him, years ago.'

'But by that time you were married, I presume?'

'Absolutely, yes. I married in 1979.' Someone spoke to her in the background. 'Look, I'm sorry to put you back to square one, but I have to go now. I'm catching a flight to a G7 summit in Vienna, and my car is waiting. Goodbye.'

'I'm not quite back at square one,' Gillard said. 'Your input could still help solve this case—'

The voice back on the line was the smooth tone of the official, who apologized for the hurried departure of his boss. 'I'll ping you my email address. Contact me if you have any further enquiries, and I'll make sure any message is passed on.' The line went dead.

–

'What on earth was that about?' Sam asked.

'Well, the riddle of who Emily Speakman is has been solved. As Emily Cavendish MP, she recently became the first female chancellor of the exchequer.'

Sam laughed. 'I've heard her called boring, but not dead boring.'

'The thing is, even though she's not the Emily we're looking for, we now have a definite incident to pin this whole crazy story against. The theft of her handbag and bank card would probably have been reported, and with luck we can get a place and date.'

Sam looked puzzled. 'So what you're saying is that somebody called Emily came into possession of Emily Speakman's credit card, and then got murdered? Two Emilys seems a bit of a coincidence.'

Gillard shook his head. 'No, the likeliest prospect is that the woman in the photograph either stole the handbag or somehow got hold of the card, and used it as an alias, at least with Philip.'

'Well, with friends like him who needs Emilys?'

Gillard groaned and dropped his head into his hands.

Chapter 26

The list of questions Gillard sent to Emily Cavendish's office was acknowledged but remained unanswered for a week. Finally, he was invited to meet the chancellor on Tuesday at a nondescript government office near Reading after she had been to a photo opportunity 'with hard hat and trowel for HS2' as the smooth-voiced official described it. 'You'll have half an hour,' he told Gillard.

In the event, the detective was left kicking his heels in a conference room for an hour and a half, until the Right Honourable Emily Cavendish MP marched in at the head of a swarm of lanyarded Treasury and PR officials. 'Christ, I need a coffee,' she announced to no one in particular. 'Why do they always stand me in a wind tunnel of cement dust? I suppose I've reached the age when I should apply foundation, but I don't need sandblasting.' She smiled at Gillard. She was dressed in a grey suit and black tights, with matching pearl necklace and earrings. Gillard took in her pale complexion and angular figure, which confirmed that she could never have been the woman in the photo- graph.

Once coffee and cake had been served, and all minions evicted bar Toby, the smooth-talking assistant, the chancellor took control of the conversation. 'DCI Gillard, after our conversation the other week, I looked through my diaries and found that I had reported the theft of my handbag to the police on 4 July 1973. Does that accord with your records?'

'I'll be able to check now,' Gillard replied. 'Crime reports of that era were not computerized, ma'am, so there was no way for me to search nationally for the record with your name. Only if we'd had a conviction might it have been possible, by searching on the culprit's name. What I really need to know is where you were when this crime took place.'

'I believe I was in a pub in Leeds city centre. I don't recall the name.'

'Okay, that's a good start – I now know where to look for the records. I take it you weren't ever told of an arrest being made or the recovery of any of your property?'

'I don't think so.'

'I know it's an awfully long time ago, but did you have any suspicions of who may have taken your bag?'

She shook her head. 'I remember the pub being very crowded. It was a weekend lunchtime, so it could have been anybody.'

'What was in the bag?'

'My purse and flat keys. I think they were the only important things.'

'The only thing I found was your Access card. But there are some other clues I would like to run past you.' From an envelope he produced a series of enlarged photographs of the clothing found in the vanity case. 'Did you see a young woman in the pub wearing clothes that matched these?'

The chancellor laughed, and turned to her aide as she looked at the photograph of the pink boots. 'I think I would have remembered these,' she said.

He smiled superciliously. 'Absolutely,' he said.

She flicked through the other pictures, wearing a slightly bemused expression.

After a few minutes she looked up. 'Condolences on the death of your uncle, by the way.'

'We weren't close,' Gillard replied. 'And I'm increasingly convinced he did commit murder, even if he didn't know the name of the person he killed. I think we can find out who she was.'

'Good. Please notify Toby here when you've cracked it.' With that she swept out.

Chapter 27

PC Nick Kite sat in his favourite chair by the fire, and waited while his wife brought him a supper of beans on toast with bacon, which he habitually ate from a tray while watching the football on TV. 'They were poking about in the loft the other day,' Ursula said as she set the tray across his lap.

'There's nothing incriminating up there,' he said, shaking brown sauce liberally across the plate.

'Yes, but what happens about the house now he's dead?'

'I don't see any reason why we can't carry on living here,' Kite said, spearing a piece of streaky.

'But the sisters will inherit, and they're bound to want to sell.'

The PC chewed ruminatively 'I don't think they would dare, considering what we know.'

'That's blackmail, Nick,' she said, her arms folded.

He looked up at her, his porcine face impassive. 'I'm not blackmailing them, am I? I'm just enjoying a very cheap rent that was agreed a long time ago. I haven't noticed you complaining about it either,' he said as he lifted a slice of beans-laden toast to his mouth.

'It'll all come out in the end,' Ursula said. 'You can't keep murder hidden.'

The constable shrugged and pointed the remote at the giant wall-mounted TV. Ursula, seeing the conversation had crashed into the inviolable temple of football, stalked out.

–

The next day Nick Kite powered his Mitsubishi Warrior down the rutted, twisting track to his father's small-holding. Since the divorce, and his subsequent retirement from the police, Vince Kite had spent most of his time working the vegetable patches, tinkering with his antique John Deere and doting on the dogs. That was a good 30 years he'd been on his own, only returning to the house to sleep. Vince had always been on the uniform side, reaching the rank of sergeant by 1982, but never bothering to take any subsequent exams for promotion. That might have taken him out of the district, and Vince Kite was always happy to be a big fish in a small pond.

Nick didn't like to spend much time at the cottage. His father never had the heating on, had done barely any housework and had left everything pretty much as it was before his wife departed. He could swear there was washing-up still on the draining board from 1988.

He brought the 4 × 4 to a halt by a metal gate and clambered out. He unlocked a hefty padlock and swung the squealing gate open. Immediately, a chorus of barking began from cages within the smallholding. 'Just wait a minute, boys,' he said. Kite dragged out a heavy polythene sack from the bed of the truck, shouldered it and made his way into the compound, closing the gate behind him. To his left, half a dozen dogs, big boisterous crossbred animals, threw themselves at the wire mesh of their cage, having scented the contents of the bag.

'Don't worry, you'll get your turn,' he said as he approached a larger enclosure with thicker mesh and a blue polythene roof. He put down the sack as he crouched to unlock the padlock and donned thick leather gauntlets, making care to pull them well up his forearms. Only then did he ease the cage door open. He peered into the shadows but saw nothing, and heard no sound. Nervous, Kite recalled how 18 months ago he'd almost lost a hand to the animal within. His father was the only one who could safely approach it, the only human it trusted. It had originally been bred as a deerhound, to chase and bring down young red deer which live on Exmoor, but its temperament made it unsuitable, and it preferred the easier prey of sheep.

The policeman reached in for the rusted metal bowl which it fed from and, unsealing the sack, poured in half of the two gallons of sheep viscera that it contained. Ironic, really, that Hollow Coombe farm ended up providing this offal cheaply only because the animal to whom it would be fed had killed several ewes. It was Vince's pound of flesh, extracted a couple of times a year, from the woman who had spurned him.

Food regulations prevented any meat from such a kill entering the human food chain. His eyes flicked up and he saw the creature in the shadows. A German shepherd cross, it was higher in the hip and broader in the shoulder than a pure-bred Alsatian. Its coat was thick and very dark: charcoal grey on the top with brindled, sandy streaks on the flanks. Its eyes were not the typical dark brown of the pedigree, but a much lighter shade, almost amber, as if a light burned within. But the most chilling aspect of the animal was its intelligence. Instead of rushing at the food, like a typical dog, it assessed the situation more like a cat, sniffing the air and the ground, eyeing its jailer. Kite retreated out of the cage and closed the door, leaving the animal to gorge itself at its leisure.

Chapter 28

The Red Lion in Victoria was typical of the pubs at London rail termini: enormous, frenetic, noisy, litter strewn, with sticky carpets and lots of people on the move. There were no free seats, but Gillard found space to lean on a pillar underneath a big screen showing sport. He scanned the many commuters for his quarry, a true crime author called Timothy Smeeth who had agreed to meet him here.

It had been three weeks now with no leads, Christmas was just two weeks away and this was his only hope for a breakthrough. Everything else had come to nothing. He had used Google Street View to investigate the addresses that Philip had lived in the 1970s. The one in Coventry had been demolished to make way for a dual carriageway; the Northampton one, which seemed not to have ever had a garden, was now a vet's practice; and only the Kidderminster address was really recognizable as a much-enlarged private house. He had only lived there briefly at the start of his days as a salesman. Gillard doubted it was, yet, worth using up a day's leave on a trip to any of these locations.

On the face of it, he had done better looking for Emily. There were over 300 messages or approaches for friend-ship on his newly created Emily Speakman Facebook page

– overwhelmingly trolls, spammers, perverts and fraudsters. West Yorkshire CID couldn't find the real Emily Speakman's theft report from 1973. The civilian staffer he spoke to admitted that the records for most of that year had been mislaid. Gillard wasn't surprised.

It was Smeeth's email which promised to change everything. The message was pretty simple: I know who the girl is.

Gillard had found several images of the author on Google and was scanning the crowd for a thickset bespectacled fellow with a moustache. But the scruffy raincoated individual who sidled up to him had neither spectacles nor a moustache. 'Tim Smeeth,' he said, offering a hand.

'You look a bit different.'

'Ah yes. All the pictures you'll find of me relate to my book about Beverley Allitt the murderous nurse, published in 1993. Since then I've shaved off the tash and discovered the wonders of disposable contact lenses.'

Gillard exchanged a clammy handshake with him and they went off in a vain search for a quiet and secluded table. The one they eventually found was tiny and right next to the kitchen door, but if they could only just hear each other over the sound of pans, cutlery and shouted orders, at least they knew they would not be overheard.

'You're keeping me in suspense,' Gillard said, once they had sat down.

'Well, that's always part of my job,' Smeeth said with a slight smile. He had a crumpled face, wild eyebrows and a mass of unruly hair. 'I was looking through the missing person files for my new book on Harold Shipman. I think there are more victims. Anyway, I stumbled across the Speakman photograph you posted, and recognized it.' He looked triumphantly at Gillard and then announced: 'The woman in your picture is Chrissie Frost, aged 17. She was murdered by Christopher Colin Harrow in 1973.'

'Harrow? The M1 murderer?' Gillard asked.

'The very same. Harrow was one of the most interesting serial killers in Britain but hardly anyone has heard of him. Have you read my book? No, of course you haven't. It's out of print now anyway.' He snorted a harsh little laugh, fabricated from years of disappointment and oiled by injustice. 'He killed at least four young women between 1967 and 1974. There are a couple more missing, but thought to have been killed by him. Poor Chrissie is one of them.' He passed across a creased black-and-white photograph, one of those stark and unflattering images used in police murder investigations of the 1970s, in which the victim somehow looks aware of her own imminent death. There was no doubt she was the Emily that Philip had identified from the photo found in the suitcase.

'Tell me about her,' Gillard asked.

Smeeth had a prepared tale. 'Chrissie Frost was the eldest of two, brought up in a troubled household in Bradford. Shy, sly and desperate for affection, she was taken into care, first with a foster family then in children's homes. She became something of a petty criminal, then absconded aged 17, never to be seen again. Her body was never found.'

'When exactly did she disappear?'

'Bear with me.' Smeeth consulted a hardback notebook, thick with cuttings. 'July second, 1973.'

'If that's correct, that ties in with the theft of a handbag in a Leeds pub two days later. That bag belonged to a woman called Emily Speakman. It's possible that Chrissie

Frost adopted Ms Speakman's name because it matched the credit card she had stolen.'

'Was the card used?'

'I'm not sure. It was certainly reported stolen, but neither the issuing bank's records nor the police incident report survive. It was in the days of paper records. No doubt if the theft had been linked with the disappearance of Chrissie Frost there would still be copies of all the relevant paperwork.'

'This is an interesting line of enquiry,' Smeeth said, stroking his chin. 'Because the Chrissie Frost case *is* still open.'

'What about Harrow. Is he still inside?'

'He died three years ago. I was the last person to interview him.'

'Plans for a second book?'

Smeeth emitted a huge, exasperated sigh. 'Well, I was certainly thinking about it. The trouble is, Harrow is still not really well enough known. Unfortunately, he was overshadowed by a contemporary, active in the same locale.' When Gillard didn't fill in the blanks, Smeeth blew another sigh. 'Peter Sutcliffe, the Yorkshire Ripper? There are plenty of books about *him*. My publisher doesn't think there is a market for another book about Harrow unless there is some new twist in the case.'

Gillard nodded. 'I see. And you are hoping I might provide the twist?'

'Well, we shall see, won't we?' Smeeth gave him a peculiar lopsided smile. 'It's a thin living being a true crime author. If I help you, I hope you can help me. Can I buy you another beer?'

Smeeth was as good as his word and virtually emptied his contacts book into Gillard's own notebook. The senior investigating officer for the M1 murders had died long ago, but one of the constables who had sat in on the interviews, Ivan McDougall, had just retired. Smeeth had already interviewed him. Chrissie Frost's mother was also alive, but according to Smeeth not much help. 'You'll be wasting your time with her, I'm afraid. She's in her 80s, and has no clear recollections. As far as we can establish, she hadn't seen her daughter for two years before her presumed death.'

Witness statements, however, were still available. Smeeth seemed to have photocopies of all of them and arranged for a huge package to be sent to Gillard's home.

–

It was a long Saturday trip under murky skies to the Leeds suburb of Kirkstall, but Gillard was happy to do it in his own time if it shed some light on the death of Chrissie Frost. Ivan McDougall lived in a suburban row of 1930s semi-detached mock Tudor homes, his own being marked out by a garish collection of flashing Christmas lights in the garden and an inflatable Santa just inside the bay window. Welcoming Gillard into his home, the retired detective, a gaunt and greying figure in cardigan and corduroy, was almost invisible against the twinkling baubles of his Christmas tree which dominated the lounge. He made them both a cup of tea.

'This is a good excuse to get out of accompanying Mary on her Christmas shopping expedition today,'

McDougall said, rubbing his hands together with satisfaction.

Gillard had with him his copy of Smeeth's book, *Harrow: the M1 Killer* and had gleaned as much as he could about the man who had killed as many as six young women in the 1970s. Harrow had been a regional sales representative for heating products, and travelled extensively on Britain's then quite new motorway network. It was the distinctiveness of his maroon 1971 Daimler Sovereign that finally got him convicted. Twenty-one-year-old Jill Farley, the second of his victims, was seen getting into this vehicle at the Toddington services on 9 April 1972. Her body was found in woodland in Hertfordshire two days later. She had been raped and strangled. Though the witness hadn't made a note of the number plate, there were few enough of these vehicles for the police to trace them all, though it took the best part of four years to find the conclusive evidence: a footprint near the grave which matched the shoes that Harrow wore.

McDougall, who had retired as a detective sergeant, had been a young constable at the first interview with the 34-year-old suspect in 1975. Gillard explained that he wanted to home in on a later interview, in April 1976, when the murderer had already been convicted of four killings and was serving a 25-year sentence. This was the interview, according to Smeeth's book, when the late Detective Chief Inspector Norman Lawson and McDougall had first put to Harrow the suggestion that he had killed Chrissie Frost.

'I don't think I'll ever forget it,' McDougall said. 'Harrow was always a cool customer, supercilious and smart-alecky. He wasn't a big bloke, but he had this look about him, the dark eyes and the swept-back hair, and you knew he would never hesitate to kill.' McDougall flicked open a loose-leaf folder, photocopies of the case notes. 'I asked him about Chrissie, and he leaned forward and said: "Nice-looking girl. Looks older than her age. I'd like to have done her. But I didn't. You'll not get me on this one." We went back and forwards on it for a couple of hours. We were always asking where he had left her body, but he wouldn't say anything. That was unusual because he had told us where he had left Anne Tomkins. But in this case, he just locked his hands behind the back of his head and pretended to go to sleep, as if we were boring him.'

'So what do you know about her disappearance?' Gillard asked. 'Tim Smeeth sent me this copy of a witness statement which said she was spotted at the Leicester Forest East motorway services at roughly ten o'clock on Thursday.'

'That's right. The witness was a male motorist who clearly fancied the girl and was going to give her a lift himself. But this sleek maroon Jaguar stopped ahead of him,' McDougall said.

'But Harrow had a Daimler Sovereign, didn't he? Not a Jag.'

'Yeah, but they are actually almost identical. Not much more than a badge difference. Besides, this witness was more interested in the girl than the car.'

'I don't suppose too many witnesses would admit that these days,' Gillard said.

'Different times, isn't it? The bloke gave a very good description of the suitcase she had, which was small and had stickers on it.' McDougall passed across a photocopy.

'Ah, I'd not seen that.' Gillard read the description. 'That sounds just like the vanity case that we recovered from Philip Antrobus's effects. Antrobus also had a Jaguar. It's still there on the farm.'

McDougall gripped the arms of his chair. 'We could make so much progress if these bloody people weren't dead.' He looked like a man eager to get back on the job. 'Still, have you looked in the boot of that Jag? You might find the body of Chrissie Frost.'

Three weeks without identifying the hit–and–run victim. DI Jan Talantire was surprised it had taken this long for her boss, Detective Chief Superintendent Bob Parker, to summon her for a carpeting at Devon and Cornwall Police headquarters in Exeter. As she stood in his sterile, windowless office, she took in the shelves full of golfing trophies and photographs of him with the great and the good of senior constabulary. Parker himself leaned back in his chair with his hands behind his head, a crisply ironed white shirt struggling to contain his beer belly.

'I'm a patient man, Jan, but the newspapers are full of all sorts of conjecture about the identity of the victim. We've become a bit of a laughing stock, to be honest. Useless yokels, that's what's being said behind our backs.' He shook his head in exasperation. 'I've even approved your budget request for this isotope analysis thing, but it's a lot to spend when we have to wait a month for the results. Isn't there anything more we can do?'

'It's bodies I need, sir,' she replied. 'To replace DS Stafford, who should be on maternity leave. Not just someone driving up from Exeter a couple of times a week. I need assistance on the case every day.'

'Yes, well that's beyond my control, I'm afraid. You know the human resources situation. I've read all the various forensic reports, and we seem to know an awful lot about our victim. But someone out there must've known him, must be missing him. There can hardly be a person in the country who has not seen the huge BBC website feature about him. But still nothing.'

'Yes, for that reason I'm tending to the view that he's from abroad,' she said.

'Which ties in with the shoes bought in Dubai.'

'Yes, sir. The trouble is, as you know, there is no international missing persons database, except for those concerning war, human rights violations and natural disasters. Interpol has a few cases notified, but there seems to be no apparatus to pursue them. If we knew the country he came from, we'd be able to narrow it down. That's why I was asking for extra bodies. At the moment I've got a uniformed constable laboriously going through European countries' missing persons databases, looking for people of the right age.'

'Yes, I can see why that is unsatisfactory. What about the driver? Can we charge Barbara Antrobus yet?'

'No, sir. Her alibi is pretty strong. The CPS chucked the case back at me. They won't take it unless we've got something more.'

Parker harrumphed his displeasure. 'You've got to do better than this, Jan.'

–

Talantire and DS Charmaine Stafford spent the day reviewing the evidence file. There had been no breakthroughs on either who had been driving the vehicle or who had been knocked down. The reconstruction of the journey of the Ford Ranger brought forth only contradictory accounts. No one had seen it near the phone box at Furzy Hill, and only one witness had seen it in Bear Street. They'd looked through hours of dashcam footage offered by local motorists, but found nothing. Most of the other calls following the reconstruction had ignored the day they were being asked about, but referred to the car being driven erratically in the town centre the previous Saturday. None of it shed any light on Barbara's alibi.

'If it was only her sister providing the alibi, she could have done it. I wouldn't trust either of them. But there are all these others,' Stafford said as she flicked through the witness statements.

'Not just other residents, who could easily be mistaken, but two members of staff too, including Mrs Dickinson.'

'What about Philip Antrobus?' Stafford asked. 'We know he was capable of nicking a set of car keys and getting himself into a vehicle. In this case the keys were in the car already.'

'Yes, but have you seen that Ford?' Talantire asked. 'It's quite high off the ground. It's one thing for an elderly paraplegic to ease himself off a wheelchair into a comparatively low seat like a Toyota Yaris. But to haul himself up there...'

'But we know he can stand. Samantha Gillard witnessed it.'

'If you can believe her,' Talantire said.

'Do you think she's lying?' Stafford asked.

'I don't know,' said Talantire, working the stub of a pencil across the top of her knuckles and back into her palm. 'Let's put it this way, Charmaine. If we are testing the unlikely theory that Philip Antrobus drove the hit-and-run vehicle, you need better foundations than the testimony of a woman who has an incentive to lie.'

'I believed her,' Stafford said.

'That's fine. Believe away. To put Philip Antrobus behind the wheel, you also need to believe that he woke up at a time in which he was normally asleep in his room, put himself in his wheelchair, took himself into the car park unnoticed, knew the keys were in there, pulled the door open, hauled himself up and into the cab, drove up to Furzy Hill in a vehicle he had never used before, did so without attracting any attention, knocked down our Mr Nobody, and drove it back to the road behind the care home for his sister to find, then took himself back to bed unseen.'

'The Red Queen used to believe as many as six impossible things before breakfast,' Stafford said. 'Lewis Carroll, *Through the Looking-Glass*.'

Talantire smiled. 'Charmaine, that seems to me a very strong argument for having a slice of toast before coming to work. Do your thinking after a bit of breakfast. It restores your sense of scepticism.'

'I had a boiled egg and two slices of toast,' Stafford said. Suddenly she groaned, and put a hand to her stomach. 'God, that hurt.'

'Are you all right?' Talantire said.

The detective sergeant's brown eyes flicked up. 'I'm not sure.'

Talantire knew this was Stafford's first child, and that she had been extremely nervous about it. 'Let's get you to the loo to begin with.' Talantire moved ahead to open doors while Stafford waddled to the ladies, holding her tummy. By the time they were inside, the detective sergeant's low groans had become more urgent fast-breathed howls. Talantire ducked outside, leaving her colleague in a cubicle. 'Clifford, come here,' she said to the PC, who was passing with a bundle of papers and a cup of coffee. 'Keep an eye on Charmaine. I think the baby is coming. I'll bring my car to the front, it'll be quicker than calling for an ambulance.'

The young constable's eyes bulged with terror, as if he had been asked to clear a pub full of drunken Millwall fans with nothing more than a rolled-up copy of the *Police Gazette*.

'On second thought,' Talantire said, 'here are my keys. Get my car. I'll stay with her.' The ragged scream from the cubicle confirmed the wisdom of her decision. Willow took the keys and ran.

Chapter 29

Zoe Stafford became the first child born in Barnstaple police station, delivered by Detective Inspector Jan Talantire after Charmaine's short but agonising labour, during which most of the male officers either vanished or seemed to turn into headless chickens.

It was early evening before Talantire managed to get a moment to visit Stafford at North Devon District Hospital, and after the hugs, the congratulations and the introduction to the child, the new mother confessed she hadn't had the chance to look at her emails for a while and asked if Talantire would do it. 'There shouldn't be anything much,' Stafford said. 'Except the results of the fingerprint analysis from the hit-and-run victim. I'm sorry, but I forgot to send them off at first.'

'Better late than never,' Talantire replied, getting out her smartphone. After getting the password, Talantire accessed her colleague's police email account. Scrolling down the laden inbox, past the many messages of congratulations, she found the message from CSI, forwarding a series of possible or partial matches to the victim's fingerprints. None were perfect matches, but the nearest was a partial print that had only been on the database for a few weeks.

'I don't believe it,' Talantire breathed as she looked up the origin of the best match.

'What is it?' Stafford asked.

'The best fingerprint fit to our hit-and-run victim is actually from Barbara Antrobus's Ford Ranger. From the *inside*. That partial latent print of thumb and forefinger from the glovebox we've spent weeks trying to identify.'

'You're saying he was run down by a car that he was in?' Stafford asked. As if in sympathy, her baby began to cry, a furious high-pitched mewling that made further speech impossible. Talantire kissed them both goodbye and hurried back to the scene of the accident. If it was an accident.

Chapter 30

It was almost 8 p.m. when Talantire parked her car outside the phone box at Furzy Hill and paced around on the tarmac. She had recalled that there was a slight down-ward slope from the kiosk to the ditch where the body was found, and she wanted to check whether there was any possibility that whoever stole the car could have run himself down. Even with comedic idiocy, it would take some doing. She had already looked up on the Internet two or three such accidents, when drivers had forgotten to put the handbrake on. None of them had been at the kind of speed required to cause the injuries that Mr Nobody had sustained. There were of course other occasions in which a car owner had been run down by someone attempting to steal their vehicle. This could not be the case here.

She played her torchlight up and down the road, and immediately dismissed the notion that the victim could have been the driver. There was a little camber from the centre of the road to the edge, which probably explained the way the body had eventually rolled into the ditch after having been struck, but not enough of a gradient for a vehicle to freewheel at much more than a walking pace. Especially if it had a body trapped beneath the chassis. No, she decided, her initial impression was correct: the vehicle had been driven at speed towards the victim. And that meant somebody else was involved.

However, if the victim had at some point been inside the vehicle, it gave renewed weight to a previously dismissed theory that the killing had been intentional. Someone taken to a quiet and lonely place, dumped on the road and then run over.

Only then did she realize that two other pieces of evidence supported this conclusion. One, that the victim had been stripped of ID. Two, that he had recently taken sleeping medication. No, scrub 'taken', substitute 'been drugged with'. The pieces seemed to be fitting together a bit more easily.

Having set aside the tangled knot of who was driving the car, Talantire looked again through the forensic details of what was discovered in the car. DNA from hairs and fingerprint comparisons had shown that all three Antrobus siblings had at some time been in the vehicle. That was all entirely reasonable given the four months that Barbara Antrobus had owned it. Then there were these prints from the victim. He'd either been sitting in the front passenger seat, or had just possibly reached inside for something when the door had been open. That didn't fit with the idea of a targeted killing. The normal modus operandi for taking someone to a lonely place to kill them involves the victim being bound and gagged and in the boot. So the chances are the victim did not know what was going to happen to him. In fact, it was likely that the victim trusted the driver, perhaps even knew them well. If so, that would explain him treading on Peter Yates's chewing gum too.

Talantire leaned on the fence, close to where the flowers had been tied, and stared through the darkness across the moors and towards the sea. She really had to approach this from the other direction. This was not stranger crashing into stranger. So if Miss Antrobus or Mrs Gibson had anything to do with it, it would relate to somebody they knew.

Who on earth might have suddenly disappeared from their lives?

She needed inside information on the family. Perhaps it really was a good time to return some of the many calls that DCI Gillard had left on her answering machine.

–

Gillard was at work the next day when she called him.

'This call is off the record, Craig,' she said. 'But I need your help to save me a lot of time.'

'Absolutely. I told you before, anything I can do.'

'Look, I'm only doing this because you've kept on the right side of the line and because I feel confident that I can trust you. This is absolutely confidential, just between you and me, okay?'

'Okay.'

'The victim of the hit-and-run had been in the vehicle that later ran him down.'

Gillard gasped. 'That changes everything.'

'Yes, it does. I need to ask you about anyone who might be missing from the lives of your aunts. Family members, far-flung cousins, friends, friends of friends, people who may have been abroad for an extended period. Anything you can think of.'

'I can't think of anyone in the family who is missing, except of course for Howie. Howard Gibson, Trish's ex-husband, who left her in 2008, and is now in Thailand. That's a long time ago.'

'Are we sure he's still over there?'

'Well, that doubt had crossed my mind,' Gillard said.

'Have you spoken to him recently?'

'No, not for decades, but Trish seems to regularly.'

'I'd ring him myself, if I could be sure who was really on the other end of the phone. I was thinking of combing Mrs Gibson's house for DNA to see if I can find a match against the hit-and-run victim.'

'Hmm,' Gillard said. 'After ten years it might be hard to find Howie's DNA. Jan, there is a quicker and surer route than that. I understand Howie has two older sisters in Scotland. You could do a familial DNA comparison between them and the victim. I'll dig up their addresses and email you this evening.'

–

Sam continued to fret about her husband's brooding silences. He hadn't been cycling for a week, and spent long evenings on the Internet researching cold cases upstairs in the spare room. As they sat staring at each other over a small roast chicken one Thursday evening, she asked him what was on his mind. The crease between his brows, seemingly deepening day by day, flexed as he looked up at her.

'I'm sorry, Sam, I think I've got to go back to Devon this weekend.'

Her sigh took up the next ten seconds.

'Can't you just...' Her question died on her lips, and she stared out of the window into the dark, windswept garden.

'Barbara is due to be sentenced on Monday for the assault at the police station, having finally pleaded guilty. I think Trish at least would like some moral support. However, I've got something else to do too. I want to take a look inside that rusted old car in front of his caravan. From what Barbara told me, it's been there at least 15 years. There is an outside possibility that we will find the body of this Chrissie Frost in the boot.'

'But Philip told me he remembered burying her.'

'True enough. But I have to chase down every lead.'

'Unpaid, and in your own time,' she reminded him.

'I'm doing it for Trish – she's a nervous wreck.'

'And what about you, Craig? You're like a wraith. It's eating you up. You're mumbling in your sleep and you're biting your nails.'

He looked down at his fingertips in surprise. She was right. 'I'll be fine. It's Trish I'm worried about. I think she's just living for Christmas. Howie and his family are coming over from Thailand to be with her. Last time I spoke to her, she could talk of nothing else.'

'That's very supportive of him, and his new wife,' Sam said. 'Going over to see an ex-wife.'

'Takes all sorts,' Gillard said. 'By the way, I had a call from DI Talantire this morning. I was a bit surprised seeing as she's been ignoring my calls for so long.'

'What did she want?'

'She wanted to know if any friends or family had disappeared in recent weeks.'

'Howie?'

'Maybe. We can't say a word to Barbara and Trish, but it seems that the hit-and-run victim may have been known to them.'

'Why does she think that?'

'There's some forensic connection.'

'Craig, this is getting scarier every day.'

He nodded.

'I'm coming with you,' Sam said, leaning across the table and grasping her husband's hand. 'You need me, I can see that.'

-

This time the journey down was less troubled by bad weather and Gillard needed no reminding to get a proper bunch of flowers for his aunt. A mixed bunch of red and yellow roses with orange chrysanthemums, and a box of chocolates. He had also, at Sam's suggestion, bought and wrapped the full Marks & Spencer's bath time gift collection, designed for elderly ladies, to leave at Trish's to be opened on Christmas morning. For Barbara, who always considered Christmas a waste of time, he had wrapped a good bottle of brandy and some department store vouchers. Family guilt bought off for under £100.

Trish greeted them, as before, with warmth, but her growing anxiety bubbled just under the surface. She confessed that she and Barbara had had a monumental row that morning, which had made her cry. Trish was convinced this farmhand lover boy of hers, Peter, was an unhealthy influence on her sister. 'I don't mean to sound old-fashioned, but it isn't right, is it? More than a 50-year age gap.'

'Still, when it was Hugh Hefner the other way round,' Sam remarked, 'everyone said good luck to him with all those young models.'

'That was all about wealth, surely,' Gillard said.

'Wealth!' Trish exclaimed. 'Barbara's just got debts, including a loan for the car the police are still sitting on. If Peter wants to inherit that lot of trouble, good luck to him. Speaking of a car, you've come back down to look at Philip's old Jaguar, I believe?'

'Yes, I just wondered if you remembered how long it'd been there on the farm.'

'Years and years – I couldn't tell you. I think Barbara is the person to answer that question.'

'She said 15 years, but I'm intending to ask her a little more about it after we drive over to her place tomorrow. Were you ever given a lift in it?'

'I really can't remember, dear.' Trish left Sam and Craig in the lounge while she made preparations for dinner. These were interrupted by a call. From Trish's excited tone as she walked around the kitchen, flour up to her elbows and the handset tucked under her chin, Sam guessed that it was Howie.

She looked at Gillard and saw his eyes narrow in suspicion. She was going to ask him what was up, but he walked away into the kitchen. He seemed to interrupt Trish, and was given a sharp retort. He shrugged as he rejoined Sam on the sofa.

When she'd finally finished the call and came into the lounge, she was full of news about the eldest daughter, May, eight, who was now doing very well on the violin. 'I listened to her, she was really good,' Trish said. Craig and Sam endured more family trivia while they were having their evening meal, and it was only later, while Trish loaded the dishwasher, that they had a moment of privacy.

'There is something strange going on,' Gillard whispered, checking that Trish couldn't overhear them. 'I asked if I could speak to Howie, while she was still on the line, but she shushed me. When she hung up, she said that Howie wasn't there, he was travelling.'

'And that's suspicious?'

Gillard sucked his teeth. 'It's convenient he's not there, isn't it? And it's a really odd time to even get a call from Bangkok. It's 2 a.m. over there. Would they really have the daughter up that late playing the violin for her benefit?'

'They probably called at a time to suit Trish,' Sam said.

'Possibly. But I noticed there was flour not only on the cordless phone, but on her mobile.'

'Sorry, Craig, I don't know what you're driving at.'

'I wondered at first if she had picked up the wrong phone by mistake when the call came in. Then I had an idea. After she finished, I rang 1471 from the bedroom extension to find out who the last caller was. And it was Trish's own number. She rang her landline from her mobile.'

'That doesn't make sense,' Sam said, starting to laugh. 'She'd have been talking to herself.'

'Sam, I know you think this is hilarious, but I think she was chattering away to herself for our benefit.'

'To save us from having to listen to her, you mean!' Sam was still chuckling.

'I wonder if any of this family of Howie's exists.'

Sam shook her head. 'No Craig, they must do. You haven't been subjected to the photographs, and the interminable stories, like I have. She doesn't mind that you switch off to it, but I'm expected to listen, which is the burden of womanhood. There are not only pictures of Trish in Bangkok, at various temples. She's also with the whole extended family, at a barbecue, by a swimming pool. Follow me.' She led him back out of the lounge and to the alcove next to the stairs which had been turned into something of a shrine to Howie and his family. There were dozens of pictures of a huge extended clan, all neatly framed and hanging on the wall. There were also three enlargements of a striking young Thai man, his arm around Trish in some British setting with Georgian architecture in the background.

Trish finally emerged, tea towel in hand.

'Where was this taken, Trish?' Sam asked, of one British picture.

'Bath, in 2015. Sarawut wanted to visit his old college,' she said.

'You don't have many pictures of Howie,' Gillard said.

'He took most of these,' she laughed. 'He doesn't think he's photogenic, so prefers to be behind the lens. There's a couple.' She pointed out enlargements of him with her by a hotel swimming pool. 'That's from 2008 when we went to Singapore. Our last holiday together, and this,' she said pointing to an interior shot of her and Howie at a bar. 'This is from 2015 when I went out to see him in Bangkok.'

Once Trish had returned to the kitchen, Sam said, 'Look, Craig. The whole family are coming over for Christmas. That would be a pretty big lie to make up, wouldn't it? With a definite big-bang expiry date.'

'It might be, if anyone is here to spot it.'

'Craig, you've always told me to look out for motive. When something doesn't make sense, what reason would there be for it? Why would she lie?'

Gillard shrugged. 'Well Sam, you've got me there. Trish always seems to be devoted to Howie. But it's equally clear that she's telling us about a phone call that didn't happen. It must've been for our benefit.'

Sam looked into her husband's eyes. 'There is this mysterious hit-and-run. What if she'd accidentally knocked him down?'

'Don't think I haven't considered it,' Gillard replied. 'Especially since Talantire's call. There's two massive problems with that theory though. One is that she's been going on about Howie and his family in Thailand for years. Barbara's met some of them, and on one occasion went out with Trish to Bangkok. So if I'm right and this family doesn't exist at all, it can't be anything to do with the hit-and-run, and it's a much longer-running fantasy which also enmeshes Barbara. The second problem, of course, is that Barbara isn't the only one with a cast-iron alibi for the accident. Trish was with her. They were both seen by numerous people at the home, DI Talantire conceded that.'

Sam shrugged. 'Since being married to you, I've found myself looking at reasons for murder. But I have to say in Trish's case, she gives every sign of never having got over Howie leaving her. She talks about him constantly, and I've seen genuine tears in her eyes. I think she still really misses him.'

'Let's examine this another way,' Gillard said. 'I'll sneak a look at her address book, and ring him up myself. And I'll look on Facebook. I know Trish isn't on it, but maybe some of his kids will be.'

Once they were up in the bedroom, Gillard got his own phone out and searched for Facebook entries for Howard Gibson. 'There are hundreds of them.'

'Try adding Thailand to the search,' Sam said, looking over his shoulder.

'Nope, no results when I do that.'

'If he doesn't like photographs of himself, Howie is unlikely to be a Facebook fan,' Sam said. 'I mean, that's the whole point of the thing, isn't it?'

Gillard tried searching again on Howie's wife Tangmo, but with the Gibson surname there were no results. Then he tried the brother-in-law's name, Sarawut, but realized he didn't have his surname. There were thousands of results. Eventually he gave up and they went to bed.

At breakfast the next morning, Gillard asked for Howie's email address and Trish quickly provided it. 'What about a phone number?' he asked.

'Why are you planning to ring him?' Trish responded. 'You've never shown any interest in him before. I'm not sure if he'll even remember you.' Eventually she wrote down a number for him. 'You'd best get on to Barbara's now, she'll be expecting you. You don't want to be late.'

Sam could see her husband's face drop. Still enmeshed in the expectations of his aunts, trapped in some child-hood nightmare that he was still unable to share with her.

–

They were largely silent on the half-hour journey to Hollow Coombe farm. It was a bright and breezy day, the hedgerows still full of sloes and rosehips, fed on by frenetic sparrows.

'Stop the car,' Sam demanded as they crested the ridge for the first view of the sparkling sea. Gillard did so and turned to his wife with raised eyebrows.

'Please turn off the engine.' He complied. 'We've tiptoed around this for long enough, Craig. I know there's a lot of buried pain here, but you have to confront your past. You can't do that if you keep it buried.'

'What's done is done.'

'It's not even beginning to be done. Can't you see that? It's damaging you every single day. These two poisonous creatures control you.' Getting no reply, she slammed the dashboard in exasperation. 'Craig, for God's sake! If you could just see yourself as I see you, you would recognize the intimidation that Barbara in particular exerts over you.'

'It's just baggage – we've all got emotional baggage.'

'It's not just ordinary stuff, Craig.'

Gillard shrugged.

'I want you to tell me exactly what Barbara did to you. And I want you to tell me now. I have a right to know. Because without it, I don't even know who you are.'

Gillard leaned back in his seat, sucked in a deep breath, and then began to tell the story.

Chapter 31

Sam was transfixed by the horror of what she heard. A seven-year-old boy, put to bed each night over that summer by his aunt who was then thirty. 'Come on, my little bedtime soldier.' That was always the phrase. Sam had even heard Barbara use it to Craig a couple of times in their recent trips, and she had seen him recoil. At first, she mistook it for chafing at the use of childhood terms, but she hadn't understood the implications.

Gillard had described how Barbara had drawn him into an intimacy over that summer. First by undoing her bun, unleashing her enormous mane of jet-black hair in the evenings, and asking him to sit behind her on the sofa and comb it while she watched television. He was frightened of that hair – the unleashed power of womanhood, the way it dangled over him when she came to say good night. She then began to involve him in washing her hair. She would stand at the big butler sink, wearing only underwear, and ask him to stand on a little stool so that he could tip water over her to rinse the suds away. It was no doubt intended that he could see her body. He had never seen his own mother this way. Then, in the last week, when he awoke with a nightmare during a storm, Barbara came for him and took him into her own bed. Her heat, her proximate nakedness barely concealed by her nightdress, and that terrifying scarred eye. She looked at him, the effect she had upon him, and announced: 'So, my little bedtime soldier is standing to attention. You will soon be a man.' She had slid down his pyjama bottoms and caressed him.

Sam had gasped when she heard this. No wonder Craig was screwed up. The act was brief and never repeated, though he found himself expecting it, and physically ready for it, for that remaining week. He never told his mother; he never told anybody. His shame over his own physical reaction he carried inside himself.

'It's terrible, Craig, just terrible.' She stared at her husband, who was resting his chin on his hands across the top of the steering wheel. He looked exhausted. For several minutes they embraced, across the seats, and then he suggested they take a ten-minute walk before going to the farm. Neither of them was in any condition to meet the perpetrator of this crime. At least not yet.

'She's been a victim herself,' Gillard said as they made their way along a footpath towards the cliff edge. 'Her whole life until the death of her father, Jacob. He was abusing her, as a child, as a teenager. It's he who was in those photographs they found on Philip's laptop. Her child, buried on the cliff, was undoubtedly his. That's what Trish has told me, and it makes sense. No wonder my mother fled Hollow Coombe at the first opportunity to go to London, no wonder Trish herself ran away from home.'

'When did you find this out?'

'Only a few years ago. I think perhaps it was when Howie left Trish. But it makes so much sense. Barbara, being the eldest of the sisters, was expected to stay at the farm, to look after her disabled mother and to cater to her father's drunken whims.' They walked for another half an hour before Gillard finally said, 'Okay, I'm ready.'

–

Barbara made her displeasure at being kept waiting quite obvious. No sooner had they emerged into the kitchen than she said: 'I don't have much time now, I need to bring some ewes down into the barn for worming. I made some sandwiches, so you can help yourselves.'

'It's all right, we don't need to bother you. We just need to take a look at Philip's old car. I don't suppose you have any keys for it?'

'It's rusted to buggery,' Barbara said. 'I don't know where the keys are, and don't think they would work even if you found them. You need a crowbar. There's a couple in the small stables' tack room if you want.' She went out and slammed the door.

Craig and Sam made their way back outside and found the dilapidated brick building Barbara was referring to. No horses seemed to have been kept there in decades. Instead, it was full of plastic drums of sheep feed, worming compound and dip chemicals. From the rafters hung a variety of old and rusted tools. He quickly found a hefty three-foot crowbar. He returned to the Vauxhall for his own toolbox, then led Sam up the steep muddy slope to Philip's caravan. The car still connected to it was indeed in a dreadful state: no tyres, and rusted so badly the sills were as delicate as gingerbread. Nettles surrounded it and there were weeds growing up through the chassis. The soft leather seats were streaked with mould and split in many places.

He trampled down the weeds around the boot and pressed the release button. It was rusted closed. The crowbar made short work of it, however, and the entire metal boot lid was soon prised off. The storage cavity had rusted right through from below, the spare tyre sitting on the weeds. There were no signs of human remains.

Craig and Sam then set off to find Barbara, who had disappeared towards the western end of the farm on the quad bike. They found her with the two dogs, having cornered a large flock of sheep into a pen.

She still looked angry.

—

Monday's Exeter Magistrates' Court hearing for Barbara Antrobus was endlessly delayed by a series of other more urgent sentencing hearings. It was nearly four o'clock by the time she was called, and the three lay magistrates heard a mitigation plea from the defence lawyer, which mentioned the struggles of rural farmers on the North Devon coast. They conferred briefly before sentencing Barbara to six months' jail, suspended for a year, plus 100 hours of community service and a £400 fine, including a victim surcharge.

Gillard's aunt showed no signs of relief that the sentence was suspended, but merely grumbled to Trish and Craig over the fine and the difficulty of being able to fit into the farm calendar nearly three weeks' worth of what she expected would be graffiti removal in Barnstaple.

'You should be thankful,' Trish said. 'It could have been a lot worse.'

'Bugger that,' she said as they walked down the steps into a cold wind. 'It might have been nice to have a couple of weeks sitting on my bum doing nothing.'

–

In the next week, Gillard tried on four occasions to ring the number in Thailand that Trish had given him. On each occasion an answering machine kicked in, speaking presumably in Thai, and he left a message after the beep. There were no replies.

Gillard's final attempt was made first thing one morning as he and Sam were having breakfast before heading off to work. As before, he left a message, and then returned to his bowl of cereal. 'Like I said, Sam, I don't think this new family exists.'

'Well Howie certainly existed once,' Sam replied. 'He came to your mum's funeral. There are photographs of him.'

'Nothing very recent though.' Gillard chewed his cereal thoughtfully.

'Yes, there was. There was a photo of him with Trish on that display by her stairs, when she went out to Bangkok in 2015.'

Gillard smiled. 'Yes, I had a good look at that picture. It's the bar of some hotel but it could be anywhere. The glasses she was wearing were the same ones from the 2008 pictures on the mantelpiece. But on some other pictures, supposedly from 2011, according to Trish, she is wearing different pinkish frames. Now—'

'Do you think she killed him?' Sam interrupted. 'Because to me, that's where you seem to be heading.'

Gillard shrugged. 'I don't know. I agree with you that she seemed to be devoted to him, and I can still remember how upset she was when he left. I mean he treated her appallingly, if he really did just head off to the fleshpots of Bangkok in 2008.' He rubbed his chin. 'And that's why the story of hers about befriending Howie's new family just seems so odd.'

'If the family doesn't exist, or at least is nothing to do with Howie, then it's an extremely elaborate set-up. And for what reason?' Sam looked at her husband. 'I mean, why is it so important to Trish that we believe in this family?'

'I'm not sure.'

'If there's one thing you've taught me, Craig, it's to follow the money. If there was some insurance policy, some large inheritance, then surely she would be better off admitting he was dead and trying to collect. Rather than fabricating some story to pretend that he's still alive.'

'Don't imagine I haven't been considering all that,' Gillard said, shaking his head. 'The whole thing is completely baffling.' He paused and looked at his wife. 'Well there's one way of finding out. According to Trish, Howie and family are supposed to arrive at Heathrow two days before Christmas. We could offer to go and meet them.'

Sam blew an exasperated sigh. 'There is almost nowhere I'd like to avoid more than Heathrow Airport in the Christmas rush. Why don't we just ring Trish up on Christmas Day and asked to speak to Howie?'

Gillard shook his head. 'She's too smart for that. She either won't take the call or she'll say that they're out. She's very clever.'

'Well, whatever,' Sam said. 'But let me tell you one thing now, just in case you're thinking about it. I will not be spending Christmas down in Devon just to try to catch your aunt out.'

'Fair enough. I'll ring Barbara this evening, see if I can get any insight from her.'

—

Barbara Antrobus was not particularly receptive to Gillard's questioning. 'I can't tell you the exact details of when Trish met Howie and his family,' she said. 'If I was you, I'd be spending my time trying to help me get my car back from the bloody Devon police, rather than gainsaying your long-suffering Auntie Trish. I lost another ewe last Wednesday, throat ripped out. This doesn't get any easier.'

'All right, Barbara, I understand that. I've left messages with DI Talantire about following up on the previous dog attacks, but it didn't come up when we last spoke.'

'When was that?'

'Three days ago.'

Her voice rose with indignation. 'So you spoke to her, and didn't even bother to ask her about my ewes?'

'Barbara—'

She hung up, leaving Gillard staring at the receiver.

Chapter 32

Gillard had not expected to have to travel as far as Northumberland in his research into the life of Philip Antrobus. But the phone call he had received at home during the week had offered him much too tempting a clue to ignore. A man called Ronald Grice, who had worked with Antrobus in the 1970s, had seen Gillard's notice in the pension newsletter of their former employer. The Philip Antrobus that Grice described seemed a world away from the gentle and reflective churchman that came across during his time as a homelessness campaigner.

They were sitting in a pub in the picturesque Northumbrian town of Wooler, and Grice, a cherubic pensioner with a halo of snow-white hair and an e-cig that he kept fiddling with, was shaking his head as Gillard told him why he was making the investigation.

'Well, the Philip Antrobus I knew was certainly interested in the ladies,' Grice said. 'That's for sure. But to murder one? I can't really believe that.'

'So you said you were on the same sales team with him?'

'That's right. There were a few occasions when we shared a car, because we both had client visits in the same city.'

'Did he pick up hitchhikers?'

'Oh yes. Fast Phil always picked up hitchhikers, so long as they were female and good-looking. It made the time pass pleasantly.'

'Did he get that name for his driving? Or some other reason?'

Grice just laughed. 'What do you think?'

'But he did have a Jaguar, didn't he?'

'Yes. An XJ6, I think. He was the most successful salesman on the team, and got the best car. That's why I was really surprised when he left.'

'When exactly did he leave?'

'Gosh, now you're asking.' Grice stroked his chin and said, 'The summer of 1973, I think.'

'Do you remember any particular occasions when he stopped for hitchhikers?'

'There was one time when we were travelling to Glasgow and we had these two students in the car. They'd been waiting a long time in the rain for a lift, and were extremely grateful. Anyway, we got these two girls to Glasgow, which was where they were going, and invited them for a drink at the Excelsior Hotel, by the airport.' A sly smile crept over his face. 'We each knew which one we fancied, and thought a couple of drinks might do the trick.'

'Was he the instigator of this escapade?'

'Oh God, yes, always. He had the patter. I was just the follow-up guy. He almost always seemed to get the goods. He'd book the room, have it for the first 45 minutes, and then it would be my turn with girl number two. But quite often, the girl I got would turn a bit cooler on the whole idea while waiting in the bar. I didn't have quite his charisma. But on this occasion at least, they were both up for it.' He couldn't suppress the grin. Gillard felt that this man had been dining out on this particular anecdote for many decades, almost as if it was the pinnacle of his life.

'Can you remember the date?'

'No. Only that it was raining. Still, that could be any month in Glasgow.'

Gillard waited while Grice fiddled with his vape. 'No, it was nearly Christmas. I remember there were decorations up in the hotel.'

'That's a pity. We think the event in question took place over the summer. Did you accompany him on any business trips in the months leading up to his departure?'

'No, I don't think so. There was one at Easter. Maybe the year before. I got my leg over then too.' He rubbed his hands together enthusiastically.

'Mr Grice, let's focus on Philip's movements and behaviour. Would you say he had a temper? Did you ever hear arguments at work or see any evidence of violence?'

'I can't say I did. He had a pretty big ego. I mean, at the office he would regale us with these various lurid stories, which were pretty boastful.'

'So you would say that he actively set out to seduce the women he gave lifts to?'

'Not just them. The women we met in bars, secretaries, anyone really. He thought he had a gift. "She was begging for it" was the kind of thing he would say. It annoyed some of the blokes, but most of us wanted a little bit of it to rub off on us.' He chuckled conspiratorially. 'Wives at home, big expense account, fast company car, the boys playing away. They were great times. It was before any mobile phones, so the missus couldn't check up on you.'

'He wasn't married though, was he?'

'No, but I was, and so were many of the others.'

'Any other employees who would have known him, that you're still in touch with?'

'There's a couple. I can speak to them, give them your phone number. And there is my wife of course, Brenda. Wife number two, actually.' He grinned again. 'She was a secretary, and had a bit of a fling with him before she and I got together.'

'Can I speak to her?'

Grice blew a sigh. 'I'd prefer if you didn't. She doesn't know about what went on. I never told her. It might make things awkward.'

'Surely she would have guessed,' Gillard said. 'She was working in the office with you both. It sounds like she was part of it.'

'No, she wasn't.' Grice looked offended for a moment. 'Anyway, we've never talked about it. All right. Come back to the house, have a cuppa. Just tread carefully, will you?'

Half an hour later, Gillard was sitting with Brenda Grice, a slender and delicate woman whose pale-blue eyes showed considerable intelligence. Her husband announced he was going to the shed. Gillard began immediately. 'I just wanted to ask about Philip Antrobus. I believe you knew him quite well?'

'We worked in the same office,' she said. Her eyes revealed there was more to tell.

Gillard said nothing, and held her gaze.

'Ron's told you, hasn't he? About my relationship with Phil?'

Gillard nodded. 'I think Antrobus may have murdered a young woman at around about the time that you knew him.'

She nodded. 'I'm not that surprised. He thought he was God's gift. He was good-looking, but assumed that was all any woman needed. And the sex of course. I fell for it myself to begin with. I was young and he made all sorts of promises, which he kept for precisely five seconds.'

'How did he treat you?'

'Casually, I suppose, is the best description. I was a facility that he used when he felt like it, when he came back from his trips away. I didn't see it like that at the time, of course. I was smitten. Totally smitten. I was only 17, and he was my first.'

'Was he ever violent to you?'

'No. He could be quite sweet sometimes, when he wanted something. However, he did become quite angry one time when I couldn't sleep with him.'

'Couldn't?'

'When it was my period.' Her gaze drifted away in recollection. 'He didn't hit me, or even threaten to. But he didn't like anything getting in the way of his plans. I suppose today you would call it a sense of entitlement. He certainly had that.'

'Did you know about his other girlfriends?'

She shook her head. 'No. There were rumours of course, but I never believed them. Because he told me he loved me. And, like I say, I was just 17. He bought me jewellery and promised me the earth. I think he had everything pretty well compartmentalized.'

'When did you find out about the other women?'

'Well, a few weeks after he left. He didn't even say goodbye. The girls in the office told me, rather gradually and kindly. I cried. And then I grew up.' She gave a tight little smile. 'But years later, when Ron told me about this homelessness TV programme, and that Phil was now a clergyman, I watched the programme. Now *that* was the shock. I just couldn't believe it. He seemed to be an utterly different person.'

'I just want to go back to the summer of 1973. Were you working at the company at that time?'

'Yes. I do remember when we heard he had left. It was all of a sudden, like he had been fired or something. We normally had leaving parties, but not in this case. He just seemed to slip away, and nobody heard from him again, until Ron opened the *TV Times* more than a decade later and saw this programme listed.'

'We know he moved to another company, Johnson Hoists Ltd, one which went into liquidation,' Gillard said. 'After that, he reportedly went to an ashram in India.'

'I don't know anything about that,' she said. 'But it doesn't seem like the man I knew.'

'So you had no contact with him at all after that time?'

Brenda was slow to answer. 'There was one time. He rang me up when Ron was at work.'

'When was that?'

'I can't remember exactly. Maybe 1980? He asked me if I wanted to come out for a drink. I knew what that would lead to, so I said no. And that was the last time I ever heard from him. Don't mention that to my husband.'

'I won't.' Gillard smiled reassuringly. More secrets from the past. But the real Philip Antrobus, the darkness and the light, was gradually emerging.

–

Over the next few days, Gillard spoke by phone to several of Antrobus's former colleagues. None of them seemed to be able to add any new details to the picture of a womanising single man in his 20s enjoying a buccaneering lifestyle. It reinforced Trish's view that something had happened to completely change his life. The murder of Chrissie Frost, the young runaway who was masquerading as Emily Speakman, seemed the obvious catalyst for the abrupt change of direction.

While it was tempting for the detective to continue to gradually piece together the missing pieces of his uncle's life, he had to remain focused on his objectives. There was no doubt in his mind that Philip had committed a murder, one that had been ascribed to another killer. Finding where the body was buried was essential. Only that would provide the crucial physical evidence of the killing. Yet with the perpetrator dead, there didn't seem to be any way of finding out. Even a shallow and hastily-dug grave, almost half a century on, would have become overgrown and hard to detect. None of Antrobus's former workmates could recall anything about the precise dates of his movements, and it was very rare for any of them to be with him in the car. Antrobus had clients all over the country. Assuming he had picked up Chrissie Frost at Leicester Forest East, perhaps her second lift after the bag snatch in Leeds, where would she have been heading? What kind of refuge would she have been seeking?

The last sighting of Chrissie Frost, according to Smeeth, was at ten o'clock on Thursday 5 July 1973 at the Leicester Forest East services on the M1. If the witness was correct, she got into a maroon Jaguar.

Where was she heading?

It was time to ask the people who knew her best. Her family.

–

Gillard got Eileen Frost's details from Timothy Smeeth. The author told him that the murder victim's mother still lived in the same Bradford suburb where Chrissie had been brought up. While the terraced house they had occupied had been demolished, she now lived in a social housing complex around the corner. Aware that Smeeth had said he would be wasting his time, Gillard wasn't going to visit her. Instead he rang her up. But Mrs Frost was extremely suspicious and hung up at his first mention of the death of her daughter. She didn't pick up on his subsequent attempts to ring her.

Perhaps there were other ways to pick the brain of the victim's mother. Gillard was at work when he made the phone call to West Yorkshire Police's headquarters at Wakefield. He was put through to a junior officer, DC Yvonne Colclough, who was in charge of the cold-case evidence files. She agreed to email him copies of the notes from the interviews with Chrissie's mother and father, but seemed curious that such an ancient case should be of interest to someone based at the other end of the country.

'Well, as you know, Chrissie Frost's disappearance has been linked to the M1 serial killer—'

'Christopher Colin Harrow,' she said. 'I'm just reading the book.'

'I know the author. I'll tell him you're enjoying it. You'll make his day.'

She chuckled. 'Harrow is a fascinating individual. One of our overlooked Yorkshire murderers.' She made him sound like a tourist attraction, bidding for a place in the next visitor leaflet.

'My theory is that Chrissie is one of those he didn't kill.'

'So the book's wrong?'

'Possibly. If so, there might be a new edition.'

'So who did kill her?'

'My uncle, quite possibly. Philip Antrobus. That's the theory I'm working on. He confessed shortly before he died, though he got the names wrong.'

When Gillard finally hung up, he was convinced he had thoroughly confused Yvonne Colclough, even though her interest was clearly piqued.

The emailed notes were not particularly illuminating. The bulk of the interviewing, in the early days after Chrissie's disappearance, had concentrated on the staff at the children's home and members of the immediate family. The absence of her distinctive vanity case was not noticed for a couple of weeks. Chrissie had been a frequent runaway. With a well-documented record of minor criminality and parents who were known to the police because of domestic violence, she didn't attract the same level of sympathy or media interest as some nice middle-class girl from a good family. After the first two weeks, the progressively longer gap between interviews made clear there was a drop-off in the resourcing of the case. There was only one interview, ten days into the investigation, in which the possibility of Chrissie having left the area was discussed with her mother, and even then, it was fairly brief.

Where did you go on holidays?'

'Filey, when we had us any money.'

'Was your daughter happy there?'

[Interviewee shrugged] 'Rained all the time, didn't it?'

'Did you ever take her away to visit relatives?'

'My uncle Lenny in Renfrew, couple of times.'

'Any others?'

'Once, when Chrissie was about 10 or 11, we went to see my aunt in Somerset. She had a pony and taught Chrissie to ride it.'

'What year was that?'

[Interviewee shrugged]

Gillard leaned back in his chair, arms behind his head. Somerset. The trouble was, Leicester Forest East was hardly the best place to begin a journey there. He pulled up on his screen a map of the British motorway network in 1973. It looked like a child's drawing of a dress. The M4 was the hem, the M1 the right-hand side, the M6 the upper left and the belt, the M62 the shoulders. The M5, some way from being complete, made up the lower left. The logical way to get to Somerset from Leeds at that time was to avoid London. There was no M25 until 1986. Gillard could hardly recall a time before the orbital motorway around the capital, and could barely remember how the metropolis functioned before it. So perhaps Chrissie got a southbound lift on the M1, got off at the Leicester Forest East, then hitched a lift along the M6 to Birmingham. From there she could try to grab a ride down the M5.

It was a laborious route, but if she was inexperienced, she might have taken it. Particularly the first lift, when, having snatched a bag, she was desperate to escape Leeds – she might have taken a car to anywhere.

Philip's mutterings about Emily Speakman had included references to a picnic, and a meadow with wild-flowers. That implied that the weather was good, or at least warm enough to sit outside. It also meant he must have had the opportunity to buy food for a picnic. Could he have planned to have one by himself?

Gillard was convinced that, buried somewhere within a half-hour's drive of that network, was the body of Chrissie Frost.

Chapter 33

That evening, Gillard prepared a slow-cooked casserole for Sam who was working a late shift. While he was waiting, he looked through the folder of newspaper cuttings about Philip's protest activities. There were sheaves of them, and photographs of him standing arm in arm with demonstrators in front of bulldozers. Trying to make sense of this, Gillard googled the obituaries of his uncle and found an interesting one in the *Daily Telegraph* which quoted one of his friends, Lord Kilpenning.

> From the mid-1980s, whereever homes were demolished to make way for office blocks or shopping centres – almost anywhere in the south of the country – Philip would be there, giving an interview to a journalist. While he never seemed to explicitly back the more extreme tactics of some protesters, he was able to explain their objectives and make them seem both reasonable and proportionate. The building companies hated him, especially as he seemed to have allies both in the House of Commons and in the Lords. By 2002, he seemed to be more of a green campaigner, fighting to save woodland from being bulldozed – in some cases, rather

ironically, for new homes. Usually, the protesters ended up losing. But not completely. Philip was occasionally able to broker a compromise in which a green area would be set aside near one of these new developments, to be enjoyed by residents in perpetuity. They were known as peace gardens, or more informally as 'Antrobus acres', though very few were as big as an acre. Allies of his in the Commons managed to get these acts of mitigation incorporated into what later became Section 106 of the Town and Country Planning Act 1990. It was a significant achievement.

Gillard soon found the peace gardens online, now known as 'urban peace gardens', run by a trust based in Battersea. Their website detailed each of the seven sites, all but two of which survived. The first seed of a clue was beginning to germinate in the detective's brain.

He had assumed that Philip Antrobus's seemingly random personal journey, from troubled rural childhood to wide-boy salesman, from sexual predator to atoning priest and then campaigning churchman had been driven purely by angst. But to Gillard, part of it now was looking more calculating. If he was right, the Rev Philip Antrobus had been a whole lot cleverer than he had assumed.

–

When Sam arrived home, her husband had not only filled the kitchen with the aroma of a delicious meal, but said he wanted to share a theory about the murder of Chrissie Frost. He poured her out a glass of wine, served up the food and said: 'I believe the Reverend Philip Antrobus incorporated the covering up of this murder into his later campaigning.'

'Tell me more,' she said, taking her first tasty mouthful of slow-cooked shin of beef in red wine and garlic.

He smiled. 'Philip's first great environmental battle wasn't about the demolition of houses to make way for offices. It was actually the Broxbourne Park development near Gloucester. It was the county's first out-of-town shopping centre, 130 acres near the M5. The land was originally greenbelt, some of it woodland.'

'I don't get what this has to do with the murder,' Sam said, sipping her wine.

'Bear with me,' Gillard said. 'Now imagine. Philip Antrobus in 1973 was a buccaneering salesman, used to seducing female hitchhikers with expense-account meals and hotel rooms. But this first week of July was particularly warm, in fact the only week of decent weather that month, according to the Met Office records. And he had suggested a picnic to the woman who innocently thumbed a lift with him. So they bought food together, and may well have had a perfectly innocent picnic in the flower meadows along the banks of Brock's Bourne, as the stream was known originally. It was only a 10-minute drive from the M5. Of course, that's not enough for Philip who, as we have learned, has to try it on with every girl he meets. We'll never know quite what happened, but my guess is Chrissie Frost rejected his advances and he raped and strangled her. There were woods nearby, and that is where he buried her body. It would have been light until ten o'clock at that time of year, so he had plenty of opportunity to see what he was doing until late in the evening.'

'And now they have put a shopping centre over it?'

'That's my guess. But it's a little more subtle than that. I have to make some more phone calls tomorrow to see if I'm right. If I am, I might be able to find out precisely where poor Chrissie is buried.'

Friday, 14 December

Detective Chief Inspector Craig Gillard spent most of the next day in a meeting with a senior lawyer from the Crown Prosecution Service and half a dozen other officers discussing the fraud in which his team had increasingly become bogged down.

The only relief came during a coffee break when he was able to check his phone, and found he had received an email from a Mrs Lakshmi Kendall in response to his advertisement in the *Times of India*. She confirmed that she had met Philip Antrobus in 1979 when he was in India, and they had met up again in Britain for a few months in the 1980s. Mrs Kendall said she lived in St John's Wood in London and had a grown-up family, but had had the advertisement drawn to her attention by a relative in Delhi. She invited Gillard to ring her for more information.

The fraud meeting dragged on until the late afternoon, and it was nearly 6 p.m. before Gillard had the opportunity to make the call. Fortunately, Mrs Kendall was in, and was happy to cooperate. 'Philip and I were an item for several months in India, and I met up with him again in Britain during the first season of his TV programme.' She had an almost regal tone, with a delightful lilt in her voice. Gillard could quite see how she would captivate anyone she talked to. 'But we were never married or engaged. It was a long-running joke that we had run away and got hitched, mainly to tease my parents,' she said.

Gillard referred to a historic case they were investigating but skated around the details. 'Do you know the addresses he lived at in the mid to late 1970s?' he asked.

Mrs Kendall thought she had travelled with him to Liverpool in the first months of his appointment to the diocese there in 1980. 'I don't have any exact addresses there, I'm afraid.'

Gillard left the crucial question until last. 'Did he ever discuss previous girlfriends with you?'

There was a long pause. 'Well, I don't recall exactly, but he did have a lot of emotional baggage. I think he had rather hurt somebody in the past, and felt guilty about it.'

'Do you remember the name?'

'I don't think so.'

'Could it have been someone called Emily? Emily Speakman?'

'Yes, now you come to mention it. Yes, he mentioned an Emily.'

'May I ask why it was that you broke up?'

There was a considerable pause. 'He was a troubled man, Detective Chief Inspector, he was in turmoil. I wanted to get married, actually, but he wasn't ready. We kept in contact for a long time, during his first months in Liverpool, when I think he was lonely. I was hoping for a change of heart, but by then he had a different passion. The Church. And very soon I met someone else. I often wonder what might have been. I was sorry to hear of his death. I don't know what crime you are investigating, but I think I can say without fear of contradiction that he was a good man.'

Gillard, not wanting to needlessly damage a cherished memory, did not contradict her. He thanked her and said goodbye.

–

The rather amateurish website of the Peace Gardens Trust showed its premises were a dilapidated office above a women's hair salon in Battersea, south-west London. Gillard's subsequent phone call led him to its single part-time employee, a young woman called Sue. 'There have been no new peace gardens for many years,' she explained. 'Though the trust fund hasn't been added to for many years, the income generated is sufficient to maintain the five gardens we still have.'

'I'd like to ask you about the very first garden, Brox-bourne Park,' he said.

'Long before my time, I'm afraid. The cuttings we have show just how contentious the whole business was. Reverend Antrobus was arrested, along with many others. But ultimately there was negotiation with the developers, who altered their plans to allow a garden area to be incorporated.'

'Who attended those meetings?'

'Well, Reverend Antrobus for sure. I have copies of the minutes somewhere.' He heard the metallic groan of a filing cabinet and the flapping of paper. 'Yes, he was accompanied by Frank Minting, one of our original trustees.'

'Is he still alive?'

'Oh yes. He's 92, but he still comes to our AGM.'

Gillard thanked her and called the number that Sue had given him. The phone rang and rang, and was eventually picked up by a man who answered by laboriously reading out the entire number. Frank Minting listened carefully while Gillard introduced himself and explained that he was chasing up leads in the unsolved disappearance of a young woman. 'Good heavens,' Minting replied. He spoke slowly, but his mind was sharp and so was his recollection of that very first meeting with developers.

'They were quite insistent that their plan would go through unchanged. They wanted a two-storey shopping centre, with a continuous roof. Philip had brought along an alternative design, in which the atrium, where the escalators were to go, was actually open to the sky and had a small peace garden in the centre. Their architect rather liked the idea, and persuaded the developer that it could actually save some money too.'

'How big was the peace garden?'

'Well, Philip's original idea was that it would be a 40-yard-diameter circle. In the end, it was 18 yards, I think, and square. But the original trees, silver birch mainly, were undisturbed. That, I think, was Philip's biggest point of principle, to preserve a little slice of undisturbed country-side.'

'Thank you, that's extremely helpful. I think I shall go and take a look myself.'

'I'm delighted to be of assistance,' Minting said. 'But I can't see how all this can help you very much. Did this young lady disappear while shopping?'

'No. As far as we are aware, she was having a picnic.'

Monday, 17 December

The Broxbourne Park shopping centre, a few miles south-east of Gloucester, had seen better days. The vertical concrete slabs which marked the entrance from a windswept car park were originally seen as futuristic architecture but would now be seen as brutalist. Water stains and pockmarks marred the originally smooth surface, and the offices above sported a continuous stripe of rusting metal windows sandwiched between pale-blue panelling. Passing through the sliding doors, Gillard let himself be carried along in a stream of Christmas shoppers. He made his way along the main thoroughfare flanked by the usual high street retailing names, and spotted Santa's grotto next to a branch of JD Sports. Behind the grotto, and its queue of excited children, was a patch of rather tired-looking greenery, with three or four silver birches decked with flashing lights. Two wooden benches and a narrow winding bark-lined trail marked out the full extent of Philip Antrobus's vision: a garden for peace and reflection in the midst of consumer frenzy.

It didn't seem very peaceful.

Gillard made his way along the path and sat on one of the benches. He looked up at the sky, a framed square of grey, and then down at his feet. He hoped he was right about this. There were originally seven peace gardens, but Gillard was convinced it had to be the first one. The idea of a peace garden was so different from Philip Antrobus's earlier homeless campaigning that something must have inspired him to take on the might of developers.

Fear.

Somewhere under here, he was convinced, lay the body of Chrissie Frost. Philip Antrobus had moved heaven and earth to avoid the woodland resting place where he'd hastily buried her violated body being disturbed by construction work. Not out of respect for the dead, of course, but to cover up his crime. He must have been terrified when he heard of plans for the Broxbourne Park shopping centre, and the digging that would accompany it.

The music moved on to the familiar refrain of Slade's 'Merry Xmas Everybody'. So much had happened since 1973 when Chrissie died. But so much, like the music and the undiscovered killing, remained the same.

Chapter 34

Talantire slid out of the office early and spent a rare Monday evening with her partner Jon sitting staring at some trashy TV panel game. She had spent the entire day unsuccessfully trying to crack the sisters' alibi, the culmination of a series of interviews over the last few days in which she alternately tackled Barbara Antrobus, with a beefy DC called John Cox in attendance, and Trish Gibson. You couldn't slide a fingernail between the two women's accounts. Feeling dispirited, she just needed a few hours to decompress from this seemingly insoluble hit-and-run case. Watching some mindless drivel was perfect. She was resting with her socked feet across Jon's lap and the remains of a glass of Sauvignon Blanc warming between her fingers. She smiled to herself, thinking this cocoon of affection with her man was the perfect way to spend the dog-end of a tough day.

Turning to Jon, she saw he was asleep with his mouth hanging open, a tendril of suspended spittle vibrating gently with his breath.

A capsule of cosiness for one, then, not two.

She shook herself out of her stupor and managed to extricate her limbs without waking him. She lowered the sound on the TV, drained the dregs of her wine and began to think once again about the other end of the case. Her attempts to track down the victim of the hit-and-run had run into the sand once she enlarged her search beyond the UK. She had already spent several fruitless afternoons chasing round and round the same pieces of evidence, getting nowhere.

Going upstairs to the den, she logged on to the Police National Computer. She had been hoping for some results from the stable isotope tests. She had been waiting weeks but there was nothing yet. However, one other result had dropped into her inbox, unexpectedly quickly: the familial DNA test on the victim of the hit-and-run.

Hands shaking, she clicked on the PDF and opened it, rereading it again and again, hoping for a different conclusion to the one written in black and white in front of her. The test showed no familial DNA relationship between the hit-and-run victim and the sisters of Howard Gibson. The dead man wasn't Howard Gibson, nor a relative of his.

The devastating conclusion sent Talantire back to the fridge where she found herself refilling her wine glass to the brim.

After Gillard mentioned Howard Gibson as the only missing person in his aunts' life, the idea that Trish had run down her own ex-husband had been quite enticing. In recent days, with no other leads emerging, Talantire had increasingly convinced herself it must be true. It would take care of motive, and it would explain why the victim's dabs were in the vehicle as well as spread all over the front. It ticked all the boxes except one.

Truth.

It wasn't true. Incontestable forensics declared it couldn't be.

She took a gulp of wine and leaned back against the fridge door. For the first time in her career, she felt mocked by a corpse. Mr Nobody had retained his anonymity. Nobody knew who he was. It wasn't much consolation to know a little about who he wasn't.

Chapter 35

Someone's ears must have been burning in Robert Gordon University in Scotland. The long-awaited stable isotope tests arrived by email first thing next morning while Talantire was sitting eating a yoghurt at her desk at the station.

The report was dense, and it took Talantire a while to assemble the life story hiding behind the scientific terminology and caveats. The victim of the hit-and-run was certainly a seasoned traveller. He had recently spent several weeks in Thailand, according to his hair and nails, as well as periods earlier in his life in London. His teeth and bones, however, showed that he had spent most of his life in and around Adelaide in Australia. There were extraordinary revelations: one isotope of carbon in his bones was unique to the geology of a particular oil and gas field off the coast of north-west Australia called Gorgon, although there were isotope traces from other oilfields too, which fitted with the contaminants found in his blood. Talantire was stunned at the level of detail, and before she had finished her breakfast, she was following it up. As Dr Wellesley had suspected, the victim was almost certainly an oil worker, and a workplace link to Howard Gibson seemed the most obvious connection to pursue.

Perhaps there were quicker checks that could be done. She found the Australian Federal Police missing persons website and hit an immediate roadblock. It only allowed searches by the name of the missing person, the one piece of information that she was trying to get.

She switched to Facebook. She had previously searched for 'missing oil worker' and found too many to follow up, often relating to industrial accidents. But this time she added the word 'Australian' and found three profiles, one of which immediately stood out. Mark Hartley was the right age – 62 – and from Adelaide. The Facebook page had been set up by his two children, who had helpfully listed a series of known travels by their father after his divorce last year. It included several pictures, most of which could easily have graced the front of a cruise brochure: a pleasant, youthful, fit and outdoorsy visage with an easy smile and laughter lines. From the comments of his kids and their friends, they were very optimistic that he would turn up, which is why the police seemed not to be interested as yet. As the comments below the pictures conceded, Hartley had been through a rough time after the end of the marriage, and was probably just looking for a bit of time on his own.

Naturally, they thought he was alive.

Talantire was convinced he was dead. She was pretty sure that this apparently well liked, generous and outgoing man, who looked like he could have lived to 100, had been mown down deliberately and was now lying without a face in the chiller cabinet at Royal Devon and Exeter Hospital.

What a waste of a life.

She passed the news to DCS Parker, who congratulated her on the breakthrough. With his permission, she made email contact with the police in Adelaide. She wanted three things from them urgently: a DNA sample, credit card records and a phone trace on his mobile.

Finally, she allowed herself to celebrate. It was only a few minutes after ten in the morning, and in less than 90 minutes she had really cracked the case. Who to share the news with? Charmaine Stafford was on maternity leave, but had begged Talantire to keep her in the loop on this case. She drove round to her home and blurted it out the moment she opened the door.

'That's fantastic,' Stafford said, hugging her. 'It's amazing what secrets scientists can dig out of the human body.'

'All I need to do now is prove that he was in Barnstaple,' Talantire replied, once she was sitting down with a coffee, amid a sea of baby clothes. 'And then figure out why somebody needed him dead.'

–

Details of Mark Hartley's credit card usage arrived promptly that afternoon, showing that he had indeed come to London from Bangkok, arriving at Heathrow Airport the morning before the hit-and-run. He had bought a ticket from London Paddington to Barnstaple, which arrived at 2.33 p.m. She propped up printouts of Hartley's face next to the computer screen, again pulled up the Barnstaple railway station CCTV footage, and homed in on the arrival time.

She spotted him immediately, though he was wasn't wearing the outdoorsy clothing he was found in. He had a formal charcoal-grey overcoat and was pulling a wheeled grey suitcase. There were three CCTV cameras: two on the platform, and one covering the entrance to the car park. Hartley walked into and out of view without meeting anyone. He yawned several times, and just as he was stepping out of view the final time, put his mobile to his ear. The delay was so slight between retrieving the phone from his pocket and putting it to his ear that Talantire assumed he couldn't be making a call. Someone was calling him. Whoever that was almost certainly knew he had arrived, or was due to. That was a vital phone call. Talantire had to know who had made it.

First thing next day she found out. It wasn't entirely a surprise.

Chapter 36

It was 5.45 a.m. when Talantire reached across to the bedside table and picked up her phone to silence the soft trilling. When she saw who the email was from, she was instantly wide awake. Jon groaned in his sleep and turned over as she padded out to the en suite to read the message. Adelaide Police had forwarded the phone trace data from Australia's telecoms firm Telstra, who had requested and finally received the UK portion from their roaming partner, Vodafone. It was worth the wait.

The call to Hartley's mobile was from a landline in Barnstaple. One registered in the name of Mrs Patricia Gibson.

Talantire dressed at furious speed, and risked a very early call to a new mother. It might wake the baby, but she was sure Charmaine Stafford would want to be in on this. The detective sergeant had been pleading the previous day about wanting to have a day a week away from maternity leave, and this would be a good route back into the case for her. Talantire would pick her up on the way to visit Mrs Gibson.

There had been a good five minutes of small talk after the welcome and the greeting of cats. Only then when Talantire and Stafford were sitting with Trish at the dining table did the serious questioning begin. 'Mrs Gibson, we have established the identity of the man run down by your sister's car,' the DI said.

'Oh yes?' Trish stroked a purring tortoiseshell cat on her lap.

'Does the name Mark Hartley mean anything to you?' Talantire asked.

'No, I can't say that it does. Why should it?'

'Where were you at 2.37 p.m. on the day before the hit–and–run?'

'That would be the Tuesday,' Stafford added.

'At home, I suppose.'

'Did you ring this number?' Talantire said, passing across a piece of paper.

'I don't think so.'

'Was someone staying with you?'

'No. It was just me.'

'Someone used your landline to ring Mr Hartley at 2.37 p.m. on that Tuesday. We have that confirmation from his phone.'

Her face twitched, and her mouth tightened. 'I really can't explain that.'

'There's a lot to explain, Mrs Gibson.'

'Then I suppose I'd better get a solicitor.'

'I think that would be a good idea, because I'm going to ask these questions again at the police station. With your permission, I'm going to take your mobile phone and any computers you have.'

'I'm sorry but you don't have my permission.'

'We can easily get a warrant,' Talantire said.

'You better had, then.' Trish smiled tightly. 'In the meantime, perhaps I can show you out?'

–

It was just before noon when Gillard was pulled out of a meeting on the fraud case to take an apparently urgent call. 'Who is it from?' he asked the female PC who had interrupted.

'She says she's your aunt,' she said.

He rolled his eyes. Another call from Trish. 'I'll call her back.'

'She said "Don't let him say he will call me back because he won't reach me." She was most insistent, and said it's an emergency.' A ripple of laughter ran around the room.

'All right,' Gillard sighed as he stood up and excused himself. There were bemused looks from around the table, especially from the money-laundering specialist from City of London Police and a detective chief superintendent from the National Crime Agency who had travelled down to Guildford for the meeting, and who were halfway through their PowerPoint presentation. Just as he was closing the door behind him, one of the officers whispered: 'Say hello to Auntie from me.'

Gillard stormed up to the receiver and immediately launched in: 'Look, Trish, I've told you not call me at work. I've just been called out of an important meeting and made to look like an idiot.'

He softened a little on hearing the tears at the other end of the line. 'Craig, I didn't know who else to ring. They're telling me that this man who was run down had

264

been rung from my telephone.' Gillard waited while Trish tearfully explained what the accusations were.

'So are you saying that you didn't make that call?' He couldn't make out her reply as her voice was so choked with tears. 'Look, have you rung Barbara's solicitor whose number I gave you?' It took a few minutes to establish that, no, she hadn't.

'Craig, would you ring him for me?'

'I'm in a meeting.' Gillard's voice was steely. 'Look, Trish, it's very simple. He's a very nice man with a good reputation and he will listen to everything you say. I will ring you this evening, I promise.'

'All right, Craig, dear. Don't you worry about your poor old aunt. I'll stay out of your hair. No need to come and visit me in prison.'

'For Christ's sake, Trish, you're going to be questioned, that's all.' It took a further five minutes of reassurances before he could hang up and return to the meeting.

'Finished your personal phone calls for the day?' asked the DCS from the NCA, to a smirking audience.

'My apologies, everyone,' Gillard said, putting on a brave smile to cover the seething anger inside.

–

The warrant was issued within two hours, and Talantire and Stafford raced up to Trish's home in an unmarked car, followed by PCs Kite and Willow in a patrol car with the hydraulic door ram. The detective was kicking herself for not requesting a warrant in advance of the first meeting. Now she expected this devious old woman would be disposing of every incriminating detail that she could. She had no idea whether Trish Gibson was forensically aware, but she didn't want to take any chances.

However, even before she had reached the porch, it was clear that events had moved on. A note, signed by neighbours, said that Mrs Gibson had been taken to North Devon Hospital accident and emergency. Talantire rang this news into the incident room, and had the note checked out to confirm it was genuine. Her suspect was currently in intensive care with breathing difficulties and heart arrhythmia.

'Slippery bitch,' Talantire breathed. 'She's done it deliberately.'

'That's a bit harsh,' Stafford said. 'We've piled a load of stress on her. She's only a tiny little thing.'

'Detective Sergeant, never forget that the trickiest things can come in small packages.'

Willow arrived shouldering a ram, which looked a bit like a very large bright red spade handle. 'Can I use this yet, ma'am?' He was like an overgrown boy with a new toy.

'Not yet. Let's check next door to see if they have a key before we smash the place up, eh?'

Thursday, 20 December

It was the week before Christmas, but in Craig Gillard's car tearing down a rain-swept M3 towards Devon, there was no festive spirit. Barbara's terse text an hour ago had seen to that. Trish was in intensive care after collapsing at home. There seemed no alternative to making the 380-mile round trip from Surrey yet again.

'Poor Trish,' said Sam.

'Poor us, you mean, at her beck and call.' Gillard raced past a line of trucks. The speedo briefly flicked up to 95, the wipers at maximum to handle the blinding spray.

Sam eyed him dubiously. 'Craig, she might be dying.'

'No such luck, I'm sure.'

'Can you imagine how you would feel if she died and you never got to see her again?'

'Ecstatic.' Seeing Sam's reproachful stare, he softened. 'Look, I'm sure she'll be fine. I'll get us there as soon as I can.' He shook his head. 'Of course it would have helped if I'd managed to get hold of Barbara to see if it really is serious or just another chapter in the Trish Gibson encyclopaedia of emotional blackmail.'

'I take it Trish isn't answering her own phone?' Sam asked.

Gillard shook his head. 'It certainly explains why after peppering me with calls yesterday, she seemed to be playing hard to get today.'

'What about Talantire? She could tell you what's happening.'

He laughed bitterly. 'I've left five messages, but she isn't responding and the desk line for the custody sergeant just rings and rings. I don't blame her. The last thing you want when you're running an investigation is to have a more senior officer breathing down your neck who just happens to be related to your suspect.'

'But you've not overstepped the mark, have you?'

'No, I've been careful not to, but then Trish has been bombarding me with phone calls at work, so I felt that I had to do something.'

'So not just the big meeting—'

'That was the most embarrassing, but there's been a lot more. Trish seems to think I can wave a magic wand and make all this go away.'

The hands-free phone rang and Gillard answered. Sam could hear it was Barbara, and she sounded anxious. 'Where are you, Barbara?' he asked.

'Sitting outside intensive care. There's been plenty of activity, but nobody is telling me anything.'

'Any idea what's wrong with her?'

'She's had some kind of seizure and breathing difficulties.'

'When was this, Barbara?'

'Yesterday afternoon, apparently.'

'That must have been soon after I took her call at work,' Gillard said to Sam.

'I texted you as soon as I got the message,' Barbara said. 'But the answering machine's been on the blink, and you know what mobile coverage is like at the farm. I didn't know until this afternoon.'

'I'm not blaming you, Barbara, really.'

'Craig, I really don't think she's malingering this time,' Barbara said, as if reading Gillard's mind. 'She managed to ring 999 before collapsing.' She gave them the details of the hospital, and said she would remain until they arrived. 'And Happy Christmas, by the way,' she barked, before hanging up.

Gillard shook his head and accelerated. They were still three hours away.

'It must be the stress that brought it on,' Sam said.

'Never underestimate my Auntie Trish,' Gillard said. 'This is a very convenient way for her to postpone any awkward conversations with DI Talantire.'

'You're so horrible to say that,' Sam said. 'Poor Trish just lost her brother a few weeks ago, after terrible revelations about his past, and she's probably worried about her sister and this conviction. No wonder she can't cope any more.'

Gillard shrugged. 'That's what she wants us to believe. She's an expert manipulator, she always has been. I know.'

'You got the same blood in your veins, Craig.'

'Don't I know it? It's giving me sleepless nights.'

–

It was early evening when they got to the hospital, and they found Barbara sitting with Peter in a crowded waiting room, holding hands. Noticing Sam's stare, Barbara let go of the young man. Gillard gave his aunt a perfunctory embrace and asked: 'Any news?'

'She's conscious, but they are going to keep her in for a second night. I saw her briefly but she's asleep again now. I don't think they'll let anyone else disturb her.'

They all sat together for an hour until Barbara made her excuses. 'Got to get back to the farm,' she said. 'We got an Airbnb guest coming this evening, and I've got to get the ewes in. Here, take Trish's keys. I'm sure she won't mind if you help yourself to the spare room and whatever's in the fridge.'

It was 11.40 p.m. when Craig and Sam arrived at the house. There were several scraps of notes on the door, including one from the police. The door had not been forced, and Gillard was able to unlock it. It certainly didn't look like a full police search had taken place; in fact, it would have been hard to guess the place been turned over at all except for the official notice.

Exhausted after the long journey, Sam made her way up to the by-now familiar guest room. Gillard, however, seemed to be thinking about the décor. She saw him staring at the alcove by the stairs, which showed all the pictures of Howie and his family in Thailand.

'What were you doing?' she asked after he'd finally come to bed an hour later.

'Just a theory I'm working on.' While she waited for clarification, the landline rang downstairs. Gillard went down to answer it.

'Craig, it's Barbara, we've got another wolf attack. I need your help, right now.' She hung up.

Gillard called up to Sam: 'Barbara needs help. It's another dog attack. I'll be back as soon as I can.' He glanced at the clock. A quarter to one in the morning.

'You're not going without me,' Sam said, dressing rapidly. 'I can speak to Barbara on the mobile while you drive.'

It was a cold moonlit night as they drove at speed up from Barnstaple past Paracombe to Hollow Coombe farm. The roads were deserted. Sam managed to get more details of what had happened. Barbara's dogs had been going berserk in the kitchen, and Peter had gone up on the quad bike to check the barn where the ewes were now corralled at night. Something had disturbed them and there had been panic. At least one was dead. Several others had managed to escape the barn and then, in their terror, had got stuck in some wire fencing and would probably be lame. Barbara said she had taken a shotgun and tried to head off the creature at the western edge of the farm where Gillard had seen the animal make its escape last time. She could no longer see it.

'Craig,' Sam said, putting the phone down for a moment. 'Barbara says there's a back lane half a mile before the farm entrance, by a bench on the left-hand side. She says if you take that, it brings you up to the western boundary. We could head it off.'

'I remember it,' said Gillard, and hit the accelerator. He saw the bench in the full beam of his headlights and swung a sharp left onto a narrow lane between high-hedged banks. The dense oak trees which shrouded the lane and joined above made it seem like a ghostly primeval tunnel.

'There's someone here,' said Sam, pointing to a faint glow lighting the underside of trees far ahead. 'Could that be Peter's quad bike?'

'No, I don't think so. There's no gate out of the farm up here, so he couldn't have got onto the road.'

Round the next bend they saw a vehicle waiting in a passing place for them to come past. It was an ancient Land Rover. 'Stop and ask the driver, Craig. He's bound to have seen something.'

'No.' He drove straight past. 'We don't want to arouse his suspicions yet.' He looked in the rear-view mirror and saw the Land Rover pulling away. Gillard stopped the car and waited for half a minute, then carefully reversed back to the passing place, the only point at which a three-point turn could be made. He opened the window, sniffed and nodded, then turned the car round. 'Dirty old diesel,' he said, closing the window. He switched off the headlights and followed the Land Rover slowly, using only the faint glow of its rear lights and the pools of moonlight piercing the canopy of trees to guide him. At the junction, Gillard held back amid the last of the high hedges, watching as the Land Rover turned right towards Barnstaple.

'What are you waiting for?' Sam asked.

'That's a distinctive vehicle. I don't need to be right on its tail at this time in the morning. He's going to lead me back to where he came from and that's how we're going to catch him. Give Barbara a quick ring and ask if the dog – sorry, wolf – is still about on the farm.'

Sam did so. Barbara was impatient for Gillard to arrive, but did admit that she hadn't seen the wolf for the last ten minutes. 'We're following a Land Rover,' Sam told her. 'Craig thinks it may be connected.'

Sam had to hold the phone away for the torrent of invective that Barbara unleashed into her ear. 'She asks what makes you think this vehicle has anything to do with it?'

'I'll tell her later,' Gillard said. 'Just hang up.'

Sam said goodbye and ended the call. 'So what is it, then, Craig?'

'Last time I chased the dog, on foot during the storm, I smelled diesel fumes when I got onto the lane, just about where that passing place was. There's nothing quite like an old Land Rover to spew clouds of diesel. I didn't want to tell Barbara about it because she's convinced this is a wolf, but I had a feeling that this is about some kind of old grudge, going back decades.'

'Someone with a grudge against Barbara? Deliberately releasing a dog to attack her sheep?'

'Yes. There's a lot I don't know about her past.' He reached to the right underneath the ignition and fiddled with something. 'Right, that should do it.'

'What are you doing?' Sam asked.

'Got a little switch to shut off one headlamp. It's useful when doing night-time tailing, because if you've started by being followed by a normally lit vehicle, if you see one with just one headlamp and sidelights, you'll think it's a different car. And you certainly won't think the police are using an illegally lit vehicle.'

'Clever.'

'Yes, though it's something to be used sparingly.' He released the brake and set off, turning right, the way the Land Rover had gone.

It took a few minutes to catch up with the distinctive old vehicle, which was doing a steady 40 miles an hour. Craig hung back, leaving the Land Rover beyond the reach of his one dipped headlamp. Just before the town sign, the vehicle ahead swung left into a very narrow track. 'Quick, he just turned,' Sam exclaimed.

Gillard drove straight past. 'It's all right, we'll come back on foot.' He pulled the car into a residential street a few hundred yards further on. They pulled on thick jackets and woolly hats, while Gillard took a small knapsack from the boot of the car. They made their way back along the deserted and unlit road. Gillard used a torch, which he carefully shrouded through gloved fingers to keep the beam narrow and pointing to the ground. They found the turn-off which the Land Rover had taken and followed the rutted, unmade road, towards the silhouettes of smallholdings and sheds. Barking could be heard a hundred yards ahead, amid the faint red glow of vehicle rear lights. Stealthily they approached still nearer, until they were just a few yards behind the Land Rover. The barking indicated that the driver was somewhere inside the smallholding. Gillard memorized the registration number and peered into the cage in the back of the vehicle, whose metal gate was hanging open. There was a metallic dog bowl with a little water in it. He wiped a tissue around the edge of the bowl and, carefully folding it inwards, stuffed it in a plastic bag in his pocket for safekeeping.

He then retrieved a long-lens camera from the knapsack, and a flash unit. He indicated Sam should move back along the lane, but he crouched down to ready himself for the return of the driver whose footsteps he could hear. The man, silhouetted in his cloth cap and waxed jacket, was making his way through the gate when Gillard took the photo. The flash was dazzling for a second. Gillard ran off back down the lane, soon catching up with Sam as they sprinted back to the car.

'That was exciting,' Sam said as they drove off.

'I saw a sign on the gate that said Low Meadow Yard. Talantire should be able to trace him easily enough if any DNA test from the dead sheep matches the dog saliva on the water bowl.'

'They won't be able to ignore the attacks on the sheep any more, will they?' Sam asked.

'Not so easily, but of course my connection to Barbara inevitably casts doubt on my impartiality. That's bound to be an issue. Still, when they find the dog, they can do their own DNA tests.' When they pulled up outside Trish's house, Gillard got the camera out of the knapsack and turned it on. He looked into the viewing screen, and showed Sam. It was a good picture of the cloth-capped man, a grizzled, weather-beaten fellow in his late 60s or early 70s.

'No one I know,' Sam said.

'I'll bet Barbara knows who he is,' Gillard said. 'I'd put money on it.'

Chapter 37

They were both up before seven the next morning, and ate a quick slice of toast and marmalade on the go. The plan was to head straight back to the hospital to see how Trish was. While Sam got into the car, Gillard rummaged in the toolbox in the boot and pulled out a sledgehammer and a chisel.

'What do you need those for?' she asked.

'Not sure yet.' He turned to look at the house, squatted down and peered at the pebble-dashed wall on the rear extension.

'What is it, Craig?' Sam asked, now getting out of the car.

He didn't reply, but stood and walked to the back of the single-storey add-on, then round into the small back garden. When he emerged again a couple of minutes later, he was shaking his head in puzzlement. 'As I thought, that really is very strange.'

'Are you going to let me in on it?'

'Sorry. See this back extension? It's not big, but there doesn't appear to be any way into it. I had expected there to be a utility room entrance, something like that, or at least a back door which shows it is being used for storage.'

'Why are you so bothered about the design of Trish's house? Shouldn't we be at the hospital where she might be fighting for her life?'

'Hardly,' he said. 'You know, I remembered from years ago there being a downstairs toilet.'

'But there is one, next to the kitchen.'

'Yes, but that's modern and tiny. I may have only been young, but I remember it had a bath in it.'

Sam began to laugh. 'People make changes to their homes. It's normal.'

Gillard knelt down again by the side wall of the house. 'The rendering is raised and flaky here,' he said. He got out a pen knife and pressed it into the brittle coating. A coin-sized lump fell off, revealing the brickwork beneath.

'I don't think Trish is going to be very happy about you burrowing into the side of the house,' Sam said.

'You can say that again,' Gillard replied. He tapped at a join between two bricks, a foot above the ground, where a circular mark was revealed in the mortar. 'A wastewater pipe has been sawn off here. It used to drain into this manhole,' he said, tapping a metal plate in the concrete at his feet. 'I'm sure there's been a soil pipe too, if I was to chisel off enough of the rendering to find it.'

'What's all this about, Craig?'

He stood and looked at Sam. 'I can't work out why someone would take out a reasonable-size ground-floor bathroom, and then brick in the whole area. It's dead space. If you go inside the house, that wall by the side of the stairs, where all the pictures of Howie and his family are hanging, is over what I think would have been the doorway into this bathroom.'

'The simplest way to find out is to ask her, surely?'

'I did. And she insists the house was like this when she moved in back in the 1970s.'

'Couldn't she be right?'

'What about the bath I remember having here?'

Sam shook her head. 'Craig, you're beginning to sound a little bit like your uncle Philip. None of this matters.'

'Oh yes it does,' Craig said as he got back into the car and started the engine. 'More than you can possibly imagine.'

–

Once they were at the hospital, they made their way to the intensive care unit. They recognized several of the people they had seen yesterday, still waiting for news of loved ones. Not the greatest way to spend the week before Christmas. Gillard managed to find a senior nurse who was able to brief them on Trish's condition.

'She's very weak, and rather woozy. She's breathing better now, and the anxiety attacks have eased. It's possible she could be well enough to leave later today, but we can't really discharge her without someone to look after her until social services can assess her ability to look after herself. Are you immediate family?'

Gillard explained who he was and suggested that Barbara might be able to arrange for care as she lived locally. The nurse nodded.

He turned to Sam, who was on her mobile. She looked at him and mouthed the word Barbara, giving an exaggerated look of horror to indicate his aunt's mood. Gillard wasn't surprised that she was angry, given that neither he nor Sam had come to the farm since last night as she had asked. He hoped that when the police investigated the evidence he had accumulated, this whole idea of the wolf would finally be put to bed. Still, he was too busy to deal with it now. He turned back to the nurse.

'Have the police been here?' Gillard asked.

She gave him a sharp look. 'I believe so. The consultant was quite emphatic that she is in no condition to be interviewed.'

'But as her nephew, perhaps I could speak to her?'

The nurse said she would check. Gillard went to the end of the corridor where he could get a signal, and rang DI Jan Talantire. For once, she picked up immediately.

'I believe you've been trying to interview my aunt, Trish Gibson?'

'That's right. Don't ask me to give you any details, because I won't. I think you know that.'

'That's not why I'm ringing. I'm at the hospital, and as a member of the family will be the only person allowed to speak to her. Is there anything you'd like me to ask her?'

'I think it can wait until she's better,' Talantire responded.

'Trish said that you have identified the victim of the hit-and-run, and you claim she had been in contact with him.'

'I've told you before that you won't get a single detail out of me.'

'Okay. That's fine. I thought I'd give it a try but I'm sorry for treading on your toes.' He thanked her and cut the call.

The nurse returned and said that he could see his aunt for a short time. Craig and Sam were shown into the shared room which Trish was in. She looked tiny and pale, hooked up to various drips and machines. She managed a weak smile, but her voice was too soft to be heard easily and she had to repeat her question a couple of times.

'Are the police out there?' she wheezed.

'No. I've spoken to Talantire. They're happy to wait until you're better.'

'I can't catch my breath,' she wheezed. 'I may have pneumonia.'

'Really? That's not what the nurse said.'

'I can feel fluid, dear.'

Gillard shook his head. 'You're a very wily customer, Trish. But once the police start going through your mobile phone and computer, they will figure out what you were doing.'

Trish started to laugh, which turn into an extended coughing fit. 'They haven't got them,' she eventually managed.

'They had a warrant, and searched the place.' He brought out the police notice of entry which had been posted through the door of her home.

She shook her head. 'I already got rid of them. Before the police arrived.'

Gillard folded his arms. 'They can still find out, it just takes a bit longer. What is all this about, Trish?'

Her eyes began to water. 'It's about Howie. I miss him so much. I relied on him for everything, and couldn't bear it when he left me all alone.'

'You've got his family coming to see you,' Sam said. 'Howie and his wife and lots of his kids will be here within a few days, if you're well enough to receive them. You just have to be well enough to enjoy it.'

Trish reached out for Sam's hand, and stroked it affectionately. 'You are lovely, Sam. I'm sorry I doubted you about Podge. He really was a cantankerous old devil. You probably had no choice but to push him over.'

'But I didn't push him over,' Sam retorted. 'He must have fallen while I was squeezing out of the door.'

Gillard stroked his wife's wrist, a signal not to let matters get out of hand.

'Whatever you say,' Trish said. 'None of it will matter for me. I'll be gone soon, when the Big C comes back for me. And Barbara will lose the farm. We're all done for.'

'Don't be so melodramatic,' Gillard said gently. 'You'll live for years yet.'

A nurse came in and asked them to leave, as the consultant had to do some tests. 'You can come back this afternoon, after three, if you want,' she said brightly, and then went back to the nurse's station.

Sam left immediately, but Gillard remained behind to kiss his aunt goodbye. When he emerged a few minutes later, Sam saw that his face was grim.

'Did something just happen?'

'Yes. I asked Trish whether she or Barbara was driving the car, and she just muttered that "some secrets are best kept". I challenged her on it but instead she switched to a more personal subject.' He looked away, a crease of pain between his brows.

'Craig, what did she tell you?'

He looked down. 'Those photographs on Philip's laptop. I had recognized Barbara as one of the victims, and guessed that the abuser was Jacob, her own father. Barbara knew, and so did Trish, and when they looked at me in the caravan, they were assessing how much I had recognized.'

Sam looked at him. His eyes were closed in anguish.

'What I didn't know, and what Trish has just told me, is that the other girl is my own mother, aged thirteen. I hadn't recognized her.'

'Oh, Craig, that's awful.'

He nodded, mutely, and put a hand across his face. 'She never said a word. Not to any of us. She carried that secret to her death.'

'God, what a family,' Sam breathed, as she embraced her husband. 'Trish really knows how to inflict pain, doesn't she?'

Gillard held her close, rubbed her back and then sighed. 'Well, I've got some errands to run. I'd better go and see Barbara at some stage, but before that I'm going to take the opportunity to look through Trish's paperwork.'

'You can't just carry on as normal, can you, after that?' Sam was incredulous.

'Do I have a choice?'

'Why don't you come with me to town? We could do some pre-Christmas retail therapy, have a meal out, or even just a coffee. It may be crazy busy in town, but it will be sanity compared with this.'

'No, Sam, I've got lots of things to do. I've got to nip down to see Talantire too, and check in with the office about the fraud case.' He turned his back and started flicking through his phone.

Sam watched him for a few moments and then gave up. 'Okay, do what you want. But I'm going out. I certainly need a break, even if you don't. I need to take my mind off things.'

'Okay.' He didn't even look up.

'Bye, Craig.' She had her coat on and was waiting by the door. She got barely a grunt of acknowledgement, so she finally stepped out into the curtain of rain and slammed the door behind her.

-

Sam was tired and footsore after three hours' shopping, but despite the rain and the slog uphill from the town centre with heavy bags, was now in a better mood. Trish's house was in darkness. That meant Craig wasn't back yet. She wondered why he hadn't rung her, and on checking, saw her phone was out of juice. Fortunately, there was a charger upstairs. She stood under a street lamp as she fumbled in her bag for the spare key Craig had given her. However, when she got to the front door, she saw a note from Craig asking her to ring him, and not to go inside. She dumped her bags on the doorstep and peered through the reeded glass of the front door, but in the absence of light could make out nothing. Why had he given her a key if he hadn't wanted her to go inside? In fact, with a flat mobile phone it was obvious that the only way to ring him was to get inside, where there was a landline.

She'd become increasingly exasperated by the odd and secretive behaviour of her husband. She was thoroughly fed up with his lunatic family, and just an hour or two of Christmas shopping been a marvellous tonic from the weirdness that she had experienced with Trish and Barbara. She certainly wasn't going to wait here on a rain-swept front doorstep. She fitted the key, let herself in and brought in her bags. She used her elbow to flick on the light switch, but was so surprised by what she saw that she gave a gasp of fright and dropped her shopping.

-

The wall adjacent to the staircase, an alcove which had held Trish's gallery of photographs of Howie and his family, had been smashed right through at head height. A chair-sized section of brickwork was missing and broken, much of it lying on a polythene sheet right next to the stairs. There was dust on many of the surfaces, and a collection of tools lying around. And above all there was a smell of decay. Like bad drains, but worse.

This must be why Craig had asked her not to come in, because of all the dust and rubble. Sam shook her head in amazement. Craig must have done this. After all, those were his tools, including the sledgehammer, lying with the rubble. He had just made a colossal mess, and there would be grit and dirt on all of Auntie Trish's favourite doilies and cosies throughout this rather prissily furnished house. Sam's first inclination was to go upstairs and plug in her charger, but she couldn't walk past without peering through the hole that her husband had made. To see through, she needed to balance carefully on one of the larger pieces of removed brickwork that lay on the polythene. Finally, she rested her chin on the edge of the gap, and peered into the gloom beyond.

What she saw there made her scream in shock and run out of the house.

Chapter 38

Gillard's calls to DI Talantire had gone to voicemail every time, but what he had to tell her was too important to be left as a message. So he had driven at speed down to the Barnstaple police headquarters, hoping to catch her or a senior colleague. He was in luck. After a brief conversation with the desk sergeant, Gillard was shown into Talantire's office. Five minutes later, he was following a blue-lighted patrol car speeding back to Trish's home. His aunt was still in hospital and could be contacted later, but the person he was most worried about was Sam, whose phone number had registered as unavailable when he tried to call it earlier. He just hoped she'd got his message.

When he saw her standing on the doorstep, he hoped that he was right. But after he had parked and raced up the path, the expression on her face told him otherwise. She was shaking. 'My phone was dead, that's why I couldn't call you.'

'I hoped that you wouldn't go inside,' Gillard said. 'But I can see that you have.'

'I now realize what you were getting at when you looked around the rear extension. All this talk about bathrooms.'

Talantire and two uniformed officers had made their way past and into the house, and Gillard watched as the detective stood on the rubble to peer through the hole he had made in the wall. When Gillard had first taken his hammer to the wall, he was far from certain what he would find. But the sealed-off bathroom soon gave up its secrets. The bath was there, just as Gillard had remembered it, next to the left-hand wall. It was filled up to the brim with what looked like concrete, and protruding from one end was a football-sized lump, its concrete shell cracked.

From within peered the eye socket of a skull.

This, Gillard was certain, was the body of Howie Gibson.

–

Talantire stood on tiptoes to look into the gap. 'So I want to be absolutely clear, Craig, that you haven't been in through this gap into the room.'

'No, of course not. I'm not about to mess up the crime scene.'

'But you did make this hole in the wall yourself?'

'Yes. The modifications to the house were so illogical, and created this area of dead space in the rear extension. I just kept thinking, why would Trish have sealed off an area of her own house? And then I kept thinking about Howie who just apparently ran off to Thailand in 2008 after 20 years of marriage.'

'Did anyone outside the family claim to be in contact with Mr Gibson after that time?' Talantire asked.

'Not that I'm aware of. We only had Trish's word, backed up by Barbara, for what had happened. Of course, everyone in the family was very sympathetic to her. Howie had seemed a nice enough guy, but he always spent a long time away like oil workers often do, and I suppose it wouldn't have come as a great surprise that he had visited brothels in Thailand and other places. So, six months after he left, when Trish said she'd received a postcard from him in Bangkok, we weren't all that surprised. Neither were we surprised when she said that Howie's sisters, his only surviving relatives, had disowned him over his behaviour.'

'But all the time he was here, dead in the bath.' Talantire jerked a thumb towards the cavity in the brickwork.

As the crime scene team arrived, Gillard and Talantire moved out of the way into the lounge. Sam, increasingly shocked at the tone of the conversation, said: 'I can't believe that Trish would have murdered him. She's such a gentle soul.'

'I'm not suggesting she did,' Gillard said. 'I think he may have died from natural causes.'

'So why on earth didn't Trish notify the authorities?' Sam asked.

Gillard smiled. 'You were right, Sam, when you said follow the money. And like you, I was initially thinking about who could be richer as a result of his death. What I hadn't really thought about was who could be poorer.'

'I think you're going to have to explain that,' Talantire said.

'I only decided to go ahead and knock down this wall after I uncovered some paperwork in one of the kitchen drawers. It was about Howie's pension. He had been a self-employed oil contractor and had built up a very large pension fund which he had turned into an annuity with an insurance company. He had retired just six months before he supposedly went off to Thailand. That pension was over £60,000 a year, and according to the documents I found, was being paid into a joint account with Trish. The trouble with annuities is that they stop paying out when you die, and the entire pension pot goes back to the insurer on your death.'

'Wasn't there a widow's pension?' Sam asked.

'No. You can choose an annuity which allows for a widow's pension, but they pay out less to begin with. Anyway, he hadn't got one. The upshot is that if Trish had notified the authorities of his death, she would have lost the income from the annuity. I've seen her own pension from the relatively few years she spent as a schoolteacher, and that is a tiny fraction of what Howie's pension was bringing in.'

'Okay,' said Talantire. 'Let's go back to the beginning. Let's assume, for the sake of argument, that Mrs Gibson's husband dies of natural causes in the home. I assume she's not a bricklayer or a builder, so somebody else must have been in on it. Somebody built this tomb around him.'

'Maybe your uncle Philip?' Sam asked.

'No. His mobility was already very poor by the time Howie disappeared in 2008. I'm pretty sure he couldn't lay a brick if he tried. No, I think I know who helped Trish, and had most of the skills required—'

'Barbara,' Sam breathed.

'Exactly. I think it's Barbara who is the ultimate beneficiary of Howie's pension. The farm hardly makes a penny, and from all I've heard, there were big debts to be repaid.'

'But what about Philip's house in Lynton? They can sell that now, can't they?' Sam asked.

'I'm not sure about that,' Gillard said.

'Well we can certainly ask Mrs Gibson when she is well enough to be interviewed,' Talantire said.

'There's another thing I'd like to bring to your attention,' Gillard said. 'It's connected to the sheep attacks at my aunt's farm. I've managed to—'

Talantire turned away to answer her phone, and then walked briskly away to the kitchen. Gillard watched her face grow grave. She looked sideways at him, a brief but accusatory glance. He waited while she finished the call. She then strode back towards him with a determined look on her face.

'Do you know the whereabouts of your aunt?'

'She is in the hospital there, down the hill, as you well know,' Gillard replied, jerking his thumb behind him.

'Not her, the other one. Barbara Antrobus.'

'At the farm, I would guess. I've not spoken to her today.'

'There's been a shooting,' Talantire said.

'What?'

'Your aunt's old pickup truck was witnessed at the scene.'

'Oh my God,' said Sam. 'Is anyone hurt?'

'It's too soon to say. If you speak to her, tell her to come in peacefully.' She turned and strode away, phone pressed to her ear.

Gillard turned to look at Sam, whose hands were covering her face. 'Sam, you spoke to her, didn't you? When we were at the hospital?'

She nodded, wide-eyed, her hands still covering her mouth.

'You didn't tell her where'd we traced the dog to last night, did you?'

'Not exactly. I just said it was a smallholding, and an old bloke with a Land Rover.'

'For God's sake, why? I was going to give the information to Talantire.'

'But Craig, what was I going to say? She rang me because you'd not returned her call. She was angry and I thought I could calm her down. I mean, I thought it was good news that we'd found who owned the dog.'

Gillard pulled her into his arms and held her close. 'I suppose you weren't to know that she would be such a natural vigilante. She's never had any faith in the police. She has a long history of settling her scores personally.'

'I feel terrible,' Sam said. 'Everything I do is wrong.'

'No, it's not. Don't think that. Barbara has always been crazy, though that's not her fault either. I just have no idea how this is going to end.'

–

DI Jan Talantire could have shared the sentiment. The first call had come from Nick Kite, to say that his father Vince was being held at gunpoint in his cottage by Barbara Antrobus. His father's beloved dogs had been shot in the cages. The scene down at the smallholding was unbelievable. His voice cracked as he relayed the tale.

Talantire called her boss, DCS Parker, and asked for permission to bring in the armed response unit from Exeter. Parker was already on his way over, and trying to secure an experienced hostage negotiator from Bristol. 'I don't think we've got anyone here.'

'What on earth is this all about?' Parker asked.

'Dogs worrying her sheep.'

'Good grief, is that all?' The line went dead.

It took less than ten minutes for Talantire to get to Vince Kite's cottage, taking her unmarked vehicle as far up the lane as she could. His home was a rundown 200-year-old place with a sagging roof and tiny gable windows, set back a little from the unmade road. There were two police patrol cars parked outside, taking up almost all of the front yard and blocking the lane. The nearest police car to the cottage had a shotgun-smashed windscreen and side window. The door panels were pockmarked like measles. The first person she saw was PC Clifford Willow, crouched down behind the nearer, undamaged vehicle. Seeing her, he signalled that she should crouch down behind the cover of the drystone wall to her right. There was open ground between them; if Barbara was shooting from the window, Talantire realized she would be a sitting duck.

Willow indicated that PC Nick Kite was taking cover behind the other car. Talantire decided to ring him on his personal mobile rather than use the police radio whose loud squawk might give away his position. Just as she was tapping out the number, there was a bellow from upstairs at the cottage.

'I'll kill him if you try any funny games,' Barbara shouted. 'He's tied up, and not wearing a stitch, so won't be giving me any trouble. He's just as helpless as my poor ewes were when they had their throats ripped out by his pet wolf.' The upstairs window slid closed, and then almost immediately reopened. 'By the way, his cock is even tinier than I remember.' The window was slammed shut again.

Willow answered Talantire's call and confirmed that Nick Kite was unhurt, and had managed to scramble out of the passenger side of the car soon after Barbara Antrobus had fired at it.

'Has she said what she actually wants?' Talantire asked.

'She wants him prosecuted over damage to her sheep over many years,' Willow replied.

'There must be something else to it besides that.'

'I wouldn't try asking,' Willow said. 'She's a good shot.'

'Don't worry, the mobile firearms unit will be here in a minute.'

The two armed response vehicles from Exeter arrived on time, each with four male firearms officers, plus a support van containing Gold Commander Bill Harper and two female staffers. Talantire was surprised to see Harper, in uniform and cap, make his way towards the open ground with a loudhailer. He had just tested the device with a brief 'one, two', before a gunshot was heard from the cottage, and the thump of lead shot hitting the van. The police officers all threw themselves to the ground

'I don't want to talk to you lot, you can't be trusted,' Barbara bellowed. 'Bring my nephew, Craig. I'll only talk to him.'

'Can you see where she's shouting from?' Harper muttered to Talantire.

'From the nearest bedroom window, I think. She pushed Vince Kite to the window, and aimed over his shoulder from behind. She'll be hard to hit.'

Harper blinked and sighed. 'What a way to spend a Friday afternoon.'

Talantire reckoned that someone had told him it was a woman with the gun, and he'd assumed she would be panicky and easily intimidated. He obviously didn't know the first thing about Barbara Antrobus. Now, lying in a muddy puddle next to her, the front of his uniform soaked, his cap having dropped off into the mud, he was on a steep learning curve. He couldn't even get back into his own command van without exposing himself to further shotgun fire.

'Let me tell you about the woman inside there,' Talantire whispered. She then summarized Barbara's criminal record and background. 'Do not underestimate her strength or determination, sir.'

'I think we'd better get this nephew, then,' Harper replied. 'A DCI from Surrey, I understand?'

Talantire nodded. 'He's got a good brain on him, sir.'

'Let's hope we don't get to see it splattered on my van.'

–

Gillard and Sam arrived within 15 minutes. 'She'll only talk to you,' Harper said to him. 'Don't take any risks.'

'I won't, but please give me a chance to end it peacefully.'

'Be careful, Craig, she's nuts,' Sam said, unnecessarily.

Gillard nodded ruefully as he slipped on a bullet-proof vest given him by one of the firearms officers. He then took the loudhailer and called out to his aunt.

'Barbara, it's Craig.'

'Come out where I can see you,' she called out.

Gillard took a deep breath, then walked out into the open space between the police cars and the house. 'We can sort all this out, you know,' he said through the loudhailer. 'But you have to release the hostage.'

'No. I don't know why I didn't guess that it was Sergeant bloody Vince Kite. I've lost hundreds of ewes over the years. I've reported them to him and his useless son Nick, but they've never shown much interest. I wonder why.'

'The police will investigate,' Gillard said. 'I have the word of the commanding officer. But you have to release Mr Kite unharmed.'

'They're corrupt,' Barbara yelled. 'Been blackmailing me for years. It's put me in debt.'

Sam gave a sidelong glance to PC Nick Kite, who was emphatically shaking his head.

'Why have they been blackmailing you, Barbara?' Gillard asked.

PC Kite had sidled up to the commanding officer, who was now standing in the lee of the van, just in front of Sam. 'Is this really necessary, sir? All these ridiculous allegations in public.'

Harper shrugged. 'If she gets it off her chest, there's more chance of your father getting out in one piece.'

'I gave him money,' Barbara bellowed. 'And when that ran out, I let his son stay rent-free in my brother's house. But I never expected this. Killing my sheep.'

'Why would they do it?' Gillard asked. 'What leverage did they have over you?'

'You better ask them,' Barbara shouted.

'Sir, she's lying,' Kite pleaded to his senior officer.

Harper waved away his entreaties.

A sob came from inside the house. 'Vince knew that my old dad was abusing me since I was 12. He claimed to be sympathetic. He was just a PC then. He was the person I turned to on the day my dad died. Weren't you? And you let me down!'

The watching officers could see the hostage's head being slammed sideways against the window frame. He was gagged, and blood was running down the side of his face. They could just make out Barbara behind him, one hand knotted into his hair.

'In October 1967, my father tried to rape me, as he had done numerous times. But this time I pushed him away and ran out, up onto the cliffs. I just couldn't stand it. Vince Kite had promised me he would help me, and I wanted to go to him. I was only 21. But old Jacob caught me on the clifftops and told me he was going to have me one last time, then throw me over. He said I'd never be any use, and no man would ever want me because of my temper, and my wild eye. My old dad threw me to the ground and was undoing his belt. I was lying with my back to the cliff edge, and as he crouched down, I kicked out at him, grabbed hold of his hair, and used all my strength to overbalance him. He rolled off the cliff.' There was a sob from inside the house and Barbara resumed tearfully. 'I ran to find Vince, because he'd told me that it wouldn't be murder if I tried to kill Dad because of what he'd done to me over the years.'

'I don't think anyone could blame you for what you did,' Gillard said.

'Don't you believe it. When I went to Vince, he said he would help cover up what had happened. He said I could be in trouble because there was no proof that I'd killed him in self-defence. I was very frightened and didn't know what to believe. For a few months he did help, to get on my good side. But then he took advantage. He and I saw each other for a while, but then I realized he wasn't much better than my own dad in what he wanted, so I ended it.' There were more tears from inside.

'I think you should release him,' Gillard said.

'No! This little shit's got to pay for what he did.' There was another thump from inside, and a groan of male pain.

'Once I dumped him, the demands began,' Barbara continued. 'It started small, joints of lamb here and there. With my mum being disabled, it wasn't hard to stash away meat for him. Vince claimed that he had smoothed over the coroner's paperwork for me so it wasn't investigated properly, and I just had to take his word for it, I suppose.'

'How long did this go on?' Gillard asked.

Sam watched Nick Kite shaking his head in disbelief.

'Well, it's never stopped. When we had a good year, he expected some cash as well as meat. Then when Podge got infirm a few years ago and moved to the caravan, Vince came round and asked to rent the house for his son. I was happy to do it, because we needed the rent to help towards the care home, costs that would be coming down the line. But then, after a few months, Nick Kite decided he didn't need to pay any rent.' She got closer to the window and yelled. 'Let me say I wouldn't mind giving that weasel both barrels too. But I realized we couldn't do nothing about it. Vince even said he left a statement about the killing of my father with a solicitor, to be released in case anything happened to him.'

'Sir,' Kite whispered to the commander. 'This really is all a tissue of lies. We have an agreed rental contract and pay in cash—'

Harper waved him away.

'All right, Barbara,' Gillard shouted. 'You are surrounded by armed officers. This isn't going to end happily unless you agree to give up your weapon and release the hostage. You've had your say and—'

'Don't you tell me what to do, young man. You're tainted with the same blood as the rest of our family.'

'This isn't about me.'

'Isn't it? I think you've seen now why your mother left home. The same happened to Margaret as happened to me. Only Trish avoided it. We're all victims, us Antrobus women, and I ain't having it any more. I want to know who got hold of Jacob's filthy pictures, which ended up on my brother's laptop. I want justice and compensation for my lost ewes. Finally, now I've got this sick reptile at the end of my shotgun, you lot might finally listen.'

Sam could see the police marksmen edging closer, weapons aimed. Harper was on his radio, giving orders from the safety of the sheltered side of his van. This was going to end in bloodshed; the woman just wouldn't listen to reason. 'Barbara, listen carefully to me. The time has come for you to—'

'So my little bedtime soldier is giving orders now?' Barbara leaned over Kite's shoulder and pouted down at her nephew. 'Oh, you loved it, didn't you?'

His face twisting into a snarl, Gillard dropped the loud-hailer and ran for the front door, kicking it hard. 'Don't you try that. I'll bloody shoot you and him both,' Barbara bellowed.

Gillard paid no heed and, after a second kick, barged his way in past the splintered frame. Sam shouted for him to come back. She could also hear the crackle of radio messages coming into Harper, telling him that neither the woman nor the hostage were now visible through the window.

'What are you waiting for? Go in after him,' Harper bellowed into his radio, and four beefy firearms officers in body armour and helmets ran for the cottage door. Five seconds later there was a shout, a single muffled weapon discharge, and then a cacophony of shouting from the other officers.

A minute later they came out carrying a still wriggling Barbara Antrobus, feet first, with Gillard's arm around her neck. Sam was enormously relieved to see no injuries. Two other officers came out with Vince Kite, walking wounded, wrapped in a blanket. He was conscious, but his face was badly gashed. The police led him past the parked vehicles towards the paramedics whose ambulance was some way back towards the road. PC Nick Kite briefly embraced his father and began to lead him past Sam. A tearful Vince Kite turned to his son to say: 'The evil witch shot all my dogs. All of them. Then she came for me.'

Chapter 39

Talantire set up an emergency telephone conference call first thing on Saturday morning, moderated by DCS Bob Parker, with Miriam Gross, a senior lawyer for the Crown Prosecution Service.

'We've already got Antrobus in custody on hostage taking and firearms charges,' Talantire said. 'As soon as the doctors give the okay, we're going to charge Gibson with pension fraud and preventing lawful burial, but what we really want both of them for is murder and conspiracy to murder over the running down of Mark Hartley.'

'Conspiracy to murder is the easier of the two, as I understand there is nothing in the forensics to say which of them was driving the car,' Gross said. 'We've got all the preparatory and motive evidence we need. It's this alibi that is bothering me. The defence is going to stand up and say, "That's all very well, you've got plenty of circumstantial, but we have witness statements which show that both the accused were playing a game of Monopoly with two residents of the care home at the time the victim was killed." It's a strong basis for acquittal.'

'I understand where you're coming from, Miriam,' Parker said. 'But we can do nothing about that. What we can do is work on them in the interview room, to see if one of them cracks or implicates the other. We can play them off, over the coming weeks or months.'

'Good luck with that,' Gross said. 'What about Peter Yates? He has no alibi, and was arguably under the control of Antrobus, which gives motivation as well as means and opportunity. The jury would love the details of this bizarre affair.'

'I just don't think it was him,' Talantire said. 'I've interviewed him three times, and I just don't think he was capable.'

'It's your decision,' Gross said, with a tone that implied she wished it was otherwise. 'But a conspiracy charge would stick far more easily if Yates was included, because then you don't have to break the sisters' alibi. Think about it.'

–

The Devon and Cornwall CSI team spent two hours assessing the interior of Trish's house before deciding that removing the roof from the rear extension and using a crane to lift out the entire bath and its grisly contents would be the easiest way to make a forensic investigation. A canvas sling was constructed to fit under the bath and a polythene capsule made to fit around it and obscure from passers-by the nature of the police find.

Craig Gillard watched in his car from a distance as the crane picked up, swung and then lowered its load onto a contractor's lorry, for all the world as if it was a skip-load of rubble.

Sam, sitting next to him, asked: 'How long before they can confirm whether it is definitely Howie?'

'Most of the forensic labs will only do emergency work over Christmas, so if Talantire has the budget for it, she could get DNA results in a day or two. Luckily for her, Trish had left Howie's den like an untouched shrine for all the years he's been gone, so getting a reference sample won't be hard.' Gillard put the car into gear and pulled away.

'So it looks like you were right,' she said. 'If that's Howie in the lorry, the Bangkok family couldn't have existed, and somehow all of those photographs were faked.' Sam, having waited patiently, was hoping they would now be able to get back to Surrey, and to the comparative normality of a Christmas at home.

'Trish obviously made some friends when she did visit Bangkok, and took plenty of pictures that she could then pass off as showing Howie's family. It's a pretty clever ruse, except for the absence of Howie himself from these photos.' Gillard turned to his wife and smiled at her. 'Sam, you've really been a superstar over all this,' he said. 'I've been grouchy and difficult and evasive, and I'm sorry about it. I know that you now understand why, but I think at first it must have been very hard for you.'

'It was, I won't deny it. But thank you for acknowledging it. What I'm really looking forward to now is getting back home to have a long soak in the bath and watching some Christmas rubbish on TV.' She grinned.

'There's just one thing, a small errand I have to do before we go home.'

'What?'

'Well they only confirmed it an hour ago, and I've been trying to set it up for weeks. So it means going up to Gloucester.'

Sam put her head in her hands and howled in irritation. 'That's 100 miles out of our way! For Christ's sake, Craig, when is this insanity going to end?'

Chapter 40

Saturday afternoon

Just four days before Christmas and shoppers were out in force. Gillard, wrapped in a heavy overcoat against the sharp northerly wind, stood in the car park of Broxbourne Park shopping centre with Sam, Detective Chief Superintendent Alan Cunningham of Gloucestershire Constabulary and DI Talantire from the Devon force. Addressing them was Colin Beattie, the shopping centre manager.

'We've moved Santa's grotto to allow you access, but I have to say this could not have come at a more difficult time,' Beattie said as he led the entourage onto a balcony which overlooked the atrium over the peace garden. Gillard had spent a long time setting up this meeting, and was gratified that Talantire had agreed to rush over after her conference call to come along too. He needed all the help he could get to back up his theory that the body of a missing murder victim from almost 50 years ago lay buried at the centre of this shopping mall.

'I don't suppose there's ever a good time,' Gillard said.

'No, that's true,' Beattie said, running his hands through his greying hair. 'But can I ask what evidence you have that somebody is really buried here? I mean, it does sound rather unlikely.'

They all looked to Gillard for an answer. 'There is no direct evidence,' he replied. 'But there is circumstantial evidence that the peace garden was set up purely to avoid disturbing a body that had been buried some years earlier.'

No one said anything for a moment. Gillard looked around, hoping someone would back him up.

'I've seen the evidence that DCI Gillard has accumulated,' Talantire said, hurriedly. 'It's logical and convincing, and I believe there's a reasonable chance we will find what we're looking for.'

Gillard gave her his warmest smile. After stonewalling him for weeks, she was now riding to his rescue.

'So how long will the shopping centre shut down for over the Christmas and New Year period?' asked Cunningham.

Beattie looked astounded. 'The centre itself doesn't shut down at all, even on Christmas Day. We have a spa and gym upstairs, three or four restaurants, one or two ethnic food shops and a homeless charity kiosk which will all remain open. We close at 8 p.m. on Christmas Eve and reopen at 8 a.m. on Christmas morning. Every other day of course it will be thronged with people. So Christmas Day is your best bet.'

Gillard pointed to the perimeter of the peace garden. 'We could screen off the entire area and put a tent over the excavation. There's room to get in one of those half-tonne micro-excavators.'

'But it would be packed up here, with thousands of shoppers gawking down, not to mention the press with their long-lens cameras trying to snap each piece of evidence,' Talantire said.

'Can we not maintain a news blackout?' Gillard asked Cunningham.

'Yes, I'd be in favour of that,' Cunningham said. 'Logistically, it's all manageable. I would guess we'd only need the excavator overnight, from Christmas Eve shutdown until Christmas morning. In that time, with the centre shut, we can get contractors to cut down the trees and build a plywood screen right around the garden.' He turned to Beattie. 'You can even hang your decorations on the outside if you want.'

'If you cut down the trees, that would destroy the peace garden,' Beattie said.

'Too bad. We can't dig amongst the trees,' Cunningham responded. 'And we can't put a tent over them. It's as simple as that. For the more painstaking hand search on any subsequent days, we would get one of the long-wheelbase CSI transit vans as the operations room, and we can use our largest CSI tent to provide a seamless connection between the dig and the back of the van. The great British public won't be able to see anything even from up here.'

'Well, I'm anxious to provide you with what you want, of course,' said Beattie. 'But I want you to be aware that for already stretched retailers, this may have quite a dramatic effect on takings. We saw what happened to the centre of Salisbury after the Novichok attacks. The upheaval lasted months, and dozens of businesses closed. Can you guarantee me that this will be over within 24 hours?'

'We don't issue guarantees,' Cunningham said. 'We have to take forensic care, and we will take as much time as we need. But having said that, I'm hopeful that we'll be finished in a day or two.'

After they had finished their meeting, they left a clearly nervous shopping centre manager fretting about the economic effect of police operations. It had already taken Gillard hours on the phone and many exchanges of email to get this far. He knew that Cunningham remained deeply suspicious of Gillard's connection with the supposed perpetrator, and it had taken a phone call between Surrey chief constable Alison Rigby and her counterpart in Gloucestershire to provide reassurance that Gillard was indispensable to the case. It was agreed on condition that he would take no part in the crime scene investigation nor be allowed access to any physical evidence.

As the officers emerged into the windswept car park, against the steady flow of festive shoppers, they all prepared to go their separate ways. Cunningham put his arm around Gillard's shoulder and whispered into his ear. 'I hope for your sake that you're right about this, my friend.' He chuckled. 'Or you'll forever be known as the prat who cancelled Christmas.'

–

It was the night before Christmas at the Broxbourne Park shopping centre, nine o'clock, and it would be an exaggeration to say nothing stirred. The micro digger was in place, the high-vis jacketed contractors were revving up their chainsaws, and the first of the silver birches in the peace garden had already been felled. From the balcony of the shopping mall above, a man dressed in a hooded jacket, jeans and training shoes peered down on the hive of activity. Despite the agreement made by his boss, Craig Gillard had no intention of being entirely excluded from the investigation into the murder of Chrissie Frost. But stubbornness like that has a cost. Sam had been upset when he told her just two days in advance that he would be working away overnight on Christmas Eve. When he explained why, her indignation turned to inspiration. Within an hour she had entirely rearranged their Christmas.

'I've booked us a hotel and spa break, and you're paying for it,' she had said.

'But didn't I just tell you—'

'You did, Craig, and that's where we're going. A top-floor suite at the Broxbourne Delta Parkway and Spa. It's right on top of the centre. You're actually next to the crime scene and you can stare at it to your heart's content while I have a sauna, whirlpool bath, a Christmas facial and pedicure. I bet I have more fun than you do.' Looking at his face, she then tapped his nose with her forefinger and said: 'Don't. You. Dare. Query. The. Cost.'

Sam would by now be having her facial. Gillard waited until the arrival of the CSI van, then returned to their room to get some sleep. He set his alarm for 4 a.m., which he calculated would be around the time when the digging would begin.

–

Gillard slipped out of bed, dressed in hoody and jeans, and tiptoed out without waking his wife. It was 3.50 a.m. and he intercepted the alarm before it was triggered. He kissed Sam gently on the temple, earning himself a soft murmur in reply. Despite her sauna and other pampering, she still hadn't been entirely pleased with him. As she said, it was one thing, the job coming first, but this whole project around Philip Antrobus had been voluntary, and had succeeded in using up almost all their free time for the last two months.

For Gillard this was unfinished business. The Devon end of the family had overshadowed him for decades. There were crimes to be uncovered, but he had not expected this. A murder committed by Philip, the one member of his family who had achieved something in his life. The rest of that part of the family were crazy or eccentric. In the next hour or two, he would know for sure whether Philip was a fantasist, just as crazy as the rest of them, or whether he really had committed an act of pure evil.

The detective slid out past reception and into the mall, where the noise of the digger could already be heard. Though the corridors only had emergency lighting, he was spotted immediately by a private security guard and challenged, but when he offered his detective identity card, he got an apology. Gillard made his way along to the balcony immediately above the crime scene, which was dazzlingly lit up by arc lamps. The digger had already dug a two-foot deep trench between the stumps of some of the silver birches, but had now backed off. Three figures in bulky Tyvek suits were on their hands and knees with trowels, carefully ladling earth onto a nearby plastic sheet. He took out his binoculars and knelt down so he could peer unseen between the guard rail and the glass panelling beneath. Focusing on the gap between the shoulders of two male technicians, he watched a brush being used to clear earth fragments from something white.

Bone white.

The sheer care and delicacy of the movements of the two men, the use of a brush, the close attention, were all evidence that they had found what they were looking for. When the third technician, crouched over with a camera, flashed half a dozen times, he knew for certain that a body had been found.

Now, after weeks of anxiety and uncertainty, he felt the flood of a powerful new emotion: vindication. Finally, he could return to the warm embrace of his sleeping wife.

–

By breakfast time, and the expected opening of the shopping centre, a tent had been erected over the pit with a polythene tunnel leading to the back of an unmarked CSI van. Gillard knew better than to try to ingratiate himself with the CSI team, who had promised to call him should they need his help. But on his laptop, he was able to use the password Cunningham had given him to access the Gloucester Police database and tap into the enlarging photographic file on the case.

The pictures told a story. They had first uncovered hip and femur bones, then a woman's shoe. It was a platform shoe, whose mauve plastic uppers and heel strap had survived much better than the cork sole, which had crumbled. The first picture of the skull wasn't until much later in the series, and Gillard had to keep hitting refresh to get the latest. The hair had survived quite well more than four decades in the ground, but the colour had leached from it, leaving it white. It was now clear the corpse had been buried in the foetal position, which required the shortest grave with the smallest amount of digging. There was no clothing on the lower half, but a torn blouse and some kind of tasselled leather waistcoat or gilet on the upper body. So far, the grave was confirming a sexual assault narrative exactly like that to which his uncle Philip had confessed.

Sam, who had been having an early morning swim, returned to the room and looked over the shoulder of her husband at the screen. She recoiled at the sight.

'Is it her?' she asked.

Gillard nodded. 'I'm pretty sure it is. This waistcoat matches the one in the photograph we saw of Chrissie Frost.' He opened up another window to put the images side by side.

'Have you had any breakfast?' she asked.

'I grabbed a slice of toast and coffee earlier. I couldn't quite face the smoked salmon or eggs Benedict.'

'If I'd seen that, neither could I,' she said, pointing at the screen. 'So are you done?'

Gillard shrugged. 'Pretty much. I'd been waiting to see if they'd recovered her underwear from the grave.'

Sam's jaw hung open. 'You've been *what*?'

Gillard turned round to look at her. 'It's not what you think. If they find her knickers, they may be able to recover a DNA sample from her assailant.'

'You're taking this right to the bitter end, aren't you?'

He conceded with a small smile. 'Okay, let's go back home. No work on Boxing Day, I promise.'

Chapter 41

Barbara Antrobus and Patricia Gibson were charged jointly with murder and conspiracy to murder, the case set for the Old Bailey in July. Barbara, given her history of violence, was remanded in custody until the case began, while Trish, still being treated for asthma and heart arrhythmia, merely had to stay at her place of residence, surrender her passport and agree not to contact witnesses.

Gillard, who was expecting to be called as a witness over the discovery of the body in the bathroom, discovered how little respect Trish gave to that ruling. His work and home emails, his home answering machine and his mobile were each peppered with Trish's increasingly shrill messages asking for his help. He ignored them entirely.

Once the trial began, Sam was able to arrange mostly night shifts at the incident room so she was able to travel up to London to get a place in the public gallery for a few hours on most days. She sat in the waiting room by Court One waiting for proceedings to start at ten, taking in the absurdly narrow corridor linking the courts, the chocolate-coloured woodwork around the stained windows and the Victorian tiled walls which gave Britain's most renowned law courts the air of a public toilet.

The first few days involved procedural wrangles, with neither defendant present nor a jury, and she didn't stay long. But on the third day, the court was packed and she got the last narrow seat at the back of the public gallery. Below her, the press benches were full, and there were three times the number of lawyers she had seen on previous days. She watched the jury being empanelled, and finally the defendants were escorted to the dock.

Barbara, in unaccustomed heels, was almost a foot taller than her sister and was wearing a maroon silk dress. Her hair had been trimmed, permed and dyed a light, soft grey. It hardly softened her face, particularly as she had chosen to wear a black eyepatch to cover her wayward eye. Sam thought she looked like a candyflossed pirate. Trish, dressed in a kingfisher-blue trouser suit, struggled to see over the edge of the dock, and was almost invisible beyond the bulk of the male custody officer placed between her and Barbara.

The judge, Mr Justice Knowlesley, a thin-faced, beady-eyed septuagenarian, told the jury that Barbara had already pleaded guilty to three counts, relating to the abduction and false imprisonment of Vincent Kite, details of which he ruled could now be disclosed under the Criminal Justice Act 2003 as 'bad character'. Separately, both sisters had pleaded guilty to fraud, and conspiracy to prevent a lawful and decent burial, which being related matters were being dealt with under the same indictment.

'Ladies and gentlemen of the jury,' he said, 'the case before you today concerns two charges even more serious than those to which the defendants have already admitted guilt. Those charges are murder, and conspiracy to murder, Mr Mark Hartley.'

Charges were put to the defendants, and they each pleaded not guilty.

Sam had seen from the press coverage that the prosecution case was being led by Sir William Strutt, a well-known and flamboyant barrister, whose corpulent figure and booming voice had graced a true crime series on Channel 5. Barbara was defended by Ellen Goodhew, an articulate cross-examiner who had managed to get one of Britain's major gangland characters acquitted of the murder of a rival in 2007. Trish was defended by Alasdair Buchanan, a veteran criminal defence specialist whose command of detail was legendary.

Strutt, after describing the known circumstances of the hit-and-run, called as his first witness Mrs Muriel Hinkley, who had found the body. Neither defence barrister challenged her version of events. He then ran through the expert witnesses smoothly: forensic specialists who established time of death, tyre-track and road traffic accident experts from various universities, the pharmacology expert who analysed Mark Hartley's blood, and the DNA and fingerprint CSI technicians who narrowed down who could conceivably have been in the car. The defence barristers did not challenge or cross-examine any of these witnesses.

Strutt then called DI Jan Talantire, and Sam watched as the barrister threaded the detective's narrative into a tapestry of conspired guilt on a grand scale. She described the discovery of the body of Howard Gibson, concreted into the bath.

'But you were not the officer who actually uncovered this act of concealment, were you?' Strutt asked.

'No, it was Detective Chief Inspector Craig Gillard.'

'That is, the nephew of the accused?' he asked.

'Yes.'

'So he, on his own initiative, knocked a hole into the wall of Mrs Gibson's home.'

'Yes.'

Strutt looked down at his notes and spoke to the judge. 'We have DCI Gillard's statement, which is uncontested and does not form part of the case.' The judge nodded.

'And how long had Mr Gibson been dead?' Strutt asked Talantire.

'Forensic tests indicated that it was a number of years.'

'Was there any indication of foul play?'

Buchanan jumped to his feet. 'Please, my lord, my client has already pleaded guilty to the concealment of Mr Gibson's death. We were not made aware that the prosecution is attempting to show that the death was not a natural one.'

The judge nodded, and addressed Strutt. 'Do you have any evidence of foul play in this death?'

'No, my lord.'

'Then, Sir William, stop making insinuations to mislead the jury.'

'My apologies, my lord.' He returned to addressing Talantire. 'You have laid before us evidence that Mr Hartley stayed overnight at Mrs Gibson's home after arrival on the train from Paddington. You mentioned the telephone evidence, from her landline and his mobile, but I understand you have something more in the way of proof of an intent to kill?'

'Yes, I do. We believe that the defendants drugged Mr Hartley with sleeping medication, hoping this would kill him.'

'This is the evidence we already heard of high doses of an imidazopyridine compound found in his blood?'

'Yes. When he awoke the next morning, Mrs Gibson said she gave him a coffee. We believe that was laced with yet more Ambien. The forensic report, as we have heard, found significant traces in his blood at the point of death.'

'So DI Talantire, can you explain what evidence you have that the defendants gave up trying to drug Mr Hartley and instead tried to mock-up a road accident death?'

'There were a number of things about the body that puzzled us,' Talantire said. 'First there was no ID, no wallet, and no phone, which is very unusual. Then, as we examined his clothing, we discovered all the labels had been cut out.'

'And what did you deduce from this finding?'

'That the perpetrator didn't want us to find out that many of his items of clothing had an overseas origin.'

'When could they have cut them out?'

'Quite possibly when Mr Hartley was asleep the second time.'

Both Buchanan and Ellen Goodhew were on their feet objecting. 'My lord,' Goodhew said. 'This is simply conjecture – there is no evidence that either of the defendants administered the sleeping medication found in his bloodstream. It could simply have been taken by the victim to deal with jet lag. Likewise, there is no evidence that they were the ones who cut out the clothing labels.'

'I am merely laying out the possibilities, my lord. I would leave for the jury to decide whether it is more likely that Mr Hartley or the defendants trimmed out every single washing and manufacturer's label, and what their respective motivations might be for such action.'

Strutt returned to the witness. 'DI Talantire, let us turn to the alleged murder weapon, Miss Antrobus's Ford Ranger. Can you remind us whose fingerprints were found in the vehicle?'

'There were quite a few. Miss Antrobus as owner, her sister Mrs Gibson, her brother the late Reverend Philip Antrobus and Peter Yates, who works for her. All these people would have a reason to be either drivers or passengers in the normal course of events. Then there were two further sets of prints, one of which was identified as Mark Hartley—'

'Let me stop you there. You are saying that the man who was run down by that vehicle was also at some stage inside it?' Strutt made it sound like he was hearing this piece of evidence for the first time, and was astounded by it.

'Yes, that's what the prints show.'

'Are you able to tell whether he was a driver or a passenger?'

'The fingerprints were on the interior and exterior of the front passenger-side door. So it would indicate that he was a passenger, though it doesn't preclude that he may have been a driver at some stage – we just don't have the prints to prove it.'

'I don't want to ask you to speculate, but is it possible that one of the defendants gave him a lift to this lonely and misty spot while he was still drowsy, without any ID, and dropped him off for some supposed meeting with Mr Gibson, the man he had come to see? And then, once he had stepped from the vehicle, they ran him down?'

Both defence barristers were on their feet, but the judge was already ahead of them. 'Sir William, stop leading the witness. If you have evidence for this suggested course of events, I shall ask you to produce it, otherwise I will ask the jury to disregard it.'

Talantire was then offered for cross-examination. The two defence barristers, uneasy allies, conferred. Alasdair Buchanan, representing Trish, approached the detective inspector.

'My learned colleague, I feel, rather rushed you through the list of those whose fingerprints were found in the car. You did not complete your list, did you?'

'I'm sorry?'

'Detective Inspector Talantire, did you not find finger-prints belonging to a known car thief inside the vehicle?'

A gasp swept across the courtroom.

'No, not on the vehicle—'

'I didn't say *on* the vehicle, I said *in* the vehicle,' Buchanan interjected.

'There were fingerprints from a Mr Michael Tuffin found on a drink can that was beneath the front passenger seat,' she said.

'And Mr Tuffin, I believe, is a convicted car thief?'

'Yes.'

'I also believe that you established that Mr Tuffin and the farm employee Mr Yates had, without permission, taken Miss Antrobus's Ford Ranger on the Saturday preceding the incident in question?'

'Yes, they both admitted that—'

'And were seen driving it in the town centre in an unsafe manner by several witnesses?'

'Yes.'

'Ms Talantire, may I ask why this piece of evidence, which one would have thought highly pertinent in identifying who may have been driving the vehicle, was not brought before the court?'

'Simply because this man had been eliminated from our enquiries.'

'On what grounds?'

'CCTV showed that he was outside the NatWest bank in the centre of Barnstaple at the time which forensic examination confirms that Mr Hartley died.'

'In other words, he had an alibi?'

'Yes.'

'Detective Inspector, what do you call the collection of statements which you have seen from staff and residents at The Beeches care home which confirm that both defendants were there at the time that Mr Hartley died?'

'That's an alibi too, but—'

'So really, Ms Talantire, you've just been picking and choosing the evidence to suit your own preconceptions, have you not?'

'No, not at all.' She looked very flustered now.

'Well, it seems you prefer the story that one or both of these elderly ladies deliberately knocked down and killed this man to an explanation where a convicted car thief, who had been seen driving badly just a few days before, in this *very vehicle*,' he tapped the edge of the witness box for emphasis, 'may have accidentally knocked down and killed him'.

'But there was CCTV—!'

'Ms Talantire, there is no need to shout,' Buchanan said. 'You cannot cover the many shortcomings of this investigation by merely proclaiming the limited evidence you do have more loudly. No further questions.'

Strutt then told the judge that he had no further witnesses for the prosecution.

Chapter 42

The case for the defence began the next morning. Ellen Goodhew, Barbara's barrister, called Mrs Dickinson, manager of the care home and then carer Marcus Fitzgerald, 'Fitz', who testified to the arrival and departure times of the two sisters, and having seen each of them from time to time during the course of the afternoon. In his cross-examination, Strutt asked Fitzgerald about his duties that afternoon and what he had been doing. After a lengthy description of the various tasks, Strutt interrupted him. 'So, Mr Fitzgerald, given all of the work you had to do, it wasn't really possible for you to verify that either of these ladies remained continuously in the home, was it?'

'No, sir, as I said in my statement.'

'So it would have been possible, would it not, for either or both of them to have slipped out for a considerable time during the afternoon? Enough time to have driven Miss Antrobus's vehicle to Mrs Gibson's home to collect Mr Hartley, then up to Furzy Hill and back to Bear Street?'

Buchanan was on his feet. 'My lord, the witness is being invited to speculate about matters that he couldn't possibly know.'

The judge agreed, and with no further questions, the witness was dismissed. Mr Justice Knowlesley then told the jury that they were to hear two statements from witnesses who were now deceased, Mr George Butler and the Rev Philip Antrobus. 'Ladies and gentlemen of the jury, you should be aware of the limitations of such evidence, which is being allowed under the rules of hearsay. Indeed, in the case of Rev Antrobus, there are two further issues. One is that he was the brother of both accused, and secondly that he had been diagnosed with dementia, and on a previous occasion judged by a police doctor unfit to give evidence. So you must weigh any conclusions accordingly.'

A junior prosecution barrister then read out both statements, which emphasized the continuous presence of both Trish and Barbara at the care home while all four of them played a game of Monopoly.

Ellen Goodhew then recalled DI Talantire for cross-examination. 'Miss Talantire, we earlier heard your evidence about the culpability of the two defendants. But as you have long been aware, we have a total of four witnesses who maintain that both of these ladies were playing Monopoly with their brother at precisely the time the hit-and-run took place. Four witnesses, Detective Inspector Talantire, and in addition, we have the call log from the emergency services which gives the time the theft of the vehicle was reported by Miss Antrobus. Given the weight of this evidence, do you not agree that these two elderly ladies could simply not have committed the crime attributed to them?'

'They could,' Talantire said. 'It was possible that either of them slipped out of the care home through the back entrance, took the vehicle, and returned it to Bear Street within a half-hour time frame.'

'And who would have been rolling their dice on the Monopoly board while all this happened?' Goodhew asked.

'I'm sorry?'

'Monopoly is a game, Miss Talantire. Players take turns. A gap of half an hour in proceedings would have been noticed, would it not? Did not both these witnesses involved in the game, Mr Antrobus and Mr Butler, say in their statements that the two sisters were "continuously" present?'

'They did,' Talantire said. 'But Mr Antrobus was suffering from dementia and his testimony cannot be relied upon—'

'But he won the game, did he not?'

'I'm sorry?'

'He won the game of Monopoly, Ms Talantire – paragraph 46 of his statement.' She held it up and waved it towards the jury. 'Not the act, surely, of a man bereft of the judgement to say whether his own sisters were present or not?'

'I couldn't say,' she replied. 'I'm not much of an expert on—'

'No indeed, Detective Inspector. I think we have established that you are not much of an expert. Likewise, in Mr Butler's statement, a man, let the jury be aware, who was a commercial property surveyor before retirement, and who has no question marks over his mental facility, there is no indication that there was a hiatus or delay in the game.'

'As I said,' Talantire responded. 'These statements were just taken from initial notes made by a junior colleague on the evening of the incident, when we thought it was just a hit-and-run. They were not the detailed statements that I would have taken, had not both witnesses sadly passed away.'

Goodhew turned with astonishment to the jury. 'I have been a barrister for 27 years, and I have never before heard a serving police officer try to highlight a supposed inadequacy in her own constabulary's investigative procedures as a piece of evidence to secure a conviction.' She turned back to a blushing Talantire. 'It hardly puts matters beyond reasonable doubt, our legally required burden of proof, does it?'

'That's not what—'

'Ms Talantire, unreliable police evidence-taking, from my perspective and indeed that of any ordinary person, surely, would tend to lead towards acquittal, would it not?'

'Not when that evidence is the only thing holding up an alibi,' she shot back.

Goodhew said she had no further questions. She then requested that Barbara come to the witness stand. She made her way across court and, once installed in the box, loudly proclaimed her oath on the Bible.

'Miss Antrobus, you have run Hollow Coombe farm, alone, since what year?'

'Since 1964, when my father died.' Under further questions she went on to describe her mother's multiple sclerosis and early death, and the difficulties of farming land too rough and steep for anything other than rough grazing.

'How long has the farm been in your family?'

'More than 200 years.'

'And all your forebears managed to retain their ownership of land, through thick and thin, is that not correct?'

Barbara agreed.

'It would be fair to say, would it not, that your life has not been an easy one? And that the finances of the farm have been precarious, to put it mildly?'

Barbara agreed with both these questions. 'It's hard to turn an honest coin with sheep.' Further questions showed that the farm was mortgaged to the tune of over £200,000, and that annual losses had varied between £10,000 and £30,000 for the last ten years.

'Miss Antrobus, where does the money come from to make the mortgage payments?'

'From my sister, Trish, mostly.'

'Patricia Gibson, your co-defendant?' He gestured towards the dock at which the tiny figure of Trish, dressed in her blue trouser suit, peered over the wooden ledge.

Barbara nodded.

'Running a struggling farm must be taxing – mentally as well as physically, would you say?'

'Yes. I'm fine with the hands-on stuff.'

Goodhew shuffled her papers. 'I have here a psychological assessment that was made shortly after your arrest. Now Miss Antrobus, as part of this assessment, your IQ was measured.'

'I'm not thick, you know.'

'Indeed not, but you may be easily led.'

'Objection, my lord,' Buchanan said. 'She is being led by my learned colleague, if by nobody else.'

'Miss Goodhew,' the judge said. 'I hope you have some evidential support for this line of questioning?'

'Let me rephrase,' she replied. 'Miss Antrobus, the psychological assessment report I have in front of me shows that you have a reading age of 12, and an IQ a little below average at 95.'

'Well I hardly got the chance to read a book,' Barbara said, turning to the jury.

'Is it true that your sister Trish, who went on to become a history teacher, used to help you with your homework when you were an adolescent?'

'Sometimes, yes. But it's horses for courses, ain't it? She still doesn't know one end of an ewe from the other.'

'But she did occasionally help you with the accounts at the farm?'

'Yes, I'm not much good with numbers or computers.'

'But, in her statement, your sister said that it was you who thought up the plan about her ex-husband's annuity.'

'Well that's rubbish. She sat me down and told me, after he had died, that the money wouldn't come through any more.'

'Was it you or she who thought up the plan to pretend he was still alive?'

'It was her but, fair's fair, I was fully up for it. Once it was explained.'

'Miss Antrobus, I would like to take you back to the afternoon of Wednesday 7 November last year. The prosecution has detailed at considerable length the circumstances of the hit-and-run accident in which Mr Mark Hartley met his death. It is their contention that you or your sister were driving this vehicle at the time, and deliberately killed him.' She looked up at her client. 'What do you have to say to that assertion?'

'It's not true. Someone stole my Ford, when Trish and I were at the care home.'

'Indeed, may I remind the jury that we have no fewer than four witness statements to that effect. So what was your reaction when the police came to tell you that your vehicle had been used in a hit-and-run?'

'I was horrified. Absolutely horrified.'

'No further questions, my lord.'

—

Prosecuting counsel Sir William Strutt took the opportunity to cross-examine Barbara. 'Miss Antrobus, my learned colleague has done an excellent job of illustrating the privations of your upbringing on a struggling hill farm. We have also heard that both your sisters, Patricia and Margaret, ran away from home during adolescence. Can you tell me why they did this?'

'They weren't happy at home.'

'Indeed not. And were you happy?'

'No, sir. I had all the farm work to do, and to look after my mother who had multiple sclerosis.'

'And of course, you watched your older brother go to university, leaving you behind.'

'Yes, sir.'

'And what of your father, Jacob Antrobus?'

Barbara looked at the judge and said: 'I don't want to talk about him.'

'My lord, this line of questioning is not relevant to the alleged crime,' Goodhew interjected, backing her client up.

Strutt responded. 'I will establish its relevance, my lord, as a contribution to the character and state of mind of the defendant, from which other actions spring.'

'You may continue, with care,' the judge said.

Strutt then repeated the question, and Barbara replied. 'I hated him.'

'Is it not true that he abused you over a period of six or seven years when you were a girl?'

Barbara looked down, and her broad shoulders sank. She appeared to be trembling. The judge told her to take her time. Her eventual answer, yes, was so soft that it could only be heard because the court had fallen utterly silent.

'And is that not why both your sisters ran away from home? To escape abuse?'

Barbara nodded. 'Yes, it is.'

'Did the fact that you were left to face his abuse alone make you angry?'

'What do you think?' she shouted.

'Miss Antrobus, with all due respect, I'm here to ask the questions and not answer them. That is your job.' He waited a moment, and then rephrased. 'Would you say you are an angry person?'

She shook her head. 'Only when I'm riled.'

'Were you riled when Detective Inspector Talantire interviewed you about the loss of your sheep? When you punched her on the nose?'

'It wasn't about the sheep – that's why I was angry. She was asking about this hit-and-run. I was angry because they never show any interest in the deaths of my ewes.'

'But you did punch her on the nose, did you not? And only a few weeks later you took hostage a retired police officer, while wielding a shotgun, and threatened to kill him, did you not?'

She made no reply.

'And did you not shoot all of his beloved dogs, at point-blank range, in their cages? Including a puppy of only ten weeks?'

The jury collectively gasped. Barbara looked down and said nothing.

'Well, Miss Antrobus, you do not answer but you have already pleaded guilty to that crime too. A nasty act of cruelty—'

'His dogs attacked my sheep!'

'The court undoubtedly feels sympathy because of the privations of your upbringing, but none of this excuses the cruelty and gratuitous violence of your behaviour, does it?'

'No, sir.'

'For example, we have several witnesses who testified that you slammed the head of this retired police sergeant Vincent Kite into the frame on an upstairs window while holding him hostage, causing cuts and severe bruising. Do you remember what you said?'

'Yes, I said "Now that's what I call a quality kite mark."' A ripple of laughter ran around the court and a slight smile played on Barbara's lips.

Strutt looked up and waved his spectacles at her. 'I think the jury can see, Miss Antrobus, that you laugh and make jokes even as you inflict pain. You are a cruel person.'

She shook her head in denial.

'Would it not be fair to say that you get riled, as you put it, on a regular basis? That you are always prepared to take matters into your own hands?'

'No, not always—'

'That in fact, when sufficiently riled, and in order to save your farm from bankruptcy, you are quite capable of running down an innocent man in your large and powerful car, and dragging his body under the wheels, causing him grievous and ultimately fatal injuries in the process?'

'Absolutely not.'

'No further questions.'

Buchanan, representing Trish, then made his way up to the witness box to question Barbara. 'Miss Antrobus, you are quite handy with your fists, aren't you?' There was no reply. 'It took four police officers to restrain you after you hit DI Talantire, as we have already heard.'

'I work with my hands. I couldn't do it if I was weak.'

'You are, what, five foot eleven? And you weigh... how much?' Buchanan leaned on the witness box where, because of the step, Barbara overshadowed his six-foot frame.

'Twelve stone three, according to them quacks at the prison who weighed me.'

'Your diminutive sister—'

'Only got one sister now.'

'Indeed, and she is rather small and frail.' He smiled winningly at the jury.

Barbara coughed her scepticism. 'She uses her weakness to get others to do things for her.'

'But wouldn't it be fair to say that she is intimidated by you? And feels she should do what you want?'

'No. She does what she wants.'

'When you were both teenagers, did you not break her arm during a fight?'

Goodhew jumped to her feet. 'My lord, I really must protest. It certainly demonstrates desperation if counsel for Mrs Gibson feels she has to reach into the rough-and-tumble of adolescence half a century ago to support her contentions.'

The judge smiled at her. 'If so, Miss Goodhew, I'm sure the jury can be relied upon to reach the appropriate conclusion about its relevance.'

Buchanan continued. 'Can I remind you, Miss Antrobus, that you and your farm are the sole beneficiaries of this financial ruse, which was to pretend that Mr Gibson was still alive? She gains not one jot, financially. So is it not true that you bullied her into this arrangement?'

'No, that is not true.'

'Is it not true, Miss Antrobus, that it was you that was the driving force behind this plan, and indeed slipped out of the care home to pick up a rather groggy Mr Hartley from your sister's home—'

'That's cobblers,' Barbara yelled. 'Neither of us did it.'

'Then who did?'

'I don't know. Nobody knows, except whoever did it.'

Chapter 43

It was the next day when Trish Gibson was called to give evidence. Gillard's aunt had dyed her hair blond, and put it in a ponytail. She was wearing a blue pinafore dress and a frilly white blouse, and black patent leather T-bar sandals with white socks. This childlike attire stood in contrast to her evident infirmity as she was helped by a court official to make her way across from the dock, in front of the jury, and up to the witness box. She fumbled and dropped her newly acquired walking stick as she laboriously climbed the four not particularly difficult steps, grasping the small banister as if she was on an ascent of Everest. She then produced an inhaler, taking copious breaths, before Alasdair Buchanan was able to ask his first question.

Gently, he asked her about her relationship with Howard Gibson, beginning with their first meeting at a restaurant in Barnstaple in 1977, where she was a waitress and he a diner. 'It was his lovely blue-grey eyes that I first noticed,' Trish said, smiling at the jury and getting some warm looks in return. Sam noticed Trish had developed a slight lisp, and a stronger Devon accent. These, together with her apparently shy demeanour and small stature, made her seem more like a schoolgirl than the woman of 70 she actually was.

'He had a lovely Scottish burr, which sounds a bit exotic down our way, or at least it did back then.' Coaxed skilfully by her barrister, and with regular stops to dab her eyes, Trish set off on a reminiscence that produced wistful nods and smiles from the jurors. Interruptions from Sir William Strutt and Ellen Goodhew about the relevance of the tale were rejected by the judge, and Buchanan cruised on to his final triumphant question: 'Tell us about the evening you found your husband's body in the bath.'

Trish needed two minutes of preparation with inhaler, handkerchief, and steadying herself on the witness stand before she was ready. She described how she had prepared him his usual evening cup of tea with two plain chocolate digestives, his favourites, to have while taking a long bath, and walked into the bathroom. 'I screamed and dropped everything.'

'Why did you not call for an ambulance?'

She shook her head, shoulders trembling. 'It was too late, you see? I saw him there, his head lolling on one side, his mouth open and partially underwater, and I knew he was gone. It was all my fault.'

Every eye in the court was now focused on her face.

'Why on earth was it your fault?' Buchanan asked softly.

'Because I was watching TV, and if he called for me, I didn't hear. I was late with his tea. If I had gone in during the previous adverts, he might still be alive.'

A female juror sighed and wiped her eyes.

'Mrs Gibson, please tell the court about your decision not to report your husband's death.'

Trish then described phoning her sister, and the half-hour of sympathy she was given. 'And then she said: "What about his pension? Will we still get it?"'

There was a gasp of disbelief from the dock. Barbara's jaw was hanging open, and she was shaking her head.

Buchanan then asked: 'What was your response?'

'I was shocked. My poor Howie still lying there, and she was thinking of the money, his pension money—'

Barbara's roar of outrage echoed around the court and she stood, knuckles tight on the guard rail. 'That is not *true*. You sneaky, lying, conniving bitch.' The judge's call for silence had no effect. 'It was *your* idea, I didn't know anything about it,' Barbara bellowed. 'How *dare* you!'

The custody officer was asked by the judge to remove Barbara to the cells. But for all his nightclub bouncer size, he was hard pressed to shift her an inch, and it looked like an equally matched wrestling bout. The arrival of two more officers, and a noisy couple of minutes, led to Barbara's removal. Ellen Goodhew, tasked with upholding Barbara's innocence, sat with her head in her hands.

After a moment for the court to recompose itself, Buchanan turned to his witness, but Trish got in first, addressing the jury: 'You can see why I'm scared of her, can't you? But sometimes you just have to tell the truth.' She gave a sad little smile.

'Mrs Gibson, please confine your observations to the matters you are asked about,' the judge said.

Buchanan then elicited from Trish further detail of the plans that she said were made, at Barbara's instigation, to cover up the death. 'She may not be great with computers, but she spent a long time on mine, researching how we could delay reporting my husband's death, and build a false life for him.'

'And how would this be achieved?' Buchanan asked.

'Well, the pension stuff and the documents were the easy bit. The money kept flowing so long as we never reported his death. But of course, there was the matter of poor Howie's body, still at this point lying in the bath.' Trish began to weep, and after a pause continued. 'I couldn't see what on earth we were going to do.'

'And who hit upon the idea of sealing off the bathroom?'

'Barbara suggested it to me that evening. I was shocked. I just couldn't bear the idea that we wouldn't give my husband a decent burial. But she had thought it all through. She's a very practical person, and can lay bricks and plaster walls to a decent standard. There was also the plumbing to deal with, lots of DIY-type considerations.'

'I presume this upset you?' Buchanan asked.

'Enormously. I couldn't bear it. We argued about it for two days, until Barbara said that I should go away for a couple of days, and she would deal with all the unpleasant details.'

Ellen Goodhew stood up and intervened. 'My lord, in the interests of justice, my client should really be able to hear this testimony, which goes beyond details given in the witness statements and is clearly prejudicial to her interests.'

The judge nodded. 'I had been thinking the same. We will adjourn for lunch, and during that time, Miss Goodhew, please explain to your client the importance of self-restraint. Another outburst like the one we had earlier, and I will have no hesitation in continuing the rest of the day's evidence without her.'

–

They resumed with a cross-examination of Trish by prosecuting counsel Sir William Strutt, who asked her about her childhood, and at what age she ran away from home.

'I was 16, your lordship.' She smiled at the jury, and almost seem to curtsy.

Strutt looked at her over his half-moon spectacles, a gesture familiar from the TV series in which he rehashed infamous crimes of the twentieth century. 'You can call me Mr Strutt, Mrs Gibson, this isn't a witch trial. My understanding is that, even if found guilty, you will not be burned at the stake.' He flicked through his papers. 'I understand that you stayed with the family of a school friend in order to avoid the attentions of your father, is that correct?'

'Yes, Mr Strutt, sir.' The curtsy again. 'I cleaned house for them until I was 21.'

'Mrs Gibson, you have already pleaded guilty to some very serious crimes. Involvement in the covering up of the death and perpetuating a fraud are far from trivial matters.'

'Yes, sir.' She bit her lip and looked down. 'It was to help my sister,' she murmured.

'Very noble of you, Mrs Gibson, I'm sure. You did go to extraordinary lengths, did you not?'

'I did what I had to do.'

'Well let us then hear the details. I wonder if you would lay out for me the process by which you created this fictitious family to cover up the death of your husband in June 2008.'

'Yes, sir. My sister suggested the story about Howie going abroad, but I soon realized that this might lead to as many questions as answers. He has two sisters in Scotland, both devout churchgoers, so I needed something strong enough that they would be disgusted with him. So that's where the trip to the brothels and everything came from. I rang them up and told them my story, and I said that I had been told all this by a work colleague of his.'

'What was their reaction to this unwelcome news?'

'They were horrified. I think at first they were reluctant to believe it. I knew I needed more evidence. So I set up an email account in the name of this fictitious work colleague, who claimed to have seen Howie with his arm around a girl in a brothel, and forwarded the email to them. They replied that they would never speak to Howie again.'

'What about the other parts of the story? The new family, the sons and daughters? How did you invent that?'

'That wasn't too difficult. Barbara and I went to Thailand in 2011. We made friends with some local people we met there, and visited many of the same places that I'd been to with Howie on our previous trip together in 2006. So that's how I was able to meld together the family, so Howie and I were apparently on the same trip.'

'Let me understand this correctly,' Strutt said. 'You were fabricating a past for your late husband by befriending a local family?'

'Yes. We took them out for meals, and took lots of photographs. The one snag was that there was never a picture of Howie and his supposedly new wife Tangmo together. But making friends with them brought some unexpected benefits. I really did meet Sarawut and his son Buma and go to Bath with them. It all added some depth to the story. I also wrote some postcards back to myself, impersonating Howie's scrawl, and asked Tangmo to drop them in the post one at a time, once every three months, and when they arrived, I pinned them up at home. Tangmo doesn't speak or read English very well – not that English is much help when it comes to my version of Howie's handwriting.'

'So your husband, whom you claim to have loved, was dead all along, while you were making up these terrible stories about him.'

Trish's eyes filled with tears, and she blew her nose energetically. 'That was the worst thing. I missed him terribly, still do – he was everything to me, and I should never have let her persuade me to cover up his death. He was a good man, and I had to make out that he was a bad one. That was the most painful thing.'

'For someone who was supposedly reluctant, you seem to have found plenty of inventive ways to spin the story out.'

'We were just worried that people would ask too many questions. In fact, nobody did, until my nephew came long.'

'Detective Chief Inspector Craig Gillard. He had his suspicions, didn't he?'

'He did.' Trish nodded.

'Now Mrs Gibson, when did you first hear from Mr Mark Hartley?'

Trish sighed and shook her head. 'Well a year ago I got this phone call out of the blue from Australia. Mark had been trying to track Howie down because they were old mates. Being a man, I suppose he wasn't quite as appalled by the story of sexual misdeeds I had to tell, though he was quite sympathetic to me as the jilted woman. He had phoned Howie's sisters originally to find out where he was, but the address I had given them didn't actually exist any more.'

'Recovered texts and emails show that it was a building site. You claimed your husband had moved some time previously, didn't you?'

'That's right. Mark was very persistent, and quite suspicious, though more of Howie's supposedly new family than of us. Barbara was insistent that we had to do something about Mark, or he would eventually uncover the truth. I thought because he was in Australia it wouldn't matter, but she had other ideas. So she invited him over.'

Strutt removed his glasses and looked down at his notes. 'Your sister rang him?'

'Yes.'

'Not you?'

'No.'

In the dock, Barbara was vigorously shaking her head in disagreement. Sir William Strutt turned to look at her, and then back at the witness. 'Your sister seems to disagree. Indeed, Mrs Gibson, police records show that there isn't a single phone call between any of Hartley's phone numbers and Barbara's landline or mobile. They were all to your home landline.'

'Barbara rang from my phone.' She turned to the jury. 'I've got a cheap international calling plan, you see. Anyway, she rang from my house, and told Mark that Howie had come home to Barnstaple and was now staying on her farm. He was extremely depressed, but if Mark really wanted to meet him, he could come and stay with her.'

Barbara again signalled her disagreement, shaking her head, her arms folded sternly across her chest.

'So Mr Hartley agreed?'

'Yes.'

'In reply to one of his emails, accessed by the police, you told Mr Hartley that your former husband had returned to Devon because of the failure of his new marriage in Thailand. You told him that Mr Gibson was severely depressed, and you made Mr Hartley promise not to tell anybody, neither their former colleagues nor family. Is that correct?'

Trish nodded.

'Why the secrecy?'

'It's obvious. We didn't want everyone traipsing round to see if they could meet him.'

'Indeed. In fact, it sounds like covering your tracks in advance, in preparation for killing Hartley, because no one would know he had come to visit.'

'No, no, it was not that way at all.'

Strutt flicked through some documents until he found what he was looking for. 'Really? You emailed Hartley to say you and your sister had been looking after your husband since his breakdown. You said he no longer used his phone or emails and had become a recluse. Mr Hartley was warned his visit should be kept entirely secret as it would make a great surprise and most certainly cheer up your ex-husband. That was a pack of lies, wasn't it?'

'Yes, obviously—'

Alasdair Buchanan jumped to his feet and objected. 'My lord, my client has already pleaded guilty to covering up her husband's death, yet now she is being tried for it by my learned colleague as if she had denied it.'

Strutt turned to the judge. 'My lord, I'm attempting to show the intimate connection between the defendant's preparations for covering up her husband's death, and those subsequently concocted to preserve that secrecy by luring Mr Hartley to his death.'

'You may continue,' the judge said.

'To return to my previous question, Mrs Gibson—'

Trish interrupted. 'We weren't trying to lure him to his death. We wanted to mislead him.' She stopped to wipe her eyes and blow her nose. 'I would have much preferred if it *was* true, don't you understand? I miss Howie so much.' She turned to the jury. 'It gave me solace to imagine he was still alive. Even if he had strayed, I would happily have had him back.'

'Let's return to the day of Mr Hartley's arrival,' Strutt said. 'Did you go and meet him from the station?'

'Yes. I parked nearby, up the hill, but told him where to find me.'

'Why didn't you park by the station?'

'It's usually full.'

'On a Tuesday afternoon? Mrs Gibson, may I suggest that the real reason is that you didn't want to have your car identified on CCTV?'

'I've no idea about that. I met him a few hundred yards away. I got him home and he was pretty tired after flying in the previous evening.'

'And then, shortly after he arrived, you drugged him, did you not?'

'No.'

Strutt smiled sceptically. 'Mrs Gibson, the forensic reports and the expert witness we heard earlier indicate that Mr Hartley's blood was saturated with sleeping medication.'

'I don't know anything about that. He must've taken it himself.'

'Well I'm sure the court would love to ask him, Mrs Gibson, but we cannot, can we? Because he was run down by your sister's car and killed.'

'I assume that's a rhetorical question,' Trish said.

'Mrs Gibson, do you have sleeping tablets in the house?'

'I don't know. I wouldn't have thought so.'

'Your medical records, accessed by the police, show that for a period of several years you have been prescribed Ambien, a drug of the imidazopyridine class, the exact same compound that was found in Mr Hartley's bloodstream at the time of his death.'

'I assume it's a common medication. But I no longer needed them, so I don't think there are any in the house.'

'Indeed, Mrs Gibson, they were not found in your medicine cabinet when the police searched. One may suppose that you have disposed of them.'

Buchanan objected, and Strutt retracted his last assertion before continuing. 'No trace has been found of Mr Hartley's phone, nor his wallet, passport or other essential documents. They were not on his body, and he seemingly didn't leave them at your home. Do you remember seeing any of them when he arrived?'

'I'm sure I saw his phone and laptop.'

'So where are they?'

'I don't know.'

'Neither of them were ever used again, for telephone calls or the Internet, after his phone call to you from Barnstaple railway station.'

'We don't have a very good signal.'

Strutt looked down at his papers. 'Indeed, so you have said. Mrs Gibson, your Internet search records show that you searched for "how to disable a laptop". Which method did you use?'

'That wasn't me.'

'It was from your computer.'

'As I said, my sister did the research.'

'Miss Antrobus said in her statement that she saw you put Mr Hartley's laptop in your freezer after he had fallen asleep.'

'That's not true. She may have done it, I don't know.'

'She also says that you levered open Mr Hartley's mobile phone with a nail file, removed something smaller than a fingernail, and microwaved it in your kitchen.'

Trish's mouth narrowed and her face tightened.

'That would be the SIM card, would it not?' Strutt asked. 'The essential brains of any mobile phone, without which it is useless.'

Trish shook her head. 'I'll take your word for that, sir. I'm a pensioner. I don't understand modern technology, and wouldn't have a clue about that.'

Strutt shook his head. 'Come now, Mrs Gibson. Both you and your sister profess ignorance of sleeping pills, no clue to methods of disabling communication devices, and indeed no knowledge of which of you was behind the wheel when Mr Hartley was run down. Yet someone slipped him drugs, someone prevented him using his mobile phone and laptop, and someone drove that car.'

Trish said nothing.

'What time did Mr Hartley wake up in the morning on the day that he died?'

'About 10.15 a.m. He was very groggy.'

'And, according to your statement, you made him breakfast and a coffee?'

'Yes, but he dozed off again on the sofa before he finished it—'

'And that was because you had slipped him some more sleeping pills?'

'No. And there's no "more" about it. I hadn't slipped him any.'

'So what did you do then?' Strutt twirled his glasses in one hand.

'I waited for nearly two hours for him to wake up. Barbara drove over, which allowed me to go out, pick up a bit of shopping and then go to the care home.'

'You left your sister alone with Mr Hartley?'

'Yes.'

Barbara was shaking her head, her knuckles tight on the edge of the dock.

'She joined you at the care home at 1.30 p.m. That seems clear at least from all the witnesses.'

'Yes.'

'So how do you think Mr Hartley happened to be in Furzy Hill at the time of his death?'

'I don't really know. I presume he woke up after Barbara had left and then decided to walk to Barbara's farm.'

Strutt shook his head. 'So Mrs Gibson, your best explanation of this tragic occurrence, and forgive me if I paraphrase, is that a jet-lagged Mr Hartley wakes up, decides not to use his mobile phone or laptop but instead sets out to walk the 17 miles to your sister's farm, a place he had never before visited and which presumably he didn't have directions or a map to, and then coincidentally got run down several hours later by your sister's Ford Ranger driven by a car thief?'

'I'm not saying that happened. I wasn't there. You asked me to speculate, and that's just what I did.' Sitting nearby, her barrister Alasdair Buchanan smiled wryly at Trish's deft response.

'But Mrs Gibson, I didn't ask you to lie, did I?'

'I'm not lying.'

'Isn't it the truth, Mrs Gibson, that you and your sister were planning to kill him at your house, and lost the courage to do it?'

'No, of course not. I was just in a panic because he wanted to meet Howie, and Howie wasn't there, and in the end, I wouldn't be able to explain it. It was just all a panic really.'

'I hope you won't take it amiss, Mrs Gibson, if I say I find your story utterly lacking in credibility.'

Strutt took off his glasses and waved them in the direction of the jury. 'From all the evidence and your witness statement, you would apparently have these twelve fine and true members of the public here believe that you were merely caught up in some entirely understandable act of charity to your nearest and dearest.' He twirled his spectacles again for emphasis. 'But is it not the truth, that the evidence we have heard, from the entombing of the body of your husband, the siphoning off of his pension, the creation of an entirely fictitious family for your husband to cover your tracks, and finally the enticement of the entirely innocent Mr Hartley to his death, show that you are the mastermind of this plot?'

'No, sir.' Trish curtsied again.

'Do you expect the jury to believe that you, as the educated, highly intelligent and more worldly sibling, played no major part in this plot?'

'As it's the truth, I hope they will.'

'Mrs Gibson, have you ever driven your sister's Ford Ranger?'

'Well, it's a bit big and powerful for me. I don't like it. I'm only tiny. I can hardly get in.'

'Oh come now, Mrs Gibson. You have been hiding behind a façade of quasi-disability and helplessness throughout this, haven't you?'

'No, sir. I'm not well.'

'So you would have us believe. However, the medical records that we have here show that you are reasonably fit and well. Is that not true?'

'No, sir.'

'The interview notes from your first, second and third conversations with Detective Inspector Talantire mention that in the last 15 years you survived both breast and uterine cancer, is that not correct?'

Trish looked down, prompting the judge to request that she answer the question. She nodded her assent.

'In fact, according to your medical records, you have never had cancer, have you?'

'I wanted a second opinion,' she muttered. 'I think they missed it.'

Strutt struggled to keep a straight face. 'Mrs Gibson, if you had developed cancer and the doctors missed it, I suggest you would not be in a position to stand here giving evidence, would you?'

Trish turned to the judge, hoping for a more sympathetic response. 'I'm finding it a struggle, actually, because of my illnesses.'

Strutt continued, 'I would suggest, Mrs Gibson, that the main struggle you have is with the truth. The main reason that I have delved into your medical history is to show the jury that, far from being an honest and truthful person who recently told "a couple of porkies" to aid her struggling sister, you are in fact a long-standing mistress of misleading, a lady of lies, whose untruths are so carefully woven into her own life that she is barely aware of where the fabric of fact ends and the fabrication of fibs begins. Is that not so?'

'No.'

'What year did you claim to have suffered breast cancer?'

'I don't remember.'

'I think you do.' Strutt picked up her statement and took it over to the witness box. 'What year does it say there?' He tapped halfway down the document.

'I can't read it, I've got my wrong glasses.' She fumbled for her small clutch bag and then dropped it, disappearing into the depths of the witness box in search of it. Chuckles could be heard around the court as she scrambled unseen, muttering to herself.

The judge intervened. 'Mrs Gibson, this is not a comedy venue. Please stand up.'

As she did so, Strutt said: 'I'll save you the trouble, Mrs Gibson. You first reported suffering from cancer in 1983, according to the school you worked at, and from where you took an 18-month sick leave on full pay. It was a lie, one you have kept on what we may term "lie support" for over 35 years.'

'No, it wasn't a lie.'

'Mrs Gibson, did you at around 3.50 p.m. on Wednesday 7 November, take your sister's Ford Ranger—'

'No, I did not.'

'—and, stopping to pick up Mr Hartley, drive it to Furzy Hill—'

'No.'

'—where you persuaded him to leave the vehicle, and then—'

'No, it wasn't me.'

'— drove it at him, at speed, dragging his body face down along the road, causing him horrible injuries, and then took from his ruined body any remaining identification to cover up your crimes?'

She continued to shake her head.

'Mrs Gibson, have we or have we not established that you are an inveterate liar? One who has lied, again and again, under oath, to the police, and to the court?'

'I'm telling the truth.'

'Then if you didn't drive this car, who did?'

Trish blinked, and said nothing.

'No further questions, my lord.'

Chapter 44

Craig Gillard arrived to join Sam for the afternoon session. She met him just beyond the security gates, bursting to update him on events. 'I can see exactly what Trish is trying to do,' she told him. 'Make herself out to be helpless. She's already charming the jury, you can see it.' She summarized the evidence being presented. 'She's really blaming Barbara for everything.'

'What about the question of who was driving the car?' Gillard asked. 'That's the crucial issue.'

'They've each denied it, but I'm sure the barristers will come back to it later in the day.'

Barbara was returned to the dock for the afternoon session, with a custody officer sitting either side of her while Trish continued to give evidence. Alasdair Buchanan began by refreshing the court on the evidence that Trish had given that morning. Gillard's gaze was locked on Barbara, who scowled remorselessly at her sister, occasionally shaking her head.

'So Mrs Gibson, you said that your sister had encouraged you to take a couple of days away while she dealt with the rather delicate details of preparing your husband's body for being entombed.'

Trish nodded, and her 'yes' was barely audible.

'Did she ever tell you exactly what she had done?'

'No. But I discovered that she had taken a book out of the library about serial killers and their victims, and had done some online research. I didn't want to know the details.'

Buchanan looked down at his papers. 'However, Mrs Gibson, you heard earlier in the trial expert forensic testimony, and I trust you have read the report which the police made available.' She nodded again. 'For the benefit of the jury, and without wishing to amplify your discomfort, let me remind them that your husband was entirely drained of blood, through a cut made in his throat, and there appeared to be some residues of surgical spirit or some kind of preservative which was poured or pumped in, to replace it. Can I ask you, Mrs Gibson, if you had anything whatever to do with this?'

'No, of course not. Barbara has butcher's training. She did all that. I wasn't even there, I went to stay with Podge in Lynton.'

Gillard saw that Barbara's mouth was working, muttering inaudible but clearly hostile comments.

'And can I further ask you about the concrete that was poured into the bath, up to its rim. Were you present, and did you help with this?'

Trish again denied playing any part in it. Buchanan then went through every stage of the cover-up process, asking her again if she contributed, and in each case, she said no. Finally, he asked if there was any part of the physical process of sealing her husband inside her house in which she had taken part.

'Yes. I helped with the wallpapering, making sure it matched what I already had.'

Then Buchanan returned to the central question of the trial, the one for which the charges of conspiracy to murder and murder had been laid.

'Mrs Gibson, earlier in this trial you heard your sister testify under oath that neither of you were driving the car that so tragically killed Mark Hartley. Let me ask you the same question, and remind you that you are under oath. Were you driving that car?'

'No.'

'Was your sister Barbara driving that car?'

Trish didn't speak for a while. 'I honestly don't know.'

Buchanan, taken aback by this reply, looked down at his papers which included the witness statements where the two sisters had backed each other's version of events.

'You don't know, Mrs Gibson?'

'No.'

There was a low animal growl from the dock, where Barbara was on her feet, knuckles white on the metal rail that encircled it. Her eyes were lasered on her sister, radiating an astonishing enmity.

The judge leaned over and turned to Trish. 'Mrs Gibson, you previously testified under oath that neither you nor she could have been driving, because you were both continuously present at the care home with your brother at the time the incident took place. Are you saying that is not true?'

'My lord, I am saying that I cannot account for all the time my sister was there. She absented herself—'

Barbara could no longer restrain itself. 'Judas! We had a deal. I'm going to kill you for this. I'm going to rip out your lying throat.' She made the sign of a knife across her throat.

Being unable to silence her, the judge directed the custody officers to remove Barbara, and cleared the court for the five minutes it took to do so. Her screams and shouts of rage could be heard even out in the external areas of the court, where lawyers, witnesses and the general public were standing, shocked.

'To return to the previous question,' Buchanan said. He shuffled his papers, then looked up at his client. 'You say your sister Barbara absented herself during the time you were playing Monopoly?'

'Yes. She said she was going to the loo.'

'And how long was she gone?'

'About half an hour, I suppose.'

Ellen Goodhew stood and objected. 'My client needs to be able to hear this,' she said.

The judge shook his head. 'Your client needs to appreciate the standards of behaviour expected in Crown Court, and has forfeited her right to be here.' He turned to Alasdair Buchanan. 'You may continue.'

'That half-hour absence must've interrupted the game, surely, Mrs Gibson?'

'Well it did. When it was her turn, I went to look for her, and not finding her in the toilet, came back and said I would roll the dice for her. I ended up buying Pentonville Road, which I suppose seems ironic now.' She gave a smug little grin.

'But Mrs Gibson, your own brother and Mr Butler both said she was continuously present during the game.'

'That's because every time it was her turn, I walked out to the loo to pretend to ask what she wanted to do on any given square. But she wasn't there.'

'Did you know where she was going?'

'I presumed she was going to check up on Mr Hartley, to see if he had woken up. I had no idea she had plans to kill him.'

—

Ellen Goodhew finally took her opportunity to cross-examine Trish.

'Mrs Gibson, your original account and this one are incompatible. So you have lied under oath, have you not?'

'Reluctantly. I did it to protect my sister—'

'I think the jury may prefer to decide that you did it to protect yourself. After all, by blaming my client for driving the car, you may hope to escape blame yourself.'

'That's not true. I pleaded guilty to the crimes I committed: the fraud and covering up the death of my husband. But I pleaded not guilty to murder, and I stand by that.'

'Yet we have heard compelling forensic evidence that sleeping tablets were administered to Mr Hartley at your home.'

'Not by me. He probably took them himself.'

'And are you saying that he also threw away his own wallet, his own mobile phone, and cut the labels out from his own clothing?'

'Well I certainly didn't do it.'

'So Mrs Gibson, what was your plan for Mr Hartley, seeing as you had enticed him halfway round the world to come to visit you? How did you intend to persuade him that your late husband was still alive?'

'I was going to show him all the photograph albums.'

'Come now, Mrs Gibson. You could have sent him those photographs by email.'

She did not reply.

'Mrs Gibson, is it not true that your sister Barbara is an innocent in this. That it was you who devised the plot in its entirety, and researched it on the Internet?'

'No.'

'As my learned colleague has shown, you have lived a life of lies, and finally being caught in a web of your own making, it was you alone who decided that Mark Hartley must die, and you who callously took your sister's vehicle to commit the crime, so that in the final analysis, if your alibi fell through, you could blame her. As you are now doing.'

'No, that's not true.'

'Really, Mrs Gibson? Did you or did you not less than an hour ago under cross-examination change your evidence to implicate your sister?'

'I'm telling the truth.'

'Well if so, it would be a first,' Goodhew said, dropping her documents noisily onto the desk in front of her. 'I rest my case.'

Chapter 45

The prosecution summing-up concentrated heavily on the motivation of both women. 'There has been a great deal of detailed and contradictory evidence presented, but I must ask you to keep in mind the main incontrovertible facts,' Sir William Strutt told the jury. 'A defendant's car killed Mr Hartley, and both defendants were responsible for enticing him to come and visit so this heinous crime could be committed. While both these women blame each other in varying degrees, you do not need to know which of them was behind the wheel in order to convict for conspiracy. The list of crimes to which they have already pleaded guilty shows that neither of them has any compunction about conspiring to break the law, and it is conspiracy which lies at the heart of the case.' He then went on to list every charge they had admitted, emphasizing the degree of co-operation required between the two. 'What we have, ladies and gentlemen of the jury, is a litany of evil. Not a crime of passion, undertaken in the heat of the moment, but a precisely planned, premeditated if imperfectly executed conspiracy.'

Ellen Goodhew concentrated in her summing-up on the extenuating circumstances of Barbara's life, and the frustrations and difficulties of struggling to keep a sheep farm solvent. While acknowledging Barbara's outbursts of violence and pointing out that she was certain to go to jail for a substantial period for the crimes already admitted, the barrister said she was a wronged woman. 'A careful examination of the evidence makes clear that she was the junior partner in all this. Mr Hartley was invited to stay by Mrs Gibson, from her telephone; it was she who created the elaborate ruse of building her dead husband a phantom family abroad; it was her computer on which the research was done; it was she, surely, who had the most intimate knowledge of her husband's pension arrangements.' She then pointed towards the dock, the two contrasting women sitting there. 'You must not judge by appearances, but by intentions, by actions. You will have no doubt which of these two women was the organizing genius, and which the labourer.'

Alasdair Buchanan took an entirely different tack, leaning heavily on the physical intimidation that his client felt from the bullying older sister.

'Ladies and gentlemen of the jury, can you really believe that this tiny, elderly lady, an esteemed history teacher, who has never been in trouble with the law, would commit a brutal murder? You will have seen, from the photographs of their wedding, and of subsequent years together that Mrs Gibson and her husband were deeply in love. Her only crime was to try to cover up the natural death of her beloved husband to help her sister, who would otherwise lose the family farm because of the debts incurred. Mr Gibson's annuity, as uncontested evidence shows, would not have provided for his wife after his death, and her own means were insufficient to keep her sister's farm afloat. So Mrs Gibson, out of a surfeit of love for her troubled sister, committed the – albeit serious

– crime of covering up her husband's death in order for her to continue to receive his pension. But that is not the crime with which she is charged here.'

Buchanan approached the jury, making eye contact which each of them. 'She is charged here with an act of homicide, the deliberate running down of another human being with a vehicle, and with conspiracy to commit such an act. As we have seen, no fewer than four people have attested that she could not have done this, because she was at The Beeches care home playing Monopoly with her brother Philip at the time when she was supposedly committing murder. The prosecution has tried repeatedly to cast doubt upon the witness statements signed by two members of staff of the care home and two residents. To my way of thinking, this lady, who has considerable health difficulties I think it is fair to say, would have to have had the energy and determination of a veritable James Bond to be able to accomplish the logistical acrobatics required to commit this crime in the time available. Look at this lady, ladies and gentlemen, and make up your own mind. I would remind you that if there is even a slight doubt in your mind whether this upstanding and selfless lady would be capable of committing such a heinous act, then your duty, both legal and moral, is to acquit.'

–

The judge's summing-up leaned heavily on the conspiracy angle. 'Following a Supreme Court ruling in 2018, it is not sufficient merely to suppose that a defendant might foresee that a co-defendant may commit a crime. You need to be satisfied that this really was a joint enterprise.'

The jury was sent away, and did not return for several hours. They spent the night in a hotel, apparently unable to agree, but delivered a verdict the next morning.

When they did, Barbara Antrobus was convicted of murder but cleared of conspiracy. In the dock, her face was grimly set and she shook her head in denial. When it came to Trish and the charge of murder, the clerk of the court asked if they had reached a verdict on which they were all agreed. The foreman, who resembled a stereotypical bank manager, said no. Further exchanges revealed that there were too many dissenters even for a majority verdict, with a narrow majority for not guilty.

The judge's announcement of Trish's acquittal produced a howl of outrage from Barbara. Her lunge towards her sister took the custody officer sitting between them by surprise. He struggled to get a grip on Barbara, who had managed to get one hand around Trish's throat, and was banging her head against the wooden edge of the dock. It took the intervention of two more custody officers to overpower Barbara, leaving Trish cringing and whimpering on the floor of the dock.

As she was carried out, kicking and screaming, Barbara said one thing over and over again: 'Trish was driving, not me. It was her, it was her.'

Chapter 46

Barbara Antrobus was sentenced to eleven years. Trish Gibson, acquitted of all the most serious charges, but having admitted fraud over the failure to declare her husband's death, was sentenced to four years in jail.

'The jury is not convinced,' Mr Justice Knowlesley said to Trish, 'that you were an entirely voluntary conspirator, and are giving you the benefit of the doubt as to what extent you were intimidated into co-operating with your sister. Unlike her, you were of previously unblemished character and you stood to gain nothing from the scheme. Given that conclusion, I see little benefit to society in imprisoning you for a misguided act of generosity towards your violent and overbearing sister. So I suspend the sentence for one year. You are free to go.'

There were gasps from the public gallery, and one tall figure, smartly dressed in a suit and tie, yelled that it was a stitch-up. Gillard couldn't see his face, as the man was four steep rows below him. He sat down at the judge's insistence, and it was only when the hearing was over and the public was filing out that Gillard recognized him. Peter Yates, with a severe haircut and, for once, no earbuds.

Immediately after the case, Talantire thanked Gillard for his co-operation and said he and Sam were welcome to join the prosecution team for a drink. 'Of course, if you prefer to wait for your aunt to celebrate her acquittal, I would understand.'

'I'm sure you'll understand if we don't join you,' Gillard said. Sam watched complex emotions travel over his features. 'This isn't a victory for anyone, least of all me.' He turned to Sam. 'But I don't think we'll be spending any time with Trish. We don't want anything to do with her ever again.' He turned back to Talantire. 'I can't believe she has got away with it.'

Talantire smiled and raised a finger. 'I'm not done yet, Craig. There are possibilities for a retrial with some fresh evidence. We'll have to see.' Leaving the enigmatic comment hanging in the air, she turned and walked away.

–

It was nine o'clock the next evening when Sam took a phone call, expecting it to be Gillard to say what time he'd be back from work.

'Hello, Sam dear,' Trish said. 'I saw you in the public gallery, and looked for you afterwards after my acquittal.'

Craig and Sam had deliberately avoided running into Trish. Sam didn't know what to say now. 'I'll tell Craig you rang.'

'Hollow Coombe farm is up for sale. The debts are too much, and the bank wants its money, especially now Barbara is inside. I've arranged to sell a lot of the equip-ment, but wondered if Craig would come down and help me sort through the stuff.'

'Oh,' said Sam. 'Isn't there anyone else who can help you?'

'Well you're my only family, and I'm too wobbly now to do much myself. Craig needs to be there to look after our family interests. So I'll expect him down this weekend.' She hung up, and Sam shook her head in despair. *This never ends. It just never ends.*

When Gillard arrived and she broke the news, his jaw dropped. 'I'm not going down there. She's got Peter to help her, if he's willing to. I want nothing to do with her.'

—

DI Talantire heard about the yard sale at Hollow Coombe farm from PC Nick Kite. 'There should be some bargains this afternoon. There's a quad bike I've got my eye on, amongst other things,' he told her as they stood by the coffee machine in Barnstaple police station.

'Frankly I think you should stay well away, considering the allegations made against you and your father.'

'There's nothing to worry about. The rental paid was cash in hand. There was no rent book. There's no formal complaint against me from Antrobus or Gibson.'

'Not yet, perhaps.' Talantire sipped her coffee, which tasted like burned tar. 'So who is running the auction? Have they got formal auctioneers in?'

'Yes, but I think Trish Gibson is running it herself. There's that Peter Yates – I expect he's going to help her.' He looked at his watch.

'What? Are you crazy? We've had him drunk and disorderly in the town centre with Micky Tuffin twice since they put Barbara Antrobus away.'

'Yeah,' Kite smirked and folded his arms. 'The grab-a-granny escapade is over for him.'

Talantire pursed her lips. 'He's obviously really upset. He was clean as a whistle before this, and he's gone off the rails now she's inside.'

Kite stared at her with incredulity. Empathy clearly wasn't his strong point.

'It takes all sorts, Nick.' She started to walk away and then turned to him. 'You did that Section 30 on Hollow Coombe farm, didn't you?'

'We revoked the licence months ago, and Willow went round to get the guns.' Kite looked at his watch. 'Good, off shift now. See you later.'

Talantire called Willow on his radio. She wished she had used Section 30 of the 1968 Firearms Act years ago, given that Barbara Antrobus would have been judged of 'intemperate habits' even before her convictions for murder and kidnap. 'Clifford, you did get both of Barbara Antrobus's shotguns when you went round there, didn't you?'

'There was only one, ma'am.'

'No, Clifford, there were two. There were always two. Who did you speak to?'

'That Peter Yates.'

'For God's sake, Clifford, don't you see what's going to happen?'

–

Talantire ran to her unmarked car. PC Kite's private vehicle was already gone. She wanted to ring him to tell him to keep an eye out for Peter Yates. But the person she was most worried about was Trish Gibson. She had seen Peter in the public gallery of the Old Bailey on the last two days of the trial. The look on his face when his lover was sentenced was one of horror. She had seen him again in the public area of the court, weeping. A week later, she had taken the statement from him after his arrest in Barnstaple town centre. He was a fizzing bomb of anger and nervous energy. The detective had no doubt in her mind who would be the one person he blamed for having Barbara taken away from him. A woman who had retreated into her home since being cleared of murder. The woman whose first day in public since the trial was today.

Trish Gibson.

The detective arrived at the farm in half an hour, just as the auction was about to start. There was an improvised car park on the meadow filled with 4 × 4s and pickup trucks. She slotted her own vehicle in and made her way on foot down towards the farmhouse. There was an array of largely rusty and antiquated farm machinery laid out on tarpaulins and straw bales, being picked over by a scattering of local farmers. Three young men in auction house overalls were policing the equipment. Talantire spotted Nick Kite, in conversation with his father, by a collection of chainsaws. There was no sign of Trish, but her Nissan was right there at the front.

The detective walked up to Kite and asked if he had seen Trish. 'No, and I haven't seen any sign of that quad bike that I want to buy either.'

Trish emerged from the house, walking shakily with a stick and issuing orders to the overalled staff. She then, with some assistance, mounted a straw bale so she could address the small crowd. 'It is with great sadness that I have to preside over the break-up of this once great farm. We had a bit of family trouble, you might've heard about it...' There was considerable laughter at this. 'But that will be your gain, I hope.'

The low-frequency noise of a vehicle intruded on her speech. Talantire turned to see a green quad bike with a lanky black-clad figure hunched over the controls emerge from behind Philip Antrobus's caravan and speed down the hundred yards towards the farmhouse. The rider was wearing a full-face crash helmet, but Talantire had no doubt who it was. She yelled at Trish to move out of the way and sprinted towards the bale on which she was standing. Nick Kite ran towards the quad bike, which slowed to a halt just a few yards from the bale. Talantire reached Trish and glanced left to see that Kite had interposed himself between Yates, shotgun now in hand, and her. Talantire threw herself at Trish, knocking her off the bale, just as Yates fired. There was a deafening boom, a scream, and a squall of red, stinging rain spattered Talantire's face and coat. Trish pinned below her, Talantire peered over the edge of the protective bale to see that Kite was writhing on the ground, screaming piteously and holding his face. The crowd had fled, or dived, and Peter Yates, his visor open and the shotgun now to his shoulder, was aiming straight at Trish. Talantire ducked down, just as the second blast went off, and she felt an agonising pain in her shoulder. She was vaguely aware of the farmers and officials now struggling with Yates, and the single repeatedly bellowed word: 'Judas!'

Chapter 47

Peter Yates, horrified at the injuries he had inflicted on Kite, gave himself up on the spot. Talantire looked far more injured than she was. Though she had been speckled with pellets in the shoulder and was splattered with Kite's blood, she was able to oversee the arrest while awaiting police reinforcements. PC Nick Kite was gravely injured in the attack, disfigured and losing the sight in one eye. He subsequently retired from the force due to ill health, avoiding the investigation of a complaint against him by Barbara Antrobus. Though there was suspicion that he had 'lost' all the evidence files relating to dog attacks at her sheep farm, and had been complicit in attempts to blackmail her, there was no appetite in the police force or CPS to take things any further against him. However, six months later, when DI Talantire finally found the time to have Philip Antrobus's laptop forensically examined, it was discovered that the device had originally belonged to Vince Kite, sufficient files being recovered to indicate it had been used for his correspondence. The original Polaroid photographs, taken by Jacob Antrobus in the 1960s, had been recovered by Kite senior during his investigation of the old man's death. Nearly 40 years later, in the late 1990s, he scanned in those pictures for his own enjoyment, including those of Jacob's abuse of a teenage Barbara and her sister Margaret. When he upgraded computers, he hadn't realized that his wife Ursula had got rid of the old laptop, which Philip bought for £5 from a charity shop. There was no evidence that Philip had ever used it.

Peter Yates was sentenced to 14 years for attempted murder and grievous bodily harm. A week into that sentence, being served at Long Lartin in Worcestershire, he was found hanged in his cell. In a final act of contrition, he left behind a letter for Barbara.

> Dear Babs,
>
> Things have not gone well for me since you were put away. I have struggled and struggled with the injustice of what happened, and have done terrible things for which I am truly sorry.
>
> I cannot live with all this, and I cannot live without you, who showed me so much kindness and love. So I can tell you now that it was me who took your car when you were in the care home with Trish and Philip. I'd heard what you were discussing, and I thought it would help. I picked Hartley up at Trish's house, meaning to take him back to the station and out of your lives.
>
> But he told me that he thought there was something fishy going on with Trish, and he kept fiddling with his phone, which didn't seem to work. So I gave him a lift to the phone box, and said you can make a call there. He got out

of the car, and then turned back to me
as he realized it wasn't a proper phone
booth. That's when I drove at him. It was
horrible.

I'm so so sorry about all the trouble
I have caused, and hope my confession
means you will be let out of jail early.
I hate to think of you, a woman of hills
and countryside, caged up. It's not right.

I'm going now, to make my peace, and
hope I get your blessing.

All my love,

Peter

Talantire read the letter, her jaw hanging open. She had
never believed Peter Yates capable of murder, though his
attempt on Trish's life had proven her wrong. Logistically, it would certainly have been easier for Yates to
kill Hartley than for either sister. Still, the letter did not
entirely convince her. But hunches, however strong, do
not match the weight of a posthumous confession. The
CPS's Miriam Gross, in a hastily convened conference call
with her, concluded there was absolutely no point now in
using the new forensic evidence Talantire had discovered
to seek a retrial of Trish Gibson. 'I think that's a shame,'
Talantire said. 'It seems obvious to me that Yates is making
a gift to the woman he loves. I don't for a moment think
he was driving that car.'

'I don't have an opinion, but an emotionally charged
confession is gold dust for the defence,' Miriam Gross said.
'So we've got even less chance of getting Mrs Gibson now.'

Weeks earlier, when the trial was already well underway, Talantire had by accident found a small unexamined evidence bag in the Barnstaple police warehouse, misfiled with another crime. The label showed it had been collected months ago by CSI, just inside the back door at Trish Gibson's house, but it had never been properly recorded, examined or added to the trial evidence. It was just a single frayed washing instruction label, clearly cut from an item of clothing. The brand label, Myers, turned out to be an Australian department store. Talantire had waited on tenterhooks for a DNA and fingerprint examination from the glossy man-made fabric. She waited many tantalising days, and only got confirmation of a partial thumbprint matching that of Trish Gibson after the jury had begun to deliberate on its verdict.

As evidence of intent it was dynamite. The defence had managed to persuade the jury that there were other possible explanations for the drugs in Mark Hartley's system, and the absence of labels in his clothing. But here, arriving too late to be used in the trial, was incontrovertible proof of Trish's calculating premeditation.

In the light of Peter Yates's confession, for now at least, Miriam Gross and the CPS wanted none of it.

–

Sam was glad to be able to get Craig away for an extended summer holiday, hiking in the Atlas Mountains of Morocco. For three glorious weeks they could forget about everything, just soak up the arid beauty of the stark mountain scenery, beyond the reach of the smartphone and email. It was in the last week when Sam disclosed to her husband that she thought she was pregnant. It brought a huge grin to his face as he scooped her off her feet and held her close. Finally, when their time away was up, they reluctantly headed back to the grey skies of England, and whatever awaited them in the world of work.

Driving them back from Gatwick Airport, Sam watched a crease of care return to her husband's brow as he sat in the passenger seat going through a bulging inbox on his phone.

'Some from Trish?' she asked.

'Yeah, loads. But I'm not going to open them.' He flicked down until he got to various work-related emails.

'I thought it was a bit rich of social services to ask us to take her in,' Sam said.

'They're just following policy rules, I suppose. We are Trish's only relatives, apart from my sister. Given the publicity from the trial and her increasing infirmity, she'll find it pretty tough to keep living down there in Devon.'

As they turned into their own street, they saw a big blue 4 × 4 parked in their drive. A Ford Ranger, 2012 model.

'What in hell is going on?' Gillard asked. He looked down at his phone: next-door neighbour Roger Davies had just sent a text.

Saw this little old lady outside looking a bit lost. Seems your aunt arrived early for her visit, so I let her in with the spare key and explained that you would be back in a couple of hours. Hope that's okay.
Roger.
PS She's such a sweet little thing, driven all the way up from Devon!

'Jesus Christ!' Gillard exclaimed. 'Trish is in the house, and has parked her murder weapon right on our drive.'

Sam stared at her husband. 'I don't believe it, how does she do it?'

'Right,' said Gillard as they pulled up outside. 'I'm going to sort this out once and for all.' He flung open the door and jumped out, for all the world as if he was going to tackle an armed drug dealer. He was only halfway to his front door when it opened and Trish was standing there with her arms outstretched and her lips puckered for a welcome kiss. 'Hello, Craig, so wonderful to see my favourite nephew. Did you have a nice holiday?'

'Trish, you're leaving. I'll just get your stuff out,' he said. Sam watched her husband avoid the embrace and push past her into the house. Trish rolled her eyes at Gillard, then made her way down the front steps and along the drive to greet Sam.

'Sam, how wonderful to see you,' Trish said, arms wide. Sam stepped back warily, her hands involuntarily moving to her midriff.

'Oh, my dear, you're finally pregnant. Congratulations.' Trish's eyes widened in glee. 'How lovely! And I'll be able to babysit.'

Sam fought the chill that crawled down her body. 'Trish, I'm sorry, but you won't be able to stay. I heard Craig tell you.'

Trish's eyes narrowed and she reached out a claw-like hand to grasp Sam's wrist. 'Well that's all right, because I've just bought the bungalow opposite.'

Sam turned and looked in horror at the 'for sale' board in the garden behind her. It had seemed to be there for years, but now sported a single word. Sold.

She turned back to look at Trish, who had opened the door to the Ford. 'One more thing, dear. Is there a good Ford dealership around here? I'm not familiar with the garages in Surrey, and have so much to learn for my new life close to family.'

'I have no idea,' Sam whispered, as the full enormity of this development sank in.

'I just need to get the brakes fixed.' She looked up and held Sam's gaze, a smile widening on her face. 'They've never been any good, have they? Not even from the first time I drove it.'

Acknowledgements

I am indebted to Hester Russell, Head of Crime at GWB Harthills LLP who guided me through the legal intricacies of Old Bailey trial. Tanya Keelty of Lloyds Banking Group and credit card historian John Whitworth helped me on old credit card records, while retired DI Kim Booth steered me on police procedure. I would also like to thank Father Geoffrey Thompson and sheep farmer Karen Becskehazy. For the purposes of the story, I inflicted on Barnstaple police station, and on Devon and Cornwall Constabulary in general, a kind of worst-case staffing crisis, though it is not a world away from reality in parts of rural Britain. Like all the characters in this book, the hamlet of Furzy Hill and Hollow Coombe farm do not exist. I would particularly like to thank Michael Bhaskar and his hard-working team at Canelo. Above all, I owe everything to my wife Louise, always my first and most insightful reader.